BARBARA SHOUP

HYPERION BOOKS FOR CHILDREN
NEW YORK

FIRST EDITION

1 3 5 7 9 10 8 6 4 2

Library of Congress Cataloging-in-Publication Data
Shoup, Barbara.
Wish you were here / Barbara Shoup—1st ed.
p.   cm.
Summary: A high school senior tries to cope with the shifting patterns of his life while struggling to come to terms with his parents' divorce, his best friend's sudden departure, his mother's remarriage, and his father's near-fatal accident.
ISBN 0-7868-0028-3
[1. Interpersonal relations—Fiction.   2. Divorce—Fiction.   3. Remarriage—Fiction.   4. Parent and child—Fiction.   5. Identity—Fiction.]   I. Title.
PZ7.S55884En   1994
[Fic]—dc20   94-9368   CIP   AC

For Ralph Bedwell
and The Rockets

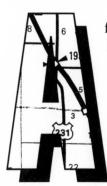fter the divorce, my dad's shrink told him it was important for the two of us to do things together, so he bought this book called *Amazing America* and arranged our vacations so that we could visit some of the strange places it described. He took me to the Tupperware Museum of Historic Food Containers, the Etch A Sketch factory, and the National Cowgirl Hall of Fame. We'd see Dollywood, he promised. The Museum of Drag Racing, with the top fuel slingshot dragster that exploded and blew off Big Daddy Don Garlits's foot. And, of course, Graceland.

I didn't have the heart to tell him I hated going away. After the disastrous vacation our family had taken right before the divorce, I'd made up my mind that the safe thing was to stay put. To be normal. I was happiest in the hours between the time school let out and my mom came home from work. She felt guilty leaving me alone, but I liked it. I'd eat whatever snack she'd left and watch reruns of *Ozzie and Harriet*, *Father Knows Best*, *The Donna Reed Show*.

Those people never went anywhere; they hardly left the kitchen. They were happy. Which made me even more certain that our vacation had caused the divorce. I know that sounds stupid. But I was only nine.

When I told my best friend, Brady, about how Dad got so mad at Mom while we were in the Ozarks that he hitchhiked to the airport and flew home two days early without us, Brady said, "Maybe that's why they got divorced, Jax; maybe it isn't. The important thing is, don't ever tell them what you think." He was an expert on divorce; his parents had been divorced since he was five. I paid attention to him when he told me, "What you want to do is figure out what they want you to say and say that. Otherwise they'll freak out and send you to a shrink."

"Sometimes people love each other, but they just can't live together." That's what Mom and Dad told me the night they sat me down and explained why Dad was leaving, so that's what I repeated every time Mom got worried and decided we should talk.

"You really understand that, Jackson?" she'd ask.

I'd say yes, even though I didn't understand it at all.

Sometimes she'd leave it at that; sometimes she'd say, "But how do you *feel?*"

Brady had coached me on this, too. "Don't act like you think the divorce is no big deal. Act, you know, kind of stunned. Like you haven't exactly figured it out yet, but you're working on it."

So I'd tell Mom, "I'm sad about the divorce. I really miss Dad. But I love you guys, and you love me, so I guess things will work out okay." I'd try to look hopeful, trusting. "Won't they?"

She'd get all teary eyed and hug me. "They will, honey. I promise you. You're such a good boy, Jackson," she'd say. "You really are."

My biggest problem according to Brady: being good.

"People *think* I'm good," I always told him when he said it.

"No. You *are* good, Jax. Face it, man."

I can hear him laughing his wild, hooty laugh, and it makes me wish I'd told him, "You face it; you're the good one." Because it's true.

Last year—junior year, when we'd all go over to Hardee's after school, Brady was the one who talked for hours about the way the world should be, the one who cared about making it better. If people weren't so obsessed with being comfortable, they'd think twice about trashing the earth the way they do, he said. And if they weren't so greedy and paranoid, they wouldn't let little kids starve because they read once that some person on welfare cashed in his food stamps and bought a Cadillac.

Once we were walking through Military Park downtown, and this old black guy sitting by the fountain said, real polite, "You boys got any change to spare?" It was November, just starting to get cold, and the guy was wearing this grody, ripped-up windbreaker. Brady gave him five bucks and said, "Stay right there, man. We'll be back." We went over to Ayres then, and he bought the guy a down parka with his dad's charge card. He got into all kinds of trouble for it.

See, that's the difference between me and Brady. People think I'm good, but really, I'm just too scared to risk getting in trouble. Brady has the guts to do what he believes is right.

Like leaving.

I guess it's the fact that Brady really did it, that he's really gone, that's got me thinking about my parents' divorce.

he thing is, Brady and I had made this plan. First, he psyched out his mom. He refused to get a summer job, and lay around the house all day with the stereo blaring. He got drunk every night. It worked like a charm. When the first of August rolled around and he told her that he wanted to get an apartment for his senior year, she thought it was a great idea and talked his dad into paying for it.

Our senior year was going to be so cool. "The beginning of the end," Brady said when we talked about it. The apartment would be a place where all our friends could hang out, one place they'd always feel welcome. Where, he assured me, one way or another, both of us would get ourselves laid before the lease was up. He'd be in charge of music and conversation. I'd make sure that things didn't get too wild.

He never doubted that my mom would let me move in with him. "She's in love, Jax," he said. "Impaired. She'll let you do anything."

As usual, it turned out he was right. Mom wasn't crazy about the idea, but her boyfriend, Ted, had spent a few nights at our house lately, and I knew she felt guilty. I guess she figured that if I wasn't living there, I couldn't get wrecked by what she was doing. Plus, there'd be no excuse for Dad to show up and make his usual wisecracks about the situation, to act amused by the idea of Mom with someone else in their old bed.

Then the week before we were supposed to move in, Brady and I were vegged out in the living room at his dad's house, making plans. We could borrow his mom's boyfriend's truck to move our stuff, Brady said. We'd have our beds from home; we could use those plastic crates instead of dressers. His mom, Layla, had an old couch in the basement we could have, a couple of beanbag chairs. She'd promised to tie-dye some sheets and make them into curtains. My mom would donate kitchen things.

"Can you dig it, Jax?" he said. "One week from today, we'll be grooving in our own pad. Totally jerk-proof." He laughed this kind of heh-heh-heh cartoon laugh and looked over at his dad's stereo system—an incredible setup, top of the line. "All we need now is the Great Wall of Music."

"Right," I said. "Just ask him nicely. Dad, sir, could I please have your stereo?"

"Ha, ha," Brady said. "He won't even let me use it when I'm here. A boom box is good enough for me." He looked over at the Great Wall again. "Want to hear the new R.E.M.?" he said.

"Sure." I got up to head for his room, where the boom box was.

"No, man. Here. Deluxe sound."

"Brady," I said, "jeez, don't piss him off now. What if he says he won't pay for the apartment?"

"He won't know," Brady said. He put the CD in, turned the volume way up.

That's why we didn't hear Mr. Burton come in early from work. Brady and I were stretched out on the white couches, totally into the music, our eyes closed. Mr. Burton got all the way over to the stereo and hit the stop button on the CD player before we realized he'd come in. He stood there in the sudden quiet, probably counting to ten in his head. He prided himself on being a rational guy.

5

"Brady, I believe I asked you not to use my stereo," he said.

"Hey, I'm your kid," Brady said. "Remember? What's yours is mine."

"No," Mr. Burton said. "What's mine is not yours. My stereo system is certainly not yours. You may remember that I gave you a stereo of your own to use when you're here."

"Boom box," Brady said. "Big deal."

"A very expensive boom box," Mr. Burton said. "And you're damned lucky to have it. This may surprise you, Brady, but the very best of everything isn't owed you simply because you exist. If you don't figure that out pretty soon, you're going to be in sad, sad shape when it's time to face the real world."

"Oh yeah," Brady said. "The real world. *Your* real world. Hey, old man, what makes you think I'm ever going to have anything to do with that?"

Mr. Burton raised his hand, as if he might hit him. Then he just lowered it, as if in surrender, and shook his head. "You know, Brady, you're absolutely right. On this issue, I defer to you. You'll never have anything to do with the real world. You can't hack it." He walked out the front door and drove away.

Brady said, "Do you believe this, Jackson? Do you believe he dissed me like that?" He started pacing back and forth across the living room, muttering, "Asshole, asshole."

"This is news?" I said. "So your dad's an asshole. So what?"

He kicked the leg of an end table, and a Chinese lamp teetered on its base.

"Come on, Brady," I said. "Chill out."

For a second I thought he would. He walked over to the picture window and pulled back the curtains as if to look out. Then suddenly he yanked them so that the brass rod pulled away from the wall and hung at a slant across the window. Plaster rained down onto the end table.

"Brady!" I said. But it was as if I weren't even there.

He started pacing again, and now every time he crossed the room, he wrecked something. First a blue ceramic ashtray on the coffee table. He just picked it up and dropped it, shattering it on the wood floor. Then he ripped up an *Architectural Digest*.

6

I'd never seen him like this before. He was the one who always told people, "You want to freak out your parents? Don't get mad. It drives them insane." Now it was as if he'd drunk some kind of potion. The truth is, it scared the crap out of me. Watching Brady trash his father's living room, I felt paralyzed—exactly like I used to feel when I was little and something I was watching on TV suddenly turned scary. Just get up and turn it off, I'd tell myself. But I never did. I'd stare at the screen, all the while a dark place opening wider and wider inside me, just like it was now.

I did try to calm him down once. He stopped in the middle of the room, looking a little confused. He was drenched in sweat, breathing as hard as if he'd just come in from a run. I went over to him then, spoke his name, and put my hand on his shoulder. But he shrugged me away. For a second I thought he might hit me. Instead, he turned to the shelf of tapes behind him. Methodically, he pulled each cassette from its plastic case, then ripped the tape from the cassette. Pretty soon the room was covered with what looked like brown ticker tape. As if there'd been some kind of weird parade.

Finally, he threw himself down on one of the couches and stared at the mess he'd made.

"You are in deep shit," I said.

"Screw it," he said. "Screw you. Screw everyone."

"Come on, man," I said. "Don't be a jerk. I'll help you clean up what we can. Then let's get the hell out of here."

"No way," he said.

"Okay, let's just leave then."

"You leave, Jax," he said.

I didn't think I should leave without him. But when I tried to convince him to go with me, he grabbed me and pushed me to the front door. "Go," he said. "I mean it. Just leave me alone." So I did. There was no arguing with Brady once he'd made his mind up. Plus, by then I was pretty pissed off myself, and disgusted by what he'd done. I figured Mr. Burton was going to come back any minute, and I didn't want to deal with that.

Two days passed before I found out Brady had run away. Ted went to visit his kids in St. Louis, and my mom came out of her rosy fog long enough to realize that the grass hadn't been cut for weeks and my room was a pit. She put me to work. Then, in a fit of nostalgia, she decided we should go school shopping. Like I was a fifth grader, thrilled to buy a couple of pairs of jeans and the three-ring binder of my dreams. I humored her. I didn't want her to get mad at me and change her mind about the apartment. We were supposed to move that weekend, over Labor Day.

Friday I called him.

"Brady?" his mom said. "Haven't you heard? He took off in his dad's Chevy—you know, the car Jerry keeps to drive to the airport so he doesn't have to leave the BMW in the parking lot. I figured you knew. He left the day he trashed Jerry's living room— you were there then, weren't you?"

I didn't answer.

Layla hated Mr. Burton's guts. She couldn't quite keep the serves-him-right tone out of her voice when she said, "Jesus, what a mess. You *were* there, weren't you, Jackson? Jerry said you were."

"Yeah," I said.

"He's pissed out of his mind," she said cheerfully. "You know what a chintz he is. It's killing him that he's already put down that three-hundred-dollar deposit for your apartment. God, he's so predictable. So gettable. I said to him, 'Jerry, it's not like this is the first time Brady's pulled a stunt like this. Just cancel the credit cards and he'll be back. Why get bent out of shape? That's exactly what he wants you to do.' "

She laughed. "Anyhow, I figure he'll run out of money pretty soon. He'll get hungry. When he shows up, I'll have him give you a call."

She hung up then, but I sat there for a long time with the phone receiver in my hand. My room was spotless. My stuff was packed to move. I thought, She's right. He'll be back; don't sweat it.

I remembered the time Brady got mad at his mom and spent a week holed up at his dad's cabin in Michigan. Another time, he and this kid we knew from junior high decided to take off for California. They ran out of money before they got to Kansas City, and turned back.

But the whole weekend went by. Tuesday, the first day of

school, I woke up to the sound of my mom's voice. "Up and at 'em, Jackson," she said. God, there she was at the foot of my bed, terminally perky, exactly as she had been every school day since I'd started kindergarten.

"Oh, man," I said, and it hit me like a Mack truck: I'm stuck in this house, this life. Brady's gone.

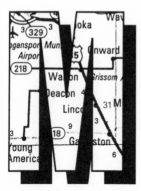om felt bad for me, sure. But the truth is, she'd always thought Brady had a bad attitude. And though she didn't come right out and say so, I knew she wasn't all that sorry he was gone. She wasn't sorry that the apartment deal had fallen through, either. She admitted it not long after he left, when we were talking and watching Saturday morning cartoons in the kitchen— something we've done together since I was a little kid.

"I have to say I'm glad you didn't move to the apartment, Jackson," she said. "This time next year, you'll be off to college. That's soon enough. I'm not exactly in a hurry to get rid of you, you know." She gave me a funny look. "Honey, you didn't think of running away with Brady, did you?"

I said, "I wasn't invited."

She shook her head and sat there for a while, running her fingertip around the rim of her coffee mug. She said, "You know,

Jackson, Brady—" She paused. "Brady has a lot of problems—"

"Oh, *really?*" I said.

"His parents—"

"They're screwed," I said. "He's better off without them."

"But he isn't ready to be without them, Jackson. It's dangerous out there for a person like Brady, who—"

"He's tougher than you think," I said. "He's the smartest person I know."

She gave me this look like she thought I was suffering brain failure.

I said, "You think he's dumb because he blew off school, don't you? Give me a break. Do you really think there's anything worthwhile going on there? It's nothing but a big waste of time."

"Maybe," she said. "But it's what you're *supposed* to do at this time of your life. It's your job." That's what she always said about school. Anytime I ever complained about how stupid it was, she'd say, "Sometimes life demands stupid things of us, Jackson." As if that made stupidity okay. Still, she'd drummed this sense of responsibility into me so successfully that I'd already gotten through that first week of school like a robot.

By the second week, the rumors about Brady were thick. He was in Pennsylvania: Beth Barrett was sure she recognized him when the TV camera panned the crowd at an antinuke rally. The guy she saw had ratty blond hair like Brady's, that same teddy bear body. He had on a psychedelic T-shirt—hot pink and blue, with "Grateful Dead" on the back—just like the one Brady always wore. Eric Harmon heard that the Arizona State Police had called Brady's dad and asked him to send Brady's dental records to see if they matched up with a dead kid they'd found in the desert. At a dinner party, Tom Best's parents heard that Mr. Burton's Chevy had been found in a Shell station in Wyoming. Supposedly, when Brady realized he couldn't charge gas anymore, he'd ditched the car and set out hitchhiking.

Stephanie Carr told us she dreamed of Brady every night. He was serene, she said. He was in a quiet place, surrounded by trees. She saw a lake in one dream, turquoise, deep. First period, while the images were still fresh, she'd sit in Western Civ with her eyes closed, thinking *where, where, where,* like a mantra. When the bell rang, she'd reach across my desk and borrow my notes, which she'd copy all through Conversational French.

Even teachers were talking about him. I was an office messenger one period of the school day. I'd sit there, pretending to study, and eavesdrop on their conversations. They loved to one-up each other. They'd hash over absurd conferences they'd had with Jerry and Layla—the two of them having called a truce and united forces just long enough to come in and blame the school for whatever mess Brady was in. A lot of teachers said flat out they were glad to get rid of him. The nicer ones worried. "That kid has no common sense," they said. "Something terrible is going to happen to him." But they didn't miss him.

Mrs. Blue was the only teacher who was truly sorry he ran away. But then, she was the only teacher who ever figured out that there was a lot more to Brady than he let on at school. Sometimes we talked after Western Civ class, and she'd bring up something he said or did—usually something outrageous or funny or secretly nice. Once she said, "Jackson, I always thought Brady could've been a good writer if he'd just put his mind to it. You know, he did a great job on that pioneer journal assignment we did last year. But when I told him so, he started acting even worse than usual in class. . . ."

She felt so bad about what had happened, as if she'd failed Brady somehow, that I had to tell her he really did care about writing, he really did try. I said, "He's probably writing every day—wherever he is. Science fiction, that's what he loves." I even told her about the novel he wrote when we were in the sixth grade—how Layla had it printed and bound and gave it to all her friends for Christmas without first asking him if she could. After that, I told Mrs. Blue, Brady never showed his stories to anyone, not even me.

"So it wasn't you," I told her. "It wasn't anything you did."

"Thanks, Jackson," Mrs. Blue said. She put her hand on my shoulder for a second, then turned away. Jeez, she was practically crying.

It gave me some kind of weird power knowing what to say to make people feel better about Brady, having information nobody else had. Before, it seemed like no more than the love-me-love-my-dog syndrome that made me part of our group. I was Brady's friend; I tagged along. For the most part I was invisible. Now our friends stopped me in the halls, phoned me in the evenings, came over to talk to me at parties. They'd say, "Now, what exactly happened that day at Brady's dad's house?" Then they'd listen intently while I repeated it. They acted as if Brady's disappearance were a story problem from sixth-grade math: *If a boy says ABC to his father, wrecks X number of tapes and other household goods, then steals Y number of credit cards, Z amount of cash from his dad's top drawer, plus a blue 1983 Chevy, where will he end up?*

Since I was Brady's best friend, everyone figured he'd let me know where he was. I figured he would, too. I'd go home every afternoon fully expecting to find a postcard from some exotic place. Or to hear the phone ring at an ungodly hour. "Collect call for Jackson Watt from Brady Burton," the operator would say. I'd say, "Do it," and there'd be Brady, barking at me, telling me how great it was on the road, saying, "Jax, come on, man. You've got to come right now."

I just might have gone, too. The way I felt those first few weeks—cool for the first time in my entire life—I might actually have had the courage. But as time passed and there was still no word, people lost interest in what had happened to him, and I began to feel like a fool for still caring. For believing that once Brady made it to the wider world he'd give me a second thought. He'd laugh if he realized what a big deal his leaving was to me. How I'd used him to make me feel like a player. Get a life, Jax, he'd say. The more I thought about it, the stupider, the smaller I felt. Me, run away? Oh, right. By the end of October, I could hardly even drag myself to parties.

Not that I'd ever been the party animal Brady was. He loved to chug a few beers, then entertain everyone doing imitations of our principal, Mr. Parker, who read the morning announcements like a zombie, mispronouncing every third word, and our history teacher, Mr. Nowicki, who'd packed a radio in Vietnam and eventually managed to turn every class discussion to what it had been like there, how everyone in his unit had been perpetually stoned.

Alcohol made Brady weirdly amiable. When it was time to

go home, he'd say, "Okay, Jax. Who's too wasted to drive?" He'd usher the ones I named into my VW bus: "the Magic Bus," he called it. He'd pop in a tape—usually some mix he'd made—turn up the stereo full blast, and pretty soon everyone would be hooting out the windows, laughing and singing. He'd yell, "Halt!" if someone had to puke, and I'd put on the brakes. I'd drop them off at home, one by one, Brady last. "Thanks, dude," he'd say, and weave up to the front door like one of those harmless drunks in a movie from the fifties.

Now parties were awful. I sat and watched everyone get loaded, knowing I'd never have the nerve to say anything about their driving without Brady there to jolly them along. In fact, without Brady there making a joke out of everything, some people turned downright mean.

The night of homecoming I said, "Remember last year when Brady's car got a flat tire in the parade?"

Eric Harmon said, "Is Burton all you can talk about, man?"

Tom Best said, "Face it, dude, Brady is history."

"Yeah, Watt, have a brew for once," someone else said. "Loosen up."

Kate Levin giggled. "Hey, we should get Brady's picture put on one of those milk cartons. Like those kidnapped kids. Some lady in Toledo would spot him in the grocery and call in."

"Or in Kalamazoo at the Burger King," Tom said. "With Elvis."

Had they all forgotten how close we once were? How close Brady made us right from the beginning? How when we were freshmen he thought up the idea for the club?

We had to make these time capsules in World History class. "Choose a series of artifacts or visual images that are representative of American adolescence in the latter part of the twentieth century," Ms. Redmon had said. Some people turned in real capsules with real things inside: Walkmans, photos of rock stars, football programs, friendship bracelets, neon-colored Chuck Taylors, *TV Guides*. Ms. Redmon said we could interpret the assignment creatively. Brady was the only one who really did.

He got one of those black-and-white speckled composition books, wrote "DIVORCE: A DAY IN THE LIFE" in big letters on the front, and asked everyone in our class whose parents were divorced to write something in it. He got an F.

"You didn't really do any work," Ms. Redmon told him. "And your topic is too narrow."

"Screw it," he said after class. But I knew he was upset.

Usually, Brady threw away all his school papers, whether he'd gotten a decent grade or a poor one. He kept the notebook, though. And in spite of the fact that he was mad at Ms. Redmon about his grade, he admitted that her assignment had been worthwhile. The idea of the time capsule nagged at him. We *should* be responsible for recording our lives, he said. That's when he started the club.

Anyone whose parents were divorced and who wanted history to remember the effect of divorce on their lives could join. We'd be totally available to each other. A member could call another member at any time, day or night, and that person was honor bound to help him. Like AA, Brady said.

The thing is, just being together made people feel better. We'd get together at someone's house every few weeks, eat pizza, and talk. It got so that we'd try to one-up each other with the crazy things our parents had done. Like Eric's parents having the Grandparent Ticket Lottery for his brother's graduation because there were eight grandparents instead of the usual four. Or Pam Flowers's parents, who'd gone steady in high school, going to their twentieth class reunion together as a joke—her mom wearing her dad's class ring on a chain around her neck. Brady put me in charge of writing everything down.

After a while, the club got to be less formal. The gatherings became parties for all our friends. But because Brady had made us comfortable with the idea of talking about our lives, there was always a group sitting around, deep in conversation. I still wrote down the things people said, but not right at the time, like I had before. I wrote later, alone, sitting on my bed—like I am now.

I still have that notebook, and I've kept it up these past two months even though Brady's gone. I've quit going to parties, but

I write down the news I hear, eavesdropping in class, at lunch, in the halls. In fact, keeping up the notebook is the only real reason I can see for being in school at all.

I hate being there. I sit in class and stare at our so-called friends one by one, thinking, Hey, remember the time Brady drove you down to IU for Journalism Institute when your dad had to go pick up his girlfriend at the airport? And you—remember the time your mom had the car accident and he drove you to the hospital every night to see her? And how about that T-shirt he gave you, asshole, when you told him your parents were splitting up? The one he had made specially for you, with a picture of Beaver Cleaver and his family silk-screened on it, circled, with a line slicing across the middle?

Screw 'em, Brady's voice says inside my head. *Screw it all*. But that's all it says—nothing about what to do instead of caring, since I don't have the guts to run away.

Walking down the hall, I feel like I have ankle weights on. Just getting from one class to another and then, finally, home, exhausts me. But when it's time to sleep, I lie on my bed, bug-eyed, watching the digital clock click off the seconds, minutes, hours.

Tonight I got up, though, and got the divorce notebook out of my desk drawer. I wrote for a while in it, the usual thing. Then I turned the notebook over and upside down so that when I opened it, it seemed like a blank book again. On the first page, I wrote everything that had happened since Brady left, all I felt. I'll keep on writing in it until he comes back.

I have to believe he'll come back. When he does, he'll grab the notebook and throw himself on my bed to catch up on the divorce data. When he's done, I'll say, "Flip it over, man."

He'll read what I've written about my life; then he'll fill in his half of the conversation. He'll say, "Okay, Jax, here's the program."

And everything will fall into place.

ad picks me up for our regular Wednesday night dinner and says, "Jackson, I bought a family membership at the health club so the two of us can work out together." He tosses me a bag from Capitol Sporting Goods. Inside are two pairs of gym shorts and some tank tops, the kind with deep-cut armholes, like bodybuilders wear. There's socks and a new pair of Reeboks. There's a new gym bag with a couple of white towels in it. Oh, great, I think. He's feeling guilty about not spending quality time with me. Or he's freaked out because I don't hate Mom's boyfriend. Or he feels sorry for me because I'm so pathetic since Brady left. I hate it when he gets responsible. I'm starving, but I don't say a word when we drive past the steak place where we usually eat.

Walking into the club, we're blasted with music: there's a different song playing in each one of the four aerobics classrooms. The girl at the desk smiles as my dad explains the sign-in process to me. "Welcome to The Peak," she hollers over the din.

In the locker room, there are mostly yuppie guys, loosening

their paisley ties, stepping out of their pin-striped suits. As usual, my dad's wearing jeans and one of his dozens of concert T-shirts. Tonight: George Thorogood and the Destroyers. He's in pretty good shape because of the work he does—he's a carpenter and rigger with the stagehands union and spends a lot of time hauling equipment and climbing around stage sets—but now, as he changes into his workout clothes, I notice that he's bigger than he used to be. The muscles in his arms are bulging. His gym shorts are tight around his thighs.

He sees me looking, and grins. "I got tired of looking like a wimp," he says. Then, "Speed it up, bud. I've got someone lined up to show you the machines."

I put on the red pair of shorts, one of the tank tops. The new Reeboks are so white they're like beacons. Anyone who hadn't already noticed the way the tank top flaps around my chest would take one look at these shoes and laugh his head off because it's so obviously my first time here. That's not the worst thing, though. The walls are mirrors. I have to look at myself.

Dad introduces me to Kim, his trainer. *Our* trainer. She's twenty-something. Pretty. Five-two, tops—but built. Curly blond hair. She's an exercise physiologist, he says. From his tone of voice, you'd think he was telling me she was a brain surgeon.

Bingo. I get it: his new girlfriend.

"Jackson," Dad says, "Kim'll have you looking like Arnold Schwarzenegger before you leave for college."

"Oh, Oz." Kim giggles; then I see her realize I might think she's giggling at the hopelessness of his promise. She rearranges her face into a more professional expression—or at least as professional as anyone could hope to look, dressed the way she is: shiny black tights, bright pink bralike top that matches her long pink fingernails, a pink headband the same color, and pink socks that fall around her ankles.

She opens a file cabinet, takes out a chart, and hands it to my dad. "You get started, Oz." She checks her watch, pink also. "Twenty minutes on the StairMaster, right? I'll come check on you in a few minutes, after I've done Jackson's profile." She takes out another chart and prints my name in block letters across the top.

"So," she says brightly, "what do you want to work on?"

"Hey—" I attempt a grin. "You're the expert. You tell me."

"Hmm," she says, looking me up and down, scribbling on the chart. "Pecs for sure. Lats." She gestures toward one of the Nautilus machines. "We'll put you on the pull-down for those. You'll want to build your biceps, of course. Everyone wants good biceps. And lots of legwork."

"I've got a terrific mind," I say. But her blank look tells me she doesn't get the joke.

Brady would die laughing. At Kim, because she's such a dim bulb. At the machines that look like high-tech skeletons, at the dorks working out on them, moaning and grunting like they're having orgasms. He'd love schlepping around this place with his gut hanging over his gym shorts, ogling the women jogging on the treadmills and pedaling the stationary bikes. He'd figure out some way to rub up against Kim's breasts when she helped him get situated in the Nautilus machines, all the while cracking jokes, so instead of getting mad she'd think he was the most amusing person in America. It used to drive me crazy sometimes, the way he always managed to make girls think he was so charming. I mean, what's the attraction? He's got a lousy body, a big mouth, and hair that looks like it got caught in a Mixmaster.

"Body is not the same as body language" is how my mom explains this phenomenon. According to her, girls like Brady because of the way he moves: loose and slouchy, his arms always open, his hands rising palm up, as if saying, Who cares?

Obviously nothing like my own uptight self. It's pathetic. I have to make a conscious effort to unhunch my shoulders and unfold my arms, so Kim can guide me into the machines properly. I pretend it doesn't bother me a bit that nearly every time, my whole body starts shaking after a few reps, and she has to set the weight lower. Nearby, Dad's finished his twenty minutes on the StairMaster and is now doing squats over by the big-screen television, sweat flying off his hair like rain. I can't believe he's subjecting me to this.

"Hey, look on the bright side," Brady would have said. "The humiliation pretty much guarantees a hard-on's out of the question. At least you won't have to deal with that."

19

"This is going to be great for you, Jax," Dad says over dinner. "Put some muscle on that frame. Six months from now, the girls will be all over you."

"Yeah," I say. "Six months from now I'll probably be as big a dude as you are. My life will be a veritable love buffet."

He grins. "Blow off some stress, anyway," he says. "You could use that."

I shrug.

He takes a long drink of beer from his frosted mug. "You know, buddy, your mom's worried about you."

"Mom always worries," I say.

"True," Dad says. "I can't argue with that. But every now and then there *is* a reason for it. She thinks you're unhappy—and I have to tell you, pal, you don't seem so great to me, either."

"Jesus, what is this?" I say. "I'm happy. Read my lips: I am delirious. Will you guys get off my back?"

"Okay, okay." He holds up his hands, palms toward me. "I hear you. Your call, man. You know how you feel. I'm not trying to lay a *Father Knows Best* trip on you."

"Good," I say.

Our food comes. Dad flirts with the waitress, orders another beer.

"So," he says. "Still no word from the latter-day Kerouac?"

"Nope."

"Serious business this time, hey?" he says. "A clean break."

I have to say, I surprise myself. I guess I didn't realize how pissed off I've been at Brady for taking off, for dumping me, until Dad started with the third degree. "That asshole," I say. "He didn't have to make a clean break from me."

"Whoa!" Dad kind of rears back in his chair. "I thought you were on his side."

It's none of your business whose side I'm on is what I'd like to say, but I'm not stupid. The more upset he thinks I am, the harder he'll try to dig information out of me—especially since Mom sent him on this spy mission. So I go rational on him. I say, "What side? If he's not here, there is no side."

He shakes his head and gives me this patient look, like I'm a slow learner but he's doing his best to deal with it. He goes, "Jackson, pal, sometimes you gotta do what you gotta do."

And I'm home free. I know exactly the direction in which this conversation is about to turn. I could leave the table, go play the video game in the lobby a couple of times, and come back, and Dad would still be telling the story of his life. How he left college with nothing but his guitar, went out to San Francisco, got high, met the Dead, and lived happily ever after. Until he hooked up with Mom, who tried and failed to civilize him.

I think about how Brady used to say, "Jax, we ought to trade dads, you know? Your old man would cut me some slack. My old man would chill out. Dude, he loves the way you do things right."

"The way I'm uptight," I'd say.

He'd laugh. "Yeah, Jax. Uptight. A virtue, according to the Jer. If some of us weren't uptight, the world would be far too mellow. Nothing would ever get done. Me? I think, Who cares?"

Listening to Dad drone on about how some people just have to get out there and learn things the hard way, I think, Why do I care? About Brady. About Dad, who couldn't do a *Father Knows Best* trip on me if his life depended on it. Man, I'm in worse shape than I thought if Mom's on *his* case to help me.

"You've got to get a life, Jax," he says to me now. "You can't wait around for Brady."

"Yeah, yeah," I say. "I'll get right on that."

Get a life. Fine. I'd love to get a life if I just knew how. I go around for the next few days in a total rage. Get a life, get a life, I keep thinking. Screw you, man. I feel like calling him up and saying, hey, did you ever think about this? Maybe if you hadn't ditched me and Mom, I could've depended on you instead of on Brady. Maybe I wouldn't be so screwed up now.

And I am screwed up. I am clearly screwed up. Even I know I ought to be over the divorce after all this time.

"Jackson," Mom says. "What is the matter with you?"

"Nothing," I say.

"Honey, I know you're—"

"You don't know anything about me," I say. "Just leave me alone."

I go to the gym when I know Dad won't be there, and I work out until my muscles hurt so bad I can't think of anything else. I rake the yard. I slam the rake down into the leaves, which is the closest I can come to hitting someone. But then I start thinking about when I was little and Dad used to rake the leaves into a big pile and leave them in the corner of the backyard for weeks for me and Brady to play in, and I'm not mad anymore. Just depressed.

It makes me want to go back and be that age again: Dad sitting on my bed every night, the two of us goofing around when I was supposed to be going to sleep, Mom yelling, "Calm down, you guys! I mean it!"

When I was scared, he'd make me sing, "Wild thing, you make my heart sing. . . ." We'd both sing at the top of our lungs to show the monsters in the closet that we weren't one little bit scared of them. "Heck, we like monsters!" we'd say.

Halloween night, I drop Snickers bars into the trick-or-treaters' bags and think of how Dad used to be the one in charge of handing out the candy when he lived with us. He'd dress up like a pirate and open the door with one of my rubber knives in his teeth.

Kids come in a steady stream. The usual astronauts, gypsies, and queens. Tiny ghosts and goblins trundle up and hold out their bags. Their parents wait on the sidewalk, and in the weird light of the flashlights they carry, they look like ghosts themselves.

When it's over, when the street is dark and quiet again, I go up to my room, put in Springsteen's *Nebraska,* and turn it up loud. I listen to Bruce sing about losers so I don't have to think about what a loser I am myself. So I don't have to think about Dad and how it used to be.

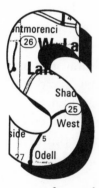

aturday. Mom's gone for the day—she and Ted left ungodly early for the IU–Purdue game. Ted's a big fan. He has one of those thousand-dollar reserved parking places right near the stadium. Every home game, he motors down to Bloomington in his red-and-white van, with a cooler full of beer and every kind of deli food you can imagine. He has dozens of tapes of sixties music that he blares on a jam box while everyone eats. They invited me to come along, but I said I couldn't spare the time.

College applications, I said. I knew that would do the trick with Mom since she's been driving me crazy to get them done. I did work on them for a little while. I got the easy blanks filled in on all of them. Name, address, high school, parents' employers. It's the essays that stopped me.

In various forms, they all say "We want to know more about you." I could comment on foreign policy or on an issue that I believe is crucial to my generation. I could name a character in fiction, talk about why I'd like to know that person—what role

I'd want him or her to play in my life. I could write about my career goals. I could describe some significant experience that changed me.

But I don't care about foreign policy. There is nothing I can say about any issue affecting me and my generation that I think will make any difference at all. I'd like to know Holden Caulfield— God, what a cliché. I have no career goals. The most significant experience of my life is my parents' divorce, and that's nobody's business but my own. So I quit writing.

When the mail comes—still nothing from Brady—I swipe Mom's Victoria's Secret catalog, take it up to my room, and jack off looking at the models. Even that's depressing. It gets me thinking about what a disaster I am with real girls, worse than ever now that Brady's gone. I run through all the girls at school that seem the least bit attractive, the least bit possible. Face it, fool, I think. You can't even talk to them—forget screwing them. Like you'd even get the chance.

Since noon I've been lying on my bed, catatonic, the stereo blaring. When I hear the doorbell, I think, Brady! Then, Ha, forget it. No way. Which pisses me off so bad, I think when he *does* finally show up the first thing I'll do is deck him.

The doorbell keeps ringing, and now I feel catatonic and agitated both, if that's possible. Please, I think. Whoever you are, just go away. I get up and look out the window. Grandma's Cadillac is in the driveway; I'm doomed. She has a key. She comes right in whenever she feels like it, and today is no exception.

"Jackson," she hollers. "Come down here. I can hear that awful music of yours. I know you're there."

She's standing in our kitchen, dressed in her country-club clothes. The minute she sees me, she says, "Sit down. I want to talk to you. Do you realize you've got your mother worried sick?"

I slump into a kitchen chair.

She yanks at the back of my shirt collar. "For Pete's sake, sit up straight," she says.

I gag, hoping to distract her or make her laugh, but she just stares at me with this sad-dog expression, obviously trying to convince herself that I can't be as hopeless as I seem.

"You're such a nice-looking young man," she says. "Why do

you sit like that, as if you want to disappear? Now—" She lights one of her cigarettes, the long, thin kind with pastel flowers printed on the filters, and I can't look at her because I'm thinking about how Brady and I used to crack up over them. "Interesting marketing concept," he'd say. "Kill yourself with pretty cigarettes."

Grandma takes a long drag. "We're *all* worried about you, Jackson. You just haven't been yourself lately."

"Senioritis," I say. "Early diagnosis."

"Oh, nonsense," she says. "According to your mother, you haven't even touched your college applications, and here it is November. If you really can't stand high school anymore, I'd think you'd be a bit more enthused about planning what you're going to do when it's over. If you don't get those applications done before Thanksgiving, who knows where you'll end up?"

"IU is fine with me," I say. "Those other schools are Mom's idea, not mine. I don't want to go to law school or med school. I don't want to be a yuppie with an M.B.A. So what do I have to go to Yale or Harvard for?"

"Jackson, don't be ridiculous. You are seventeen years old. How do you know what you don't want?"

"I know," I say.

"Well, you don't know a thing about how tough it is out there in the real world. You don't have any idea about what you may be called upon to do in your lifetime."

That gets her going on who'd have ever thought Mom would end up divorced, struggling to make ends meet on a music teacher's salary—which leads her handily into the subject of Ted.

"Jackson, I hope you're not going to spoil things for your mother," she says. "We both know Ellen can only be happy if you're happy. If she's worrying about you, how can she enjoy her relationship with Ted; how can the two of them attend to their own lives? I wouldn't be a bit surprised to see them get married if things go right. Your grandfather, God rest his soul, would've been crazy about Ted. He's just the kind of man he always wanted for Ellen. Responsible. And he obviously adores her. Your grandfather was heartsick over all Oz put her through. Just heartsick." She lights another cigarette.

I hate it when she gets on this track. I know Dad's no prince, but it makes me mad when she bad-mouths him to me, and today, for some reason, it makes me even madder than usual.

"Yeah, it's really a bummer that Mom ever married Dad in the first place, isn't it?" I say. "If she hadn't, she could've spent her whole life blissed out at tailgate parties in the IU stadium parking lot. And, hey, you wouldn't have had me to worry about at all. Because I wouldn't even exist."

"Jackson!" Grandma looks as if I've just slapped her.

"Okay, I'm sorry," I say. "I'm *sorry*. But give me a break, will you, Grandma? Why would I screw up the thing between Mom and Ted? Have I ever acted like I didn't want Mom to be happy? Just tell her to quit hounding me, and I'll be fine."

She takes a Kleenex from her purse and dabs at the corners of her eyes, careful not to mess up her makeup. She collects herself, tilts her head, and looks at me with a sneaky smile. "So, getting back to IU," she says.

"What about it?" I say.

"Ted loves IU."

I go, "No shit, Sherlock. What gave you the clue? The picture of Bobby Knight he keeps on his bedside table?"

She gives me her pruny look. "You know I don't care to hear that kind of language from you, young man."

"Sorry," I mutter.

"Like I was saying, Ted loves IU." She leans toward me. "Now, Jackson, use your brain. Ted would be very pleased if *you* loved IU, wouldn't he?"

I have to laugh. She can't help herself, always trying to fix things. I say, "Jeez, Grandma. All the world's a stage, and we're your puppets, right?"

"Think about it, Jackson." Grandma reaches into her purse and takes out a twenty-dollar bill. "Buy something for yourself, honey," she says.

"Is this a bribe?" I ask.

She winks at me the way she used to when I was little. Then she's gone.

Back in my room, I tear up all the college applications except the one for IU. I filled it out a long time ago. There's no essay if you live in-state, so it was easy. I put it in its envelope and slap on a stamp.

Suddenly I'm starving. I grab my car keys, cruise past the post office, and mail the application; then I head for Hardee's, where I order more food than I've eaten for the last three days combined. It's kind of crazy how much better I feel just knowing where I'll be a year from today. Not that I think some miracle is going to happen just because I'm in a different place. For all I know, I'll end up by myself; I'll spend my Saturdays eating crap food in a Hardee's there. Where will Brady be then, I wonder? For just one split second, I get this light feeling inside me, and I don't care.

or Mom's birthday, Dad has forty black roses de-livered by Merry Messengers. Normally, she'd have thought this was hilarious, especially the fact that the delivery guy is dressed up like Methuselah and sings that Simon and Garfunkel song that ends "How terribly strange to be seventy." He sings "forty" though, drawing it out, "for-hor-ty," to fit the rhythm. But lately Mom's been edgy, not her usual self. I could have told him they would upset her.

Not in the way they upset Grandma when she calls about two minutes after they're delivered. She's appalled that Dad would have sent black flowers, that he would have made such a big deal about Mom turning forty: she still believes it's perfectly accepta-ble—sensible, even—for a woman to keep her age a secret. My mom's upset because the flowers are so extravagant and because they're from him.

I don't know. Maybe Dad did do this on purpose, like Grandma says. To spoil her birthday. But he's not a mean person, and it's not as if he and Mom haven't played jokes on each other before. More likely, if Dad did upset Mom on purpose with the flowers, it was to remind her exactly how different he and Ted are.

Well, if that's the case, he certainly proved his point. Ted arrives to take us to dinner at Grandma's about a half hour later. He's got forty roses, too. But beautiful pink ones, with a string of real pearls hanging from one of the stems.

Predictably, this gift makes Grandma ecstatic. She fusses over Mom, arranging the necklace just so on her fuzzy sweater. She fusses over Ted, too, oohing and aahing over his extravagant gift. She actually drags out Mom's senior picture from high school to show him. Mom's wearing borrowed pearls in that picture— Grandma's: the ones my grandfather gave her. She gets the two of them settled in the living room, drinks in hand, then bullies me into the kitchen, acting as if she's desperate for help with the hors d'oeuvres. "I told you," she stage-whispers.

"Come on, Grandma," I say. "You never said one word about Ted giving Mom pearls for her birthday."

"You know what I mean," she hisses. "I told you things were going to work out between them. Pearls are just one step from an engagement ring."

"Oh," I say. "Let me get my notebook and record yet another rule from the *Doris A. Boyles Guide to the Civilized World*—"

"Very funny, young man," she says. She thrusts a tray of stuffed mushrooms into my hands and swats me back toward the living room.

Later, in the van, Mom reclines the seat and throws her arm across her face. She fakes a strangling scream: "Aaaarrgh." Then she makes her voice sound like a movie announcer's: "The mother from hell. She incites you with niceness. She makes you murderous with gratitude."

"It wasn't so bad," Ted says. "She meant well."

"Please," Mom says. "The fact that she approves of you is already making me extremely nervous. If you won't admit what a pain she is, I swear I'll never see you again. I'll keep the pearls and send you packing."

"She does have a certain frantic—uh, *birdlike* quality," he says.

"Birdlike," Mom says. "Don't you love that, Jackson? *Birdlike*.

Vulture, maybe. Listen, she's crazy about you, Ted. I just hope you're fully aware of what this could mean. She adores you. You're the man of her dreams." She starts laughing hysterically, then suddenly she's crying.

"Ellen!" Ted pulls to the side of the road, stopping so abruptly that Mom bounces in her seat like a rag doll. "Ellen, are you okay?"

"Oh, God," she says. "Don't pay any attention to me. Mother always makes me insane. Really. Doesn't she, Jackson?"

Ted looks back at me hopefully, and I nod. "It's true," I say.

"It's the roses," Mom says, when we've gotten going again. She resets her seat to a normal position before she continues. "Oh, Ted, I wasn't going to say anything—it's so stupid, really. But since the goddamn roses have gotten me all out of whack it only seems fair."

Ted looks stricken. "I shouldn't have brought you roses?" he asks. "I—"

"No, no," Mom says. "Not your roses; they were wonderful. Oz sent me roses. Forty black ones."

"Black roses?" Ted says. "He sent you *black* roses?"

I shift to the far corner of the seat, trying not to smile, but Mom glances back and sees me, and she starts smiling, too. When Ted repeats, *"Black roses?"* one more time in a wondering tone, we can't help it; we both crack up. Ted looks at Mom with this oh-no-not-again look on his face, which only makes us laugh more.

We calm down eventually, but Ted's still looking anxious when we get to our house. He pulls into the driveway and stops the van. We all sit there awkwardly until Mom reaches over and turns the engine off. "Come in?" she says. He smiles then, a slow smile that seems to spread throughout his whole body. The two of them seem rooted there, their eyes locked on one another.

Oh, God. Again. Lately, the two of them are worse than teenagers. Mom's always coming in with her lipstick smeared and her clothes wrinkled, acting embarrassed and apologetic—as if I'm her father instead of her kid. I feel like her father sometimes, pacing the floor, worrying that she's dead in a car accident, or getting myself all upset imagining her and Ted together at his apartment. It's driving me crazy. I mean, shouldn't I be the one sneaking around having sex? Shouldn't I be the one forgetting there's anyone in the world but me? Okay, here's how bad it really is: I can't even imagine myself with a girlfriend, let alone imagine myself forgetting there's anyone in the world but me and her. The way things are going, I figure I'll be the last person of my entire generation to have sex, if I ever have sex at all. Which I could adjust to a whole lot easier if I weren't continually subjected to these two.

It's begun to rain, a cold, steady downpour that streaks the windshield silver. "You guys wait here," I say. "I'll get Mom the umbrella."

I slide the door of the van open and bolt for the front porch. From the little window near the coat closet I can see them. Their two shadows become one for a long moment, and I'm ashamed of how I feel. Jealous. It's pathetic. What? Do I want Mom to be miserable just because I am? Apparently I do because I have the urge to do something really terrible. I don't even know what, just— terrible. Mean. The kind of thing Brady used to do to Layla when he thought one of her romances was getting too serious: stroll through the living room stark naked with a hard-on, maybe cut the tips off the rubbers in the drawer of her bedside table.

Get a grip, I tell myself. Get real. And I turn the porch light on to give Mom and Ted fair warning that I'm on my way back to the van.

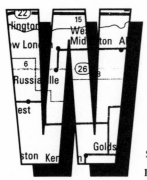hen Dad calls the next day and I try to explain to him why the roses weren't such a great idea, he says, "Bud, what you're telling me is Ellen's lost her sense of humor. Love'll do that, you know." He laughs. "I see it's going to be up to me to provide a little balance in your life until she gets her shit together. A little craziness. Drugs, sex, rock and roll. Well, rock and roll anyhow—after all, I am your father. So, hey, I'm working Crosby, Stills & Nash tomorrow night. You want to go?"

"I guess so," I say. "Yeah, I'll go."

"You want to take a friend?"

Like who? I feel like saying. In case you haven't noticed, I don't have friends anymore. Well, actually, I could invite Stephanie Carr. Flaky as she is, she's been nice to me since Brady left. She worries about me; she's constantly trying to talk me into going out and having some fun. But if I invited her, Dad would assume I had something going with her, and it's not worth trying to convince him that I don't. So I just say, "No thanks."

"Okay if Kim goes with you, then?" he asks.

"Kim?"

"Yeah. Kim. Is that some kind of problem?"

"No, no problem at all," I say, and spend the next twenty-four hours in a state of total anxiety.

But for once things go better than I hoped. I pick her up at Dad's house around six, and she says, "Well, hi, Jackson," as if it's the most normal thing in the world to be going out with me. Dressed in jeans and a sweater, her curly hair pulled back in a barrette, she looks younger but also not as ditzy as she looks in her workout clothes. She chats about people at the health club, tells me about some book she's reading that supposedly proves that red meat can kill.

When we drive by Pizza Hut, Tom Best and Eric Harmon walk out. They wave when they see me; then they see Kim in the front seat and stop dead in their tracks. Their eyes bug out. They think she's my date.

Yes! I think. I get this kind of loose feeling inside and run this mind trip, imagining she really is my date and what we'll do together later in the back of the van.

"Jackson?" she says, jolting me back to reality.

"Yo!" I say, thankful for the darkness that hides my red face—not to mention any evidence of my hard-on. I reach for the dash, rummage through the tapes there for *4 Way Street*, stick it in the tape deck. I calm myself down telling her about how Brady and I always had a preconcert concert to get ourselves in the mood for the real thing. I tell her about the time we told our parents we were going to a leadership conference with the student council but really drove to Chicago to see the Grateful Dead. How Brady forgot his tape case and we didn't dare go back to get it, so all we had was one Dead tape that we found in the glove compartment. How he said, "Tradition, Jackson. That's the trouble with people these days: they don't care about tradition," and insisted that if *Aoxomoxoa* was all we had, then we'd play *Aoxomoxoa* for the whole four-hour drive.

"Who is this guy, Jackson?" Kim asks. "Brady."

"My best friend," I tell her. "He ran away."

She asks me when he ran away, then why, then what do I think about it, how do I feel? She's truly curious to know what would make a person do something that drastic. Which makes talking about Brady easier. Plus, she doesn't know him; she can be objective. He's never done anything to piss her off.

She says, "What does he look like?"

"Pudgy," I say. "Kind of like an oversize eight year old."

She laughs. I tell her how he won't wear anything but T-shirts and jeans. How his hair sticks up in the back like Alfalfa's, his shoelaces are always untied. How he always wears his baseball cap backward.

I think this will make her laugh again. Instead, she asks, "How does Brady feel about himself, about the way he looks?"

"He doesn't give a damn," I say. "He likes being a mess. It drives his dad crazy. Mr. Fitness, you know? Mr. Burton gets up at five every morning so he can get in a six-mile run before he goes to his law office."

"But I bet Brady doesn't actually like being a mess," Kim says. "Don't you think everyone would *like* to look good? Don't you like it, Jackson? You certainly seem different since you've been working out. I mean, look at you, sitting in the driver's seat not even slumping," she teases. "And I was noticing yesterday at the gym that your body's starting to change. Here, for instance." She reaches over and squeezes my right bicep lightly.

It tenses—Jesus, *I* tense all over at her touch, and even though Kim does this kind of thing all the time, I have to say to myself, Stay *right* here, man, okay: breathe, no wet dreams. It's funny, really, the way she regards each human body as a particular challenge—the way a sculptor might view a block of marble. I actually like her.

Here's the shocker, though: I've gotten to like working out, too. At first, I went just to keep Dad happy. I couldn't have been more surprised when, in no time, Kim was adding weight to the machines. I'd nearly kill myself to do the full number of reps because I thought it was hilarious what a big deal she made about my progress. I don't tell her so now, but she's right about my body changing. I'm no Mr. America, but if I stand in front of the mirror in my bedroom and flex my arm, I can see it harden.

We get to Market Square Arena early enough for the sound check. First the amps, then the mikes. The stagehands call out, "Test Graham, test David, test Stephen." The band roadies test the guitars, the keyboards. The percussion roadie strikes the drums repeatedly.

"Where's Oz?" Kim asks, and I point him out high above us, crawling around on the rigging like a circus act. At first, it scares her to see him up there. But she calms down when I tell her he's been doing it since before I was born and he's never fallen yet. Stephen Stills comes out at one point, and Dad scrambles down the rope ladder. Stills points at one of the amplifiers. Dad nods, making a gesture that seems to say, No problem. Stills slaps him on the back, laughs, and disappears.

"Does Oz know him?" Kim asks.

"He knows them all," I say. "All the groups from the sixties that still go out on the road, anyway. He was on road crew for all of them at one time or another, before he came back and married Mom."

"Wow," she says, her eyes glued to Dad back up on the rigging.

She's in love with him. I've watched plenty of women fall in love with him, so I know the signs. It won't be long before she starts thinking about marriage. Part of me says, Oh, not again. Part of me fantasizes that things might actually work out between them. I mean, marrying Kim wouldn't be the worst thing that could happen to Dad. I worry about him. He's not the most careful person in the world. Bouncing around from girlfriend to girlfriend the way he does, he could get AIDS or some other disease. Or he might not. It's the good news/bad news thing: if he does manage to stay healthy, he'll get old. He's a good-looking guy now, young looking, but that can't last forever. What happens when the women he wants don't want him?

Not my problem, I know. Brady was right when he used to say, "Hey, your parents are supposed to worry about *you*."

So I concentrate on not worrying, on watching people fill up the auditorium, and pretty soon Dad scrambles down from the

35

rigging, his work temporarily done, and takes us backstage to watch the concert. Stage right, we lean against speakers twice our size, careful of the tangle of thick black wires all over the floor. We're so close to the musicians that the changing lights make us change color, too. We can see the order of songs taped to the floor.

Spotlights crisscross the audience. Faces leap out, white as mimes' faces, then disappear. Arms wave as if in slow motion. Smoke swirls up like fog. Brady would crack up: I get a perfect shot of his mom and her friend Marlys. The two of them are out of their front-row seats, boogying, holding up their cups of beer. There are these college guys next to them, loving it, egging them on.

I can't help getting pulled in by the music myself. When they play "Our House" near the end, I swear I get as sentimental as if I were forty, remembering that song from when I was young. Actually, I *do* remember it from when I was young. Really young, though—maybe three. It was Mom's favorite song then; we used to sing it together.

Mom asks me later, "Is she nice? Your dad's new girlfriend?" She's leaning against the kitchen sink, watching me eat a slice of pizza.

"She'd never feed me this crap," I say. "Her entire reason for living is to convert the universe to tofu and bean sprouts." I feel a twinge of guilt making fun of Kim, but I know Mom expects it, needs it. "Man, the two of them bicker constantly about food—the other day, it's Dad who starts in. He goes, 'Over my dead body we're having tofu for Thanksgiving.' "

"Thanksgiving," Mom echoes. "Jackson, you're not serious."

I raise my right hand, pizza and all. "I swear it," I say. "And Kim says, 'It might just *be* over your dead body, Oz. The human body is like a car. If you want it to run well *and* look good, you've got to keep it tuned up, cleaned, and waxed. But you've got to give it the right fuel, too. You wouldn't put steak or greasy pork chops in the gas tank of your car even *once*, would you?' Dad goes, 'Oh, for Chrissake.' "

Mom giggles. She says, "Why does this remind me of Laura?"

I roll my eyes.

Laura was his last girlfriend, a recent convert to the New

Age. *She* said too much attention to the body was a clear sign of a soul trapped in the lowest chakra. Older, wiser souls understand that the body itself is of no consequence—it exists merely as a shelter for the spirit. According to Dad, it was this kind of thinking that caused her to go from a size eight to a size fourteen in less than six months, thus causing him to move on.

Sometimes he says to me, "Jackson, never trust a person under thirty." A couple of years ago, he went through a phase of testing every woman he met. Bottom line, if she hadn't heard of Che Guevara, he wouldn't even consider dating her. But it didn't take him long to conclude that relationships with women who *had* heard of Che Guevara involved a smorgasbord of deeper problems: children to raise, jobs they'd love to quit the moment they got married, brains fried by acid. Dad said that too many of them held the tiresome conviction that if women ran the world, it would be a better place. And, invariably, they had bad thighs. Very bad thighs.

What he really wants is a woman who will adore him and not need him: a pretty unlikely combination, if you ask me—but he never asks, so I don't say. I stay mellow. Dad's girlfriends come and go. They're nice, most of them. They want me to like them, and usually I do. But I don't get attached to them.

"Is she nice?" Mom asks again.

"She is," I say. "She's no rocket scientist, but she's nice."

"Well, that's good." Mom sighs, and I remember the thing that both of us are always trying to forget. She still loves him. Looking at her lost in her own thoughts, I have a sudden vivid memory of her standing in exactly the same spot years ago, watching Dad. He was sitting at the table—in the same place I'm sitting now—eating chocolate ice cream, his favorite food.

It was night. I was supposed to be in bed, but I was thirsty, so I'd come downstairs to get a drink of water. When I got to the kitchen door, though, and saw them there, I stepped back into the little bathroom across the hall.

I could still see them. Dad lifted a spoonful of the ice cream and offered it to Mom. It was soupy and a big glop fell on the table. She laughed, took the single step you have to take to get across the small room, and in a dancelike move, bent and licked

37

it up just like a cat. She knelt then and let Dad feed her the rest from the spoon. He looked at her a long time. He took his fingertip and slowly painted chocolate lines on her cheeks, her nose, even on her eyelids. Then just as slowly, he licked them away, both of them laughing, a strange laugh I'd never heard before.

Obviously, I know now what was going on between them. I know what happened when Dad picked her up and carried her to their bedroom, and knowing only makes it hurt more to remember. I mean, maybe I wouldn't feel so bad about the divorce if I thought they'd never loved each other. Or even if they'd loved each other once and then something happened to make them stop. But Mom never stopped loving Dad. I see it on her face sometimes—for no more than a split second—when he walks into a room. And Dad still loves her, too. Or who she once was.

When he talks about the way Mom used to be, it's as if he's talking about a friend who died or disappeared, someone I can never meet. Her hair was long and wavy. She wore floaty clothes, bracelets that jangled. Once I heard him say, "The way Ellen held the guitar, singing, you'd have thought it was made of gold."

They don't say it, but I know it was having me that changed her. It's not my fault they got divorced. I know that. But I can't help believing they'd still be together if I hadn't been born.

know things are seriously cranking up between Mom and Ted when Mom says, "Jackson, Ted would like to take you down to Bloomington for the day. You know, show you around. Honey, it would please him if you'd go."

It's the last thing I want to do. I mean, what are we going to talk about? I imagine horrible dead silences between us. But I say, "Sure, fine," because I'd look like a real jerk if I said no.

Ted's okay, though. He's got this brand-new CD player in his van that has a "random" function; he's like a little kid with a new toy. I get in and he hands me a pile of CDs and says, "Pick ten." He sets up the machine then, and we're perfectly happy cruising along the highway, constantly surprised by what plays next. I say what a great invention the random function is, and he agrees and somehow we get on the subject of weird inventions, gimmicks that've made people a million dollars. I think of Brady then. The way he was always coming up with something no one else would even consider.

I tell Ted about the science project we did when we were in

the fourth grade. "That year everyone was into Atari," I say. "Our moms were always yelling at us to go outside or read a book, but all we wanted to do was play Pac-Man or Donkey Kong or Space Invaders. We'd sit in front of the TV screen for hours on end, clutching the joystick.

" 'Absolutely no more,' Brady's mom said finally. 'I can't stand it.'

"That's when Brady had the idea for the science project," I tell Ted. " 'Does Atari Really Improve Your Hand-Eye Coordination?' "

I tell Ted about the skills test he made up. How many times could we bat a tennis ball against the garage wall without missing one; how many baskets could we hit in a row; how many volleys could we get in before the Ping-Pong ball went flying across the basement floor, out of control?

"Then, of course, we had to play Atari to test our hypothesis," I say. "We'd do the skills test first every day, recording the results on a chart. Then we'd play Atari for thirty minutes, sixty minutes, ninety minutes, two hours at a stretch and test ourselves again to see how the various lengths of time affected our hand-eye coordination."

When Ted groans, I tell him Brady's dad thought the project was the most ridiculous thing he'd ever heard of, too. "This is completely unscientific," he said to Layla. Of course, she thought it was brilliant. But then, Layla always thought Brady was a genius.

"So what happened?" Ted asks.

"We got an honorable mention," I say. "Layla was pissed. Practically everybody got an honorable mention. But we got on TV. Channel Six. This feature story on kids and science. As far as Layla was concerned, that proved we should've won. She was sure Brady was the next Einstein."

Ted just laughs. He's cool. I know Mom's told him about Brady running away and how freaked out I've been about it, but he doesn't use what I told him to segue into emotional territory and try to weasel anything out of me about how I feel. We just drive on a while longer, grooving to Steppenwolf, until we exit the highway and the stone gates of the university come into view.

We have lunch at Mother Bear's, then spend the rest of the afternoon wandering around the campus.

"I always feel strange when I come down here," Ted says. "Like I'm the person I was when I was in school. Like I could actually be that person again if no one could *see* I've gotten older. I suppose that sounds crazy."

"No," I say. "Anyway, no crazier than the way I feel."

Ted cocks his head, waiting for me to go on.

"Like, just now, I'm already the person I'm going to be. You know, when I come here."

"Déjà vu in reverse," he says, and smiles.

Later, when I told Dad I went down to see the campus, he said, "So did Ted get you one of those dork driving caps, like the one he wears?"

In fact, Ted bought me a sweatshirt that cost forty-two dollars and a cool red wool baseball cap, but I knew if I told Dad he'd say Ted was trying to buy me. He'd have acted like he was kidding, said something like, "Your price is too low, Jackson. You should have held out for a red Jaguar, with IU plates." But his feelings would have been hurt. It's bad enough that Ted's a successful businessman, a successful businessman who graduated from the college my dad flunked out of. Dad says he dropped out, but Mom told me that he took off for California because his grades were so bad, he knew it was just a matter of time before he got the letter telling him it was all over.

I dread telling him what happened tonight. I was doing my homework at the kitchen table when Ted came to the door. I said, "Sorry, Mom's gone to the PTO meeting at her school." But he just stood on the porch, his hands in his pants pockets. He said, "I know. Jackson, could I talk to you?"

Ted is a big man. Not fat. Stocky. "Beefy," Dad says. However you want to describe him, it was disconcerting to see a man Ted's size, dressed in a suit and tie, looking anxious about whether or not his girlfriend's kid was going to invite him in.

I opened the screen door, and he stepped into the kitchen. "Want a beer?" I asked.

"Oh, yeah, great," he said. "Thanks a lot."

I pulled the tab on a Michelob and handed him the cold can. He took a long drink, then twisted the can around and around in the palm of his hand. He looked at my homework spread out on the table. "I'm interrupting you—"

"My pleasure," I said. "I hate physics." I snapped my book shut and laughed, hoping he'd laugh, too. He didn't, though.

"Listen, Jackson," he said, "what would you think about my girls coming over from St. Louis for a visit. Say, Thanksgiving?"

"Sure," I said. "Why not?"

He cleared his throat. "The thing is, I don't exactly know how they'll act. They're still so upset, you know. Just nine and five. They're still, well, they're still upset—"

"About the divorce," I said.

"I guess you know how that is," Ted said.

"Yep," I said.

"So, if they acted . . . lousy at first, you'd understand."

I said I would.

He said, "Good. Good. It really matters to me how it works out, you know, in the long run." Then, out of the clear blue sky, he said, "Jackson, I want to marry your mom."

I looked at him for some clue to what he expected me to say, but he looked as stupid and in-over-his-head as I felt. I said, "You're asking me if you can?" My voice cracked like an eighth grader's.

Ted didn't laugh, though. He didn't want me to feel like the fool I was; I could tell. He sat down on one of the kitchen chairs, set his beer on the table. "I guess I'm asking you what you think." He paused. "What do you think, Jackson?"

"Does my mom know you're here?" I asked. If he said yes, I was going to kill her.

He shook his head. "We talked about Kristin and Amy coming. We both wanted to be sure you'd feel okay about it. A holiday and all. She probably wouldn't be surprised to know that I dropped by to see what you thought about that. I don't know. Maybe she would be surprised. Maybe she'd have wanted to talk to you first. Or maybe she *has* mentioned the girls coming?"

Ted went on before I could answer. "Listen, I had no idea I

was going to say that other to you. About wanting to marry Ellen. It just came out. I haven't really talked to your mom about it yet. Not seriously."

He heaved a big sigh. He put his head in his hands. "God, I just don't want to screw this up," he said. Then he told me all about his ex-wife, how unhappy they'd been together right from the start. She was a painter, he said. An abstract painter. He had an M.B.A. They should've known it wouldn't work out. Apparently, everyone *else* knew. When they told their friends they were splitting up, every single one of them said, "I can't believe you guys hung in there as long as you did."

"My own parents said it," Ted said. "They never could stand Susan. She was too . . . unusual for them. I loved her, though. When I was with Susan, I felt like a more interesting person. When we were younger, that is. The last few years I was with her I felt like a nerd. When she left me, she said I was an embarrassment."

He said, "For a long time, I wanted to kill her."

What was I supposed to say to that?

"Oh, Christ, I shouldn't be talking about any of this with you, Jackson," he said. "I know that. It's just—I really do love Ellen. You'll probably think this is stupid, but I fell in love with your mom on our first date. She's so—I don't know, she's so good. I know how she feels about your dad. I mean, I know she still loves him. I know she'll never really get over it—"

He paused and looked at me, as if to make sure I knew that piece of information about my mom. I shrugged to show him that I did.

"I can handle that," he said. "But, Jackson, do you think maybe she could be happy with me?"

I had to tell the truth, even though I knew it meant kissing off the life it had taken Mom and me so long to get used to, starting all over again. "Yeah," I said. "Yeah, I do."

"You do? Really?"

Brady probably would've said something silly like, "Yes, my son," to break the tension. I just nodded.

Ted took a deep breath and let it out. He laughed then, a

kind of weird laugh. "This is ridiculous, isn't it? Talking to you this way. As if you were Ellen's father."

"It's okay." I felt the heat rush to my face, heard my voice go a little out of control again when I said, "I appreciate, you know, that you care what I think."

Ted leaned over and punched me on the shoulder. "You're one in a million, Jackson," he said. "You're not like other kids."

How true, I thought. Depressing. If only he knew what that actually meant: Jackson, you're a loser. But I must be getting used to it because, at least right then, I felt perfectly comfortable sitting there at the table with Ted, the King of the Dweebs.

He took out his daughters' school pictures and showed them to me. "They really are good girls," he said. "Just upset, you know?"

"It's hard," I said. "I remember that."

He nodded. "I think you'll be good for them, Jackson. I think you'll be a help to them. But, believe me, I know it's been just you and Ellen for quite some time now, and I'm counting on you to let me know if Kristin and Amy bug you or if they get in the way of your privacy. Or if I do, for that matter." He blushed. "Assuming Ellen agrees to marry me, that is—"

A kind of awkward silence fell between us then, until Ted grinned and said, "So, what do you think about those Hoosiers?"

We were still talking IU basketball when we heard Mom's car in the driveway. She walked in and looked at us with a puzzled expression.

Ted glanced at me, then he stood up. "Ellen," he blurted out, "will you marry me?"

"What?" she said. "Oh, my God. Yes." And burst into tears.

When she calmed down, Mom called Grandma to tell her the news, and then she cried some more. Ted grinned goofily. The three of us sat around in the kitchen a long time. Ted's normally a fairly quiet guy, but tonight he couldn't quit talking. He told Mom how great their life was going to be, starting now. He told her all the things he was going to do to make her happy. We were all going to be happy, me included, he said.

He didn't mean anything by it, I knew, but it depressed me. Mom, yeah. Ted has a good shot at making Mom happy, and I hope he does. But me? Sometimes I think I won't ever be happy again. I'm not even sure I want to be happy. I mean, I was once, when I was little, and look what happened. But I figure things aren't going to get worse with Ted around, and I'm satisfied with that.

When I got up and said I'd better be getting to bed, he said, "Jackson, I don't exactly know how to say this, but—well, you know—I'd like you even if you weren't Ellen's kid."

Mom cast me a grateful glance when I reached out, shook his hand, and said, "Ted, as stepfathers go, I couldn't think of a better person for the job. Plus, you might let me drive your van sometime, with the random CD player." That made him laugh.

"Absolutely," he said. We shook hands again; he clapped me on the back.

"He's some kid, Ellen," I heard him say to my mom as I headed upstairs.

I crawled into bed with my clothes on. I was so tired from all that had happened this evening, I felt like I was dying. I thought I'd conk out right away, but I couldn't sleep. So here I am writing in the notebook again, trying to make sense of my life.

Why can't I just be happy for my mom? I *am* happy for her. God, I've known for a long time that she and Dad were never going to get back together. So why am I getting all bent out of shape about the divorce again—as if Dad had just left yesterday?

There's no answer; there never is. Why try to make sense of it? What I really want is out of my life for a while. Or I want Brady back in it.

If he were here, he'd dream up some weird, amusing plan to make me see beyond my own small, pathetic life. Hell, if Brady hadn't run away, I'd be at our apartment right now, living a real life. What's happening between Mom and Ted wouldn't affect me at all.

45

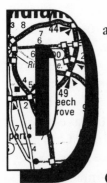ad's blasting the horn at 8:45 on Thanksgiving morning for the Turkey Trot, an event Dad and his friend Tom cooked up a few years ago when they started running. The idea is if you run five miles on Thanksgiving, you can eat whatever you want the rest of the day. Like most things Dad has anything to do with, it's gotten slightly out of hand. Last year the theme was "America: the Cornucopia," and Dad and Brady and I went as a bunch of carrots, dressed in orange mechanics' jumpsuits and orange stocking caps with plastic ferns stuck on top. This year's theme is "Your Favorite American Freedom."

"Too bad Brady can't make it," Dad said when he told me. "He could've been a road."

It annoyed me. When he said, "So what should we be, pal?" I said I had my own idea for a costume, thinking it would hurt his feelings. But if it did, he didn't let it show.

I get in the car this morning, and there he is dressed in regular running clothes, with the brown hairy arms of a grizzly bear costume fastened over his own arms and a little sign hanging around his neck that says "The Right to Bear Arms." Kim shows off her pink Lycra suit plastered with bumper stickers—she's freedom of expression.

I wait for Dad to turn and say, "What, no costume?"

Then I whip a red bandanna out of the waistband of my sweatpants and tie it across my mouth. I hold up an index card that says "The Right to Remain Silent."

"Perfect," he says, just the tiniest bit edgy.

It is perfect. I feel weirdly happy. I like having annoyed Dad. I like wandering around Tom and Mary Beth's yard without feeling like I have to make conversation.

"Where's your friend Brady?" Mary Beth asks.

I give her the hitchhiker's thumb.

Like always, the costumes are cool. Tom's made a sandwich-board American flag with flames painted at the top of it. Now and then he lights up a cigarette to get the effect of smoke. Mary Beth is dressed as a fountain pen: black sweats with a gold band around her shoulders. She's made a nib out of gold cardboard that sits on her head like a crown. She's the Declaration of IndePENdence. Each of their three kids is dressed in red, white, or blue sweats, "We The People" emblazoned on their chests, one word per kid. A bunch of their friends are there, too. They have poster board printed with phrases from the rest of the preamble to the Constitution hung around their necks, and with a signal from Tom they make a long line, each one reciting his or her part.

Dad and Tom pass out Styrofoam cups of champagne to the runners. Mary Beth serves powdered doughnuts on silver trays. Near starting time, they herd us all onto the front porch for the pageant, which consists of everyone singing "Old Mr. Turkey" at the top of their lungs. Then it's time for the Blessing of the Shoes.

I've never run the Trot before. I've always hung out at the house with Brady. Kim talked me into doing it this year. "Surprise your dad," she said a few weeks ago. "You're in shape; you can do it."

"Go for it," she says now, and gives me a little push toward the starting line.

"You're running?" Dad asks.

I nod.

A guy dressed up like a Catholic priest invokes God and Notre Dame to help us run fast. Tom's littlest kid shoots the ritual popgun, and we're off.

"Go, Jax!" Kim yells. She's not running herself. She hates being sweaty anywhere but the gym.

The pack of thirty or so runners spreads out after the first block. Dad and Tom stay with the front group, leaving me to jog at an easy pace near the back. I click off the first mile, my body warming, loosening. It's easy to quicken my pace—so I do, passing people now and then. I like that. I've never been into sports much, but now, running, it occurs to me that maybe it's because when I was a wimp I was never any good at them. Kim's right: I like my new body. I like feeling strong. I catch up with Dad and Tom at the four-mile mark and stay with them right to the finish.

"Yes!" Kim yells, her bumper stickers flapping as she jumps up and down. "Jax, you did it! You did it!"

"Christ," Dad says to her. "Whose side are you on? I buy the kid a goddamn health club membership, and you train him to use it against me." He grins and tries to give her a big sweaty hug, but she screeches, "Oz!" and makes him chase her across the yard.

Mary Beth rolls her eyes. "Isn't Kim a trip?" she says. "God love her. She's so—"

"Enthused?"

"Yeah, that's exactly it. Terminally enthused. Apparently, she's got you spending all your spare time over at the gym, too." She holds me at arm's length. "Well, it's working. You look different—older, better. All grown-up, I guess. And what's this I hear about your mom, hon? Oz says she's getting married."

"Next month," I say. "Christmastime."

"So soon!"

"That's what Grandma says," I say.

Mary Beth laughs. "She probably still wants the wedding she had her heart set on when Ellen married Oz."

"I guess so."

"A hippie wedding. God, she was so mortified! I remember her wringing her hands and saying, 'Honey, you can't want this. A dress like a nightgown and a garland of weeds in your hair!'

Ellen looked so beautiful that day, though. Oh, Jax, do you think she's going to be happy?"

"I think so. Ted's nice. They have a nice time together."

"Oz said that, too."

"He did?" I say. "I thought—"

"You thought your dad didn't like Ted." Mary Beth sort of smiles. "Oz said, and I quote, 'He's a real Neil Diamond kind of guy, what can I say? But he's good to Ellen. I think she really loves him.' "

"Yeah," I say. "She does love him."

"Good," Mary Beth says. "I'm happy for her." She gives me a quick, fierce hug, then she hurries away, leaving me to Dad, who looks at his watch, grimaces, and says, "Go change your clothes, pal. We're outta here. No way am I risking the wrath of Doris, getting you back late for the bird."

Driving to Grandma's, I want to say something to him about what Mary Beth told me; I want to say I'm glad you feel okay about Ted. And I am glad. But I don't speak. I can't risk getting all emotional about Dad right now. I have to concentrate on how not to blow it with Kristin and Amy.

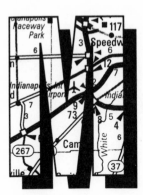

om and I have been through this a million times in the last few weeks. Do we make a big deal of their visit? Do we go for a more low-key approach? Mom regards me as the expert, even though I tried to explain to her that this is not like anything that ever happened between me and Dad's girlfriends.

"Even so," she said. "What did they do that you hated most? What made you like them?"

I said mainly I liked them if they didn't obviously resent me or try to compete with me for Dad's attention or treat me like some generic kid. I hated to be fussed over, though. I liked to be respected as a person but at the same time left alone.

"Well, that's something," she said. "That would favor the no-big-deal approach, wouldn't it? What I think we ought to go for is a kind of no-threat charm."

"Good plan," I said. "First we get some Valium—"

"Jackson!" she said. "Be serious."

But she looks so mellow when she comes to Grandma's door to let me in that I'm not so sure she hasn't gotten some Valium, after all.

"How's it going?" I whisper.

She beams and gestures for me to follow her into the kitchen. Once there, it doesn't take long to figure out that Grandma has taken charge of suckering Ted's kids into loving us. She does it in her usual way, partly with presents and special treats, partly by sleight of hand. She's put a wrapped gift at each girl's place at the dinner table. She's rented tapes for them to watch on the VCR. On the kitchen counter, there's a big glass jar full of Gummi Bears. The sleight of hand part is how she acts as if none of this is a big deal, how she catches them off balance by already knowing who they are.

"You like Gummi Bears, honey?" she says, sounding so surprised when she sees Amy eyeing them. As if she keeps two pounds of Gummi Bears around all the time, to snack on herself while she's watching Phil Donahue. "Here. Let's put some in this little dish for you."

"Is that right?" she says when Mom mentions that Kristin takes ballet lessons. "Well, isn't it funny that I happened to pick out that *Swan Lake* tape to treat myself for doing all this cooking? Kristin, maybe you'd like to watch it."

I happen to know that she's talked to Ted a dozen times in the last week, trying to get a fix on the girls. Kristin, the oldest, is thin and long-legged. "She grew three inches over the summer!" Grandma whispers, coaching me out in the pantry. "She hasn't gotten used to it yet, so don't mention it. Tell her that she looks just like a ballerina. Or that she has pretty hair; Ted says she's vain about her hair. That's what's in the packages, you know. Barrettes and those ruffly bands girls are wearing now to hold their hair back."

Kristin does have pretty hair. It's silky blond, like Ted's—long and straight. Amy's hair is pretty, too. Also blond. But thick and boingy, like Shirley Temple's. But I don't say so. I figure Kristin and Amy probably hate my guts already; they probably think I'm stealing their dad away from them, so, at least right now, it seems better to say nothing than to risk saying something

51

wrong. I'll just watch them a while; that's what I've decided. Take my cues from what they do.

So far, they've ignored me. Ted introduced me right when I came in.

"Hi," they said. That's all.

Ted gave me this look like, Jeez, I'm sorry, but I just smiled at him.

I'm fine, really. I can be patient. I graze on the hors d'oeuvres on the kitchen counter, leaf through a couple of magazines. When Mom asks about the Trot, I tell her about beating Dad, and everybody laughs. Well, the adults laugh. Kristin has disappeared into the den to lose herself in the ballet. Amy's there in the kitchen, leaning against Ted's leg, but she keeps her eyes downcast. Ted keeps his big hands on her shoulders. Now and then, distractedly, he combs his fingers through her curls. Mom watches them.

Grandma's like that Hindu god with eight arms, taking things out of the oven, putting other things in, basting the turkey, checking to make sure that each serving dish has its silver spoon. If anyone tries to help her, she says, "No, no. Out of the way!" She won't let us into the dining room until everything is in place: the turkey looks as if it were cut out of a magazine ad, the steaming vegetables, the mountain of mashed potatoes. The good china, the sterling silver, the starched lace tablecloth.

I think of Dad and Kim, and wonder whether they really are having tofu for dinner. It would be perfect in a way. It would serve him right. I mean, it certainly would be untraditional—nothing at all like what Dad calls the Doris A. Boyles Annual "Over the River and Through the Woods" Holiday Burlesque.

"Why can't we have our own Thanksgiving?" he used to say when he and Mom were still married. "Cook a bird, have a few friends over. Be laid-back for a change. Why do we have to put on church clothes and go over to your mother's?"

Mom always said the same thing. "It's a family tradition, Oz."

"Bull," he'd say. "You weren't so hot about traditions when I met you. We were going to make our own traditions, remember? What happened to that?"

It was the same thing at Christmas, on Easter Sunday.

Mom never argued with him, but we always ended up at

Grandma's, and it was always a disaster. Dad in a foul mood. Mom a nervous wreck, worrying about what he was going to say or do next. I suffered in my own way for being the traitor I was, for letting Grandma sucker me in every single time, just the way she's suckering in Kristin and Amy today.

"Do you want Jackson to be like your parents, Ellen?" I'd hear Dad say after I'd gone to bed. "Do you want him to believe in what they believe in? God, didn't we say we wouldn't raise him the way we were raised? Didn't we say we wouldn't subject him to all that crap?"

I'd put my hands over my ears and lie there, my stomach churning with too much turkey, my whole system surging with sugar, and the room would start to spin. It was just a matter of time before I'd throw up and start to cry.

"See?" Dad would say. "It isn't good for him to be there."

Mom would tut-tut over all that rich food, but it wasn't that simple. Something inside me knew that the only way to feel better about having sided with Grandma was to purge myself of the whole day.

It's depressing to think about it. I watch Grandma charm Ted's daughters now. She tells them how sweet and pretty they are. She asks them questions in her polite, persistent way, and they answer her as if she's a queen. Of course, once Grandma's out of the picture, things immediately start to go down the tubes. On the way to our house after dinner, the girls start bickering over the invisible line they've drawn down the middle of the seat in the van.

"She's touching me," Amy whines. "Mommy says she's not allowed to touch me when we're riding in the car."

"Not a car, stupid," Kristin says. "A van."

"I'm telling Mommy you called me stupid," Amy says. It's the first time I've heard either of them mention their mother all day, and even I know Ted should read it as a signal. He should take them back to his apartment and spend the evening with them, alone. I glance at Mom, whose smile keeps looking more and more anxious.

"Hop to, kiddos," Ted says when we get to our house. He slides the van door open. "Let's go, hey?"

Inside, Kristin parks herself on the couch, drawing herself into the corner of it, as if trying to disappear. Ted sits down on the easy chair, and Amy climbs onto his lap.

I thought I was prepared for things getting uncomfortable; I told Ted it was no big deal. But now I see I'm not prepared at all. I felt like a stranger, odd man out, at Grandma's all afternoon. Now I feel that way in my own house. What I'd like to do is to go up to my room and put on some music—*Stop Making Sense* would be good, since nothing does anymore. Or maybe *Dark Side of the Moon*. But I don't want Ted to feel any worse than he does, so I stick around. I can't stand just sitting there, though, the tension gathering around us like smog. So I get up and turn on the television. "You guys want to watch *The Simpsons*?" I ask. I spin the dial to find the station. "I'll bet it's a Thanksgiving special."

"We're not allowed to watch that show," Kristin says. "Our mom says it isn't good for us."

"Turn it off, Jackson," my mom says.

Jeez, I've never seen a more miserable group of people in my life. I can't be mad at Kristin, she looks so sad. Ted is mortified. Both Mom and Amy look like they're about to cry. Me? I feel like I'm about eighty years old. I wish I could say to Kristin, Listen, I've been through this. What you're doing is only going to make things worse. But kids don't listen. They can't. Kristin will have to work it out herself, like I did. Like everyone does.

I hope she has someone to help her through it, though, like Brady helped me. He was there. No matter how mad or hurt I am about the way he ditched me, no matter what he's like when he comes back, there's always that. I'll never doubt that that part of our friendship was real. I'll never forget it.

"Hot chocolate, everyone?" Mom says in a hopeful voice. "With marshmallows?"

"Sure, great," I say.

Ted and I talk about IU basketball while she's in the kitchen. Well, Ted talks. I let him. Amy and Kristin sit so still they might pass for a couple of the dolls in Mom's collection.

"Here we are," Mom says, breezing back in with a tray of mugs. She passes them around and sets a plate of cookies on the coffee table. She turns on the stereo: music from the *Nutcracker*, which she and Ted plan to take the girls to see tomorrow. Even so, it feels awkward, too quiet. We all sit like game pieces waiting to be moved.

Then Ted starts babbling about what a great person my mom is, how swell I am, and what a great time we're all going to have in the future. Oh no, I think. Don't do this. I rack my brain for some way to shut him up or turn the conversation in another direction, but I can't think of a single thing to say to him that wouldn't seem rude.

"Ellen and I are going to buy a new house," he says, digging himself in deeper. "A nice big one, with a room for each of you in it, your own room that you can fix up however you want. Ellen will help you. And we'll take neat trips together; we'll have a good time."

Amy gets up to use the bathroom, and when she comes back, she goes to sit next to her sister on the couch, as near as she can get without touching her.

"And look," Ted says. "Ellen's gotten us all these travel magazines to help us pick a place so we can all go on the honeymoon together at Christmas." He flips the pages of one. Beaches, cities, deserts, mountains, forests blur, all making one place: not home.

Amy says in a small voice, "We can't go away at Christmas, Daddy. What if Santa Claus can't find us?"

"Oh, you are so stupid," Kristin says bitterly. "There is no Santa Claus."

"Kristin!" Ted says.

Mom looks stricken. And I feel pretty bad myself. Poor Amy. Does she need to know this on top of everything else? And poor Kristin, too. She'll probably feel guilty all her life for what she just did. Not yet, though. Now she just needs to keep hurting Ted, and she does.

"Well, Daddy, there isn't any such thing as Santa Claus, and you know it," she says. "You're Santa Claus. Mommy told me that a long time ago—why can't Amy know? You buy the presents. And now we have to go wherever you want us to go on Christmas or we won't get any."

"Ah, Kristin." Ted goes to her, kneels so that their eyes are level. But she flinches when he tries to draw her to him, pulls away. Amy sits at the very edge of the couch cushion, her little back perfectly straight, no doubt waiting for her father to assure her that Kristin was lying.

Just then Mom motions me to follow her into the kitchen, to leave the three of them alone, so I don't know exactly what Ted says or does next. But soon I hear Kristin's voice saying, "I hate you, I hate you, I hate you."

Then Amy's high, reedy voice. "Daddy, please, can we go home?"

Mom and I don't say a word, just look at each other. What could we say? We stand there, exiled in our own house. We hear the front door close; we hear Ted start the van; we hear the gravel in the driveway crunching as he pulls away.

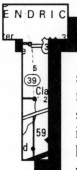

ed calls after midnight, and he and Mom talk a long time. I can hear Mom's voice, I can pick up the rhythm of her speech, but I can't understand what she's saying. It's like listening to a person speak in a foreign language. It reminds me of lying in this same spot, falling asleep to the sound of Mom and Dad talking, laughing long, long ago. Later, their angry voices keeping me awake. Now when I hear the click of the receiver, I wait five minutes, then go downstairs, as if on my way to the kitchen. I act surprised when I see Mom sitting in the living room, wrapped in her favorite afghan.

"I woke you, talking," she says.

I give her my best blank look.

"You didn't hear me?" She nods toward the phone. "Ted," she says. "We were talking about the girls. Honestly, Jackson. Sometimes I think your dad's right. Life's cheerleader, he used to call me. Here I was perfectly willing to believe that everything was hunky-dory just because Thanksgiving dinner went okay. Thanksgiving at my *mother's* house. Like it hasn't taken me my whole life to realize that nothing that happens there is exactly real—

"And Ted's just as gullible as I am," she says. "What a pair we'll make. Oh my God."

"Come on, it wasn't that bad," I say. "They were tired and they got cranky, that's all. Ted should've taken them home right after Grandma's. Believe me, about this part, I am an expert. I *know*."

She gives me a weak smile.

"Mom, you told me just yesterday you knew it wasn't going to be easy. That it would take a while. Remember?"

"That's me," she says. "Worrying about the wrong thing again. I put in all that time and effort worrying about Thanksgiving dinner and forgot there was the whole rest of the weekend to worry about. Not to mention the whole rest of our lives. Kristin and Amy are still little children. They're going to be around, they're going to need Ted for a long time—"

"As opposed to me needing anybody?" I say. "Does this mean that since I'm not a little kid anymore, since I'm practically out of here, you're transferring all your worry to those two?"

"Oh, Jackson," she says, and starts to cry.

I feel like a real jerk then. "Mom, I'm kidding," I say. And I was. Or at least I thought I was when I said it. Boy, I can just imagine some shrink drilling me. Are you feeling threatened, Jackson? Do you feel that having stepsisters will cost you some of your mother's love? But now's no time to think about that.

"Mom! Get a grip," I say. "Come on, I was kidding. Really. I always thought it would be cool to have a little sister. Now I'll have two."

Mom dabs at her eyes with the afghan and sniffs. "Did you wish you'd had a sister, Jackson?" she asks. "You never said so."

"Oh, sometimes. . . ," I say. I don't tell her that it was only after the divorce that I had even considered it. Until then, just the three of us together, life seemed perfect. After the divorce, though, I wondered sometimes whether having a sister or brother would have made things easier. Someone to split the pain with. But I don't want to upset Mom more, getting into that, so I turn the tables on her. "Did *you*?" I ask. "Want more kids, I mean."

"I'd've liked another child," she says slowly. "I—your dad and I decided that having more than one wouldn't be good for us."

"For him."

She gets that look she's always gotten when I'm treading on territory she wants to avoid. She's always been careful not to criticize Dad in front of me, she's always tried to be matter-of-fact about what happened between them, not to lay blame. That's good, I know. But sometimes it makes things harder because it means that I can't get pissed off about Dad in front of her. I have to work a lot of stuff out just watching and thinking, which takes a long, long time.

"It's okay," I say. "About Dad. I know he didn't want *any* kids. I'm over feeling bad about that."

"Your dad loves you, Jackson."

"I know that, too," I say. "It's okay. I know who Dad is."

"You do, don't you?" she says. "That's good. Sometimes I think *I'll* be sorting that out for the rest of my life. Who he is, who he was, who he might have been. What we might have been together. And I hate it when he's so damn nice. You know what he said to me the other day? We were talking about the schedule for this weekend, when he might spend some time with you, and he said, 'Don't worry, Ellen. This thing with Ted's kids will work out fine. They'll be crazy about you; they're lucky to have you.' "

"They are lucky," I say.

"It's not that, Jackson. Whether or not what he says is true. It's just that he said it. That it was even on his mind. Oh, I should quit thinking about him. I know it."

"Yeah, I'd stick to one worry at a time," I say. "You started out worrying about Kristin and Amy. Be consistent. That's what you're always telling me."

I thought she'd laugh, but she looks like she's about to start crying again.

"Oh, honey, I just feel so bad for them," she says. "Those poor little girls. If they like me, they betray their mother. If they don't like me, they lose even more of their dad than they've already lost."

We sit in the dark living room a long time—her on the couch

wrapped up in her afghan, me in the rocking chair, cold, but pretending I'm not. The porcelain faces of my mom's dolls are white in the moonlight. Pretty little children, I think. Without problems.

In a little while, she sighs. "Here I go, Jackson," she says in a wobbly voice. "Looking on the bright side again."

"Oh no," I say, and roll my eyes.

Finally, she laughs. "Seriously, now—it *was* nice at Mother's, wasn't it? Kristin and Amy can't help but admit that, at least inside, even if they don't say so. And what happened later certainly wasn't as bad as it might have been. I mean, it wasn't, or didn't seem to be, a reaction against *me*."

"It wasn't," I say. "You're right about that." Which is, of course, a flat-out lie. It had everything to do with her. And with me. And the whole stupid concept of people getting divorced in the first place. But she doesn't want to hear that.

"And don't you think they're nice little girls?" she goes on. "Better than you thought they'd be?"

I nod.

"That was a big relief to me," she says. "I actually liked them. What if I hadn't?"

"Yeah," I say. "What if they'd turned out to be like Brady? You want to talk about looking on the bright side, Mom, think about what it would've been like if Ted had showed up with a couple of kids who acted like Brady. Boy, he used to cook up some great ways to sabotage Layla's romances. Wouldn't you just love to get him as a stepkid?"

"Oh, God," she says. "I love Brady, but he's a handful. He'd be way too much for me to take on as a stepkid, no matter how madly in love I was with his dad. Oh, ugh—"

We both start to laugh at the thought of her—or anyone—being madly in love with the Jer.

Then she goes serious on me again. "I'll tell you something else, Jackson," she says. "Tonight, the way what happened with the girls hurt me made me realize how much I want things to be all right with them. How much I want to be with Ted. You know, I've run this through my mind over and over. I love him, but is it *real* love? I mean, the way I feel about Ted is nothing like the way I felt—"

She lets out a long breath and gives me this look like, Man the torpedoes, full speed ahead, and I get this feeling of dread in the pit of my stomach. I know exactly what she's going to say.

"It's nothing like the way I felt about your dad."

I've always known how much Mom and Dad once loved each other. I've always known it was a special, wonderful kind of love—at least for a while, and that has always been the saddest thing to me about the divorce. It's hard enough just to know it. But when Mom speaks the words, actually admits how she feels, it all seems so hopeless: love in general, I suppose. Life. I mean, what's the use of loving someone if it turns out you can't live together, can't make each other happy? It makes me never want to love anyone for fear that in the end all I'll have is this terrible, terrible love and no place for it to be but trapped deep inside my heart.

"I probably shouldn't even be telling you this," Mom goes on. "Oh, honey, I know all this is so painful. I hate the way my getting married is putting your life in turmoil all over again. But if I'm going to do it, well, it seems like the least I can do is to help you understand the way things are. God help me, I still love Oz. I always will."

"I know that," I say, my voice breaking.

"You do, don't you?" She sighs. "You know all kinds of things you shouldn't have to know at your age. Jackson, I'm so sorry for that."

I shake my head just a little, as if to say it's all right. It isn't, though. It will never be all right. But we both know that, so why say it, even if I could? And it seems important to her to finish saying whatever it is she means to say to me. I just let her go on.

"Before I met Ted, I thought, Well, if I can't stop loving Oz—and I know I never will—I guess that's that. I didn't know you could love two people at the same time. But—" She pauses, presses her fingertips against her eyes, and her voice goes wobbly again when she says, "What I'm learning is love doesn't measure like anything else. The more there is, the more there is—

"Honey, I know this is true. When I'm not crazy, when I'm

not worrying about how all this is going to affect other people—you, Ted's girls—it's the thing that amazes me. I don't have to quit loving your dad to love Ted. The way I feel about him can be there inside me just as it's always been, a kind of ache. A balance almost. Without it, I wouldn't realize how different what I feel for Ted is. How possible. How right—

"Jackson, does this make any sense at all?" she asks.

"Yeah," I say. And right then I think I love my mom more than I've ever loved her in my whole life. Which would explain why I feel sick inside thinking that soon it will be Ted she'll be talking to about her life. He'll be the one who'll hear her secrets. She stands, the blanket still wrapped around her. She pulls me out of the chair, puts her arms around me, hugs me. "Oh, Jackson," she whispers, "what would I do without you?"

I don't answer. I can't.

She holds me at arm's length, looks at me a long time, then hugs me again—this time quickly. "Let's get some sleep," she says. "Good grief, it must be nearly morning. We have children to entertain tomorrow. Hearts to win, yes?"

"Roger," I say, my own heart nearly bursting.

TWELVE

n the first weeks after Brady left, I stopped by to see his mom a few times, but she seemed distracted, aloof, as if my *not* having run away were a kind of offense. But I wake up the Friday after Thanksgiving remembering that Brady, Layla, and I have spent that day together every year since he and I were in kindergarten, and I'm sure Layla is remembering it, too. This was her favorite day of the year, she once told me. She loved the idea of Christmas coming, which she thought of as something apart from Christmas itself. *Christmas* depressed her. So she counted on that first official day of the holiday season to trick her for a little while into being the child she once was, the child she's convinced still lives deep inside her.

Layla's big on freeing the child within, which she is quick to point out is not all that easy. "The world believes the child in us is dangerous," she says. She says that only by returning to the state of childhood can people feel free to express their true emotions.

I always say, "Yeah, yeah, right," when she gets on that track.

It's either agree with her or admit that I think life would be even more of a mess than it already is if people went around expressing their true emotions every time they turned around.

But Brady loved to bait her. Last year, on the day after Thanksgiving, he was vegged out on the couch, watching TV. Layla tried to get him enthused about helping us decorate the house. "Honey, there's a child hidden somewhere inside you that just loves the magic of Christmas," she said.

He said, "Ma, I *am* a child. Every time I want to do something that's the least bit interesting you tell me, 'Brady Burton, you're just a child.' Then you tell me, 'No.' So if I'm a child and if putting up a bunch of Christmas junk seems incredibly boring to me— ergo boredom *is* my true emotion! Did you ever think of that?"

But Brady's cynicism hadn't dented Layla's armor of good cheer. She tromped around the Christmas tree lot in frigid weather for an hour until she found the perfect tree. She sang, carrying the boxes of Christmas decorations down from the attic.

I expect to find her in a similar state this morning, especially when I pull up and see that she's already hung a huge wreath on the front door.

I ring the bell twice, three times. Still no answer. I'm just about to turn away when I see a shadow move across the bay window in the dining room. Moments later, Layla opens the door. She's wearing one of her silk kimonos; her long hair is all tangled. I'm used to that.

"My other kid," Layla used to say when Brady and I were little, and he'd drag me into her bedroom or even, once or twice, into the bathroom when she wasn't fully dressed. She'd just laugh.

But now she pulls the robe tighter around her, combing her hair with her fingers as if embarrassed by the fact that I've caught her in this state.

"Reporting for duty," I say, after we stand there a long, awkward moment.

"Ah, the Friday after Thanksgiving." She attempts a smile. "I should've known you'd show up, Jackson. Come in, honey," she says. "I'll fix us a cup of coffee."

She talks to me over her shoulder as we walk down the hall

toward the kitchen. "I got the wreath up. That's as far as I got, though. I went back to bed. The doorbell woke me and—"

She waves off my apology. "No, no. God, it's time for me to be up. It's nearly eleven. What I started to say was that when I heard the bell I thought for just a second that it might be Brady. You haven't heard from him, have you, Jackson? That's not why—"

"No," I say.

She sighs, busies herself with the coffee. The kitchen looks as it always has: cluttered, the sun blinking through the plants that are tangled in the window. A prism catches the light and casts rainbows across the old wood table. We spent hours sitting here when we were little, Brady and I. Layla would put a plate of cookies out, fix us mugs of sugary coffee with lots of cream, and cinnamon sprinkled on top. She'd sit down with her own mug of black coffee, and we'd talk. Gerbil tricks. Baseball cards. Ecology. It was all equally fascinating to Layla. "You boys," she'd say, and shake her head in amazement, as if we were the two smartest kids ever born.

Now there's nothing but a stripe of light at Brady's place.

"Remember when I taught you guys Gregorian chant for your Christmas project?" Layla says.

"Fifth grade," I say.

Layla says, "You sounded like angels."

"Then the next year Brady did that report on the pagan origins of Christmas and got in trouble."

"Mrs. Carpenter," says Layla. "That bitch. When I called to talk to her about Brady's grade, she said, 'I clearly told the children to do a report on Christmas, Mrs. Burton.'

"Of course, I totally blew it. I said, 'You think Christmas began everything?' Boy, she really had it in for Brady after that. You know, Jackson, I never could quit getting in the middle of Brady's problems. But he always meant so well, and—

"Honestly, sometimes I rack my brain trying to figure out how Brady could've ended up such a mess when he was such a bright little boy, so sweet. When I loved him so much. *Loved.* See, I think of my own child in the past tense. It's depressing."

65

"He'll come back," I say, though today I'm not sure I believe it.

"You want to know what I feel worst about?" she asks. "What makes me feel so ashamed? Jackson, the first few weeks I didn't even miss him. It was a relief to me to have him out of the house. He'd been so—difficult all summer. I felt battered. But now I'm scared, Jax. I just want him to come home. I don't care what a pain in the ass he is. I just want him back with me. . . .

"I miss him so much, I'm about to die. And, honey, I miss you, too, you know? I miss the old days, all the fun we had. You boys were always so close. You had such a special friendship."

I nod.

"You miss him, don't you, Jax?"

"Yeah," I say. "I miss him." And I do. But I'm also pissed off at him, and hurt. Sometimes I wonder whether ours was such a special friendship, after all. But I keep that to myself.

Layla sighs. "I'll tell you something crazy," she says. "Some nights I turn Brady's stereo on full blast—that U2 tape he left in the tape deck—and I pretend he's in there sulking, dreaming about running away, or maybe on the phone, cooking up some outrageous plan that's going to get him into trouble again—

"My support group says I have to accept the fact that he's gone," Layla says. "My therapist says it's time to get my act together, that I've done all I can for Brady and I should move on, do something for myself for a change. The guy I've been dating says, 'Hey, you have me.' But—"

"Really, he could come back anytime," I say. "For Christmas . . ."

Layla looks away from me.

The kitchen clock says 11:45. I'm supposed to meet Dad for lunch at noon, but I could call him and say I'll meet him later. I hate to leave Layla here alone. "I could stay a while if you want," I tell her. "Help you decorate. Then if Brady does come home—"

"I think I'm done with Christmas," Layla says. "It's just one more damn trick the world plays to keep you from dealing with the way things really are. I mean, even if Brady did come home for Christmas, you and I both know it wouldn't make a bit of difference to him whether or not the house was decorated. Oh, damn him," she says, crying, "goddamn him," pressing the heels of her hands hard against her eyes. Then she reaches across the table and puts her hands, still wet with tears, over mine.

"Honey," she says. "Let go. We've both got to let go of what Brady's been to us. All those people with all their good advice are right about that. Even when he does come back—if he does—he may not be anything like the person we remember."

She laughs a little, a kind of mean laugh. "And we may seem different to him, you know? I wonder if it ever occurs to him that we might change while he's out there doing what he damn well pleases. That maybe we already have . . ."

Her words make something shift inside me. Whether Brady's changed or not, I don't know. But I have. I've had to change to fill in the blank space he left, and in some ways I'm not sorry. I imagine taking Brady to The Peak with me to work out. He'd insist on wearing those ridiculous baggy surfer shorts and his orange Chuck Taylors with the laces untied. All the while I explained the Nautilus machines to him, he'd be smirking.

"Okay, man, I think I've got the program here," he'd say. "*Fifteen reps times ten machines times four times a week plus sweat minus IQ equals Rocky Balboa.* But what's the point? Come on, Jax, we're outta here. Let's go get some pizza."

Would I say no?

he week after Thanksgiving, Mom and Ted buy a big house on Washington Boulevard. It's white, with green shutters and those windows that jut out on the second story. Cape Cod, Mom calls it. There's a huge maple tree on either side of the brick sidewalk, each with thick ivy growing in a perfectly trimmed circle around it. An old-fashioned arched gate opens onto the brick patio in the back.

"Can you believe it?" she keeps saying when they take me to look at it. "*This* house? Jackson, how many times do you suppose I've driven past this very house and said, 'Now, that's what a house is supposed to look like!' "

"About a million," I say. "And that's only counting the times I was with you."

I can have the attic room, they say. It's the most private place in the house. The girls' rooms are the ones you see from the street, each one exactly the same size, with a little bench seat built into the window that juts out over the yard. Ted and Mom's room is over the garage, huge, with its own bathroom. Near the kitchen, there's a little greenhouse, where Mom can keep flowering plants all through the winter.

The house is in great shape—and empty, so Ted and Mom decide to move in right after the wedding.

"I can take a leave of absence from school till the first of the year," Mom says. "If we really work hard at it, we ought to be able to manage it. It makes sense, don't you think?"

"Sure," I say. Any other answer and I'm going to have to try to explain why the thought of moving so soon gives me this turned-inside-out feeling. I don't know why I feel that way; I just do, at the same time that my rational self sees that doing everything at once makes sense. It would be stupid for Ted to move into our little house and then out again. And in my case, a clean break with the past is probably the best thing. With only two weeks to get organized, there won't be any time to worry about how this new life is going to be.

Every day, Mom goes out armed with lists. She tromps around buying the things we need for the new house. When I get home from school, the two of us begin the nightly task of boxing up our stuff. We get slowed down because we keep remembering things. Emptying out the curio cabinet, Mom dusts each object: pretty cups and saucers, teapots, dishes, funny salt and pepper shakers, old fountain pens, an antique fan. She unearths the heavy silver tea set Dad's parents gave them for a wedding present. "Just imagine this next to some of the other presents your dad and I got," she says. "A hundred-pound bag of brown rice, a pinecone wreath, a copy of *Be Here Now.* I ought to give this to Oz, you know. It belonged to his mother's family. . . .

"You never knew your Grandma Watt, Jackson, but she really was a lovely person. Oz adored her. It wasn't until she died that he became completely estranged from his family. . . ." Her voice trails off. She wraps the tray in newspaper, sets it carefully in the box.

Before we pack the photo albums, we have to look through them, laugh at the forced holiday shots, the goofy vacation shots: me in different places, getting taller and taller, growing into myself.

"Remember when Grandma dragged us all to Disney World?"

69

Mom says. "Spring break, the absolute worst time to go. The crowds were horrible. Your dad snapped when we were watching the parade on Main Street, getting elbowed and stepped on by full-grown adults trying to get closer to Mickey Mouse. He said to my dad, 'Earl, you Republicans make fun of the Red Chinese the way they put pictures of Chairman Mao all over the place and worship them. But look here. All these Silent Majority types falling all over themselves, worshiping a mouse. It isn't even a real mouse!' *I* felt guilty, of course. Here my parents had spent all this money on a vacation—

"Honestly, Jackson," she says, "I hate to think of how much of my life I've wasted trying to please one person I loved without upsetting some *other* person I loved. I still haven't gotten used to being with Ted, who acts as if every single thing I do or say is an act of genius."

Hey, I want to say. What about me? Don't you remember I think you're wonderful? But I'm afraid that if I try to tell her how I feel, I'll start crying. Or worse, admit that I'm jealous of Ted sometimes and scared of how she and Ted together will affect, forever, the way she is with me.

Brady would say, "You're crazy, man. You're always worrying about your mom; you're always feeling responsible for her. Can't you see this lets you off the hook? Can't you see this is your exit?" But I'm not ready to exit yet. Everything is changing too soon.

God, I hate this. I hate all our stuff in a mess around us. I'm scared to move. In a new place, how will I know who I am? And what happens if Brady comes back, comes looking for me here, and I'm gone? That, at least, is sort of funny to think about. I mean, imagine it: he skulks into town in the dead of night, bangs on the kitchen door in his usual inconsiderate way, and scares the crap out of the nice young couple who will be living here after we're gone. Yeah, it's funny. Hilarious, really. But thinking about Brady making a fool of himself isn't enough to zap my anxiety.

At school, I can't concentrate. Every night when the packing's done and Mom's gone to bed, I drink cup after cup of coffee trying to stay awake to do my homework. Then, when I've finally finished, I'm too wired to sleep. I pace my room, stopping to touch the scarred walls, the desk and bookshelves my dad made when I started school, the bulletin board that's displayed everything from pictures of Big Bird to the "Just Do It" poster that's pinned there now. It's cold up here; it's always cold up here. I scratch my name in the ice that's built up in the corner of the window glass. The world framed in this window is the world I saw when I was a baby lying in my crib.

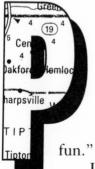

arty at my house tonight," Stephanie Carr says to me Friday afternoon. "Want to come? I miss you, Jax. Why don't you quit being such a hermit?"

"Maybe," I say, embarrassed at how many times I've turned her down.

"Go," Mom says when I mention it to her. "Honey, it would be good for you to do something fun."

I get to Steph's house a little after nine, a big brick Tudor near where our new house is. I recognize most of the cars parked along the street, but the house is dark. Standard operating party procedure when someone's parents are gone. In the kitchen, by the light of the open refrigerator, a few people are milling around, talking, drinking beer from the keg that's iced down in a baby's plastic bathtub.

"Yo, Jackson!" Tom Best says, and raises his glass.

I wait for him to tell me to get myself a beer, or even to draw one from the keg for me and make me refuse it, but he just holds out his palm for the high five. "What's up, dude?" he says.

"Little," I say, and head down to the basement to find Steph. She's dressed in a long, gauzy black skirt, a black sweater that would fit a person twice her size, combat boots, a bunch of silver bracelets, and a necklace of carved wooden unicorns. Her dangly earrings are made from tab tops. She flies over to meet me in her usual dramatic fashion.

"Oh, Jax," she cries. "You came!" She gives me a big kiss on the cheek and makes me dance with her a while. Then she takes my hand and leads me back upstairs, into the living room. White furniture, white carpet, glass tables illuminated in the moonlight. "So," Steph says, pulling me down beside her on the couch. "Talk. Tell me everything."

"What everything?" I say.

Her eyes shine with tears. "You're not okay, Jax. I know you; I see. You haven't been okay since Brady left."

I'm stunned by the relief her words bring, the sudden lifting of this secret from where it had been wedged inside me. I'm probably a heartbeat away from telling her how lost I feel when she says, "Primal scream. You've absolutely got to come to this group with me. These people are incredible! No kidding, Jax, they are so real. You won't believe how good it feels to let out your feelings."

"I don't know," I say. "I've been really busy."

"Too busy to get sane? Jax, you can't afford *not* to take the time to do this." She leans toward me. "Listen, I heard about your mom. You know, getting married. Bummer. I mean, I figure this Ted guy's got to be an asshole. I heard you guys bought that white house down the street from us—he must be as big an asshole as my stepfather if he's rich enough to afford that. It's okay if you don't want to talk about it, Jax. But, you know, I miss the talks we used to have when—"

She glances around, as if to make sure no one is listening. "Jax, have you heard from Brady?"

"No," I say.

"Well, talk about assholes. Can you believe him? Taking off like that and not even sending a postcard. Like we don't matter anymore. Like we don't even exist. If I weren't so worried about him, I'd be pissed out of my mind. Jackson," she whispers, "he's in danger."

73

"How do you know?"

"Dreams. Every single night since Thanksgiving. He's in this dark, loud place. Like something in the *Inferno*. In the dreams, I hear his voice. I look everywhere. But I can't find him.

"What made me know for sure that something was wrong, Jax—I went to this psychic. It was so bizarre. He was this old guy. He wore tons of Indian jewelry, and he sat in front of this shrine with burning candles. You know, an altar, like. With this gold Egyptian ankh and a Buddha and a crucifix. Anyhow, he calls up these spirit guides—mine—and he's talking to them. No shit, Jax, he told me things about my life nobody could have known but me. Or someone watching over me. That's why I believed what he said about Brady.

"He didn't have to say his name," she said. "I mean, he said, 'a friend,' and I knew. He said, 'It is someone very close to you. I see him traveling on a road. It is not a safe road.' It had to be Brady. I'm totally, totally freaked out about it, and I keep trying to tell the others, but they just think I'm crazy."

Her eyes look weird; she's flushed. "Are you tripping?" I ask.

"That is not the point," she says. "Whatever I'm doing—if I'm doing it—doesn't change the fact that Brady's in trouble." She grips my arm. "We have to find him."

There's clearly no point trying to reason with her, so I say, "You're absolutely right." I almost smile saying it, remembering that Brady's favorite *Saturday Night Live* skit is the one in which a guy responds, "That's true, you're absolutely right," to every single thing anyone says to him, and it ends up they all think he's a genius.

"Oh, Jax," Steph says. "Thank God. You always know what to do. I knew you'd be the one to help."

I imagine Brady grinning at me as if to say, See! I do smile this time, but Steph must think I'm smiling to reassure her, or maybe my smiling doesn't have anything to do at all with why she suddenly takes my face in her two hands, and kisses me again— this time hard and long, on the lips, her tongue flicking like a lizard's tongue on the roof of my mouth.

It blows me away. I shudder, heat rushes through me, and I get the biggest hard-on of my life. Steph looks at me with this dreamy look on her face, the same one Layla used to get sometimes when she was telling Brady and me what great kids we were.

"You are a decent human being, Jackson Watt," she says. "I love you."

Then she drifts back downstairs to the party as if nothing the least bit unusual has happened. Idiot! I think. You idiot! You could have done anything, she would have let you do anything. Christ, she probably wanted it, and what do you do? Sit there like a zombie.

I can't calm down. I get hard all over again picturing myself leading Stephanie up the dark stairway to her bedroom. But then what? As usual, considering the logistics of sex is as good as a bucket of cold water. I have never yet been able to get through a whole fantasy, starting at Point A, the kiss—fully clothed—and going step-by-step all the way through to being naked, screwing in a bed.

I don't want to go back to the party; I don't want to see her. So I slip out the front door, hoping no one will notice that I'm leaving—and no one does. It's a nice night, cold but clear. In the moonlight, the big houses on the street remind me of the dollhouse Ted and Mom bought Amy for Christmas. It has tiny furniture: tables, chairs, couches—even a Christmas tree, with minuscule ornaments and a ribbon garland. A little plastic family came with it, too: a mom, a dad, two children, and a dog. In the real houses I pass, there are real Christmas trees, real televisions with flickering blue screens. Real people. But they seem fake. Our house, the one we'll soon be living in, is totally dark.

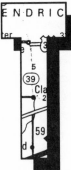

he day before the wedding, I pull up and park in front of the new house, ready for duty. Grandma's Cadillac is in the driveway, Ted's van behind it. At the last minute Mom and Ted decided to have the wedding there, instead of in the judge's chambers as they'd originally planned.

Grandma freaked, of course. "An empty house?" she said. "You're having your wedding in an empty house?"

"Our empty house," Mom said.

You could just see the little wheels in Grandma's head turning, trying to come up with a way of talking her out of it. "Those carpets! Everyone tromping around on those beautiful white carpets. Spilling! Honey, in an empty house they won't think to be careful."

Mom said, "The carpets have to be cleaned anyway. Ted's arranged to have them done right after the wedding. They'll be clean and dry in time for us to start moving in on Wednesday."

Grandma lit up, took a long drag. She put on her martyr expression. "Well, Ellen, if that's what you want . . ."

Mom said, "It is."

"I insist on doing flowers, though," Grandma said. "Just a cold, empty house . . ."

"Absolutely," Mom said. "Flowers would be wonderful."

Now the house is full of them. In the entryway, the staircase curves up, its banister bearing pine boughs wound with red ribbon. Red poinsettias sit on every stair, and there are red and white poinsettias on either side of the fireplace in the living room, too. Garlands of green decorate the mantel. A Christmas tree stands ceiling-high in one corner of the room, bare except for twinkling white lights and the angel on top, gold like the Renaissance angels in my Western Civ book.

Last night, Mom and I went through our Christmas ornaments. She and Ted decided that we'd contribute our favorites and that he'd take Kristin and Amy to shop for some new ones of their own before he brought them over this afternoon. That way, the tree would belong to all of us.

It was a good idea. Well, it seemed like a good idea until Mom and I got our ornaments out and started trying to choose.

"Pretty tacky," she said, holding up a sequined guitar that reminded me of Dad. She must have caught on because she didn't say anything else about it, just put it in the "keep" pile.

I picked up one I thought I could part with, a cheap plastic teddy bear that must have gotten too close to the lights. The brown paint looked like melted chocolate.

"Jackson," Mom said, retrieving it. "That was the very first ornament I ever bought for you."

This went on for about a half hour, until we'd been through three of the five boxes and agreed on only four ornaments that could be left off the new tree. Mom reached up and massaged the base of her neck. "I don't think I can do this, honey," she said in a small voice.

I told her to go to bed; I'd finish. I picked out the prettiest ones for the new house, regardless of their history. The others I took to my room. I'll put them on my own tree someday.

But now, compared to the beautiful angel and the delicate, old-fashioned glass ornaments Ted bought, even our best ornaments seem shabby.

This is harder than I thought it was going to be. I stand alone in the living room. Voices in the kitchen murmur like a wordless song. Quietly, I climb the front stairs, then the second narrow stairway to the room that will be mine. It seems huge, isolated. In the yard next door, there are children playing, two little boys. A third one zooms up the street on a blue bicycle. Up here, I hear nothing but the occasional whoosh of a car. I'll get used to this place, I tell myself. Next week, my own things will be here, and it will seem more like home to me. Next week. I can't really imagine it.

On my way downstairs, I see Kristin. She's hunched in the window seat of the room that will be hers, her long skinny arms wrapped around her bent legs. She looks like one of those bendable rubber dolls. After Thanksgiving, I deepened my resolve to bide my time, to let Kristin and Amy show me in some way that they might want my attention. But Kristin looks so miserable all alone in the empty room that I can't just walk by. I stop in the doorway.

"Weird, isn't it?" I say.

She jerks up, freezes like a frightened animal.

I go over and sit beside her—not too close, though. "I was just up in my room," I say. "I was trying to imagine myself actually living in it, but I couldn't. It just seems like a big old empty room to me. A nice room, but not mine."

"I'm not living here," Kristin says. "Not ever."

"True," I say. "You'll probably be here sometimes, though."

"Well, even if I have to come here sometimes, this won't ever be my real room. I don't care what they do with it. I don't know why my dad keeps asking me."

"He's worried about you guys. You know, because of the way he and my mom decided to get married all of a sudden. He doesn't want you to think he doesn't care what you want. So he asks you about fixing up the bedroom too much."

Kristin gives me a stony stare. "How do you know so much about him?" she says. "He's not your dad."

"No," I say. "I have my own dad. He hasn't lived with me and my Mom for a long time. But I still miss him. Your dad's nice, though. He's been nice to me. I like him.

"You know, Kristin, it's okay if it takes you a long time to get used to all this," I say. "Nobody expects you to fall in love with me and my mom overnight. Hey, we're not all that lovable. We know that. And just in case we might forget it, my grandma reminds us all the time." I mimic Grandma's voice. "Ellen, I don't know why you insist on going around in those old jeans of yours when you have perfectly lovely clothes to wear. Looking your best is a matter of personal pride. And Jackson, for goodness sake, quit slouching!"

"Jaaackson!" Grandma hollers from downstairs. "Why didn't you let me know you were here? Come on down wherever you are. It's time to quit dillydallying and get this tree done. Do you hear me?"

"Coming, Grandma," I shout. "See?" I say to Kristin.

She still won't look at me, but her lips quiver, fighting a smile, and when I sigh and say, "Gotta go," she gets up and follows me.

I don't look back. Think of a cat, I tell myself. Think of how a cat may jump up on your lap but jump right back off again if you try in even the smallest way to make it stay there.

She doesn't speak to me or even look at me directly while we decorate the tree, but she sticks close to my side. Now and then, she hands me an ornament, points to a spot on the tree higher than she can reach, and I hang it there. No one seems to notice. Grandma and Mrs. Harper are busy being in charge. Amy's trotting back and forth from the tree to the cookies on the kitchen counter, her face dusted with crumbs. Mr. Harper's leaning against the counter, out of the tree-trimming picture entirely. He's watching basketball on the tiny television that he pulled from his pocket to show me earlier. Who knows where Mom and Ted are. They keep going off by themselves, supposedly on forgotten errands, returning flushed—guilty as teenagers.

"Now, we'll meet Ted and Ellen at the club at five-thirty, is that right?" Mrs. Harper asks Grandma. "They know where they're going. . . ."

"Everything's all set." Grandma raises an eyebrow at me, as if to say, And you thought I was fussy.

"Do you think it'll snow?" Mrs. Harper asks, peering out the window.

"It's forecast," Grandma says.

"Goody, I love snow!" Amy whirls. Her arms pass like spokes through the circles of light cast by the brass lamps on either side of the mantel. Her curly blond hair is haloed by the white lights on the tree.

"Settle down, dear." Mrs. Harper catches her and draws her into a hug.

"I hope it does snow," Kristin mutters, so that only I can hear. "I hope it blizzards."

"If it does, I'll come get you guys in the morning in my VW bus," I tell her. "It's great in the snow! We can go sledding."

"Jackson!" Grandma orders me up on the stepladder to finish the top part of the tree.

From my perch, I watch Kristin wander over to the window.

"So, is that your very own, that orange van?" she asks me.

"Yep. My dad bought it for me when I got my license."

When the tree is finished and it's time to leave for the country club, she whispers something to Amy, who announces, "Me and Kristin want to ride with Jackson."

"Okay by me," I say, careful to sound as if it's no big deal one way or the other, even though it pleases me. I did the right thing, stopping to talk to Kristin, I think. Maybe they'll end up liking me, after all.

"I don't know . . . ," Mrs. Harper says.

"Please," Amy says. "Please." She looks to Kristin for moral support, but Kristin ignores her. She has to keep up her image. I know that.

"Jackson is an excellent driver, Ruby." Grandma smiles her mellow trust-me smile. "I'm sure Ted won't mind a bit if the girls go with him."

Kristin and Amy hurry to get their coats before Mrs. Harper has second thoughts. They scramble down the sidewalk. By some unspoken arrangement, Kristin takes the front seat in the bus, Amy the middle. I pop in a tape, a mix of B-52s songs, hoping the goofy lyrics will amuse them. Amy giggles at the song about a poodle called "Quiche Lorraine."

"That's funny, Jackson," she says.

Kristin just looks straight ahead, her hands folded in her lap.

But then, just before we reach the country club, the snow begins to fall. Fat, lazy flakes. They land on the windshield and stick there like sequins. "Oh!" Kristin says, reaching out as if to touch them. Her pleasure is so deep, so surprising, that for one second she forgets herself and turns and smiles at me, her eyes shining.

That moment it's as if she's my real sister, telling me a secret. I wish I knew the right way to say to her, Don't worry, you're safe with me. But since I don't, I keep quiet—and later, when we get to the country club and she acts as if the moment never happened, I think it's a good thing that I did. At the dinner table, she looks sullen, she picks at her food. She won't drink the kiddie cocktail Ted ordered for her. If anyone speaks to her, she turns away. Every now and then, I look over and see that she's watching me. She's watched me all evening, even though she hasn't spoken to me since she got out of the bus, or even come near me. Now, catching her eye, I smile, but poker-faced, she tilts her head and gives me a mean look as if to say why are you watching me?

It's stupid how it wounds me. I look around to see if anyone noticed the exchange, and for once I'm grateful to realize I'm invisible. It's easy to slip out of the dining room, then outside onto the wide porch that runs along the back of the country club. I stand there a long time, watching the snow fill up the golf course, wishing that, somewhere along the line, I'd learned to be bad.

I think of Brady's dad's wedding dinner here, a few years ago. Mr. Burton didn't come right out and say so, but I knew he had invited me to help keep Brady in line. It was during our freshman year, when Brady acted so horrible all the time that Mr. Burton wouldn't take him anywhere unless I went along. He was convinced I had a calming effect. Well, if I did, it didn't work that night. Brady sneaked a whole bottle of champagne from the waiter's cart and got blasted in the rest room. He faked it okay until it was time for the toasts. Even I thought he was hanging in there. Then he stood up. He raised the one glass of champagne his dad had allowed, grinned that goofy grin of his, and only managed to get out, "Dad, Cara—" before he puked onto his dessert plate.

"He's been feeling sick for a few days now," I told Mr. Burton, who wanted desperately to believe me. "The flu, probably. It's been going around."

Now, standing in the freezing cold, I realize I should've paid more attention to how Brady managed to get what he wanted by being an asshole instead of following him around like a stupid lackey, trying to make things right. Still, I know exactly what he'd tell me if he were here. Kristin will like you if she thinks you're as pissed off about the wedding as she is. She'll be crazy about you if she thinks you hate her dad as much as she hates your mom. Dude, tell her what she wants to hear.

But I could never do that. And I might fantasize about going back into the dining room and doing something outrageously bad, but even if Brady were here to egg me on, I wouldn't go through with it. It's better not to think of him. Tonight, here, he wouldn't be any help.

Just go back, I tell myself. Just get through it.

"You were awfully quiet at dinner," Mom says later.

"Tired, I guess. All that packing."

"I know," she says. "This is all so stressful, isn't it? Living in this mess the past few weeks. And now trying to please all these people we don't even know. God, I hate that."

"Yeah, well maybe we ought to take some pointers from Kristin," I say. "*Don't* try to please them. Be rotten instead; then they fall all over themselves trying to please you."

Mom sighs. "She was difficult at dinner, wasn't she? When Mother told me the girls had ridden over with you, I'd hoped— what happened, Jackson? How was it that you ended up driving them over in the first place?"

I tell her about finding Kristin in the empty bedroom, about the way she followed me downstairs and shadowed me while we decorated the tree and all that happened afterward. I tell her about the moment in the bus, when Kristin turned and smiled at me.

"I must have done something wrong, though," I say. "You

saw how she acted to me at dinner. I must've done something to make her decide not to like me, after all."

"I'm sure it wasn't anything you did, honey," Mom says. "It sounds like she just scared herself—you know, let down her guard and then decided she'd better make up for it by being nasty. I think it's a good sign what happened this afternoon. Actually, it's a lot more than I'd hoped for. We've talked about this thing with the girls, you know. About how we have to be patient—"

"Jesus, you sound like Grandma," I say. " 'Be patient, be patient.' Like I have all the time in the world just to make a couple of dumb kids like me. Like it's the only thing in the world on my mind."

"Oh, Jackson," Mom says, and I see that she's near tears.

I feel awful. It's our last night, just the two of us, so what am I going to do—spoil it by being as stupid and cranky as Kristin was at dinner? I had thought this might be a special time, that Mom and I might stay up late watching an old movie or playing Scrabble the way we used to on Friday nights when I was a little kid. I don't know why it hasn't occurred to me until just now that anything we do that isn't sleeping, we'll have to do cramped in the living room, amid the packing crates. Too depressing.

Anyway, Mom looks exhausted. I hold out my hands to her, pull her out of her chair, and point her in the direction of her bedroom.

"You doing okay, honey?" she asks, pausing.

I nod. "Fried, though. With Mrs. Harper around, it's like having Grandma squared."

Mom smiles. "While you guys were decorating the tree, Ted and I drove around in the van, swearing," she says. "Screaming the worst words we could think of at the top of our lungs. Honestly, I think it's the only thing that got us through dinner."

"Thanks a lot," I say. "Leaving me with Doris and Ruby: tag-team decorators." I fake a laugh. She'd feel awful if she knew how bad it hurts me, the thought of her ditching me to sneak off with Ted. Yeah, sure, I know it has nothing to do with how much she loves me. But I can't quite shake the image of the two of them driving around together, gleefully alone.

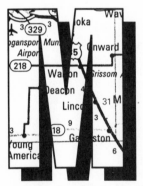orning comes, hard and blue, with just a dusting of snow. I tell myself that if we'd gotten a real snowfall, I'd have driven over to the Holidome to see if Kristin and Amy wanted to go sledding. After all, what I said while we were decorating the tree yesterday could have been taken as a promise. But without snow as an excuse, it would look phony to go over there. It would be trying too hard, which would probably make Kristin even more stubborn about not liking me. So I decide to go work out instead.

Kim's the first person I see when I get to the gym, and she's dying to tell me about the argument she and Dad had last night. She follows me to the StairMaster and says, "You won't even believe this, Jackson. I was working on one of my aerobics routines in the living room, making this tape of old stuff to use for my class, and he went totally berserk. Honestly, like it's sacrilegious to use the Doobie Brothers to work out to! I said, 'Oz, a lot of

84

the people in the class are your age, and every time I use an old song, they love it.'

"And he goes, 'They're idiots, then. Goddamn yuppies,' and stomped out the door without another word and didn't come in until two this morning and *then* he didn't even come to bed. He fell asleep on the couch in the living room with all his clothes on."

She pauses, like I might want to comment. But I just put on this grim, balls-out athletic expression and increase my efforts on the mechanical stairs. This machine is like a bad dream, I think. I climb and climb and Kim's still right there beside me.

"I think it's the wedding that's got him all bent out of shape," she says. "I mean, it's not that he doesn't want your mom to get married and be happy, it's just, you know, it's hard—"

"Don't even talk to me about Dad and the wedding," I say. "I mean it."

Amazingly, she shuts up. Yes! I think. Be assertive! Then I glance up and realize that Kim probably didn't even hear what I said. She's halfway across the room, walking toward Dad. He's bleary eyed; he hasn't shaved yet. He's got on old, ratty sweats, his beat-up jacket from the Fleetwood Mac tour, and a Harley-Davidson baseball cap that's seen better days.

"Okay, I'm an asshole," I hear him say.

"You are." Kim's voice is wavery.

"So I brought you a present." He grins and pulls a big red gummy rat out of his pocket.

Kim says, "Eeyuu, Oz, that is gross." But she giggles. She takes it and holds it up by its tail. "*You're* the rat, you know."

"Yeah? Then eat me." Dad steps closer to her, takes her shoulders in his hands, pushes his knee lightly between her legs, almost as if they're slow-dancing.

"*Oz.*" Kim glances meaningfully toward me.

He makes her struggle for just a second before he lets go of her.

I set the StairMaster a level higher and keep pumping.

"Yo, Jackson," he calls. "Afraid your tux won't fit this afternoon?"

Stairway to Heaven, Dad calls this machine. Right now, it

could be a stairway to anywhere but here and I'd be happy. I'm in no mood for his jokes. "We're not wearing tuxes," I say.

"Straitjackets, then." He laughs. "Going all the way."

"Screw you, Dad. Just screw you, okay?" My eyes are burning, so I close them and pump harder. My whole body's burning; my thighs feel as if they're going to explode.

He hits the button that makes the machine wheeze and come to a slow stop. "Sorry, buddy," he says. "Really, Jackson, I'm sorry."

"You want to marry Mom?" I say.

He shakes his head.

"Then just leave it alone, will you?"

"I ought to do that. Christ, I don't even know why I say this shit. Truce?" He holds his hand out, palm up, for me to give him the high five, and I do.

But I'm not letting him off that easy. I grit my teeth and beat his record on the StairMaster. Later, I beat him by twenty sit-ups. I up my weight ten above the weight he can bench-press. I'll show him he's an old fart. I'll make him remember he's the god-damn father here: he should be worrying about how I feel instead of getting into stupid arguments with his girlfriend. Gummy rats. Jesus. My anger makes me feel pure, like a machine in perfect working order.

Dad stands there and watches me. When I finish he kind of shakes his head and says, "Bud, I have to tell you I'm impressed. Who are you, Clark Kent?"

I hate it when he makes me smile when I'm mad. I hate the way he knows he's got me. Still, I hold my own. I agree to go to breakfast with him when we're through working out, but the first thing I say at the diner when I slide into the booth across from him is, "Just don't ask me if I'm okay. I swear to God, the next person who asks me if I'm okay dies."

He shrugs, holds up his hands, palms forward, as if to ward off blows.

"And by the way," I continue. "I decided not to come over to your house after the wedding tonight. I've got stuff to do. Packing. Homework."

He looks kind of funny then, like I've hurt his feelings. But he doesn't argue. He believes you ought to let people do their own thing—he'd tell you himself it's about the only thing he believes in. That and sixties music, the topic our conversation turns to now.

He tells me about a friend of his who's out on tour. His voice sounds almost wistful, which surprises me because while he loves to tell stories about being out on the road, if anyone asks him why he quit, he says, "Shit food. Bunking on a bus. I got real tired of the life."

"Would you ever go out again?" I say. "You could, couldn't you?"

"Things come up. I had the chance to go out with the Moody Blues a while back."

"So why didn't you?"

He lights up a cigarette. "You, pal. No way I'm going out on the road as long as you're around."

God, I can't even look at him. Dad, the flake who threw away his chance at an education, threw away his marriage, really, for his renegade job. He's legendary for doing exactly what he wants to do. It's never even occurred to me until this minute that he'd have made any real sacrifice for me, let alone a sacrifice that I can see is a thousand times larger than any my mom has been called upon to make.

"No guilt trip," he says, reading my thoughts. "No regrets. The truth is, I was ready to shoot Ellen when I found out she was pregnant, but, hey—I got attached to you. If God appeared right now, right here and said, 'Oz, give me your kid and I'll reunite the Beatles,' I'd pass. No shit.

"But who knows, man. Maybe I'll take a shot at it again next year. You'll be outta here. Off to college. You won't need me anymore." His voice has its old familiar mocking tone but with a sad edge that I've never heard before.

Oh yeah, I'm totally in control here. I'm so calm. I mean to be cool, to say, I'll need you, man. Who am I going to beat the shit out of at the gym if you aren't around? But I only get as far as, "I'll need you." I can't go on.

"Jax, bud, are you okay?" Dad says. Then he must remember what I said a few minutes ago about not asking me that, because he looks totally freaked out, like I really am going to do something horrible to him. Like I really could. "Jax?"

"I'll survive," I say.

It's strange. I'm not sure exactly how it happened, but for the first time in my life I feel like I have the upper hand with Dad. I could nail his ass; I could forgive him. But right now, I don't want to do either. I want a break. I want to eat my breakfast. I want to sit here in the booth with Dad, shooting the breeze for a little while, as if this were just another day.

It's not, though. It's the day of my mom's wedding. I go home, put on the gray slacks and blue blazer Mom bought me for the occasion, and when the time comes the two of us step into the white limo Ted sent for us. We stop by to pick up Grandma, who trips out to join us in her mink coat and high heels.

She gives me the once-over and tells me how handsome I look all dressed up—I ought to dress up more often. Then she eyes Mom's long white skirt and her sweater, which is exactly the same color. The pearls Ted gave her for Christmas look pinkish against it. Her white suede high heels. "Honey, you look absolutely beautiful," she says. Then, "Thank goodness we didn't get all that snow. Your lovely shoes would have been ruined."

Which is exactly what Ted's mother says once she's finished carrying on about how great Mom looks and how happy she is to have her for a daughter-in-law.

Ted doesn't say anything. He just looks at Mom, grinning like a goof.

Everyone's there waiting: Ted's family, the judge, my uncle Mike and my aunt Nancy. Grandma fusses over Kristin and Amy, who look pretty in their red velvet dresses and patent leather shoes.

Soon the judge, a friend of Ted's, positions himself in front of the fireplace, gestures to Ted and Mom to stand facing one another in front of him. Sunshine pours in through the big bay window, making a carpet of light at their feet. The wedding ceremony itself is brief. No "dearly beloved." No prayers. Just the legalities. The minute it's over, the caterer enters carrying a silver tray with glasses of champagne for everyone.

Another friend of Ted's takes pictures; the party guests begin to drift in. I've never seen a person look as happy as Ted does.

All the while he's greeting people, talking to them, he holds Mom's hand. He keeps glancing at her as if to make sure she's actually beside him. Amy sticks pretty close to them, smiling shyly when Ted introduces her to people. Kristin is perched halfway up the staircase, reading a book. Ted keeps an eye on her, smiles when she looks up, but he's smart enough to leave her alone.

I do what's expected of me. I greet Mom's friends, meet Ted's. I eat my piece of wedding cake. I look happy. Time goes by. At seven sharp, the white limousine reappears. The caterer passes around little net bags filled with rice, and we line the front walk, shivering, to throw the rice at Mom and Ted as they hurry away.

Not long after that, I say my good-byes. Dad's expecting me, I tell Grandma. She's so distracted, rehashing the wedding with Mrs. Harper, that she forgets I don't have a car. She just gives me a kiss on the cheek and a quick hug and says, "You're a lucky boy, Jackson Watt. Not everyone gets as nice a stepfather as the one you got tonight."

I agree. I mean, Ted *is* a great guy. It's not his fault I'm feeling like if I don't get out of there right this second I'm going to scream.

I walk home in the cold, dark night and sit in our echoey living room feeling sorry for myself. I can't get warm. Frigid air seeps in through the curtainless windows. Packing crates loom like big, square animals. As cars turn the corner onto our street, their headlights move across the blank walls, then fall onto the crates, hurry over them like long fingers. Get a grip, I tell myself. Get a life. I consider all the things I might do tonight. Do a movie marathon. Read. Jack off. Veg out totally: turn the lights off and stare at the fluorescent galaxy my dad and I pasted on my ceiling when I was in the fifth grade. Could I still name all the constellations?

To avoid thinking about that, I go upstairs, pop a Talking Heads into my stereo, and turn it up loud. I get warmed up, finally, by jerking around like a nutcase the way David Byrne does on MTV. I feel just about as stupid in my wedding clothes as he looks wearing his gargantuan white jacket, so I peel them off and dance naked for a while. I sing along with "What a Day That Was." Then "Life During Wartime" comes on, a favorite of Brady's.

Oh, yeah, Brady. Lately, any thought of him is guaranteed to deflate me, and tonight's no different. He'd say, "Call Steph, man. The two of you alone. All night. Who'd know?"

She'd do it, too.

Suddenly I don't want to be here with all these possibilities, with my whole life packed up all around me, so I put on jeans and a sweatshirt, and head for Dad's after all. He and Kim are playing poker, empty beer cans stacked in a pyramid in the middle of the table. They don't act a bit surprised to see me.

"Yo, Jackson," Dad says, and deals me a hand. "So how was the wedding?" he asks.

"Fine," I say, and that's that.

The three of us play till after midnight, stopping only when Dad gets up to change the music on the stereo. We listen to the new Eric Clapton, the Traveling Wilburys, the R.E.M. tape that Brady made for him and was so pleased that he liked. Nothing old, I notice. Nothing that might make him think of Mom, downtown in the bridal suite at the Hyatt, starting her new life.

SEVENTEEN

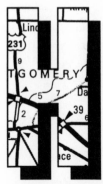oliday parties are strictly against the rules at our high school, but Mrs. Blue is great at setting up what she calls "educational experiences." Parties in disguise. We've been reading the *Canterbury Tales* in Western Civ, so the last day before break, we're telling our own stories. We're having a "traveler's repast."

It's the first time I've enjoyed myself at school in a long while. Everybody's mellow for a change, telling funny stories about family vacations or road trips that turned out to be a disaster. I tell about the time Dad insisted on taking a hundred-fifty-mile detour through Cawker City, Kansas, so we could see the *second*-largest twine ball in the world. Everybody laughs.

We drink the cranberry juice that Mrs. Blue brought as a substitute for the wine Chaucer's pilgrims drank. We eat bread and cheese. Then Tom Best goes to his seat and gets the grocery sack he's been carrying around all morning.

91

"Medieval nachos," he says, and whips out five bags of corn chips and a huge Tupperware container of jalapeño dip.

Even Mrs. Blue thinks it's funny.

Just before the end of the period, we do our gift exchange: something appropriate for a pilgrimage, Mrs. Blue had said. There's a lot of screaming and laughing as people open their presents. A mix tape of road songs, *The Hitchhiker's Guide to the Galaxy*, an all-day sucker, a squirt gun. I get a Hot Wheels race car from Kate Levin, who says, "Remember how you and Brady used to race these in the back of the room in second grade, when Mrs. Carver wasn't looking?"

"Yeah," I say, and think of him out in the world now, searching, a real pilgrim.

I drew Stephanie. I was relieved, in a way, because I knew I couldn't keep avoiding her. She called me a couple of times after the party. Sorry, I can't talk right now; sorry, I can't go out, I said. The wedding, moving. I felt bad about it. So when I drew her name, I figured, what the hell, and spent more than the limit to buy her this thing called a dragonfly's eye. You look through its prismlike lens and see multiple images of whatever's in front of you, kind of like a collage, only everything is the same thing.

"Whoa, far out," she says when she puts it to her eye. "What a trip! You guys, this is blowing my mind."

She hands it to me. Through it, I see rows and rows of her smiling face, her wild hair. I turn it slightly and she shifts, as if dancing.

"Oh, Jax, what a cool present," she says, and throws her arms around me.

Mrs. Blue smiles and takes a turn. "This is wonderful!" she says. "And useful, yes. A pilgrim must learn to see in new and different ways."

After class, Steph is waiting for me. "Listen," she says, "I've been thinking, like, maybe we could do something together sometime. You want to do something, Jackson?"

She stands there, twirling a strand of her long hair on her finger.

"Yeah," I say. "Yeah, definitely." But I chicken out again. "After Christmas—"

"Sure. After Christmas," Steph says quickly. "Hey, have a good one, Jax, okay? We're rich now; we'll probably get all kinds of shit, right?" She kisses me on the cheek and leaves me standing there, my hand on my face, as if I've been slapped.

"Carr cracking on you, Watt?" Tom Best laughs as he passes, giving me a friendly punch in the arm. "Hey, go for it, man."

Exactly what Brady would have said. He isn't even here; he didn't say it. But he's the one I'm mad at. Again.

I'm mad at Dad, too. At least sick and tired of his annual holiday snit, which has now moved into high gear. We go to breakfast Sunday morning and all he wants to talk about is the variety of ways Kim's driving him crazy.

She put red- and green-wrapped Hershey's Kisses in his boxer shorts, he tells me. He found the same candy in his mailbox, in his jeans pockets, in the glove compartment of his Jeep. She bought toilet paper that plays "Jingle Bells" when you unroll it. "If she doesn't quit trying to cheer me up, I'm going to kill her," he says.

Later, at The Peak, I try to explain to Kim how what she's doing only makes things worse.

"It's like you and steak," I say. "There's nothing in the world anyone could do to make a steak look good to you. Nothing that could make you look at it and not think, Blood."

"Yeah," she says.

"Just don't try to make Dad like Christmas, okay?"

"But then *my* Christmas is spoiled," she says.

Jesus, I think. This is hopeless. To tell the truth, I'm about up to my ears with Christmas myself. Mom's doing this *Better Homes and Gardens* thing, baking cookies like a maniac, buying all the presents she's never been able to afford to buy. I haven't done anything. "Take the charge card," she tells me. But what can I buy her now that she has everything? And what do I buy for Ted? For Kristin and Amy, my *sisters?* I don't even know them!

I wander around at the mall for hours but can't make up my mind what to buy. There are too many things to choose from. I sit on a bench and eat a frozen yogurt, watching all the kids lined up to see Santa. When it's their turn, a girl dressed up like one of Santa's elves escorts them to the throne where he sits. I'm too far away; I can't hear what they're saying. But I suppose they're asking for all the things they see advertised on television, like Brady and I used to do. We'd sit up in his room every day after school, making and remaking our Christmas lists. It's one of the advantages of divorce, he'd say: the way parents feel guilty when the holiday season rolls around. So we might as well play it for all it's worth. He cashed in big-time. He got every single thing he ever wanted, even the G.I. Joe doll that Layla was opposed to because it glorified war and Mr. Burton was opposed to because he felt that giving Brady a doll, any kind of doll, might plant the seeds for homosexuality later in life.

I got a lot myself, though not as much as Brady. I never told him, but I never gave Mom the list we made together. I made a different, shorter list. It had some toys on it but also books and clothes. Those first years after Mom and Dad were divorced, neither one of them had much extra money. Even so, they tried a lot harder than Brady's parents did to make Christmas as nice as it could be. Yeah, they felt guilty. But it was obvious that they also felt depressed and sad. Somehow, there was no fun in taking advantage of that.

hristmas keeps getting closer and closer, and Mom still hasn't said a word to me about what plans she's made with Dad this year. Ted's the one who finally says, "Jackson, Ellen tells me that you and your mom and dad have always had Christmas breakfast together. If it's okay with you, I thought I'd give Oz a call and invite him here."

Even Dad had to admit it was a decent gesture. He appears a little past ten, carrying my Christmas present— a CD player, a good one, and the complete Beatles on CD.

"Dad," I say. "Jeez—"

"For your new room." He gives me a rough hug. "I'll set it up after we eat."

I give him his present, a T-shirt that has a picture of Elvis on it with "I'M DEAD" in big letters beneath. Dad puts it on immediately. "Graceland," he says, and shields his eyes as if he's having a vision. "We've got to go there!" Then he looks at me kind of funny. "It's been a long time since we've done one of our trips, Jax," he says.

Mom brings out the waffles and melted butter, the bacon, the fruit salad, the fresh-squeezed orange juice. Dad doesn't make a single remark about the hokey Christmas centerpiece on the dining-room table or the George Winston Christmas album on the stereo. He doesn't say how strange it is to be spending Christmas morning here instead of in our old, crowded kitchen.

We talk about the weather, make good-natured fun of Grandma. Ted asks Dad a lot of questions about music, and we end up sitting at the table a long time, all of us talking at once.

"Peter, Paul, and Mary," Ted says. "Man, I loved Peter, Paul, and Mary. I saw them in concert in Bloomington, must have been '65."

"You like folk music?" Dad says. "You should have heard Ellen sing that stuff. She was terrific." He pauses and glances at Mom almost apologetically. Quickly, Ted starts talking about something else.

After breakfast, he shows Dad around the house. We've been here less than two weeks, but from the way it looks—everything is in place—we might have been living here for years. He shows him up the stairs to my room, then leaves the two of us alone.

"Nice digs," Dad says. "Like an apartment." My bed and dresser are on one side of the room. On the other, near the built-in desk and bookcases, are the couch and coffee table from our old house. My music posters are tacked up on the cork wall. "Nice house," he says. "Your mom belongs in a house like this—"

Here it comes, I think. We've avoided talking about how Dad feels about this marriage for months, and now, Christmas morning, he's going to nail her, and I'm going to have to defend her, and we're both going to end up feeling bad about it. But he surprises me.

"What I mean is, I know a house like this is what she always wanted," he says. "And I'm glad for her, Jackson. I really am. This marriage is a good thing for her, for both of you. Ted's okay. He won't mess you up. That's what used to scare me. That Ellen would fall in love with someone that wasn't right for you. But Ted—he sees who you are."

I get that same feeling I had in the diner the morning of Mom's wedding, like a camera focusing, allowing something new about my dad and me to come into view. I mean, I've always known that Dad loved me. In his way. That's the phrase Grandma's always used when she talks, grudgingly, about Dad loving me: in his way. Even Mom uses it sometimes: he loves you in his way. Translation: he loves you as well as he can. Somehow less. And I guess, over time, I'd come to believe it was true. Now I see it's not like that at all. Dad's way of loving me has nothing to do with some idea of what a kid is or what a father should be because he doesn't really have one. *That's* why it's different. His way of loving me has only to do with *me*. Jackson. Whoever I was or am or will be. I earned his love somehow, like a friend would: that's what I suddenly understand, and I feel proud and a little bit emotional about it, like if he keeps on with this conversation I might start to cry. I would for sure if I tried to explain it to him, so I don't.

"Jax," Dad says, his voice a little anxious. "You do think it's a good thing, don't you? Your mom and Ted?"

"Yeah. I think it's a good thing."

"Whew." He grins. "Ellen has a history of falling in love with the wrong kind of guy, you know."

"You're not that bad," I say. "Don't give yourself so much credit."

"Shit," he says. "Don't tell Kim that. She thinks I'm the biggest badass since James Dean."

"I'm sure," I say, and we both laugh.

"Okay," he says, opening the box with the CD player in it. "Let's set this thing up." He checks out my receiver to see where all the wires should go, then asks me where on the wall of shelves I want to put it. I choose a place, and he goes to work.

Stretched out on my unmade bed, I remember how I used to love to watch him work when I was little. You'd think a kid would be bored or jealous or even scared when his dad was concentrating so hard that he'd completely forgotten him. But I liked being with Dad when he was that way. I liked his tuneless whistle, the same whistle I'm hearing now. I liked the way his hands hovered, his fingers pressing here and there, almost as if they were making music instead of connecting wires or smoothing wood.

"There are so many things that Oz could do," Grandma used to say. She'd list them: engineering, building, computers. . . . "I don't know why he insists on keeping that ridiculous job. Honestly, a stagehand."

Mom understood what he loved. She never wanted Dad to be anything other than what he was. The problem was that after a while, what he was didn't fit with what she was becoming.

"Your dad thinks I want life to be easy," she said to me once. "I don't. I want to do the right thing. It's just that the right thing turned out to be smaller than I thought it would be.

"Oz thinks I've sold out. If I'm in the system, *I am* the system. Responsible for every terrible thing that happens. He's so angry about the world. 'Don't get any on you,' he says. I swear, he acts as if doing the right thing is no more than *not* doing the expected thing, never doing whatever they think you should do. Whoever *they* are . . ."

It's true. Mom and I laugh sometimes. For being so allegedly laid-back, Dad can be as judgmental as Grandma. And he's so full of contradiction. He rants about workaholic yuppies, but nobody works harder than Dad does. He loves work. He'll work twelve, fifteen hours at a stretch, and never complain.

But why wouldn't he work those hours if it makes him feel the way he obviously feels now? He steps back, thinking, steps forward, fiddles with some knobs, adjusts a wire. The whole world could disappear around him, and he'd never even know it.

When, finally, he's satisfied, he inserts a CD, and "Sgt. Pepper" fills the room. "There you go, pal," he says. "Okay, I'm outta here."

"You don't want to stay and listen?" I ask. "This is great. It sounds great."

"Can't do it. Got some stuff to do at home; it's a pit. And Kim gets back from her parents' this afternoon. Besides—" He glances at the piles of clothes on the floor, my open, empty suitcase. "You've got packing to do."

Downstairs, he gives Mom a kiss on the cheek, shakes Ted's hand. "Don't get burned," he says, and we all laugh.

It's another beautiful winter day. Clear and not so cold that I can't walk him out to the Jeep with no more than a sweater. Dad opens the car door but doesn't get in right away. He looks up and down the block. Little kids are out playing with their Christmas loot. Bicycles and skateboards whiz by. Little girls pushing their dolls in strollers.

Suddenly I think, Don't go. I feel awful about looking forward to the trip, about liking Ted as much as I do. If I hadn't liked him, right now Dad and I might be taking off on one of those weird trips we used to take together.

"Well . . . ," he says.

"Listen, thanks, Dad," I say. "The CD player. I never expected anything like that. It's so cool."

He jangles his car keys. He takes his sunglasses from the pocket of his leather jacket, blows the dust from them, puts them on. The sun glints off the gold rims. "I love you, pal," he says, punching me on the arm. "Don't you forget it."

randma takes us to the airport in her Cadillac. "Now leave your heavy jackets," she says. "They can stay right here in the trunk until I come back to get you."

Ted unloads our luggage and carries it to the curbside luggage handler. He has all our tickets. We wait, watching our fellow travelers hurry up and down the concourse, while he checks in at the desk. "All set," he says. We send our carry-on bags through security. Our timing is perfect. The plane for Miami will be boarding in fifteen minutes.

It's an uneventful flight. I doze in the window seat, half listening to my Walkman. Beside me, Amy colors. Kristin reads *Tales of a Fourth Grade Nothing*. Across the aisle, Mom and Ted have the Jamaica book out and are making a list of things we might like to do.

I look out the window, beyond the silver wing that looks too big to be real, down through the wispy clouds to the turquoise blue water—the same color as the ink Steph always uses. No, don't think about her, I tell myself. I focus on a boat below, just a black dot trailing a white wake, like a jet stream. In time, Jamaica appears, like a papier-mâché relief map: carefully modeled mountains painted gray and forest green, green-checkered farmlands, silver threads of river. There's a wavery white line where the land meets the water. The engines shift as we circle around to begin our descent.

The heat hits us like a wall. Ted goes to get the rental car and picks us up out front with the air-conditioning turned on full blast. "No way will I ever get in one of those jitney cabs again," he says as we cruise past the line of vans along the curb. "When I came here for a conference a few years back, we had to stop twice for people to throw up. Honest to God, the driver nearly killed at least three schoolkids who were walking in the road. Not to mention nearly killing us—"

"Ted!" Mom shrieks. "Left lane, remember?"

He swerves, then when we're safe in the lane we're supposed to be in, he reaches over and pats her hand. "Like I was saying, if we're going to get killed, I'd rather kill us myself."

"Oh, what a comfort," Mom says. But she's smiling.

The road to Ocho Rios follows the coastline. To our left, the ocean stretches out forever, striped in a half-dozen shades of blue. Everywhere else it's ferns and palm trees. Occasionally we pass resort areas, where the vegetation has been cut back and manicured. The hotels and guest houses are brightly painted, surrounded by extravagant flower beds. People dressed in the same bright colors cruise around on golf carts with striped awnings.

The native villages we pass through are gray and dusty, though. Wiry black kids play in the streets, shouting and laughing. Men lounge, smoking, outside houses that are like shacks, really. You can look right through the open front doors and see beat-up furniture and more kids inside.

"They're so poor," Mom says—exactly what I'm thinking. "And here we are on our way to a fabulous resort. It seems strange. Not right."

"I know what you mean," Ted says. He slows way down as he passes a church, where a group of people spill out into the street. "There's food here, though. So much grows wild, even. I

101

guess it's better than being poor in a cold city." Then, as if he knows I'm thinking how much mileage my dad would get out of a remark like that, he adds, "I know that sounds like a cop-out. Another rich tourist—"

A van careens around us on the right, its horn blaring. The man at the wheel grins and waves.

"I'm having culture shock," Mom says.

Amy's fast asleep, her head resting against my shoulder. Kristin keeps reading. Mom glances back at them as we leave the village with the noisy, smiling children behind.

It's late afternoon by the time we reach our resort. The bellman wheels our luggage down a garden path toward a row of thatched bungalows, talking nonstop in a voice that sounds like music, like Bob Marley. "You love it here," he says. "The sun always shine in Jamaica. Here, people always happy."

"We'll hold you to that." Ted smiles, and tips him. "That's why we came."

Everyone but Kristin heads straight for the deck off the living room. It's outfitted with director's chairs and an umbrella table. There are huge tubs of pink flowers. Wooden stairs lead down to the pool and the beach just beyond.

"Ted, I think you should know what a shallow person I am," Mom says. "I'm totally over my culture shock. Oh, this is so beautiful. Isn't it, Jackson? Can you believe we're here?"

I guess I'm over my culture shock, too, because the scene spread out before us seems wonderful: the shimmering turquoise pool, the white lounge chairs all around it. The ocean dotted with colorful sails. Near the surf line, gulls swoop and dive, bringing up their silvery catch.

"Can we go down?" Amy asks. "Daddy, can we?"

"You bet," Ted says. "As soon as we stash our stuff and change. Come on, sweetie." He swings her up and carries her back inside.

There are two bedrooms; I'll sleep in the loft. I go up the ladder sideways, balancing my suitcase. Ted hands my backpack up to me. There's a bed, a dresser, a desk and chair. Nothing fancy, but I like it. No one can see me, but if I look down, I can see the whole living area. If I look straight across, there's a great ocean view. The whole back of the house is windows.

While I change into shorts, I watch Mom. She adjusts the draperies, opens and closes all the doors of the built-in cabinets. "Oh, God, more champagne," she calls out, finding the bottle that's peeking out of the huge basket of tropical fruit on the coffee table.

"For later," Ted says, kissing her, holding her for a long moment before he takes the bottle to the kitchenette.

Both of them disappear into their bedroom to change. Kristin has been sitting primly on one of the couches, still in her traveling clothes. Now from my perch I watch her get up and go over to the big window that overlooks the ocean.

"Get ready, Kristin," Amy says, joining her. She looks so funny in her fluorescent yellow bikini and little beach shoes, her sunglasses shaped like daisies, that I can hardly keep from laughing.

Kristin regards her like the traitor she is. "I bet you don't even have sunscreen on," she says. "Mommy said we can't go anywhere without sunscreen on, no matter what. I'm telling."

I grab a T-shirt and my sunscreen and scramble down the ladder. "I'll put sunscreen on for you," I tell Amy. "You can use mine."

"You're nice, Jackson," she says, and sighs.

My hand, spread out, practically covers her whole back. I rub the sunscreen in, careful to cover every bit of exposed skin. "Here, give me your arm," I say, and rub it there, too. "Other arm. Okay, now your legs." I squirt some in her hands so she can rub some on her stomach and up near her collarbone.

Going down the stairs, Amy takes my hand. "Is your dad sad without you?" she asks.

"I don't know. Maybe."

"Our mom's sad. She's very sad for us to be gone so long. She said we can call her if *we* get sad. She wrote down how for Kristin. 'Cause she's older. Almost ten," Amy says. "Kristin can read."

"Kristin's smart," I say.

Amy nods solemnly. "I don't have to do everything she says, though."

I wait for her to go on, wondering if she's going to say that she knows she doesn't have to feel the way Kristin feels, either. But she just giggles and in her fluty voice says, "Mommy says the two of us are like night and day."

We step from the shade of the palm trees that border the deserted pool deck. The fierceness of the afternoon sun has dissolved, and a few people are stretched out on the lounges, enjoying the breeze that's blowing up from the ocean.

There's a girl about my age on the lounge next to the one where I help Amy spread her Little Mermaid towel. She's lying perfectly flat. She has a plastic contraption covering her eyes, so I know she can't see me looking her over. She's pretty: long blond hair, kind of like Kristin's. She's thin but not skinny. Her skin is pinkish with the beginnings of a tan. She has blue sunscreen on her nose. A book rests, turned over and open, beside her. When she stirs, I look back toward the ocean. From the corner of my eye, I see her sit up, stretch her arms over her head. Oh man, I think. Out of my league.

Thank God Brady's not here. He'd take one look at a girl like that and belch or fart or do a cannonball into the pool and get her soaking wet just to establish the fact that he didn't give a damn what she thought about him.

"Hi," Amy pipes up. "I'm Amy. We just got here."

"Really?"

"Yep," Amy says. "We came all the way from Indiana. In a airplane."

"*Did* you?" The girl glances at me and grins. "I bet that made you thirsty. I know where you can get something really good to drink. In fact, I'll even go get it for you. That's okay, isn't it?" she asks me.

"Oh, sure. Thanks." Just relax, I tell myself, resisting the impulse to hunch my shoulders. She gets up, in a single move flicks her hair over her shoulders, and pads over to the bar. She returns with a foamy pink concoction that has a sparkly swizzle stick and a pink paper umbrella sticking out of it. Drinking it, Amy looks like a little shrunk-up Hollywood star.

"She is so cute," the girl whispers. "Your sister?"

"Stepsister," I say. "As of two weeks ago."

"No kidding," the girl says.

I shrug, mortified to have offered that bit of personal information. Like she'd care. I'm relieved when Mom and Ted appear—until I realize that it would be inexcusably rude to walk away and join them and equally rude to stay and not introduce them to this person I've been talking to. Jeez, I don't even know her name.

Amy saves me. "Daddy, look!" She raises her glass, and the drink sloshes out on either side and drips onto her stomach. The girl wipes it away with her own towel. "My friend bought this for me," Amy says.

"Great," Ted says. "You've got a friend already? That's great."

"I get to keep the stuff in it, Daddy." Amy shows him the swizzle stick and the little umbrella.

"Neat," he says. "Hey, can I borrow that umbrella if it rains?"

"*Daddy*," Amy says.

"It doesn't rain here," the girl says. "It's not allowed."

Mom smiles. She nods at the girl. "I'm Ellen Harper," she says. "This is Ted." She assumes, like any normal person would, that I've already introduced myself.

The girl says, "Amanda Clark." She chats with Mom a few minutes, then excuses herself. "You take care now," she says to Amy. She turns to me and flutters her hand.

"See you," I say lamely.

"Amanda," Amy says when the girl has gone. "That's a *A* name. Just like mine."

he next day Kristin sullenly agrees to join us at the beach, but when she emerges from the bedroom, she's wearing a long-sleeved shirt, sweatpants, and what looks like a rain hat.

Ted says, "Honey, you're going to boil in all those clothes."

"Mommy says the sun is terrible here. We have to be very careful not to get a sunburn."

Ted points out the long row of bright blue umbrellas near the shoreline. "You can rent them," he says. "You get under one of those, you'll have plenty of shade."

Poor Ted. She gives him an okay-I'm-a-prisoner-I-accept-it look and puts her bathing suit on. When we get to the beach, she chooses the most remote umbrella, plops down in the canvas chair under it, and sticks her nose in a book.

"Want to take a walk?" I ask her.

Without looking up, she shakes her head no.

"Me!" Amy says. "I want to." So the two of us set out.

We don't go far, but it takes forever. Amy stands and watches the waves roll in and out. She mimics the sandpipers skittering along the sand. She stops to pick up shells and puts them in her plastic bucket. All the while, she's asking me a million questions. Jackson, can octopuses kill you? Do fish live someplace or do they just swim around all the time? Do birds get sunburned?

"Eeyew," she says when I show her a jellyfish that's been washed ashore.

I poke at it and gross her out again. I say, "What I want to know is, are there peanut-butter fish?"

"Jackson, there's no such thing." But there's a trace of uncertainty in her voice that makes me smile.

We turn and head back. Close to our umbrellas, she starts to run. I figure she's going to show Ted her shells, but she runs right past him. That's when I see the girl we met yesterday, Amanda. She's sitting under the umbrella next to mine, even more gorgeous than I remembered.

"Hi," she says when I get there.

I wave vaguely toward her. I'm as bad as Kristin. To avoid dealing with Amanda, I get my book out of Mom's canvas bag and pretend I'm totally absorbed in it. I watch the two of them from the corner of my eye: Amy presenting her treasures, Amanda exclaiming over them. Kristin is watching them, too. Pretty soon, she lays her book down, stands, and marches over to Amanda's chair. Amy and Amanda are so absorbed in spreading the shells on Amanda's beach towel that they don't notice her until she says in her bossy voice, "Amy, if you want to go swimming now, I have to go with you. Mom said I'm in charge of watching you in the water."

"But I don't want to swim," Amy says.

Kristin shrugs, but she doesn't go back to her chair.

"That's my sister," Amy says. "Kristin."

"Hi," Amanda says. "Why don't you bring your stuff over here?"

The next time I glance over, Kristin's sitting on the footrest of Amanda's chair. Amanda's adjusted her chair to a slant and flipped her long hair over the back of it so Amy can brush it. Her eyes are closed; she has this look on her face like she's dreaming. Amy giggles when the long strands of Amanda's hair stick to the brush, and I think of how when we were little, Brady and I used to rub balloons on our heads to make our hair stand on end. When Amanda smiles, I have this weird idea that she's smiling at what I am remembering.

"I can French-braid," Kristin says.

"She can," says Amy. "Our mom taught her."

"Really?" Amanda sits up. "Will you do one in my hair?"

"Okay." Kristin's voice is cool, but when she takes the brush from Amy and brushes the underside of Amanda's hair so that she can gather it all in her free hand, her expression is rapt. Now Amanda sits Indian style, her back perfectly straight, her hands in her lap. Kristin begins to braid in a cautious but graceful rhythm. When she's nearly finished, she says, "Do you have a rubber band?"

"Darn," Amanda says. "I don't." Then, "Wait a minute. Amy, give me my shoe, will you?" Not changing position, not looking down, she unlaces the orange shoestring in her Reebok, feeling with her fingers for the eyelets. "There you go."

"Come here," Kristin tells Amy. Like a little slave, Amy jumps up and holds the end of the braid so Kristin can tie the shoelace around it. Something about the three of them reminds me of a painting we studied in Western Civ, one I can't remember the name of. Someone and her handmaids.

Suddenly I get this burning feeling, like if I don't get up and do something right this second I'm going to go crazy. I pull off my T-shirt, throw it on my chair, and take off running.

"Jackson?" Mom calls.

I don't look back. I'm like a machine, pumping, pounding. When I know I've gone far enough that they can't see me, I throw myself down on the warm sand and breathe hard. Just chill, I tell myself. She probably didn't even notice you were acting weird. Why would she? Waves crash and recede, sometimes licking me, and leaving a bubbly white foam on my skin. When my heart stops pounding, I head back, jogging at a steady comfortable pace, planning exactly how I am going to slow down, walk to my beach chair, towel off, and sit down with my book as if I'm a perfectly normal person with no interest whatsoever in anyone but myself. I remind myself that, thank God, I can actually pull this off because

I don't look like a wimp anymore. I may feel like an idiot, I may be an idiot, but I don't have to be embarrassed by the way I look. Then when I get back Amanda's chair is empty.

"She went running," Amy says, pointing vaguely in the opposite direction from which I've come. "Like you, Jackson. She can run really fast."

Kristin says, "She asked us to watch her things."

I shrug, like it's no big deal to me what Amanda does. I drape my towel over my head and lie down on the lounge chair as if exhausted from my run.

"Isn't she the sweetest girl?" I hear Mom say to Ted. "Did you hear her telling me she was an only child? Her parents are older, retired. From San Francisco. She's in boarding school out East somewhere, some girls school. They take her on these fabulous vacations when she's on break, but I gather they're not much fun. They stay in the condo and play bridge, she says. I think she's lonely."

"She's a knockout," Ted says.

"Hmmm," says Mom. "I'll bet she doesn't know it."

This I find hard to believe, but when Amanda comes back from jogging I think maybe Mom is right. Or at least I think that if Amanda does know she's pretty, maybe it's not the most important thing in the world to her. I mean, most girls I know will sit by a swimming pool for hours and never go in the water for fear of messing up their hair or their makeup. But Amanda comes flying down the beach, all sweaty, and dives into the ocean to cool off. When she comes out, she takes a baseball cap from her beach bag and puts it on, flipping her long braid through the hole in the back. She plunks down on the sand to play with Kristin and Amy.

Amy has a bunch of little pastel-colored ponies, and they decide to make a stable for them. They make a round wall, then build up little stalls inside, one for each of the ponies. They make a forest all around by dripping wet sand into tall treelike forms. An evil forest, Amanda says.

"But these are magic ponies. Two beautiful little girls have been kidnapped by bad spirits and only these ponies can get their parents through the forest and take them to the right place to rescue their children."

109

Amy gallops one of the ponies over the sand to Amanda, then another one right up the arm of my chair. "Okay, you and Jackson be the parents," she says. "You and Jackson ride the magic ponies to the forest and find us, and then we all live happy ever after."

I sit, paralyzed, my book in my face, praying that Amanda will either ignore her or suggest another game. But she reaches over and jiggles my bare foot. "Dear," she says in a high whiny voice. "Would you *please* stop reading and get on the magic pony, so we can find our poor lost children? And then could you give me a hand building a walled fortress, so we'll all have a place to live happy ever after *in*?"

Amy giggles wildly. "Come on, Jackson," she says. "Play."

That's how I end up down on the sand so close to Amanda that I feel like I might have a heart attack any minute.

"Here," she says, handing me a Coke cup. "You can make the turrets."

I can handle that: scooping wet sand, packing it, then turning the cup over just right, so that a perfect, round turret appears. With the sharp edge of a shell, I make elaborate markings on each one.

"Like a medieval craftsman," Amanda says. "Did you know that sometimes they used to carve really bizarre things in cathedrals? Way up or in dark places, where it's hard to see?"

That gets us to talking about school and various classes we've taken, and I tell her about my favorite class, Western Civ, and how we had to make up our own circles of hell when we read the *Inferno*.

"Like for televangelists," I say. "They'd have to spend eternity preaching to adoring old ladies who are totally poor. And food-packaging people. They'd be buried in their own paper and plastic crap, forever one breath short of suffocating to death. Righteous vegetarians—"

"Eating cheeseburgers." Amanda laughs. "McDonald's Quarter Pounders. How about people who hate art? Put them in a dark room watching slides of great paintings forever and ever. And every day, there's a test. I loved the *Inferno* when we read it," she says. "But we never got to do anything fun with it, like

110

that. My school is so serious. So predictable. Everybody's exactly the same."

"That's one problem we don't have," I say. "Everyone being the same." I tell her about the weird mix of people in the city school I go to.

"I think I'd like that," Amanda says.

"It's real," I say. "It's got that going for it. Like this friend of mine, my best friend, actually—Brady—used to say, 'This place may be a dung heap. But it's real.' "

"I could use a dose of reality," Amanda says. "I go from my little girls school in its boring, antiseptic little town to my parents' condo in San Francisco, to places like this." She waves her arm toward the resort behind us. "Your friend, what's his name—Brady?—he's right about real being worth something."

"He's just about always right," I say. "He's incredible, the way he sees through things."

"What do you mean, 'sees through things'?"

I start to say he has a great bullshit detector, but I'm afraid that might offend her. So I say, "It's like he has radar for anything that's phony. He hates anything phony."

Amanda nods.

"The thing is, though," I say. "He more than hates it. He does something about it. He always does what he thinks is right. Like, at the end of last summer he just left."

"Ran away?"

"Yeah," I say. "I've never known anyone who actually had the guts to do that. His parents drove him crazy. School drove him crazy. He thought his life was totally pointless the way it was, so he left."

"He told you that?"

"Not exactly," I say. "I haven't heard from him. I just assume that, knowing how he felt."

"And you're not mad?" she asks. "He's your best friend and he ran away and you haven't even heard from him and you're not mad?"

"I was," I say. "At first—"

She's looking at me with this sad expression. I swear to God, she knows I'm lying.

111

"Actually, I'm still mad at him," I admit. "I'm pissed out of my mind." And suddenly I'm telling her everything. How close the two of us were. How strange the school year has been without him, how it freaks me out to think that there are things, really important things, in my life that Brady doesn't even know about.

Ted and Mom take the girls inside to rest, and I keep talking. "Like I have these sisters," I say. "He doesn't even know about them."

"I can't believe he just disappeared," Amanda says. "It's terrible that he wouldn't at least call or send a postcard. You don't think something bad happened to him, do you?"

"No," I say. "Some people think that, but I don't. It's just Brady. He does what he wants to do."

"Oh," Amanda says. "But you said he always did what was *right*."

Weird. For some reason her pointing that out to me doesn't make me mad.

"It's selfish," she goes on. "Running away. Oh, I know. Parents and school are a pain. But doesn't everyone have those problems? Big deal. You just get through it. That's what friends are for. You help each other get through. You don't run away and leave them on their own. Not everybody has a friend like you, Jackson. Brady should've realized that." She stops suddenly, and even though her face is tanned, I can tell she's blushing. "I should just shut up," she says. "I'm sorry."

"No," I say. "You're right. I just hadn't admitted it to myself before now. You're right. Brady can be selfish."

A silence falls between us. I think, Well, that's that. It doesn't matter how I look. I'm still a wimp. She knows it.

Then she smiles at me. "Hey, I thought of another circle for our Inferno," she says. "For people like Brady who don't appreciate their true friends. How about a Sisyphus and the rock thing? They spend eternity trying to please someone who doesn't give a damn about them."

This cracks me up. "Excellent," I say. "Brady Burton: Eagle Scout, Harvard Law."

All through this, I'm still scooping. We finished the walled fortress long ago, and now I'm making a line of turrets as far as I can reach.

Amanda leans back against the lounge chair, takes her baseball cap off, and loosens the braid Kristin made in her hair. She combs it with her fingers. "Look, Jackson," she says. "You're making a nuclear power plant. I like that, you know? A walled fortress with its own nuclear power plant. How handy."

I'm in deep shit, man. I'm totally in love with her.

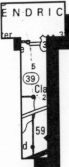 hat night I can hardly sleep, worrying about whether I'm going to get weird around her the next time I see her, like I did watching Kristin and Amy braid her hair. Worse, what if we go down to the beach tomorrow and she's not even there? But when we go down right after breakfast, there she is, already in her chair, reading.

"'Manda!" Amy shouts, and takes off running toward her.

Amanda looks up and smiles. She opens her arms so that Amy can throw herself into them. She pats the place at the foot of the chair for Kristin to sit down beside her. "Hi, Jackson," she says. She pulls an empty plastic cup out of her beach bag, holds it up, and grins. "Today, Castle World!"

And it's as easy to be with her as it was the day before. We fool around with Kristin and Amy, building a whole town of castles, then taking a beach walk to collect shells to decorate them. Ted brings us all lunch from the bar. When it's time for the girls to rest, Amanda says to me, "I think I'll go for a run. Want to come?"

I say, "Sure." I have to smile, thinking of what Dad would say if he were here. *See, bud, I told you a body could be a good thing!* Still, when we take off down the beach, I can't quite believe the person running with Amanda is me. We run a couple of miles, then walk back, talking the whole time—about everything under the sun, the way we did the day before.

"So, do you wrestle?" she asks me.

I must give her a blank look because she says, "You look like a wrestler. You know, you're strong. I thought maybe you might be on the wrestling team at school. Anyhow, never mind. I was just being nosy again. God, I know I drive people crazy asking them questions all the time. It's not like you have to tell me every single thing about yourself."

"I don't care what you ask me," I say. "It's just, I'm a total klutz, that's all. What you asked just surprised me."

"You are not a total klutz, Jackson. Why do you think that?"

I shrug. "I don't know. Before this fall the only exercise I ever got was picking up a book. Maybe playing a video game. I was horrible at Little League and all that. I only got into working out after my friend Brady left. Something to do. I'm no jock, though. Believe me."

"God, I am," she says gloomily. "My parents are always trying to get me to act like a girl. They hate this—" She pulls her soaking wet shirt away from her body. "You know, when I sweat."

"I think it's great," I say.

"Sweat?" She laughs. "Can you believe we're actually having this conversation? Honestly, my parents are right. I need to go to charm school."

I meant I thought it was great the way she is. The way she *doesn't* act like a girl. But before I can say so, she says, "Race you in," and takes off running toward the beach chairs, where Kristin and Amy are waiting.

That evening, I see her in the hotel restaurant with her mom and dad. She's wearing a pretty flowered sundress that makes her look really tanned. Her hair is held back with a headband made of matching fabric. After we eat, Ted and Mom stop at their table to say hello.

Ted and her dad shake hands. "Beautiful little girls you have there," he says to Mom. He turns to me. "And you must be—Jackson, is it?"

"Yes, sir." I give him my firmest handshake.

"Well," he says, "Amanda's told us all about you."

"She *has?*" I say, and immediately want to kill myself.

Amanda looks as mortified as I feel. What she undoubtedly told her parents about me is that I'm Kristin and Amy's step-brother, an okay, harmless kind of guy. She's probably thinking, Oh, great. He's going to think I'm madly in love with him.

So what's my next line? Don't worry, I'm not? Or worse, the truth: Actually, I am in love with you, Amanda. But don't worry, I don't expect you to love me back. Ha. I'm not stupid enough to make a fool of myself again. I keep quiet.

Her mother says, "Won't you all sit down?"

"Well, sure!" Ted says, and pulls out a chair for my mom.

The adults order a round of after-dinner drinks. Kristin and Amy have their usual Shirley Temples. Cokes for me and Amanda, in crystal glasses. No way you'd want to make sand castles using those. Mom says she loves Amanda's dress and Amanda says they make the same dresses in little girls sizes and wouldn't it be fun to get them for Amy and Kristin and they could all match? Amanda's father asks me a couple of lame questions about school and what I plan to do with my life, and I answer them but can't think of a thing to say next. So I just sit there, a total dweeb, staring off at where I suppose the ocean must be. Jesus, then the band starts, people start going out onto the dance floor, and Amy peers over the rim of her cocktail glass and in her little-queen voice orders, "Jackson, you and Amanda dance."

"Oh, do," says Amanda's mother.

I hate to dance; I never have learned how to do it right. But we go out there, and I step on Amanda's feet for a while anyhow. I don't even want to think about why she looks so miserable. Finally, the song is over, and I *think* that the most mortifying experience of my entire life is over. But making a fool of myself dancing looks like an excellent option when we go back to the table, and Amy pipes up and says, "Amanda, now is Jackson your boyfriend?"

There's this kind of embarrassed titter all around the table.

"Amy Harper!" Ted says. "Honest to Pete. What have I told you about asking people questions all the time?"

Amy looks stricken, as if she's about to cry; but Amanda scoops her up and hugs her. "It's okay, Mr. Harper," she says. "Amy can ask me any question she wants." She tips up Amy's face with her finger. "Jackson is a boy and he's my friend, okay? And you're a girl and you're my friend. Everyone who dances with me is my friend. So there." She dances a giggling Amy around the restaurant.

Amy looks so funny and cute, with her legs dangling down and her hair ribbon all askew that, thank God, everybody starts laughing and taking turns dancing with her, even Amanda's mother.

Later, back at the condo, I overhear Ted tell Mom he feels terrible about Amy embarrassing me. Don't, I feel like saying. It could have been a lot worse. At least I know where I stand: Amanda wants to be my friend. Which, of course, makes no difference whatsoever in the way I *feel*. I still love her. I still think of how it would be to touch her. I can actually picture it: kissing her, walking hand in hand to a dark, quiet place, then taking each other's clothes off, melting into each other, making love. I just give up any hope that it will ever happen. No way I'm about to make a fool of myself or embarrass her by trying to make our relationship more than what she wants it to be.

So I chill out, grateful to be able to be with her at all. Every day, we go down to the beach, and she's waiting. We fool around with Kristin and Amy till lunchtime, building castles or whatever—then she and I go for a long run. On the way back, we talk.

Mom was right. Amanda is lonely. She says to me, "You want to know something, Jackson? What I really want is to fall madly in love and have kids when I'm still really young. And for all of us to be together. It's probably awful to say that. I mean, my parents want me to be successful. And I do want a career. I don't want to be an idiot. But a family . . ."

"I want that, too," I tell her. "I want to be married to the same person as long as I live."

"What was it like when your parents got divorced?" she asks.

"Awful," I say. "I was totally confused. It wasn't that they didn't love each other, they said. Because they did. They just couldn't go on living together. How could that be? For a long time, I thought that they'd get back together. But they never did. I've never told this to anyone before, but my mom and dad still love each other. Even now."

"Now?" Amanda looks shocked.

"Yeah, now," I said. "I don't mean my mom doesn't love Ted. She loves him in a totally different way than she loves my dad. She and Dad were never going to be able to live together and be happy. They disagreed on too many important things, and neither one of them was going to change. That really was what the divorce was about. It just took me a long time to understand it. If you met my dad, you'd get a better idea of what I mean."

"What's he like?"

"Dad's, well, different. He doesn't want what most people want. It turned out that he and my mom didn't want the same things anymore. I was the only thing they had in common."

"It's so sad, though," she says. "If two people really, really love each other, why—"

"Sometimes things just don't work out," I say.

"But they can if both people really want them to. Don't you think they can then?"

"Yeah," I say. "At least I hope so."

Later, when we're wandering through the street market together, I buy a T-shirt for Dad. It has a phony college crest with a marijuana plant in the middle. "Ganja U."

"Okay, I'm beginning to see what you mean about your dad being different," Amanda says. "God, my dad would freak out if I even *bought* something like that—let alone as a present for him."

"Dad'll love it," I say. "He may be a total screwup, but he's cool."

"Is he really all that screwed up?" she asks.

"No," I say. "I shouldn't have said that. Some people, like my grandma, think he's a real loser. But they just can't accept that it's okay not to want the same thing as everybody else. I mean, Dad may have a weird job, but he's really good at it. He works hard. And as fathers go, he may be a little flaky—he's no Ward Cleaver, that's for sure—but there's never been a time he hasn't at least tried to give me what I need."

"You're lucky, really," Amanda says. "My parents are so perfect. They do everything right. They didn't have me until they were absolutely sure they could give me everything they never had. The best clothes, the best toys, the best schools, trips to Europe. All those things, giving me all those things is so important to them that I have to act like they make me happy. But all I've ever wanted is them.

"It's not that they don't love me," she adds quickly. "They do. It's just, they don't know who I am."

I know you, I want to say. I love you. But I don't. See, there's nothing in the world I wouldn't tell Amanda—except the way I feel about her. It's nothing like I've ever felt before. I want to be with her all the time; I look at her and think about what it would be like to be with her forever. Maybe even to have two little girls like Kristin and Amy someday.

They might as well be our kids now, the way they always want to be with us. "Just tell me if they're bugging you," Ted says every day. "I'll keep them out of your hair." But I don't mind. I love to watch Amanda's face light up when she sees them running toward her. I love to watch her play with them. I'm like Nick Carraway in *The Great Gatsby*, sucked into a love story, pretending I'm just an observer. I keep quiet. If I spoke, my feelings would be as pitifully obvious as his were.

Kristin and Amy say, "Oh, Jackson, isn't she pretty, isn't she nice, isn't she so much fun?"

"Yeah, yeah." I laugh and roll my eyes, as if indulging them.

They insist that Amanda go along with us wherever we go.

Mom and Ted think it's hilarious the way they're so smitten. "Maybe we should adopt Amanda," Mom says. "The way we've expanded in the last month, what's one more?"

"Or hire her," Ted says. "You know, give her some fancy title. Liaison to the Children."

But when they're being serious, they both admit it was a

lucky stroke that Amanda appeared. Because Kristin and Amy are so attached to her, it's given Mom and Ted some guilt-free time alone, a real honeymoon. Plus, Amanda met us for the first time as we are now. She just assumes we're a family, even though we haven't gotten used to it ourselves. I think we act more like a family because of her.

It won't last, I know. We'll go home and there'll be problems. Kristin will remember to be mad. I'll go back to feeling guilty about liking Ted. Meanwhile, we're as happy as people in a TV sitcom. We go to Dunn's River Falls and climb up the slippery rocks for a spectacular view of the ocean. We tour a plantation, bouncing along the dirt roads on a tractor-drawn jitney, viewing groves of banana, cocoa, lime, and coffee, stopping to watch a Jamaican boy climb up a coconut tree barefoot.

"This is so much fun," Amanda says again and again. "You guys are so fun." Sometimes when we're alone she tells me about her life at school, how lonely she is there. "There's nobody like you there, Jackson," she says once. "Nobody I can really trust. They're all so worried about what people think, they don't care what people *are*. I hate that. Honestly, before I met you I was beginning to wonder if I would ever find anyone I could really talk to. It's pathetic, you know? You're the first *real* friend I've ever had."

"No boyfriends?" I say, careful to make my voice light.

She sort of laughs. "Oh, that never works out," she says. "It always turns out to be, you know—about something else."

And I am ashamed of what I imagine when I'm alone, in the dark. I'm ashamed of what I want. If I really love her, and I do, I should be the friend that she wants and needs me to be. Not that being her friend feels at all like a burden. I need a friend myself, what with Brady's defection; and just these few days with her have made me consider the possibility that a different kind of friendship could be a good thing. Amanda asks questions; Brady had answers. Amanda says, "That's interesting"; Brady always said, "You should—" The way Amanda values my opinion makes me realize that Brady didn't value it much. I needed him a lot more than he needed me. For the first time, I see how our friendship depended on my letting him always be in charge. I see that

120

before I met Amanda I didn't really know what friendship could be.

Sometimes I half convince myself that I'm not really in love with her. I mean, if I actually did love Amanda, how could it be so easy between us and so good? It must be friendship, after all. Then she'll look at me a certain way or come around a corner when I haven't seen her for a couple of hours and a kind of shock goes all through my body. Why kid myself?

TWENTY-TWO

The last day of our vacation is a day like all the others, warm and blue. There is the whisper of the waves, the whisper of the wind in the palm trees. There is Amanda in her lounge chair, reading, when we come down to the beach. She smiles.

Amy and Kristin fly to her; they won't let her out of their sight. Kristin braids her hair. She brings her pineapple juice from the pool bar. "If I write you a letter, will you answer it?" she asks.

"Sure," Amanda says. "Will you send me copies of the pictures your dad took?"

Kristin nods eagerly.

"Too bad you're not Kristin's new stepsibling," I say, only half joking, when Kristin's out of earshot. "If Ted had married *your* mom, she might not have been so traumatized."

"Oh no," Amanda says. "Kristin loves you, Jackson. She just doesn't dare show it. Not yet. Not till she figures out that loving you doesn't mean she doesn't love her mother. I mean, how could she *not* love you?"

I swear my heart stops. I feel the way I did that first day when I sat down beside her to help build the castle. Chill, I tell myself. She's saying *Kristin* loves you. She's not saying anything at all about the way she feels herself.

Obviously, I'm right because she changes the subject and we're off talking about books and people again, solving world problems. We take our last run. I stay a little behind her so that I can watch her long ponytail fly out with every step, so that I can memorize the way she looks flying toward the horizon. Walking back, she says, "Jackson, I'm going to miss you so much. You'll write, won't you?"

"Sure," I say. "Definitely." Above us, gulls swoop and soar, and I think of the words I will write to her. I'll write them so well, so carefully. I'll send them off across the sky, into her life, and they'll make her happy, and in time maybe she'll realize the words *are* me, that it's me who makes her happy. No, not maybe. She will want me. I'll make her want me. The late afternoon sun makes the water shimmer. The breeze picks up, and I have the feeling that if I took off running, it would lift me like a rainbow kite. I could see everything, know everything. But I keep walking beside Amanda. It's enough right now just to be with her.

She has dinner with us that night, comes back to our bungalow to play old maid with Kristin and Amy until it's their bedtime. "I told my parents you'd walk me back," she says to me after she's hugged the girls and kissed them goodnight. "They're paranoid. Do you mind?"

Outside, it's breezy. It smells of gardenias. Amanda picks one and sticks it in her hair. "Want to take a walk on the beach first?" she asks.

When I don't answer immediately, she says, "We don't have to. I mean, I know you have to get up really early—"

"No," I say. "I mean, yeah—sure, let's walk." I start off, taking huge strides, trying to figure out how to act. I mean, after this afternoon, I had it all worked out. I'd write, I'd be patient. Now this.

"Jackson?" Amanda says, skipping to catch up with me.

I slow down, but I don't speak. I can't.

The tide's out. The beach is hard and flat. We walk until the lights bordering the resort look like a long strand of pearls, like the pearls Ted gave Mom for her birthday. Until there's nothing but ocean and jungle before us as far as we can see.

Amanda stops suddenly, puts her hand on my arm. She's so close I can feel her breath on my cheek. I can smell the shampoo she uses on her hair. "Jackson?" she says again. Then she kisses me. Just a little kiss first, then when my arms seem to lift themselves around her, pull her closer to me, she kisses me again, a real kiss that leaves me stupid and breathless.

"That day when I got Amy the drink," she whispers, "it was because I wanted to meet you."

"Me?"

She pulls away from me then, begins walking away.

"Wait, wait!" I hurry after her, feeling like a dork actor in a movie.

She stops, and I nearly run into her. "Listen, I love Kristin and Amy," she says. "I love being with your family. I really do. Don't think that's fake. But at first, I only played with Kristin and Amy because I thought it might make you like me. Then I saw things wouldn't work out that way. I mean, I know you like me, Jackson. But I saw that you didn't want, you know—

"Oh, my God," she says. "This is so incredibly idiotic. What am I telling you this for, ruining everything?"

"Amanda," I say. Then I don't know how to go on. I just look at her, thinking, Can this possibly be real?

She waves her hand vaguely and starts to walk away again. "No, no. It's okay. I understand. Boys never, I don't know . . ." Her voice sounds wavery. "They never like me. I'm a disaster. And anyway, I mean, with us, what would be the point? We don't live anywhere near each other. So what if you did like me? I'd hardly ever see you. It's better if we're just friends. But now I've probably spoiled that." She starts to cry.

"I do like you." I practically yell because she's gotten so far away from me.

She stops again.

"I like you," I repeat when I catch up. "I love you. Jeez, I'm in love with you. I just never thought you—" Now I kiss her.

She presses against me, and it's just the way I imagined it would be, up in my loft bed. We collapse onto the sand and lie there together. I wipe her tears away. I run my hand all along her as if it is a pencil and I'm drawing her—the curve of her hips, her ribs. When I touch one of her breasts, she breathes in sharply, makes just a little sound, like someone dreaming. I put my arms around her then, hold her for a long, long time, both of us taking deep breaths, both of us shaking. She feels so small against me. I don't ever want to do anything to hurt her.

Hand in hand, we walk back to the hotel. We pull one of the rental lounges out from underneath the boardwalk, where the beach boy stores them every night, and drag it to a secluded spot. There's enough room on it for the two of us if we wedge ourselves into it just right. We lie there, kissing, talking, while strains of reggae music float down from the hotel terrace. In my whole life, I have never been so happy. My whole world is Amanda, breathing here beside me. Amanda and music, beach, ocean, vast black sky.

TWENTY-THREE

t's still dark as Ted and I load the luggage into the trunk of the car the next morning. Kristin and Amy fall asleep as soon as we get going. Mom and Ted talk in low voices. I pretend I'm dozing. Dawn breaks, and through the slits of my eyes I watch the world emerge, a flowing stream of color carrying me farther and farther away from where Amanda dreams. I can't let myself think of that. When I do, a ball of darkness forms inside me, hard and clenched, like a fist.

Instead, I think about how wonderful she is, how right she was about so many things in my life. Maybe even about Kristin starting to love me. She sticks close to me at the airport, allows me to watch her book bag when she takes Amy to the bathroom. When we board, she takes the seat next to me. The whole time, it's Amanda-this, Amanda-that. What she wore, what she said. What to write to her, how to get her to come visit. Kristin can't know that hearing her speak Amanda's name again and again is exactly what I need. If she weren't talking about her, I'd probably be doing it myself, giving away what happened between us last night just by the sound of my voice.

On the flight from Miami, Kristin falls asleep. I occupy myself composing the letter I'll write to Amanda a few days from now—not too soon—writing and rewriting it in my head. It will be funny, I decide. It will say how I feel without being sappy. I wonder how long it will take her to write back to me.

"I guess it's really over," I hear Mom say with a sigh as the plane begins its descent. "I can just see Mother right now, elbowing everyone out of the way so she can be right at the gate when we come out."

Ted laughs.

I figure Mom's right; Grandma will be on us like a rug. I'm surprised when I don't see her right away. People stop short in front of us, hugging and kissing and already starting to tell the stories of their trips to their friends and relatives who've been waiting for them. Then I spot her, stubbing out her cigarette in one of those standing ashtrays. She gets this strange look on her face when she sees us coming toward her.

"Mother!" Mom calls. "Here we are." She hands Ted her carry-on bag, about to give Grandma a hug, but Grandma takes a step back.

"Ellen," she says. "Oh, Jackson, your dad—" And bursts into tears.

"What?" I say. But she's crying so hard she can't answer me. "Grandma, what?" I'm almost crying myself. Oh, please, I think. Don't let him be dead.

There's been an accident, she's finally able to get out. A fall, a bad one. Last night. Bones broken, internal injuries. Something about surgery, intensive care, how much each moment he can stay alive matters.

"Oh," is all Mom keeps saying. "Oh. Oh. Oh."

In the car, no one speaks. Ted navigates Grandma's big Cadillac to the interstate; we pick up speed. I look through my own reflection at the cars we whiz past, at the people driving them who look straight ahead, their eyes on the road. I wonder, if one of them were to glance over and see my face, would he be able to tell that something terrible has happened?

Grandma leans forward from the backseat, sticks her head between mine and Mom's, and starts to talk. "It was Tom who called me—you know, Oz's friend. Well after midnight."

"You knew last night at midnight?" I say. "You didn't call us?"

"Jackson," Mom says.

"Tom was the one who decided. When he called the airline and found out there was no earlier flight, he said, 'There's no point calling. There's not a thing they can do but worry if they know.' Dear Lord, I've been a basket case all day," Grandma says. "Thinking about how I was going to tell you what happened to your dad." She sounds teary. "Jackson, I'm so sorry about this. I know your dad and I don't see eye to eye. You must think—

"Honey, I've been praying for him every minute since I found out." She puts her hand on my shoulder to comfort me. I try to ignore it, to pretend it's not there, but I keep feeling it anyway. It makes me feel trapped. I shrink away from her, from all of them—as close to the door as I can get.

When she starts babbling about how it was a miracle that Dad had survived the fall, how good God was to have spared him, it's all I can do to keep from saying what I know Dad would say if he could hear her. "Ha! Some miracle. If God were really on the job, I guess he'd have kept me from falling in the first place."

I try to see Dad saying it. I have the weird idea that if I can concentrate hard enough to hold him in my mind's eye, if I can keep thinking about him as his usual malcontent self, I'll get to the hospital and find him bossing the nurses around, making smart-ass comments.

But when we actually get there and I see Tom sitting on an ugly orange couch, his head in his hands, I know Dad's bad off, really bad off, and I feel like crying again. I have to clench my jaw hard not to.

"Jax," he says, and comes to me, first folding me into a bear hug, then cradling the back of my head against his chest with his big hands as if I were a hurt child. "He's pretty beat up, buddy." He's almost crying himself. "Let's sit down a minute before we go in to see him, okay? Ellen," he says, noticing Mom for the first time, grasping her hand briefly. "You sit, too. All of you. I'll tell you what I know."

I hear his voice, but as if from a distance. It happened when they were pulling the show down, he says. Something came loose on the truss, and when it tipped, Dad lost his balance, fell to the stage. One arm was broken and his shoulder. His legs were broken, nasty breaks. He's in traction.

"The surgery," Mom interrupts. "Mother said—"

"He kept losing blood." Tom puts his hand on mine. "More than he should have from the broken bones. It was his liver, it turned out. It split open from the impact, and they had to go in and repair it. Scary shit, but it's okay. The trick was catching it in time, and they did.

"It's the head injury they're watching now. 'Minor closed head injury'—that's what the doctor called it. Which, as far as I can figure, translates into a real bad concussion." Tom hesitates. "He hasn't come to yet, Jax. They think he will soon," he adds quickly. "But right now he won't know you're there. And he looks awful, all swollen from the fluids they pumped in during the surgery to make sure his kidneys would keep working. And, Jax, he's on a ventilator, a breathing machine. It's not that he *can't* breathe. . . . The machine keeps everything regular, keeps the blood flow to his brain even, and that keeps down the swelling."

"His brain's swelling?" Imagining this, imagining Dad's liver splitting like a thrown tomato makes my stomach turn. I taste bile.

"No, no," Tom says. "It hasn't so far, or not any more than they consider normal. The machine is a precaution. You ought to be forewarned, though: it looks like *Star Wars* in there. Monitors. Bells and whistles. So don't let it freak you out, okay? It just means they're taking real good care of him."

He stands abruptly. Mom and I follow him out of the waiting room, down the long white corridor, through the double doors marked Intensive Care. Just inside, he stops, puts his hand on my shoulder. "He's going to pull through, Jackson. I wouldn't have said that to you when they brought him out of surgery this morning; I didn't believe it myself. But these last few hours have been important—everything's happening the way it should. And Oz is

129

a stubborn son of a bitch," he says with a wry grin. "Yeah, he's stubborn all right. Anyone ever asks you to define irony, buddy, here it is. For the first time in his life, being the stubborn shit he is is the best thing your old man has going for him."

He keeps his hand on my shoulder as we move toward Dad's room. I'm glad to have it there because I feel weightless, as if I might float back through the double doors, back through the maze of corridors, and out of the hospital right up into the darkening sky. I glance over at Mom. All the suntan has drained from her face. She's looking straight ahead, moving as if she's being pulled by a magnet. She reaches the room first and enters.

"Oh," she says when she sees Dad, more like a breath than a word.

Then I see him. At first I think there's been some terrible mistake. This person can't be my dad. His head is huge, his features distorted so that he looks frightening, like a monster. But it is the blankness, the stillness that makes my heart twist. My real dad constantly drums his fingers, rakes them through his hair. He fiddles with whatever object he finds within his reach, taps a cigarette on the tabletop a half dozen times before he lights it. His hands shape the feel of the words he speaks. It can't be him lying here so still, his head in a brace, his legs immobilized in slings, his arms restrained—not *complaining* about being so still. Not even noticing it.

Mom grips the iron rail at the foot of the bed so tightly her knuckles are white. She's crying; I know because her shoulders are shaking. She doesn't make a sound. In fact, there's no sound in the room except for the unnatural breath of Dad's ventilator. Then the hiss of my own breath, suddenly let out. I didn't even realize I'd been holding it.

"You okay?" Tom asks.

"Yeah," I say. "Yeah, I think so."

"You can talk to him," Tom says. "The nurses say it's good to do that. Even though he doesn't show it, he might hear you."

"Dad?" I say. My voice comes out a whisper. "Dad? It's me, Jackson. Dad?"

I touch his hand. It's warm, curled in a loose fist. I lean down, working my own fingers into it so that our hands are in the same grip they're in when we arm wrestle. My forearm rests against his on the mattress. "Dad?" I say it louder this time, right into his ear. But his eyelids don't even flutter.

I lay my head on the pillow beside his head. I want to stay with him this way until he comes back, until he knows I'm here with him. But the bed rail digs into my chest painfully. My thighs are burning, bent as they are to allow this closeness to my father. My arm's falling asleep.

It's stupid, but that's what makes me start crying: the fact that I finally have to stand up, the fact that I can't be there in the bed with him. I don't even try to explain it. I just stand there sobbing.

Mom puts her arms around me and holds me tight until I stop. "We'll stay with him tonight, honey. Okay, Jackson? We're not going anywhere. Ted will bring us what we need. We're not going anywhere until we know he's really going to be all right."

TWENTY-FOUR

h, Jackson, you got here. Thank God," Kim says, bursting into the room. "Oh," she says again when she sees Mom. She takes a step back so that she's framed in the doorway.

Tom says, "You haven't met Ellen, have you?"

I sense Mom gathering herself up to do the right thing. She offers her hand to Kim. "I'm glad to meet you," she says, "though I'm awfully sorry it has to be this way. I guess Jackson and I are still in shock, but we're both so grateful that you and Tom have been here. . . ."

"I—," Kim begins, but shakes her head. She can't go on. "I've just been so scared," she says, when she regains her composure. "Last night, waiting while Oz was in surgery, I was so scared. No one knew—

"I was so scared it would go badly and Jackson wouldn't get here in time." She turns to me. "Oz loves you so much," she says, starting to cry, and then I'm the one doing the comforting. I hold her until she calms down, until she takes a deep, shuddering breath and pulls away from me to look at Dad. She leans over, takes his hand, and rubs her thumb along his thumb. She whispers his name, but he doesn't hear her, either. Or if he does, we don't know it.

"Kim, you've got to get something to eat, get some rest," Tom says. "You're a wreck. Now that Jackson's here, why don't you go home for a little while? I've got to go home myself, check in with Mary Beth and the kids. I'll drive you."

"No," she says. "I'm not leaving."

"You'll make yourself sick."

Kim shakes her head wearily. "I just can't leave, okay? I can sleep in the waiting room again. Tonight I'll be able to sleep there."

She looks as if she could nod off right where she stands. Her eyes are puffy, her clothes rumpled, her hair's a mess. Her tiny hands with their long, shell pink fingernails look like they belong to another person, someone young and ditzy like she used to be before she moved in with Dad. "I just need to be here with Oz," she says, and sinks into the chair beside his bed.

"Well then . . . ," Mom says. For just a second I see something in her eyes that says she feels Kim's overdoing it.

Kim doesn't seem to notice, though. She stays there, holding Dad's hand, whispering his name until the nurse bustles in and reminds us that visiting's allowed only fifteen minutes every hour and only two people at a time.

Back in the waiting room, Grandma and Amy are huddled together. Kristin is reading her book. Ted is pacing. His face lights up the way it always does when he sees Mom, and he folds her into his arms. They just stand there together a long time. Grandma pats the seat beside her for me to come there. She puts her hand over mine and squeezes it hard. For once, she doesn't say anything. Amy says, "I'm sorry your dad got hurt, Jackson. I hope he gets better. I can draw him a picture, okay?"

"He'd like that," I say.

She actually gives me a hug and kiss when it's time for Ted to take them to Grandma's house. Kristin heads for the elevator without having said a word, then stops and rushes back to give me a brief fierce hug that nearly knocks me over. Mom smiles at me when they've gone. "See? I told you." She puts her arm around my shoulder, briefly touching my face with her own.

But I don't want to talk about Kristin tonight. I don't want to talk at all. I indulge myself cataloging all the crap I've had to deal with in the last few months since Brady ran away. Then I get this stupid idea that what's happened is his fault—that somehow his leaving triggered the chain of events that led to my ending up here in this hospital waiting room not knowing whether my dad will live or die. If he hadn't left—what? I close my eyes; they ache from crying. I lean back and rest my head on the plastic sofa. Mom smooths my hair back from my forehead like she used to do when I was little.

I think, Oh, if I could just go to sleep. But I can't. Last night, maybe the very moment Dad was falling, I was climbing the ladder to my loft in the condominium. There, I was as sleepless as I am now. But I never thought of him. I never once thought he could be hurt, he could be dying. I thought only of Amanda: her face in the moonlight, her long beautiful hair. Now it seems selfish to have been so absorbed—as if I'd missed some shifting of the universe, as if my paying attention could have stopped the fall. I'm fully aware that blaming myself for what happened is even more stupid than blaming Brady. Blaming anyone. I mean, things happen. But telling myself that, even believing that it's true doesn't stop the image of Dad falling from jolting me like an electric shock every time I drift off to sleep.

TWENTY-FIVE

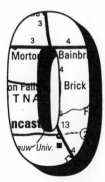nce Ted has a talk with Kristin and Amy, they settle in at Grandma's just fine. They were upset and frightened, he tells Mom. "They cried," he says. "Kristin said, 'Is Jackson's dad going to die?'

"I told her, absolutely not! Ellen, I didn't mention it before, but while you and Jackson were in the room with Oz, I talked to one of the nurses. She was very reassuring. Not that it will be easy the next few days, or that something *couldn't* go wrong. But there's no reason why it should."

Mom doesn't say anything for a long time. I'm stretched out on one of the long couches, pretending to be asleep, and I don't dare open my eyes to look at her. When she does speak I can tell she's been crying.

"Oh, God," she says, "why am I *angry?*"

I should sit up right now or at the very least do something to make them realize I'm not asleep. But I don't. I just let her go on.

"I feel like such a terrible person, sitting here thinking,

Wouldn't you just know Oz would go and do something to ruin my life again! God, as if he'd planned it."

"Ellen," Ted says. "Sweetheart, it's been such a shock. You don't know how you feel at this point."

"Oh, yes I do," Mom says. "I'm pissed out of my mind. I want to go home to our new house. Our life. All the way back on the plane I kept thinking about it. How everything was waiting—"

"It's still waiting," Ted says. "It's all there."

I hate the way I feel listening to the two of them. Bitter. I think, If Mom hadn't married Ted, she'd only want to be with me right now. She wouldn't be thinking of anything but me and what I need. And she wouldn't be angry at Dad, either. Okay, here's how out of it I really am: I think this accident might have brought them back together again. I actually let myself imagine how it would be: Dad waking to realize that Mom has been at his bedside since the moment she heard that he was hurt, that it's her voice that brought him back—

"I know, I know," Mom says to Ted. "I'm being completely ridiculous. I shouldn't even talk about this. I know I'm not really mad at Oz; how could I be mad at him? It's just so—awful, so absurd. The truth is, right now, mad is the only safe thing to be. If I weren't mad, I'd be useless. I wouldn't be able to stop crying. Ted, my heart just breaks when I think about Jackson. If Oz dies—"

"He's not going to die," Ted says. "By God, he can't die. Not after I promised Kristin he wouldn't."

Mom laughs a little, which is what I know he meant her to do, and I think, it used to be *my* job to make her laugh. But although Mom's probably right, mad is safe, I can't really work up any anger toward Ted. He's so wonderful to Mom; he so obviously adores her. Listening to them just makes me feel left out and sad. It's my own fault, I know, for eavesdropping.

"Are you still planning to take Kristin and Amy back to St. Louis tomorrow?" Mom asks.

Ted says, "Yes, unless you need me here."

"No," she says. "I can handle it. But I want you to get some rest before you go. I don't want you on the road exhausted. Oh, Ted, if anything happened to you—"

"Nothing's going to happen to me," he says.

"You're always so sure about everything," Mom says. "Sometimes that drives me crazy."

Ted sort of laughs. "I'll never be sure about you, Ellen. I don't think I'll ever quite believe you actually married me."

"God, isn't it perfect?" Mom says. "Because, just for the record, you're the one thing I feel absolutely sure about."

I expect her to go on, to add, "Well, you and Jackson." She doesn't, though. Don't be stupid, I tell myself. You know how she feels about you. She doesn't always have to say it.

I direct my thoughts to Kim, who's stretched out on the couch across from me. Is she eavesdropping, too? I don't think so. She's breathing so evenly. One hand hangs limp over the edge of the couch. She makes odd, squeaky sounds from time to time. I think she's actually asleep, that she's been asleep for a while.

When she came back from making her phone calls, she looked better. She'd combed her hair, put on some makeup. She sat down with Mom and me and told us about last night. She wasn't there when it happened, which she says she feels terrible about. Tom called from the hospital to tell her. But by the time she got there, Dad was already in surgery and there was no one around to give them even a clue about what his chances were.

"Bad," was all Tom knew. That was what the ambulance guys had kept repeating when they got to the scene. It was morning, about six-thirty, when the doctor finally appeared and they found out that Dad had pulled through, that he would probably survive.

I think Mom liked Kim better after we talked, especially when Kim said, "Maybe you'll want to go alone this time, Jackson. If you go in and sit there with him a while, you'll get used to the way he looks a little. You'll see; at least now he's not in any pain."

I did go by myself, but Kim was wrong about it making me feel better. I felt lousy. I couldn't stand to look at him. But it was even worse if I closed my eyes because what I saw then was Dad the way he's supposed to be: moving, always moving. And I could hear him laughing. I didn't stay. I went down a flight of stairs just outside the intensive care unit and walked through a maze of corridors, careful not to glance into the lighted rooms along the way. When it seemed like a suitable amount of time had passed, I went back to the waiting room.

"Yeah, I feel better," I lied. "I think I'll try to rest."

Mom and Ted fall silent. Through slitted eyes, I see that Mom's fallen asleep, her head on Ted's lap. He's sleeping sitting up, his head on the pillow he's propped behind him against the wall. I open my eyes all the way. Soundlessly, in slow motion, I sit up. It's dark in the waiting room, except for the open doorway on the far end of it, a bright rectangle of light. I don't know; maybe I've slept a while. I sure don't remember anyone turning off the lamps on the low tables or setting my backpack there within reach. My Walkman's in it, and tapes. Books and magazines. All the things I took with me on the trip.

I think of Amanda again: what she said to me last night, how it was to be with her, and I feel the way I've always felt when I come to the end of a really good story and remember it was a *story*. I wasn't in it, after all. It wasn't real.

This line of thinking makes me feel agitated, as if I'm not my real self, as if this waiting room is no more real than the beach I walked last night with Amanda. As if nothing is real. The accident can't really have happened; it can't be my dad in that room so out of it that he didn't even know I was with him. He can't die. There can't be a world that doesn't have him in it.

When I was little, at the strangest times, I used to think of people dying—Mom, Dad, Grandma, Grandpa, even myself sometimes—I'd think of all of us not *being*, and a darkness would build up inside me. I was mostly a quiet, well-behaved child, but when that feeling came upon me, I would do something wild. I'd burst out singing, or jump up and run outside, run myself silly to explode it.

"Jackson Watt, good grief, what's gotten into you?" Mom would say. But I never told her.

I don't want to tell her how I feel now. But I know if I don't get up, get out of this room, the darkness will make me do something crazy and she'll know something's terribly wrong, so I tiptoe out into the corridor.

The bright light hurts my eyes. The floors, the walls, the ceilings are dazzlingly white. The double doors at the end of the corridor are white, too. And closed, which I guess means you're not supposed to go in.

I can see my watch now, in the light. Three in the morning. I can't go see Dad. I can't go back into the waiting room. I pace up and down the corridor. I walk slowly, pausing each time at the doors to intensive care. The windows reveal nothing but another hall and the doorway to a supply room or closet. Now and then, I see a nurse pass by rolling some kind of equipment or carrying a tray of medicine, and I shrink back, so she won't see me.

I don't care how bad he looks, I need to see him. I think if I don't see him right this second, I'm going to die. I stand there, my hand on the metal door handle, my heart beating so hard, so loud it scares me. I nearly fall down when the door opens from the other side. It's Dad's nurse. She says, "Honey, if you want to see your dad, come on in. It's all right. Don't stand out there worrying."

I'm so grateful, I can't even speak. I follow her, and I'm scared witless again when we reach his room just as the ventilator alarm goes off. It sounds like a siren, like those awful Nazi sirens you hear in World War II movies. The nurse adjusts it, and it stops. He's alive.

"I'll just check these few things, give him his medication," she says, scribbling on a chart. "Then you can sit here with him a while."

As soon as she's gone, I pull the chair as close to the bed as I can get it. I prop an extra pillow between the back of the chair and the iron bed rail so I can rest my head. If I sit just right, I can see Dad's profile, and I can keep my hand over his on the edge of the bed. I doze nearly an hour that way and what wakes me is an odd sound, almost a moan. Then I feel Dad's fingers moving.

I sit straight up, so I can look full into his face. He moans again, his eyelids flutter open, and he sees me. He can't talk because the ventilator tube is crammed down his throat, but he moans again, and in the shape of the moan I recognize my name. His chest heaves, and the alarm goes off again. Dad gives me a scared look; his fingers tighten.

"It's okay," I say, praying the nurse will come, and she does.

"Don't be frightened, Mr. Watt," she says, as she works around him. "You've had an accident, but you're fine. Everything's fine. Your son's here with you."

Dad closes his eyes again; his fingers relax.

The nurse beams at me. "The minute I saw you, I had a hunch you'd be the one to bring him back," she says. "That you were just the thing he needed."

ood news," the doctor says when he makes his rounds in the morning. "Mr. Watt is conscious, though it's unlikely he'll remember anything that happens in the next few days—he's so heavily sedated. But he's as alert as I'd expect him to be under the circumstances; his vitals look good. With luck, we'll be able to begin to wean him from the ventilator within the next twenty-four hours—probably take it out about this time tomorrow. Of course, we'll keep him here in intensive care another day or so. Then another four to six weeks in a regular room, I'd say. As long as he's in traction. When we remove the pins, put casts on his legs—that's when he can go home. He'll be able to get around on crutches. But the important thing now is that he keep calm, that we watch him closely. And that you folks take care of yourselves, too." He peers at us almost sternly over his half-glasses. "It's going to be a long haul. It's going to be difficult for everyone. So try not to place unreasonable demands on yourselves these first few days."

"He's right," Ted says when the doctor's excused himself and hurried off to his next patient.

"But he's not us," I say. "Not me, anyway." I'm surprised to sound so belligerent—I didn't mean to. I didn't mean to hurt Ted's feelings, either, but I can see on his face that I have. And Mom, too. But nobody's getting me out of here, no way.

They don't argue with me. We go eat a quick breakfast in the cafeteria, then I go back to Dad's room, where the new nurse says I can stay as long as he remains stable and as long I don't get in anybody's way.

He sleeps mostly, but I like being there when he wakes. Now and then, he gets restless, pulls at the arm restraints, and I talk to him, calm him. The alarm on the ventilator goes off more often now. It's because he's hyperventilating, the nurse explains. Now that he's more aware, he's probably in some pain—plus, he has moments of anxiety and confusion. The machine has to adjust to the changes in his system that all those feelings cause.

By afternoon, it's happening more. I lean as close as I can get to Dad's face on the pillow so he can hear me over the noise, and I talk to him. It gets so that I can make the alarm stop by talking in a certain way.

I think of the right-brain exercise we did in Mrs. Blue's English class last year: she turned out the lights, made us put our heads down on our desks, close our eyes, relax—and with her voice alone she took us on an imaginary journey up a mountain path. I remember how I actually felt the night breeze against my skin so keenly that I shivered. I felt the steep rocky path beneath my feet, heard the branches of ancient trees shifting and creaking above me. As I neared the top, I saw the dancing flames of a campfire. An old man sat in front of it. He was small and wizened, dressed in a black wizard's cape that was trimmed with slices of moon. He handed me a notebook like Brady's divorce notebook, but the pages in it were blank and shining.

When it was over and we came back to the harsh light of the classroom, we were all amazed. Each of us had taken our own journey, found our own unique path, our own wise man, received his gift. We were like grade school kids, waving our hands, dying to tell our stories.

"Now you know what happens when a writer writes a story," Mrs. Blue told us. "He actually goes to that place, experiences it as something absolutely real. On another plane."

I want to take Dad on a journey now, someplace far away from this hospital, far away from pain and fear and confusion. I start with one of our weird vacations. "We're in the old Jeep," I say, "the first one you got, after the divorce. We're on a country road, looking for the Daisy BB Gun Plant and Air Gun Museum."

I actually see the factory as I speak.

"All that rickety machinery," I say. "Copper-colored BBs sliding down a chute, the ringing sound they make. The trees framed by the grimy windows. And that guide, remember him? The old man; he must've been eighty. A cigarette dangling from his mouth. 'Sixty-five million BBs manufactured here every day!' he says, the cigarette hopping. Remember, Dad? You go, 'That's a hell of a lot of BBs to stick in a lot of kids' ears,' and the guy looks at you like you're crazy."

I swear Dad smiles. He's with me. So I keep talking. "Okay, now," I say, "back in the Jeep—

"We're driving across Kansas. It's summer—July, I think— and all we see for miles is corn and sky. A farmhouse now and then, a barn, a tractor. We stop at a diner in a small town for lunch, and you flirt with the waitress. Remember? Her name is Darleen.

"I say, 'Dad, can I get two cheeseburgers?' She steps back and gives you a funny look. 'Dad?' she says. 'This is your kid? No way. You're not old enough to have a kid this age.' You shrug, like it amazes you, too. We're heading for Colorado, you tell her. To raft the river, hang out. 'Well, don't drown,' she says. 'Hey, thanks,' she says when you tip her five dollars for a five-dollar lunch. 'No kidding, thanks. You guys made my day.' "

The nurse comes in and out, smiles at me, takes Dad's temperature, adjusts his medication, empties the urine from his catheter bag. A couple of times she brings in extravagant displays of flowers. From Grandma, from the union.

I know exactly what Dad would say if he could speak: "What do they think this is, a funeral?"

Mom comes to the doorway every now and then to check in

on us. She looks sad, like she used to look waving from the driveway when Dad and I took off on one of our trips. But she couldn't come with us anymore; I understood that. And she understood, too. Dad and I still needed each other. Like now. I keep talking. Dad's with me; I know it. He watches me; his hand grasps mine. The alarm doesn't go off once.

I don't know how much time passes. We get caught in the blizzard on April Fools' Day. "Back in Colorado, Dad. On our way home from skiing. The Jeep can go through anything; that's no problem. But we have to pull off when you can't see anymore.

"It's another small town where we end up. A dumpy motel. By morning, the snow's drifted up to the fenders of cars in the parking lot. Even the interstate is closed. No way we're going anywhere. We sit in the motel coffee shop, shooting the breeze with all the other stranded travelers. By afternoon, you're squirrelly and we hike the half mile to town. Cars along the streets are buried in the snow, but there are dozens of jacked-up trucks and Broncos cruising around. The snowplows on the front of them look like armor, like knights' shields. Their tires are about as tall as we are. You'd need a ladder to climb into the cabs, they're so high up. 'That's what we need, Jax,' you say. 'In one of those babies, we could go anywhere.'

"There's a guy vacuuming the lobby of the movie theater. He's about your age. He's dressed in tight jeans and cowboy boots, an old flannel shirt. We stagger in there. He's the owner, it turns out.

" 'I'll pay you a hundred bucks if you'll show us a movie,' you say to him. 'Any movie. We're going crazy.'

"The guy laughs. 'Hell, I'd do it for free,' he says. 'But I already sent last weekend's movie back to Denver.'

"The radio's on loud, and the two of you get to talking about music, about the sixties. Pretty soon, he says, 'I'll tell you what: there is something I could show you. It's weird, though. Previews. A couple hours' worth of them I've spliced together.' He shrugs, grins. 'A six-pack, a little weed maybe. Some popcorn. You roll the film, and what the hell do you know? You think you've seen a hundred full-length movies in a row.'

"So we spend the rest of the day in the dark theater, just the

144

three of us. *The Great Escape, Breakfast at Tiffany's, Fantasia, To Sir, with Love, The Longest Yard, Old Yeller.* We get totally into it, cheering, hooting, faking sobs—

"Dad," I say. "Dad, do you remember that?" Suddenly I'm exhausted, near tears. My back is cramped from leaning over the bed. Outside, the sky is beginning to darken.

"Dad?" I say again. He blinks his eyes, tries to speak, but because of the tube in his throat, he can only moan. His hand moves on mine, tries to squeeze it. But he's too weak. He closes his eyes.

All I can think about now is when the trips stopped. It was my fault. I had to work; I had summer school; I didn't want to desert Brady. Anyhow, I thought Dad didn't really care. I'd always figured the trips were something he'd cooked up to do with me after the divorce because he thought he should. But then Christmas day, when I gave him the Elvis shirt, he said, "It's been a long time since we took one of our weird trips, Jax." He gave me that funny look, like it made him sad.

"Dad?" I say, my voice cracking. "There's a lot more places we can go, you know? Remember—on Christmas, you said we should go to Graceland. A long time ago, you promised we could go. It's really weird there, man. Really, really weird. Elvis is buried right by the swimming pool. This girl at school told me it's so tacky you can't even believe it. We can go when you get better. This summer we can go. Dad, you've got to get well. I mean it; you promised."

spend the whole night there. They've cut back on his morphine, like the doctor said they would, and as the drug wears off, Dad grows restless. Once his hand comes loose, and he reaches for the tube in his throat. When I catch it and hold it, he struggles against me until the nurse comes and fastens it down again. I can still calm him by talking, but I'm so tired I can't concentrate enough to tell any more stories. I just keep telling him where he is, what's happened. I say, "It's me, Jackson." He makes guttural sounds, trying to speak in spite of the tube, but I can't understand him. "They'll take it out in the morning," I say. "If you do everything you're supposed to do, they'll take it out in the morning. Dad, you're okay. You're going to be okay." I say these things so many times, they begin to sound like something I've memorized, like a prayer.

Finally, he sleeps. I try to doze off myself, get some rest, but I can't make the pictures in my head go away. All day, I've been trying to make Dad remember happy, funny times we spent together. Now all I see is sadness. Dad's things in cardboard boxes

146

in our yard, Dad loading them into Tom's pickup truck, climbing in himself, pulling away. Mom and I watching from the window. Those first empty weeks and months after he'd gone.

"You'll get used to it," Brady said.

That seemed worse than missing him. It still does. How could I actually get used to life without my dad?

It's after seven before night begins to drain from the window. It's a gray day outside. I can see people moving around in the slushy parking lot below. Cars creep along the street: people on their way to work, I guess. I'm mesmerized by the traffic light. Green, yellow, red. Green, yellow, red. I don't know how many times I watch it change before Mom and Kim appear in the doorway of Dad's room, sleepy and disheveled.

Dr. Marshall arrives at eight-thirty. He studies Dad's chart and consults with the nurse in a hushed tone. When they're finished talking, he turns to us and says, "I'll have to ask you folks to step out for a few moments. We can remove the tube, as I hoped. It won't take long. If you'll wait in the lounge, I'll come in and let you know as soon as it's over." The nurse pulls the curtains on the window that looks out on the hall and closes the door behind us.

When the doctor comes to tell us everything is all right, Kim bursts into tears. She covers her face with her hands and takes a few deep breaths, trying to get herself under control. "I'm sorry," she whispers. "Crying at good news—"

"It's okay," Mom says, and puts her arm around her.

When she calms down, we go back to Dad's room.

He's still in the neck brace—he will be until they're absolutely certain his head's okay—so he can't move. But the nurse cranks his bed up slightly, so he can see. He is conscious—you can see it in his eyes—but obviously still not really with it. It's as if he doesn't see me or Kim at all, as if he looks straight through us to where Mom is standing in the doorway. It almost makes me cry, the way it's just like the fantasy I had last night. He's forgotten she isn't his wife. Pure happiness is the only thing you could call the look on his face.

"Ellen," he says, croaks really. His eyes fill with tears. The next words come out excruciatingly slowly. "Aw, babe—come

147

here, come on." His hand moves in the restraint, as if to beckon her.

Kim looks as if she's seen a ghost, or maybe it is that she looks like a ghost herself. She backs away from the bed, tripping over the chair behind us, and rushes out the door.

"Jackson," Mom says. I know she means I should follow her.

Kim's leaning against the wall just outside intensive care, her eyes closed. She has to make an effort to breathe evenly, I can tell.

"Kim?" I say.

"What am I doing here, Jackson?" she says, her eyes still closed. "He doesn't even know who I am."

"Remember what the nurse told us," I say. "He's conscious, not *cognizant*. All those drugs. He doesn't have a clue about what's actually happening."

"Bullshit," she says. "I'm nothing to him. No one. Another girlfriend. How many has he had, Jackson? How many women has your dad had since the divorce? Twenty? Thirty? A hundred? It could have been anyone waiting that night, praying he wouldn't die. It just happened to be me. He'll always be in love with your mother." She's shaking now, but she still doesn't cry. She crosses her arms across her chest and hugs herself tightly. "Oh, Jackson," she says. "Oh, God, I'm so sorry. I—I've got to get out of here for a while—"

Before I can say anything to her, she's gone.

Soon Mom comes down the hallway. "Kim?" she asks.

"She left," I say.

Mom nods. She obviously doesn't want to get into why. Or to talk about Dad's mistake. She looks awful, though. I think she's been crying. "He's resting," she says. "The nurse was able to sedate him again. She said he'll sleep now. He had such a hard night. Want to go down and get something to eat? We should eat."

The cafeteria is more or less deserted. There's still breakfast stuff out, but the workers are getting organized for the lunch hour.

"Oh," Mom says. "Look, Jackson. French fries."

It's a joke with us the way we're addicted to them. Sometimes that's all we eat for supper: huge plates of french fries smothered in ketchup. I have to admit, these particular french fries look great. They're big fat ones, cut in wedges. Next to them, there's a vat of cheese sauce.

"Get some," I say.

She looks at her watch. "Ten-fifteen. God, I sound like an alcoholic trying to rationalize having that first drink. Hey, live dangerously, right? I'll have an order of those," she says to the attendant.

The man puts them on a plate and reaches for the ladle in the vat of cheese sauce beside them.

"Oh, I don't care for the cheese sauce," Mom says. "No cheese sauce, thank you."

"They come with cheese sauce." The man gestures toward another pan of french fries, the frozen crinkly kind. "If you don't want cheese fries, I'll have to serve you those."

"But I don't want those," Mom says. "I'll have an order of the cheese fries. I just don't want you to put the cheese on them. I'll be glad to pay for it, though."

He shakes his head. "No, ma'am," he says. "I can't do that."

Calmly, Mom says, "Could I speak to your supervisor, please?"

The man, clearly not too bright, shuffles off and returns with a stout, gray-haired woman.

"I'd like to have an order of those french fries," Mom says. She points to the fat, wedgy ones. "But I don't want any cheese sauce on them. Is that a problem?"

"We're not allowed to make substitutions, ma'am," the woman says.

"Substitutions?" Mom waits a moment before continuing. There are other people in line now, some looking on curiously, some looking away. Mom says, "I'm not asking you for a substitution. I'm asking you for—" She glances at me. "For a subtraction." Her tone of voice is completely reasonable. "I'd like you to subtract the cheese from the french fries, that's all. Of course, I'll pay the full price," she says.

"I'm sorry," the woman says. "It's just not allowed."

Mom stands a long moment, her knuckles whitening on her

empty tray. Then suddenly she raises the tray above her head, slams it back on the metal railing. "I *don't* believe this," she says, her voice still level, but loud. She turns and bolts for the hallway.

"You can have them! Ma'am, you can have the ones you want!" the cafeteria lady calls after her. She looks almost frightened, like she's going to get in trouble for what Mom did. I feel like telling her and everyone in line that I've never in my whole life seen my mother behave the way she did just now. Like that would really negate the effect.

"Is she all right?" the man next to me asks. "Are you with her?"

"Yeah," I say, and feel myself turning red. The only thing I can think to do is walk away.

"Oh, Jackson," Mom sobs when I find her. "I'm so sorry. I made such a fool of myself. We'll never be able to eat in there again. We'll starve to death. Days from now, they'll find us dead in a hallway."

"Don't worry, Mom," I say. "We'll get some of those glasses with noses on them. You know, like Woody Allen wore in that movie when he robbed the bank. No one will recognize us."

She laughs, then, as I hoped she would, and for a moment it's like it used to be before Ted—just me and Mom together. She hugs me hard. Still holding on to me, she says, "What would I do without you?"

She'd survive; Ted would help her. The thought is like a lead weight dropping inside me. I try to cover up how I feel by being a smart-ass. "Hey, with me out of the picture, you could exit from Dad's life completely, exit this place," I say. "It could turn out to be a good deal for you." My voice doesn't come out quite right, though.

My mom's body sort of loosens, as if all the air's gone out of her. She puts her hands lightly on my shoulders, pushes me just far enough so she can see my face. I turn away. I don't want to see the tears gathering in her eyes again. But she very gently turns me back to her.

"Jackson, I know you don't really think there's any way in the world I could be better off without you. Do you?"

I shake my head.

"And your dad?" She half smiles. "Maybe I *would* be better off without him in my life. God knows, he drives me crazy. But, honey, it's too late for that. We've been through too much together, Oz and I. I'd probably be here, no matter what. I need to help him get through this; we both do."

"I know," I say.

She sighs. "Honey, I think I need to go home for a little while," she says. "Get cleaned up. I don't know, just touch base with real life. I think we both need to."

"Okay," I say. It's a relief to allow myself to be someone's kid again, to do something just because my mom says I should.

TWENTY-EIGHT

t's still gray out, and I'm glad because, having been in the hospital so long, even this dull gray world seems alarmingly vivid to me. Have there always been so many shopping centers? So many billboards and signs? Cars seem to pass way too close. Our cabby, an older man, chats in a friendly way. He was in the hospital himself not long ago, he tells us. A triple bypass. It was no picnic.

"But those docs are amazing," he says. "Body mechanics. I'll tell you what—they made a new man of me. Hope your husband pulls through," he says to Mom when she pays him. Neither of us attempts to set him straight. We just stand on the sidewalk and watch him drive away.

I feel strange here, in front of the new house. "I still can't believe we live here," Mom says, seeming to read my mind.

For a moment, I want more than anything to be returning to our cozy old house, just the two of us. I want to stand at the window in my old room and see something utterly familiar. But all that is behind me. I follow Mom up the brick walk, into the

152

foyer. There's mail scattered all over the slate floor. Mom picks it up, sorts through it. She hands me a postcard.

It's a picture of the state capitol building of Iowa. The cars parked on the street in front of it look twenty years old. I turn it over.

Jax—
Bulletin from the real world. Blew some weed in Strawberry Field, met up with some Deadheads there. We've been everywhere, it's a blast. Tell Oz the Dead live. There's nothing like the road, man. But I miss you.
Kick ass—
Brady

Relief floods through me. He's okay. Then, almost instantaneously, I think, Do I need this? What's with Brady, anyway—sending me a postcard from *Dubuque, Iowa*, with no return address? He misses me? Ha. Bulletin from the real world? Give me a break. I pace around in my room, but in the end I'm too tired to work up a real, cleansing rage. The truth is, Brady couldn't help me now—even if I *could* find him. I'd tell him about Dad and he'd say, "Jax, you ought to jet, like I did. Leave all this sorry shit behind you." I'd tell him about Amanda and he'd say, "Man, you blew it. All that time you could have been screwing your brains out." That's when I get pissed. It's as if he actually did say those things to me, and I start pacing again, smacking my fist against my hand. "You asshole," I say. "You complete and total asshole. You don't know jack shit about anything."

I need music. I grab U2, *Rattle and Hum*. Listening to it always makes me feel like I'm hitting someone. But when I go to stick the tape in the tape deck, I see my new CD player, and I'm not angry anymore—just sad and scared, the way I have been since the second I found out about Dad. I think of him here in my room with me on Christmas day, whistling, circling the project, determined to get everything hooked up just right.

It might have turned out to be the last time we were ever together.

Don't think that, I tell myself. I turn U2 up loud.

I stand in the shower a long time, letting the hot water wash over me. Last time I took a shower, I was in Jamaica, another world. Something else to avoid considering.

Next thing I know, I'm in bed. Mom's calling, "Jackson, Jackson," gently shaking my shoulder.

My mouth is sour, my body awkward, swollen with fatigue. It's not until Mom says, "Honey, I knew you'd want to go back to the hospital this evening," that I fully awaken. I sit straight up in a panic.

"What time is it?" I say. "Jesus, Mom, it's dark outside. Why'd you let me sleep so long?"

"You needed it, Jackson. I've called the hospital every hour or so, and the nurses say your dad's doing fine. He's resting."

"So what if he's resting? That doesn't mean I shouldn't be there. How would you like it if you were practically dead and everyone deserted *you?*"

She's smart enough to walk away from me. By the time I get my clothes on and go downstairs, I've calmed down.

"Sorry," I mutter.

"I know," she says. "It's all right. I defrosted some chili, one of the leftover pies. If you're hungry . . ."

Mom sits across from me, watching while I eat two bowls of chili, a whole package of crackers, and a huge piece of pumpkin pie, as if pigging out were some form of entertainment.

"Honey, we need to talk about some things," she says.

"Like what?"

"You," she says. "Now that it looks like your dad's going to be all right—"

"He's not all right now," I say. "He needs me."

"He's *going* to be all right. And, yes, it's true he needs you. But, Jackson, you can't be at the hospital all day, every day. It's not healthy. Plus, eventually you've got to go back to school. The more behind you get, the worse it's going to be to catch up. You know that."

"I'm not going back until he gets out of intensive care," I say. "Until he at least knows what's going on, I'm staying there with him."

"A few more days," Mom says. "Then we'll decide."

"You wish I'd just forget about him, don't you?" I say.

She ignores me, clears the dishes.

"Maybe you wish he'd died. Hey, it would solve a lot of problems. We could all live happily ever after in the dream house. We could just pretend Ted's my father. We could pretend Dad never even was."

To my astonishment, she marches over and slaps me. Hard. My face burns in the shape of her hand. "Don't you ever talk to me like that again, Jackson Watt," she says. "Ever. Ever. Ever. Do you hear me?"

"Yeah," I say, but I don't apologize, even though I know that what I just said is the worst thing I've ever said to anyone. I guess the slap makes me feel we're even. Or maybe I'm just afraid to speak. I'm like some warped clone of myself. If I tried to apologize, how do I know what I'd say?

We drive separately to the hospital, and once there we stay clear of each other. Tom and Mary Beth arrive. Oh, it's been such a long time, Mom and Mary Beth say. They talk about how they always meant to keep in touch after the divorce but somehow didn't do it. Ted comes, having driven Kristin and Amy back to St. Louis. Mary Beth smiles and says, "Oz told me you'd finally met the right guy, Ellen. It freaked him out, though. Even after all this time. I think he was just beginning to get used to it—

"Is. Is," she corrects herself. "Oz is going to be fine."

Tom joins in and they talk about old times, laughing, telling Ted this story or that about things the four of them did together when they were young. Ted goes for pizza, and they wolf it down. It's weird, like a party, except when one of them remembers why we're here. You can see it on their faces. Then it gets quiet for a while.

"I can't believe it," Mom says. "Two days ago I was lying on the beach in Jamaica."

She and Ted and Mary Beth settle into a Scrabble game. Tom watches IU basketball on TV. I pretend I'm reading. Every hour, I go see Dad. Alone, or Tom goes with me. I figure Mom's afraid to go after what Dad said to her this morning. Kim never shows up at all. No one mentions her.

Dad's oblivious, sleeping. The nurse says that's good. Being knocked out on drugs all those hours didn't count as real sleep, so his body needs to catch up.

Now that I'm not so scared, I can look at him more closely. His left arm is bent, immobilized in a cast that covers his hand and goes all the way up to his shoulder. Both legs are suspended, held in place by ropes and pulleys attached to the metal pins that protrude from just above his knees. There's a long vertical incision on his upper abdomen, red at the edges, held together by metal staples. Just below it, a catheter tube emerges, the yellow urine bubbling down through it into the bag hooked on the side of the bed. The IV needle is pushed into a thick blue vein on the inside of his right wrist. There are cuts and bruises all over his body. It makes me feel sick when I think of his skin bursting from the impact of the fall.

The terrible swelling in his face has gone down; that's one good thing. But without its usual animation, it is still not quite truly his face. What I notice are the wrinkles around his eyes, the creases deepening in his cheeks. The white in his curly black hair. Somehow, the fact that Dad came so close to dying makes it seem like just a matter of time before he does. I don't mean that I think he's going to die now, from the fall. Just that for the first time in my life I truly understand that someday I will actually be without him. It might be ten, twenty, even thirty years before it happens— I could be older than he is now. But that doesn't matter. Since the moment Grandma said, "Jackson, your father—," time has made no sense to me. I don't know if it ever will again.

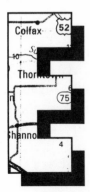

ach day he gets a little better, a little more like himself. I know he's really going to be all right when I walk into his room in the middle of the night and find him playing poker with one of the nurses, betting with Q-tips. The next day they move him into a regular room. He says, "Okay, pal, here's what I want you to do. Go over to my house and get me one of those little barbells, one of the five-pound ones I run with sometimes."

"Barbell?"

"Yeah, barbell." He raises his one good arm and waves it around. "Gotta start somewhere getting back in shape; might as well start now. So bring me the damn barbell, okay? And Christ, bring me some real clothes, too. These hospital gowns are driving me crazy."

I'm such a chickenshit, I call The Peak and ask what hours Kim will be working to make sure I won't run into her at Dad's. I haven't seen or heard from her since the day they took the tube out, but I've driven past Dad's house a couple of times and seen her car in the driveway. So I assume she's still living there, at least for the time being. Once inside, it doesn't take much time to figure out I'm right. Her workout clothes are draped all over the place in the bathroom, drying. I open the refrigerator and there's tofu and health drinks. Her sprouts are still growing on the windowsill. Her bicycle is in the bedroom. The bed's unmade, magazines scattered on Dad's side.

I never have liked Dad's house that much, maybe because it's always seemed kind of like a stopping place to me, not a real home. When Dad left, he gave Mom everything. He wanted to. Now he has one nice leather chair, but other than that chair, a great stereo system, and one of those huge TVs, he's perfectly happy with mismatched, secondhand stuff. From time to time, various girl-friends have moved in and tried to fix things up, but none of them has really made a mark. They leave and take their knickknacks and framed art posters with them.

He did make a special place for me in the extra bedroom, though. Together we painted the walls white. We bought *Star Wars* posters and curtains and a *Star Wars* bedspread. He bought me my own little TV, complete with Atari. It still works. Little spaceships float across the screen, and I zap them with the joystick. I bet if I dusted for fingerprints on it, I'd find Brady's. We must've passed a hundred Saturdays in this room, playing Space Invaders or Pac-Man or Donkey Kong, drinking Cokes, eating junk food, grooving to the Moody Blues or the Stones turned up full blast on Dad's stereo. Brady was in heaven.

It seems so quiet now with both of them gone. I grab a pile of T-shirts from Dad's drawer. Socks, sweats, running shorts. I find the barbells back in the closet, underneath a pile of Kim's dirty clothes. When I get back to the hospital, Mom's there. She's sitting in a chair in Dad's room, working on a piece of needlepoint. Dad's leafing through *Rolling Stone*. Standing in the doorway, the instant before they see me, I get that same weird feeling again, like I'm seeing something from another time. In fact, I keep having that feeling on and off all day and the next. We sit around, talking, reading, playing cards. Tom and Mary Beth come by. If I close my eyes, I can almost believe we're at the lake cottage we shared a couple of summers, making the best of a rainy afternoon. I can believe that the divorce never happened, that Ted doesn't exist. That when Dad gets better, he and Mom and I will all go back to the old house together.

It's not until I go back to school Monday morning that I begin to feel half normal. The bells, the round white-faced clocks with their black numerals make time familiar again. The ugly puke-green walls, the battered lockers, the foul graffiti in the rest rooms are a comfort after an entire week of antiseptic white.

The day is a grind, repeating the story of Dad's accident a dozen times, trying to figure out all I've missed being absent for a week, getting clear on all I have to do to make it up. It's a relief when Mrs. Blue turns out the lights to show slides in Western Civ. We look at Leonardo da Vinci's drawings with writing you have to hold up to a mirror to read, the *Last Supper*, the Mona Lisa. Then just a detail of the ceiling he painted in some castle. Trees. That's what you see at first glance. Then you notice that there are some knots of golden rope among the branches.

"But look again," Mrs. Blue says. "Look closely." With her pointer she traces the rope twisting and turning, unbroken throughout the whole design. Soon it's all I see. For a second, I get the idea that it's holding the whole world together. That something beautiful enough *could*.

Like Amanda. I get this twisting feeling inside just at the thought of her. I want to write to her; I even tried a couple of times at the hospital when I was alone. But I couldn't write the funny letter I'd worked out in my mind, and I didn't know how to begin writing about Dad's accident. If I could just see her— talking to her, it would be easier to explain. I try to imagine us sitting on the beach in Jamaica, but I can't. Jamaica seems as distant to me as my own childhood. The time with Amanda as unreal as those times before Dad went away.

"Jackson?" Mrs. Blue's voice.

The bell's rung. I didn't even hear it.

"Good grief, you're exhausted, aren't you? Your dad *is* okay, isn't he?"

"He's going to be," I say. "Those first few days, though—" I tell her how scary it was. How I used the right-brain exercise to take Dad back in time to calm him.

159

"That is really interesting," she says, and smiles at me. "Of course, probably not as interesting as the fact that school actually turned out to be useful. Or should I say 'amazing'?"

We both laugh.

"God," she says. "You don't think it's a trend!"

"Doubtful," I say. "But there was something else I thought about while I was hanging around the hospital." I tell her about being with Mom and Dad, just the three of us, the weird feeling it gave me. "Remember last year, when you told us about all the different endings of that Hemingway book?"

"Yes," she says. "*A Farewell to Arms*. Thirty-seven of them."

"That's what I was thinking about. Those couple of days with my parents were like another life. Like maybe we were trying out another version of how things could have turned out. Anyhow, it made me think about the endings and how you said writing is like real life. You just keep trying and failing till you get it right—"

"But it's not, is it?" Mrs. Blue says. "Not really."

"Nope," I say. "No rewrites."

She looks sad for one split second, then she laughs and says, "Good for you, Jackson; good thinking." I knew she would. That's why I like her: she doesn't freak out just because you say something that's true.

THIRTY

tephanie's waiting for me in the parking lot at the end of the day. She gives me a big hug and tells me she'd never have cut today if she'd known I was coming back. "I've missed you, Jax," she says. "I've been thinking about you all the time, ever since I found out about your dad. I've been imaging him better—

"You know," she goes on as if it isn't ten degrees outside and we both aren't freezing our butts off, "like you make yourself *see* the person in good health. Jogging or walking on a beach, whatever. You can image for yourself, too. Whatever you want, you just see it. You make it happen."

Waving her arms, her bracelets jangling, she goes into a long, drawn-out description of a workshop she went to at the New Age bookstore. She says she met some people there who had imaged themselves into truly happy lives.

"So anyhow, ever since I heard about your dad, I've been imaging him at a Grateful Dead concert, you know? I mean, Brady used to go on about how your dad was into the Dead, and I always thought that was so cool. Being as old as he is and being, you know, not uptight.

"You haven't heard from him, have you, Jax? Brady?"

"No," I lie.

She sighs. "I didn't think so. I bet he'd feel awful about your dad if he knew. We should go to that psychic. Remember? The one I told you about at the party? Maybe he could send Brady a message—"

"I don't have time to go to a psychic," I say. "I don't have time for anything."

Her eyes fill up with tears. "Oh, God, Jax, what can I do to help you? Like, I could run errands for you or clean your room. Really, I'll do anything. Ha, I'd give you all my notes—if only I'd been going to class. But, no kidding, I have been so fried since Christmas. I just can't stand school. It kills me, you know? I could get Kate's and copy hers for you, though. Or I could get you guys food. Like bring it up to the hospital. I could keep you company up there. It must be a drag."

"No, no," I say. "I mean, Dad's still in pretty bad shape. It takes all his energy just to do the physical therapy stuff he has to do. Too many visitors tire him out."

"So, what if I meet you after? We could do something. You really ought to do something besides go to the hospital, you know. You ought to have some fun."

I start laughing; I can't help it. I mean, is this a gender thing? Is this the line of every single female person in the world? What really cracks me up is the thought that Amanda might say the very same thing. Wouldn't that be bizarre? I work her up in my mind as being the perfect woman, a genius, and she ends up saying exactly the same thing as my mother and *Stephanie Carr?*

Steph looks hurt. All I ever do is hurt her feelings, it seems. "Listen, don't mind me," I say. "I'm crazy."

"You *should* get a life," she says.

"I know. I am. I promised Dad I'd go to the gym before I go back to the hospital tonight. In fact, I've got to do it now if I'm going to do it. But really, thanks."

She shrugs, turns away. Later, I'll deal with the way we left things between us at Christmas. I'll just tell her I met someone.

It happens. Then I am going to write to Amanda, maybe even call her and tell her what happened to Dad, tell her exactly how I feel.

I am going to get a life. My own. I actually believe this until I walk into The Peak and see Kim. She's sitting at one of the round tables in the lounge area with a prospective member. She's dressed in one of her usual ditzy outfits—turquoise today—poring over the club contract. When she glances up and sees me, she looks as uncomfortable as I feel. As I walk past her, I raise my hand in greeting. She catches it. "Don't leave without talking to me, okay?" she says, then lets it go.

It's been almost three weeks since I've worked out, and I can tell. My whole body aches with the effort it takes to lift the weight. Sweat pours off me. But it feels good. When I'm finished I feel light and strong at the same time, like taut wire. Until I see that Kim's waiting for me at the door, buttoning her heavy coat over her leotard.

"Can we go get a Coke or something?" she asks. "Take a ride?"

"I have to—"

"I know," she says. "Get to the hospital. I won't keep you long. I just don't want to talk here."

I open the door for her, follow her out.

"Has he asked about me?" she says once we've settled into the booth at Hardee's. "Tell me the truth, Jackson."

"No," I say.

"Did he tell you we had a big fight the night of the accident? Just before he left?"

"No."

"Well, we did. It was me, nagging. It doesn't matter over what. Just the usual: me wanting him to be what I wanted." She blinks back tears. "When Tom called, I thought, Oh my God, he was upset. He wasn't—"

"The truss slipped," I say.

"I know, I know. But if he hadn't been distracted, he might've felt it sooner. He might've caught himself."

"Kim," I say, "you ought to know Dad well enough by now to know that whatever happened between the two of

163

you that evening was probably the last thing on his mind."

She smiles for the first time. "Maybe," she says. "Yeah. It's part of what I'm hung up about, you know? I want a guy to think about me all the time. I used to believe Oz could do that if he wanted to."

"Forget it," I say. "When Dad's working, he's in another world."

"His own. No girls allowed. Well, I've been thinking," she says. "That day I walked away from the hospital, I thought I'd never go back. I thought I never wanted to see Oz again. I went back to the house. I was going to take all my things and just go somewhere, anywhere. But I was just too tired; I couldn't face it that night. I said to myself, tomorrow I'm getting out of here. Then when tomorrow came, I said 'tomorrow' again. Now a week's passed, and what I know is I can't leave. Whether I like it or not, Jackson—whether anybody likes it—I love Oz, and I guess I'm going to have to figure out how I can live with him. Why would I want him to change, anyway? It was him I fell in love with, not some idea of what I thought he ought to be.

"Jackson, what do you think?"

What I think is that there's a place in the world for a new kind of Ann Landers, highly specialized—a kid who knows the ins and outs of parents in love. You'd think up some yuppie pen name—Tucker, say. Or maybe something biblical, reassuring. You'd get a word processor, save certain all-purpose paragraphs on disks, handy and available for when the parents and their various significant others wrote in and asked you the same dumb questions again and again.

"I think you should go see him," I tell Kim.

"You're right, Jackson," she says. "I knew I could count on you."

Exactly what my mom's always saying to me. And Dad. And Ted. You guys are in deep shit, I think—all of you, if it's me you're counting on. But Kim's smiling again, really smiling this time, and I don't have the heart to remind her that I'm seventeen, I'm still in *high school*, which in a normal world would allow me to be the one counting on everybody else.

THIRTY-ONE

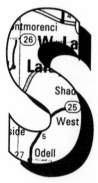 aturday is like a gift. On school days, I've been getting up at five to work out. I go through my routine with the weights half asleep, shower, dress, grab breakfast at the Hardee's drive-through on my way to school. There, I march in lockstep through my classes, taking advantage of every spare moment to keep up with my homework. I go home and eat whatever Mom's left in the refrigerator for me before I leave for the hospital to see Dad.

Today I sleep till ten. Mom fixes me waffles and bacon for breakfast, then sits across from me at the table, drinking her coffee while I eat. The little TV from our old house is on the kitchen counter, tuned to our cartoons.

"I noticed you had a postcard from Brady yesterday," she says, trying to be casual, and I curse myself for not getting home in time to get to the mail first. At least she doesn't say "another postcard," which tells me that she probably doesn't realize this is the second time I've heard from him. She was the one who handed the first postcard to me, but we were both so distracted and upset that day, I guess she didn't notice who it was from.

"I didn't read it," she assures me. "I saw it was from somewhere out West, though. The picture on front. The Indian. Is he all right?" she asks. "Brady?"

"Beats me," I say. "He's alive. It's his lousy handwriting on the postcard, that's for sure. No one else writes that bad. And he's his usual obnoxious self. He says he met some old couple in a McDonald's and told them he was a graduate student researching Native Americans. Convinced them the McDonald's sat on an ancient tribal crossroads, whatever that means. Of course, he was always reading about Indians, talking about how they'd been screwed over, you know. So he was probably pretty believable."

Mom smiles. "Layla must be relieved," she says. "I know she's been sick with worry."

Of course she assumes I told Layla about the postcard. Any decent person would have. But I didn't tell her, and I don't plan to. Maybe she's heard from him herself; maybe she hasn't. But I can't afford to get sucked into Brady Burton's drama right now. I'm putting him on hold.

"Any more waffles?" I ask, knowing Mom will forget about Layla and go get them for me. When she returns, I tell her that Dad and Kim have made up. She plans to stay at his house and take care of him when he's released from the hospital.

"He *will* need someone to help him," Mom says. "But, Jackson, do you really think that things will work out between them? You know, honey, you were right about Kim. Flaky as she is, there's something solid about her, something just—I don't know—nice. I've gotten to like her."

"And you know he's probably going to dump her in the end," I say.

Mom presses her lips together.

"It's okay," I say. "I'm no idiot. I see how he operates. All I know is this is what they're doing now."

Mom sighs. "Well, it's not my business, in any case," she says. "Except in how it affects you."

On the television, a bunch of cute little kids sing about their favorite cereal. Animated characters burst from the bowls. As casually as I can, I say, "I'm going to move over to Dad's for a while when he gets out. Help Kim take care of him."

Mom looks stricken.

"Jackson—"

"For a while, Mom. Kim can arrange her schedule to be there all day, but she works evenings. At least at first, he won't be able to get around very well on his own. He needs me."

"But move? Honey, can't you just spend the evenings there with him? I hate for you to move over there, really move. Oh, I don't know. I'm being selfish, maybe. But everything's changed so drastically these past few months—I can't seem to get the hang of my own life. If you move out—"

"What?" I say.

"I suppose I think you'll never come back. I know that's paranoid." She puts her head in her hands and starts to cry. She doesn't make a sound, but her tears seem unending. They drip through her fingers onto the woven place mat, which soaks them up.

"Mom," I say.

She waves one hand as if to say "Don't talk." So I just sit there and watch the butter congeal on the waffle I was once hungry for. I dot my index finger along the sticky line where syrup dripped on the table.

When the phone rings, I answer it. Grandma. She launches into some song and dance about how I have to keep my strength up: what have I been eating, what time have I been getting to bed at night, why in the world do I have to get up at that ungodly hour and go lift weights? She can't imagine anyone lifting weights under the best of circumstances—there are a million ways to hurt yourself. But to do it at six o'clock in the morning . . .

"I like working out. And, hey, you're the one who's always telling me I'm too skinny, I should fill out."

"You should *eat* is what I said. That's how you fill out."

"I am eating. Waffles, bacon, orange juice. I'd be eating right this second if I hadn't had to answer the phone."

"Very funny, Jackson," she says. "You know what I mean. Now tell me about your father."

"He's getting better," I say. I give her the lowdown on how

he's started exercising his right arm using the barbell I brought him. He's already starting to get some strength back.

"Well," Grandma says. "Overdoing it. Wouldn't you know?" And I feel, suddenly, supremely happy. He must really be better, I think. He must be every bit as okay as I keep telling everyone he is if Grandma's back to hating his guts.

"What are you grinning at, Jackson?" Mom says when I hang up.

"The usual," I say, and excuse myself to go up to my room.

I am determined to write a letter to Amanda—right after I read the one I got from her. When I got home from school Wednesday and saw it on the floor in the foyer with the other mail that had been pushed in through the chute, my whole body felt like my crazy bone does when it's hit hard. I carried the letter up to my bedroom, closed the door, and locked it, even though I was the only one in the house. For a long time, I just sat at my desk holding the letter in both hands, staring out at the tops of the trees. "Face it, chickenshit," I said out loud. "You're afraid to open it."

"Okay," I answered myself. "I am. So what?" I put the letter in the top drawer of my desk, the one that has a lock. I told myself, "Saturday you can open it. When you have time to think."

Now I take Amanda's letter from the desk drawer, go into the bathroom, and lock myself inside. I turn the shower on so that if Mom comes up, she'll figure I'm in there. I rip open the envelope immediately. If I wait, I'm likely to chicken out again. Inside there is a photograph of me and Kristin and Amy and one piece of pink paper, covered on both sides with pretty, straight-up-and-down handwriting.

Dear Jackson,

Hi. I thought I might have heard from you by now, but I know how hectic things get when you come home from a vacation and try to get organized. We stayed on in Ocho Rios another week, but it wasn't any fun without you and Kristin and Amy. Mother and Daddy decided to teach me how to play bridge, but it was boring, boring. I knew it wasn't the game for me when I realized that the only time I liked it was when it was my turn to be the dummy and I didn't have to pay attention. They gave up eventually. The rest of the time I sat in the sun, reading.

I was at home just a day before flying back to school. The minute I got here, I realized I should have been a bit more conscientious during break. Finals are looming, and I'm not ready. In fact, I should be studying right now, but I've been thinking about you and I wanted to write and tell you again how much I liked being with you. I meant what I said that night on the beach—that I felt different with you. Like I could be my real self. I know we won't be able to see each other very often, but I'd like for us to keep in touch. I hope you'll write back. That is, if you want to, if you have the time. Now I really do have to study.

Give my love to your little sisters. I thought you might like to have this picture of the three of you. See, I told you Kristin adores you. All you have to do is look at her face.

Love,
Amanda

I read the letter through three times, hearing her voice. I stare at the photograph she sent, seeing her just outside the frame. Her hair keeps blowing in front of the lens, and she has to use one hand to hold it back. She holds the camera in her other hand, a little crooked—which is probably why, in the photo, Kristin and Amy and I seem to be standing at a slant. "Smile," she says. We were all smiling that day.

I close my eyes and try to bring it all back, but I can't. That's when I finally get into the shower, mainly to calm myself. But it doesn't calm me. I remember that night on the beach: the feel of Amanda pressing against me, the feel of my fingers moving along her. God, whacked out like I am, I can't handle this.

Just take your goddamn shower, I tell myself. Don't start this shit now.

I turn the faucet until the needles of hot water burn my skin, and scrub myself all over hard with the loofah mitt. I step out into the steamy room, look at myself in the mirror, but I'm blurred at the edges, just the way I feel. I towel down, throw on my ratty terry-cloth robe. I go directly to my desk, sit down, and take out a piece of paper.

"Dear Amanda," I begin.

First I need to tell her about what happened to Dad so she'll know why I haven't written. It would be easy enough to write down the basics, I suppose: that night when I was on the beach with you, my Dad fell—he nearly died. But the basics say nothing about how I feel, and I want to tell her how I feel because I have the idea that, if I can say it just right, she'll understand what it means and write back and explain it to me. If I don't tell her about Dad, if I write as if everything is just the same as it was the day we parted, it would be like writing a lie.

"Jackson?" Mom yells up the staircase.

Startled, I glance down and realize I've covered the page I meant to write to Amanda with ridiculous doodles. Her name over and over. My name. Her name and my name together, just like junior high. I see, also, that well over an hour has passed. My time for thinking is gone, and I haven't even started the letter.

"Honey, are you awake?" I hear Mom's foot on the first stair.

"Yeah, yeah." I stick my head out the door to prove it, to keep her at bay.

"Didn't you tell your Dad you'd be there around noon? Can I do anything to help you get ready?"

"No!"

She looks at me oddly.

"I mean, I'm ready. I'll be right down, okay?"

Thank God she steps down, turns, and leaves, closing the door behind her. I yank on my jeans and a sweatshirt. I stuff Amanda's letter and the photograph back into the top drawer, lock it. I tear the page I've doodled on into tiny pieces, making sure that there's nothing on any one piece that could possibly be deciphered. They float into the trash can like confetti.

THIRTY-TWO

Dad has become pals with his roommate, an old farmer from Knightstown. Today the two of them have decided to order every single thing on the lunch menu just to see what would happen. When I get there, their narrow bed tables are covered with plates of food: club sandwiches, beef manhattans, Waldorf salad, Jell-O with pineapple, chocolate cake. There are plates of food on the chairs, the nightstands, the windowsill. The food servers had to roll in an extra table for the beverages alone: soft drinks, juices, coffee, and tea—hot and iced.

"Hungry, son?" Mr. Belcher asks me. Both of them crack up.

Nurses from all over the ward stop by, laughing. They nibble on french fries; occasionally one of them will sit down long enough to polish off a bowl of pudding or a piece of cake.

Mrs. Belcher looks mortified. "I don't know what made Daddy do such a thing," she says to her daughter.

"Because he could," Mr. Belcher says grandly, winking at Dad.

But the way Mrs. Belcher frowns at Mr. Belcher's act of liberation is nothing compared to the look she gives Layla when she comes waltzing in the door carrying a bunch of balloons and a *Playboy*. Layla looks great. She's wearing jeans and a big purple sweater. Her hair is wilder than usual. She's thinner than she was when I saw her the day after Thanksgiving.

"Jackson Watt," she says. "Why didn't you call me?"

I think, Shit, she knows about the postcards, and frantically I try to come up with an excuse.

But then she throws her arms around me and says, "I came as soon as I found out. Jesus Christ, what in the world are we going to do with him in this state?" She turns and grins at Dad, who grins back. "I knew you'd hate flowers," she says. She tosses him the magazine and ties the balloons on the bed rail. "And in case the balloons were a bad idea, too, I brought these." She digs in her purse and pulls out a package of darts.

She grabs me again, takes my chin in her hand. "How are you, honey?"

"Let go of me or I'll tell you the truth," I say. My voice sounds weird with my jaw immobilized.

"Okay, okay." Layla laughs, smacking me lightly on the arm. "I see you're fine."

"He's great," Dad says. "Hell, I don't know what I'd do without him."

Layla proceeds to entertain both of us, telling us about her new boyfriend, Mike, who's a biker. A real sixties kind of guy. Just last week, she went over to his house to watch *Woodstock* on his VCR. He'd spread a blanket on the floor. He had a cooler full of beer and enough pot to stoke a whole party.

"I probably shouldn't tell you this," she says, lowering her voice so the Belchers won't hear. "But Mike said we had to watch it naked, you know, to get the whole effect."

"Jesus, Layla," Dad says.

"I know, I know, grow up, right?" Layla shrugs, picks up a

piece of chocolate cake, and takes a big bite of it. "But what for? I mean, I tried that. Where did it get me?"

"Highly overrated," Dad says. "Adulthood. You're right about that."

About then, Stephanie appears. She could be Layla twenty years ago, the ghost of Woodstock past. She's dressed head-to-toe in rainbow tie-dye: tight leggings, a gargantuan shirt that comes almost to her knees. Even her socks are tie-dyed. Her long hair is caught up with pink shoelaces the same color as her Chuck Taylors. Her earrings are peace symbols, each one a different size. Even Dad seems stunned at the sight of her.

"I called your house, Jax," she announces. "Your mom said you were here."

"Stephanie!" Layla says. "Well, I'll be. Here's another person I haven't seen in a while. How are you, honey?"

"Okay," Steph says, "I guess. I miss Brady, though. . . ."

Please, I think. Not the psychic, not the dreams.

"You haven't heard from him, have you, Mrs. Burton?"

Layla shakes her head no.

I keep quiet, but I get hot suddenly, and my heart starts pounding. "Say it," I tell myself. Say you got the postcards. I know I should. But if I say it, I won't stop. I'll say, "Screw Brady. That asshole, sending me postcards from nowhere. What's that supposed to mean?" If I say it, Layla will think I'm more important to him than she is, and she'll feel worse than she already does. I let myself believe it's better not to upset her.

Dad says, "Yo, Jackson, aren't you going to introduce me to your friend?"

"Oh, this is Stephanie," I mumble, and she gushes, "It is *so* groovy to meet you, Mr. Watt. God, on the subject of Brady— he used to talk about you all the time. Really. He thought you were, well—you know—" She pauses, groping for exactly the right phrase and, as usual, comes up with, "really far out. He'd be so bummed if he knew you got hurt. I'm really, really glad you didn't, like, die."

Layla laughs. "Me, too," she says.

"Hey, thanks," Dad says, having recovered his cool. He grins at her. "I'm damned happy about that myself."

173

Stephanie beams back at him. Then she notices all the food. "Party?" she asks.

"You got it," Dad says. "Help yourself."

She works her way through five salads, all the while babbling about the politics of vegetarianism. When she finds out Mr. Belcher is a farmer, she says, "Wow, I bet it's a real trip—like, really, really spiritual—communing with the land."

"It's a lot of hard work," Mrs. Belcher says.

Stephanie regards her curiously. On the television screen, IU goes on a fast break and gets a layup, which seems to remind her why she's here. "Jax, there's a home game tonight, you know? Want to come with me?"

When I don't answer instantly, she turns to Dad and Layla. "He should come, don't you think? I mean, don't you think it would be good for Jax to go out?"

"Absolutely," Layla says.

Dad raises his broken arm, gestures toward his legs in the sling. "I'd go out myself if I weren't—"

"A cripple?" Mr. Belcher guffaws.

No way I'm going to get out of going. I see that. When Steph says, "Well? Do you, Jackson?" I say yes.

She takes off then, after presenting Dad with one of her most cherished crystals, a hunk of pinkish rock. Not long after, I walk Layla to the elevator.

"You, mister," she says. "You call me if there's anything you need."

When I get back, Dad's pulled the yellow privacy curtain and cranked the bed to a different position. His eyes are closed; the *Playboy* Layla brought is open, facedown, on his chest. I can see that his jaw is clenched. This is the kind of thing that kills me, suddenly seeing his pain. I see it in his eyes sometimes, in the way he winces when he tries to move the few movable parts of his body or when a nurse touches him the wrong way. He doesn't complain. But once, when he thought I was dozing, he made his free hand into a fist and held it for a long time against the bridge of his nose.

Now he opens his eyes, smiles weakly at the sight of me.

"Those two are a trip, aren't they? Christ, they wore me out. Hey, why don't you take off, too, pal? I'm about to rack out here. Gotta rest up for when Kim gets here later. No need for you to hang around."

He holds out his hand, palm up. I slap it the way he taught me to do before I could even talk.

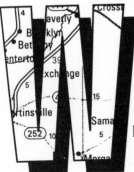hen we walk into the gym, Stephanie grabs my hand and pulls me over to the section of the bleachers where our friends are sitting. "Look who I kidnapped," she says.

"Hoo, buddy," Tom Best says, wiggling his eyebrows at me.

Putz, I think.

Still, I'm not sorry I came. I love basketball: the constant sound of dribbling, the squeak of shoes, the wonderful whoosh the ball makes going cleanly through the net. We're winning, which makes the game even more fun to watch. We count down the last ten seconds, then we all pour out of the hot, steamy gym—jubilant, as if winning a basketball game really meant something. It's a dark night, cold and starless. The first flakes of a promised snowfall are already coming down hard.

"Pray for a blizzard," Stephanie shouts, walking beside me.

"No school Monday. Hey, aren't you glad I talked you into getting a life, Jax? Isn't this way cool?"

"Yeah," I say. "Great."

We climb into the bus and join the procession of cars threading through the parking lot toward the street.

"Want to go to my house?" she asks.

Now's the time to tell her about Amanda, to make sure she understands that we can just be friends. She needs a friend, anyone can see that. The way she's looking at me, "please" written all over her face.

"Jax?" she says.

I get this weird idea that Amanda would want me to try to help her. She'd say to me, "Jackson, you know it's going to hurt her feelings. You can't just tell her here, in the car, and then let her go inside all alone."

"Yeah, I can come," I say. "For a little while."

The house is dark. Her parents are gone for the weekend, Steph tells me, leading me downstairs to the rec room. No one to bug us. She turns on the gas logs in the fireplace, puts Simon and Garfunkel on the stereo. She throws some big pillows on the floor, and we stretch out there to listen. Stephanie's calm for a change. She just lies beside me, chatting about this and that, like she's the happiest person in America.

Then out of the blue, she says, "Jackson, don't you think it's bizarre that Brady hasn't even written to his own mom—hasn't even called her? I mean, it's not like she's the kind of asshole parent who hassled him all the time. And if he doesn't even care about his own mom, maybe he doesn't care about us, either. Maybe we should just forget him. Really, Jax, do we need him? If he did care about us, wouldn't we have heard from him by now?

"Okay. I miss him, you know? I can't exactly stop missing him just because I decide to. But what I've been thinking is maybe I'm missing somebody that never was. Do you ever think that? Like maybe Brady wasn't who we thought he was at all?"

I think of the two postcards he sent me and how they don't say anything real, how they don't mean anything. How they've only made me feel worse about his leaving. "Yeah, sometimes I think that," I say. "You can make mistakes about a lot of things, you know? About people. Plus, sometimes they just change. Like me. Listen, Steph, there's something I—"

"No, not you, Jax," she interrupts. "No way." She runs her fingers along the triangle my arm makes pillowing my head. She brushes them across my chest, and I remember suddenly the way her tongue felt inside my mouth that night, the shock of it, the burning.

"You look better maybe." She smiles at me. "But you don't change. Not inside. You know who you are. You know what you want."

"I don't know shit," I say. "I mean it. Don't count on me for knowing anything at all."

She rolls over toward me, props her head on her hand. "You know where you're going to school next year, don't you? I haven't even filled out the first college application. My mom's ready to kill me—

"But the truth is, I don't want to go to college, Jax. I don't want to go anywhere. It's really stupid, but it seems so depressing to me to go away when there's no place in the world that seems like home to me to think about while I'm gone. No place to be homesick for. Am I crazy, or what? Do you have any idea what I mean?"

"Maybe that you have to have a home to leave home?" I say. "This isn't exactly the same thing, but those first couple of days when I stayed at the hospital—when my dad was really bad off— it was my room in our old house I wanted to go hole up in. I had to remind myself I didn't live there anymore. I don't think it's so weird what you're saying."

"But, see, I don't even have a decent memory of home," Stephanie says. "A bunch of crappy apartments. That's all we had before we moved to this house. Those places, I wish I could forget—

"I swear to God, Jackson, my mom thinks starting your life over is just like clearing the Monopoly board and starting a new game. The other day, she goes, 'Look at me, honey. Look at what a mess I was before I met Robert, and now I'm totally happy.

Now it's time for you to get your act together, start rebuilding your life.'

"That bitch," Stephanie says. "I said, 'Get a clue, Mom. As long as you and Daddy are divorced, parts of me are going to be all over the place. You tell me, what am I supposed to build this new life *with?*' You know what she said? 'Stephanie, you are *so* negative. You got that from your father.'

"I do miss Brady," she says, blinking back tears. "Whoever he was, he could get me laughing, you know?" Stephanie moves closer to me. "Jackson, would you just hold me?" she whispers. "Brady used to do that. Sometimes I get so scared. It's like I'm nobody. Like I'm not even here."

I put my arms around her; it would be mean not to—even though doing it, I feel the farthest away from Amanda I've felt since the plane lifted off the runway and I watched Jamaica grow smaller and smaller and finally disappear. Stephanie holds on tight, patting my shoulder from time to time, as if I'm the one who wanted to be comforted, and I have to smile. Amy did that when I picked her up to hug her good-bye the day they left the hospital. She means well, Stephanie. She's a good person, a good friend. She cares about me. She'll understand when I tell her about Amanda; she'll be happy for me. But I can't tell her now, when she's so upset. I lie there with my eyes closed and pretend that it's Amanda I'm holding. I pretend it's that last night, on the beach. I make my breathing slow and regular, like the waves.

I must fall asleep. I have to have fallen asleep because that's the only way to explain how, suddenly, Stephanie is pressing against me, whispering my name, and I am pressing back, feeling myself harden against her. I open my eyes, and she smiles a sleepy smile. She takes my hand and places it on one of her breasts. Then she outlines it there with her finger, the way we used to outline our hands when we were children.

"Steph," I say. "Wait. I—"

"Shh." She pulls my shirt out from my jeans, runs one finger along the the inside of the waistband, just touching my bare skin, and I shudder.

"No. Steph—" But it comes out a moan.

She does that thing with her finger again. Then again. Each time slipping farther and farther inside. I let her unzip my jeans, let her touch me, stroke me. "This is good for you, Jax. It's good. You need this. We both do." Somehow she undresses herself; from somewhere appears a foil package. Jesus, I think I will die when she slowly rolls the condom onto me. My whole body sings toward her, as if my head and heart have nothing to do with who I am or why I came here.

orget writing to Amanda; what I did with Stephanie made that impossible. I can't tell Amanda about it. She'd be disgusted by who I really am. I can't lie, either—and not telling her would be the same as lying.

I lie on my bed, thinking about how I felt when Amanda and I were together under the stars—large, as if the whole world wasn't big enough to hold me. It was nothing like the way I felt with Stephanie. The best thing I can say about last night is that for a while it was as if I didn't exist. It was stupid what I did. I felt lost doing it, and I feel lost now. I *am* lost. I know because when Steph calls and invites me to come over, I go, knowing full well that I'm going to let it happen again. And again and again.

I tell myself it's all right that we don't love each other. I'm being kind to her, making her feel less lonely. She's being kind to me, obliterating the real world for a little while. We're just two pathetic people helping each other through a bad time. It's only sex; what's the big deal? I might as well do it, now that I've lost

Amanda. As time passes, I half believe all this is true. Everyone at school comments on how Stephanie seems better since we've been spending time together. She doesn't drink or smoke pot when she's with me. I make her study, and she actually gets a B on a Western Civ test. Kate Levin says, "Jackson, do you realize she hasn't gotten a B since junior high?" I tell myself it's not such a bad deal. I devote myself to Stephanie, and in return she invites me to her house every day after school, we go up to her room and screw, and for a little while I forget everything I've lost.

Mom's so out of it she thinks it's nice I've got a life. Once she asks me if I ever heard from Amanda—I say no. That's as close as she comes to suggesting that Steph is a weird person for me to have chosen. I figure it's a relief to her that I have someone to be with, anyone, so she can quit worrying about me. So she and Ted can enjoy the new house and each other.

Dad knows what I'm up to, though. He's not dumb enough to say so, but I can tell by the way he looks at me when Stephanie's around—which is most of the time, since she's taken to dropping in at the hospital most evenings. Dad gets a kick out of her. She brings him candy, then eats most of it herself while she reads to us from the *National Enquirer* or the *Star*.

"Listen to this one," she'll say, wiping at the chocolate dribbling out of her mouth. " 'Man Sees the Hand of God as Elevator He's Riding in Snaps from Its Cables and Plummets to the Ground!' " Or " 'Husband and Wife Both Get Sex-Change Operations.' Jeez, can you believe that? I mean, what about their poor kids? Like, suddenly, your mom's your dad?"

Dad cracks up.

"That girl is good for you," he says one night when we're alone. "She'll set you free."

It's no use telling him about Amanda. That I was stupid choosing Stephanie when it's Amanda that I love.

"Jax," he'd say. "Love the one you're with."

Love. The very word scares me. Mom and Dad loved each other, and look what happened. I love Amanda, and all I can do is hurt her. I think of her in that school she hates, checking the mail every day, looking for a letter from me. She's probably sorry she told me how she felt about me; by now, she probably thinks

I lied when I said I felt the same way. I could make her feel better. All I'd have to do is write to her and tell her the one thing in my life that I know is true: I love her. But then I'd have to explain how the rest of my life has become an ugly lie, and I can't bring myself to do that. I'm too ashamed. I think of Mom and Dad, and for the first time I understand that it wasn't what Dad did to Mom that made it impossible for them to stay married; it was what he didn't do. It wasn't who he was; it was who he wasn't. So he loved Mom. So what? If there's something wrecked inside you, real love just won't work.

And I'm made of him, partly of him. The thought fills me with a greater dread than I have ever known. Dad's just Dad: that's how Mom and I have rationalized so many things over the years. He loves us, but he's a flake. What if I'm like him?

Yeah, "Love the one you're with" is without a doubt what he'd say if I told him about Amanda. It pisses me off just to think of it, which is pretty ironic considering it's exactly what I'm doing.

So I love Amanda. But doesn't what I'm doing with Steph prove that there's something wrecked inside me, too—just like Dad? And if that's true, if I'm going to turn out like him, then loving Amanda won't be enough. I should let go now, before I hurt her the way Dad hurt Mom.

With Steph, what I can't be doesn't matter. She's even more wrecked than I am, so just about anything I do is bound to make her life better. Maybe I even love her a little. After all, there are a lot of different kinds of love. Still, I stand in the card shop for an hour, looking for a Valentine's Day card for her without that word in it or any combination of words that might equal it. I settle for one that has a bunch of cats holding balloons that spell out "Happy Valentine's Day." I buy her a pair of dangly earrings made of little mirrors.

She adores them, she says when I give them to her Valentine's Day morning. She takes off the earrings she's wearing and puts them on. She peers into the rearview mirror to see how they look. "Cool, Jax," she says, leaning over to give me a kiss. She hands me an envelope, but I don't open it until we get to the parking lot.

I hate the card inside. There's a picture of two cartoon char-

183

acters kissing on it, and above them it says "May this Valentine's Day lead you through the steamy jungles of passion, then plunge you to the depths of wild abandon—" I open it and, Jesus, a bunch of condoms fall out, weird ones, the kind that are supposed to cause strange and wonderful sensations.

"If you like that kind of thing," Steph says, speaking what the card says inside. I guess I must look really stupid because she laughs and wiggles her eyebrows. "Later," she says, and skips off to catch up with a bunch of girls to show them her new earrings.

I stash the card and the condoms in my locker, under a pile of junk. I feel half sick all morning, just thinking of them there. "Later," Steph said. But I don't want to go to her house after school. I want to go home and rack out or maybe go back to the gym and try to pump my body clean.

I think of the valentines I got yesterday from Amy and Kristin—those funny little ones kids give in grade school. My Little Pony from Amy, 101 Dalmatians from Kristin. I remember how Mom would take me shopping and I'd pick the package of cards with the pictures I liked best. At school we'd decorate shoe boxes with cutout hearts, and there'd be a party, everyone going up and down the aisles, dropping envelopes in every box. There'd be heart-shaped cookies and cupcakes decorated with red hots. It's depressing to think about how in junior high, Valentine's Day became just one more thing to be embarrassed by. It was awful if I got a valentine from a girl, even more awful if I didn't.

"It's just girls, Jax," Brady would say. "Get a grip."

But I was hopeless. He tried to coach me, but he never really understood the way I felt. For him, girls were easy. They were always calling him about this and that; he always got loads of valentines—even though he'd come right out and say no way did he want a *relationship*. Girls were trouble in the long run, he said, always telling you what to do. Dating was a bore, a throwback to the fifties. It was Neanderthal the way the boy had to pay. Still, there was never any shortage of girls willing to put up with him. Stephanie, for one.

I glance across the classroom at her now. She's sitting, fiddling with her mirror earrings so that they catch the sun and make little rainbows on the wall beside her. I think of what she said that first night we were together.

"Hold me. Brady used to do that."

And I see for the first time how *truly* stupid I've been.

"Hey, man, we'll get this apartment, get laid," Brady said. And all the time he was screwing Stephanie. No wonder she was so freaked out when he disappeared. For all I know, the reason he ran away was that he started feeling trapped, like I do now.

Suddenly it all makes sense: the way she tricked me into coming over to her house alone that night after the game, the way she had the condoms right there, handy. "We need each other," she said.

Yeah, she needed me all right. Brady's replacement.

I feel like I've been hit. The two of them; it's perfect. Two perfect disasters. Oh boy, it would've been just great if Brady and I had gotten the apartment. Christ, I'd've ended up *living* with Steph in that case. I'd've spent every night listening to the two of them screwing in the next room. It's probably why he wanted the apartment in the first place, to be with her.

He used me; she's using me now. And I'm so stupid, I let them. It makes me feel sick inside. Yeah, what a great person I am, what a prince, what a moron. Stephanie loves you; the decent thing is to try to love her back. I can't believe I gave up on any chance that things might work out with Amanda when it turns out that all I really was to Steph was the next best thing to Brady.

I cut out of school just before lunch and drive around and around the interstate loop with my stereo blaring. I pass exits for highways that would take me east, west, north, or south, the whole time thinking, What am I going to do? It only pisses me off more to realize that if Brady were here, he'd tell me the same thing he must've told himself the day he left. To hell with Steph. Do what you want. I suppose if I had the guts, I'd take off on one of those highways, like he did. But it's getting dark; Dad's expecting me. So I exit near the hospital and head over to see him.

"Yo, Jackson!" he says.

"Yo," I say, and slump into a chair. While he flirts with the nurse who's attending to him, I look at the valentines on his tray table. There's one from Kim, along with a basket of fruit and high-energy snacks. There's a huge one that all the nurses on the floor have signed. There's even one from Layla. Dad winks at me when he sees I'm noticing the little shreds of what is surely pot taped inside. Then he squints and gives me a weird look.

"Hey, what's up, pal?" he says when the nurse leaves. "You look like shit."

"I don't know," I say. "I guess Steph's kind of driving me crazy."

"Uh-oh," he says. "What's the deal?"

I start off, telling him what it's like picking her up for school in the morning. She gets in my bus, carrying a big mug of coffee, sloshing it everywhere. She reaches up and turns the rearview mirror toward her so she can fix her hair, all the while talking, updating me on whatever she and her mom fought about the night before, whatever crappy thing her stepfather said or did. She moans about school, about the state of the world, about the weather, about the way her hair looks.

Dad laughs. "Congratulations," he says. "You've just learned the quintessential fact about women. Bitch, bitch, bitch. Hey, you learn to tune them out, that's all."

I just sit there. I don't know how to say, "No, it's not all—not even close."

"You'll figure it out," he says. "It just takes time. And experience. But, Jesus, Jackson—meanwhile, can't you just relax and enjoy the—" He grins at me. "You know, *process?*"

I look at him, all strung up to the traction bar and think, I could just take a pair of scissors and snap one of those ropes, you asshole. I imagine his bandaged legs bouncing down onto the iron rail of the bed. You screw her, I feel like saying. You relax and enjoy the *process.* The sad thing is, he probably would.

"I don't have time to relax and enjoy anything," I mutter.

"Then take the time," Dad says, his voice suddenly gentle. "You're seventeen years old. Give yourself a break, will you? You're not going to marry the girl; you're just dating her. You're not responsible for anybody but yourself."

But I feel responsible for her, even knowing what I know.

She breezes in around suppertime like I knew she would. She has a valentine balloon for Dad and a box of those awful little candy hearts with messages on them. She beams at me and offers me one that says "I love you."

"No, thanks," I say.

I just sit there looking out the window at all the cars leaving the parking lot, while Dad and Steph talk. She's flirting with him, really. The two of them have been flirting with each other all along; I just hadn't seen it until now. Would Dad screw her if he had the chance? I tell myself that this line of thought is totally absurd. Dad is weird, but he's not that weird. And he's not stupid. Still, I imagine what might happen if the two of them found themselves suddenly alone. Steph would be the one to start it. That's what kills me. I know she would. She'd convince herself she was doing good, like screwing Dad was a way of nursing him. It would make him feel better.

The way it made me feel better. No, the way it made me not feel at all.

That's what I want to do now: not feel. I don't want to feel humiliated by how stupid I've been. I don't want to feel angry at Dad—it's not his fault. I don't want to feel jealous, but I do. I don't want to be with Steph, but I don't want her to enjoy herself with anyone else, especially my dad. I feel like a fifth wheel sitting here, listening to the two of them talking and laughing.

Dad launches one of his favorite shticks: Great Rivalries in Rock and Roll. Elvis versus Pat Boone, the Beatles versus the Dave Clark Five, the Ronettes versus the Shirelles, *American Bandstand* versus *The Lloyd Thaxton Show*.

"Lloyd who?" Steph says.

"Tell her, Jackson," Dad says, giving me this look like, Don't be such a drag.

"Lloyd Thaxton," I say. "He was this California guy trying to one-up Dick Clark."

"Yeah, go on," Dad says, grinning.

"His gimmick was the Lloyd Thaxton Sit-Down Dance," I say. "It was stupid. Every day they'd do one song with everybody sitting on the bleachers, you know, dancing with just the top parts of their bodies—"

I don't tell the rest of what I remember: that Mom and Dad used to do the Lloyd Thaxton Dance when they were in a really silly mood. They'd sit on the couch, side by side, and flail around, laughing like maniacs, finally collapsing into each other's arms.

"Great for cripples," Dad says now. "Though I have to admit it never occurred to me at the time." He cranks up his bed, flips on his boom box, and starts sit-down dancing to "Twist and Shout."

"Will you be careful?" I say. "You're going to get the traction cables out of whack."

He does a King Tut move with his free arm.

"Dad," I say. "Would you quit?" There's no way to tell him that the memory, the way the memory hurts me, is the absolute last straw in one of the worst days of my life. But I swear to God, I can't stand another second of it. "Dad, I mean it."

When he keeps it up and keeps it up, I stalk out of the room, a baby, a spoilsport. Jesus, what kind of person am I, anyway? Shouldn't it please me to see Dad having a good time? Shouldn't I be grateful every second of my life that he's alive?

I tell myself that maybe my real problem is this depressing place. Too many sad, sick people. Sorrow is contagious. In another week or so, Dad will be able to go home and things are bound to get better. But I know it's not true. My real problem is what to do about Stephanie. I can't avoid her forever. I have to make a plan.

Just tell her. That would be the best thing. Say, Steph, I know about you and Brady. We both know I really can't replace him. In the long run, we'll both be happier if I don't try.

Not the whole truth, of course: that I love someone else. Why hurt her?

But, as matter of fact, I want to hurt her, and I'm afraid that once I've said the first word to her, I won't be able to stop. So maybe I should just sneak out now, while I can. Maybe go home and write her a note that tells her the part of all this that I want her to know. I could get through tomorrow, avoiding the issue. Then when we got to her house after school, she'd open the door on her side of the bus and start to get out. She'd stop when she saw I wasn't opening mine, and look back at me.

That's when I'd hand her the note. "Read this," I'd say.

It wouldn't exactly be easy; she wouldn't make it easy. She'd take the note, but I'd see on her face that she knew something was wrong. She'd say, "You're not coming in?"

I'd have to say no. But I could do that. I think I could do that.

I'm halfway to the elevator when I hear her voice. "There you are," she calls. "I've been hunting all over for you. Your dad fell asleep," she says when she catches up with me. "So do you maybe want to go out and get something to eat?"

"I can't," I say. "I have homework. I'll see you tomorrow."

"We can do homework at my house if you want. Order a pizza."

I just keep walking; she hurries along beside. "God, I just love your dad, Jackson," she says when we get on the elevator. "He's so cool. He doesn't act, you know, *old*. I wish I could talk to my own dad the way I can talk to him. My dad, ha. All he cares about are Janeen and their darling little babies."

If she doesn't shut up, I think—

"Too bad for me I didn't stay a baby, a cute little two-year-old baby, like Nicole."

"Fake it," I say. "I think you could be fairly convincing."

She stops and raises a hand to her face as if I've slapped her.

The elevator jolts to a stop and the door opens. I walk away from her, toward the parking lot. "Jax, what's the matter with you?" she asks, catching up. "How come you left school today, anyhow? It totally freaked me out when I realized you were gone. Are you mad at me? What did I do?"

I keep walking.

"Jax?"

"*What?*" I say. "Jesus, Steph, will you be quiet for one second? Please?"

"You are mad at me. I knew it." She grabs my arm, but I shrug her away. "Jax, why?"

I stop so quickly she bumps into me, and I have to catch her to keep her from falling. "I'm not mad, okay? I'm just tired. I'm tired of this shit. This—" I wave my hand around, as if to include the entire hospital. "Would you just *please* leave me alone?"

"But, Jax, I love you," she says, her eyes brimming with tears.

"Well, don't love me," I say. "Because I can't love you right now. I can't love anybody." I walk away from her, out the double doors into the parking lot. I don't look back.

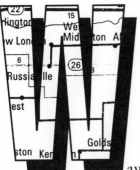

hen the phone rings later that night, I'm sure it's Steph calling to apologize for something she didn't do and make me feel even worse. Mom answers it and yells up the stairs, "Jackson, for you."

"Goddamn it," I mutter, and pick it up. "Yeah?"

"Jackson?" The voice sounds small and far away. "Jackson, is that you? It's Amanda."

"Yeah," I say. "Yeah! It's me. Amanda? Jeez, how are you?" I fall all over myself apologizing for not answering her letter.

"No, no," she says. "Listen, I know about your dad, and—"

"You do?"

"Kristin wrote me. She's so sweet; she's so worried about you. I just got her letter today, and, oh, Jackson, I am so sorry. You must have totally freaked out when you got home and found out. Kristin said he was getting better, but is he? Is he really going to be all right?"

"Yeah," I say. "He's still a mess, but, yeah, he's getting better."

"Well, thank heavens," she says. "Still, it must have been so awful for you—the fact that he might have died. I mean, are *you* okay? That's what I really want to know."

No, is what I should say, and then tell her the truth about Steph. And just having talked to her for maybe twenty seconds, I remember that she's more than the person I'm in love with. She's also my friend; I could tell her what happened with Steph and she'd understand. But right now all I want to do is listen to her voice.

"Jackson, *are* you?" she asks. "All right?"

I feel myself smiling. "I wasn't," I say. "But I am now. I was really stupid not to call and tell you as soon as I found out—"

"Don't think about that," Amanda says. "Just talk to me now. I want you to tell me everything."

We're on the phone over an hour. I tell her about camping out in the hospital waiting room that first week, about Mom's breakdown in the cafeteria. That makes her laugh. I tell her about Brady's postcards, the fact that I've kept them a secret from everyone, even his mother.

"You didn't want her to know he'd written to you and not her," Amanda says.

"Yeah, I felt bad for Layla," I say. "But I also felt like if I told anybody about the postcards, what would I say? To tell you the truth, every time I even think about them, I get pissed out of my mind. How would I explain that?"

"It makes sense to me," she says. "I mean, if someone's your best friend, he ought to be there to help you when something awful happens. What's the use of hearing from Brady if he can't help? It only makes you feel worse. No wonder you're angry."

"Yeah," I say. "I never would've thought of it that way, but, yeah, it makes sense. So, what are you, psychic? How come you know what I'm thinking when I don't even know myself?"

She laughs. "I have no idea," she says. "It's weird. This kind of thing has never happened to me before. I've never—"

"What?" I say.

"Oh, I don't know. I've never been—listen, Jackson," she says. "Do you still feel—"

"Yes," I say. "Yes. Do you?"

"Yes," she says. "Even more than I did. I miss you so much. It was so wonderful there, wasn't it? So—easy."

"It was," I say.

"Do you think it would have kept on being so wonderful?" she asks.

"Yeah," I say. "I do. Hey, maybe we should run away and find out for sure. We should, you know? Brady did it. Why can't we?"

She laughs again. "We definitely should," she says. "We'll run away and live on the beach. It's a great plan. But meanwhile, write me, okay?"

I promise her I will.

When we hang up, I'm on track, full of purpose. Okay, I think. Do it now, before you chicken out. And I dial Steph's number. I'm just going to break it off, plain and simple, and get it over with. "Hi, it's me," I say, when she answers.

"Jax," she says eagerly. "I—"

"I'm sorry I was such an asshole," I interrupt.

"It's okay," she says. "Really. I know you're still upset about your dad and all—"

"It's not that," I say. "Not only that." I take a deep breath. "Listen, Steph, a lot of weird stuff has happened to me in the last months, you know? I think I need some time out. I can't—"

She says, "It's okay if you don't love me."

"No, it's not," I say. "It isn't right what we're doing if we don't love each other. It's not fair if you love me and I don't love you back."

"I *said* you don't have to love me, Jax. And I don't love you. When I said that tonight I only meant, well—I just meant I want to be with you." Her voice is wobbly. "So don't freak out, okay? Don't make a big deal about it. I mean, even you said we needed each other, that it was good for us being together. So what's changed?"

I don't say anything. I tell myself she doesn't really need to know about Amanda. It would only hurt her more. And there's no way I'm going to make a bigger fool of myself by telling her what I figured out about her and Brady. What's the point?

"You are mad at me about something, aren't you?" she says. "I knew it when you left today. I could feel it tonight. Why won't you tell me what it is?"

"I'm not mad," I say. "I just—like I said, I need some time out. Plus, Dad's getting out of the hospital—"

"He is?" she says.

"Probably sometime this week," I say, even though I have no idea whether or not it's true.

"This week? God, Jax, no wonder you're so freaked out. But, really, you don't have to worry, you know, about you and me. I mean it. It's okay—whatever you want. And I can help you with your dad—"

"Well, maybe later," I say. "But at first, he has to take it easy. Go easy on the visitors—"

"I'm not exactly a visitor," she says in a small voice.

"No, no. Dad really likes you. It's just—well, the doctor says at first it'll take all his strength just to get around. And as for right now—like I said, I need some time out. I've got to move my stuff over to Dad's and help Kim change the living room around so we can put the hospital bed there. Then I'll have to help get Dad settled in."

"Sure," Steph says. "Sure, Jax, I totally understand. No problem. You just call me if you need any help. If you want—"

"I will," I say. But we both know I won't.

THIRTY-SIX

'm free, big deal. I'm still a liar. I *feel* like a liar; I feel like it's written all over me—and it probably is. If Brady were here, he'd see it—and he'd launch into his give-the-people-what-they-want theory for the millionth time. People hear what they want to hear anyway, so you might as well do them the favor of *telling* them that. Why not make their lives a little less painful?

"Not a moral issue, Jax," he used to say. "Don't sweat the small stuff."

But I never could get the hang of it. God, I was doomed by the time I was four. Mom swears that for weeks after she took me to see *Pinocchio*, she nailed me every single time I lied to her because the second the false words came out of my mouth, my hand would move—as if to reach for my nose, to see if it had gotten longer. Now, having lied to Steph about Dad, the fact that he *does* get out of the hospital within the week and all my time and energy *is* taken up helping Kim get the house ready and settle him in seems like visible proof of my dishonesty.

It keeps me from writing the letter I promised Amanda I'd

195

write, too. See. I'm lying even to myself. It gives me the excuse not to write it. I didn't tell her about Steph that night on the phone because I wanted to feel good for a change. So now I'm back to writing and rewriting letters in my head, trying to figure out how to tell her what I did so that the way she feels about me won't change.

I dream about her, always the same dream. We're in Jamaica, building a sand castle. Amanda shows Kristin how to dig down to the wet sand and fill our Coke cups with it to make turrets. "Sugar sand" is what she calls the hot white sand on the top. It's Amy's job to sprinkle that onto the turrets Kristin makes. I make the fortress wall. Carefully, Amanda presses shells and pebbles all along the outside of it. With her fingernail, she carves out a door, and in the dream, we enter it, leaving the girls behind.

Inside, the castle is whitewashed, with thick wood beams and tapestries. Amanda is dressed in blue, the same color as the ocean: an old-fashioned gown with gold lacing up the front. She wears one of those tall, pointed hats, with a long gold scarf floating from it. She leads me up winding stairs, around and around to the roof of the castle, so high that we're caught in the clouds.

Then I'm in bed with her in my old room. Our old house. We're sleeping at first, side by side, just our hands touching, like two figures on a medieval tomb. But the sun coming through the window is so hot that we begin to melt into each other. My hands are her hands, my legs are her legs, my heart is her heart. The whole world seems to be singing.

And suddenly we're on the beach again, ablaze, burning, our bodies human bodies again, aching, wanting, and this time I don't stop touching her.

I jolt awake every time, breathing hard, terrified by what we've done—then just plain disgusted at myself when I get my bearings, reach down, and feel the stickiness at my groin. Is that all I can think about anymore? I want to call her up and say I'm sorry. For dreaming unworthy dreams, for breaking my promise to her. I want to say, That night on the beach I wasn't lying.

Once I actually pick up the phone and dial her number. Then when she answers, I hold the receiver to my ear, speechless as a newt.

"Hello? Hello?" she says.

Click. She hangs up.

"Jackson!" my dad yells.

"Yo. Coming," I yell back.

It's just as well I didn't say anything to Amanda, I think. I couldn't have talked to her long anyhow, not with Dad needing me every ten seconds the way he does. Taking care of him is turning out to be a lot harder than I thought it would be, a real grind.

I go straight to his house after school, so Kim can get to work by four. Mom would laugh if she knew that it drives me crazy how messy Kim is. The first thing I do every day is clean. I wash the dirty dishes piled in the sink, scrub the bathroom basin, tidy the stuff around Dad's hospital bed. It wouldn't fit in his bedroom along with the huge water bed. It's in the living room, where it takes up so much space that any little thing out of place seems like clutter.

"Leave some of that for Kim," Dad always says. Like she's actually going to come home and suddenly notice the house is a disaster when she didn't notice it all day.

I say I don't mind. It's my problem if a messy house gets on my nerves.

"Well, I mind," he says. "Besides, if she's cleaning the toilet she's not screwing with my sanity, you know? She's not in here treating me like I'm a goddamn brain-dead cripple."

That gets him going on how she's driving him crazy. "Women," he says. "Stay away from them, pal."

That's when the depression hits me. It's like an elevator falling, thudding into place at the bottom of my heart. Amanda. She's sent me a few cards since we talked. Funny cards. Inside she writes things like "Hope your dad is getting better" or "Thinking of you." I know why she doesn't write more. She's trying not to make a fool of herself. She's waiting to hear from me before she says anything that really matters. I carry her letter folded up inside my wallet. I keep her cards in my school folder and take them out and look at them sometimes in class. I tell myself I'll write to her. But I'm too tired, too stupid, too sick at heart. I just can't.

197

Every time I see Mom, she says, "Honey, are you sure this isn't too much for you?"

Laying a guilt trip on her is my best defense. Like, *somebody's* got to do it. Or, I want to have this one last chance to live with Dad before I go to college. When she tries to talk me into spending some time with Kristin and Amy when they come visit, I say, "Don't you think I have enough to deal with right now?" Like it's my devotion to Dad that keeps me from seeing them rather than the fact that I can't face Kristin, who's probably written a dozen letters to Amanda by now and is bound to ask me why I didn't write to her when I said I would. Or Amy, who'll throw her arms around me and say, "Hey, Jackson, want to play?"

I can't play. I don't think I'll ever be able to play again. Every evening I fix Dad dinner. We watch a movie together. Sometimes, if it's nice outside, we take a walk up and down the block, him hobbling on his crutches. Kim comes home around eleven; that's when I start on my homework.

I don't know why it seems so weird doing calculus in that room with the faded *Star Wars* bedspreads. Maybe because when I'm in there I keep forgetting I'm not the kid I was when they were new. I never did homework in that room. It was a place I lived in on Saturdays—it was as if the room only *existed* on Saturdays. All the other days, when I was with Mom, it might as well have been as distant as the planets where Luke Skywalker and Darth Vader battled.

I try, but I can't do homework there now. The calculus formulas blur, and I drift back to that other time. I fall asleep, dream Mom and Dad's angry voices, and when I wake up I realize that it's Kim and Dad I hear.

"Oz, you *can't*. Let me help you."

"Goddamn it, I don't need help," he says.

One night I hear her crying. I knock on the bedroom door. "Kim," I say. "Don't you see it's important for Dad to do what he can for himself?"

"He can't do the things he wants to do," she says. "If he'd just calm down and let me help. If he weren't so macho, he'd get better faster. It's stupid. Can't he see that?"

"He's stubborn," I say.

"Oh, *really?*" She closes her eyes for a long moment, presses her fingers to her temples. "Oh, I'm sorry, Jackson. What am I getting mad at you for? We're in this together, aren't we? We both love him, and he's making both our lives miserable." She gives a kind of feeble laugh. "You're right. Make it easy on ourselves. Do it his way."

Things get a little better when the cast comes off his arm and he can do an upper-body workout again. He says to hell with physical therapy; he's going back to the gym where he can get serious—which may be crazy, but it gives him the feeling he's in charge. Now the first thing I do when I get to his house after school is to load him into the bus and drive him to The Peak. There, Kim and I help him maneuver into the few machines he's able to use with both legs still in casts. I look away as he struggles to move the weights that are set sometimes at half or less than they were before the accident. I can't keep myself from watching him in the mirror, though. Sweat forms in beads on his forehead. He grows pale. Sometimes his eyes blink with tears.

His pain exhausts me. I fall asleep on the bench at The Peak between sets, at school, in the kitchen waiting for water to boil, on the couch folding laundry, over my homework. It seems like the only time I don't fall asleep is in bed. Dad's taken to sleeping most of the day, napping for an hour or so around eleven when Kim comes home. About one A.M. he's ready to boogie.

It's not like he keeps me awake. I'm lying on my bed, bug-eyed, anyhow. I hear the television playing low or the whisper of his earphones when he has the stereo turned on full blast. Sometimes I hear his crutches tapping from the living room to the bathroom to the kitchen. Sometimes they tap into the bedroom where Kim is sleeping and then not sleeping. I hear their voices, their laughter when he thunks down on the bed beside her. They may be driving each other insane, but it's pretty clear from the noise coming out of the bedroom that it hasn't ruined their sex life. God knows how they do it, but they manage. It's embarrassing. When Dad taps out again, sometimes he'll stand at my door. It's closed, but I can feel him there, and I make myself curl into a sleeping position in case he opens it. I make myself breathe evenly.

199

I get up sometimes, and we talk or play cards. Maybe it's the dead of night that makes him talk the way he does. About the way things were with Mom at the end, how he felt trapped, how he had to leave. About the way he'll always feel about her, how there can never be another person like her—that's why he's always with flaky women, like Kim. Women who drive him so crazy that he's glad when, finally, they leave.

I've known all Dad's girlfriends, but since I've never lived with him, I've never lived through a whole cycle the way I have with Kim. She's leaving. She knows; Dad knows. But the thing has to be played out. Most days now, she meets me halfway up the front walk near tears and gives me a blow-by-blow account of Dad's latest harassment before she hurries off to work. I go in, and there's Dad waiting to tell me his side of the story. It's all stupid, petty crap for the most part. I don't know what to do but listen. I'd talk to Mom about it, but I'm afraid she'd worry more than she's already worrying about my living there. Dad seems to sense this, too, because when she comes by to bring us a casserole for dinner, which she does at least a couple of times a week, he's on his best behavior. When I go over to her house, I make jokes about Kim and Dad. It's like living in a soap opera, I tell her. *The Young and the Injured.*

It's not until my report card arrives in the middle of March that she figures out what's going on. Every grade has gone down at least one letter. "This is just not acceptable, Jackson," she says when I stop by Saturday morning. "We need to talk. Though, to be fair, I have to take some of the blame myself. I let you take on too much responsibility for your dad. It's got to stop."

"I have not taken on too much responsibility," I say. "Mom, I'm doing exactly what I need to do to take care of him."

"You're seventeen years old, Jackson. You're not supposed to be taking care of anybody, let alone your parents."

"Fine," I say. "I'm seventeen. So what? Who's going to do it if I don't? You?"

It was a lousy thing to say. I should feel bad when she gives me a hurt look and turns away, but I don't. I don't feel bad about my grades either. I've already been accepted at IU. It doesn't make a damn bit of difference what I do between now and August. I leave, slamming the door behind me.

Back at Dad's house, Kim is crying. Dad's hobbling around in the backyard. "Look at him," she says. "I told him, 'Oz, don't go out there. It's all muddy, the ground's all slick and lumpy. You're going to fall.' "

"He seems okay," I say, peering out the window. Dad's standing by the fence, yanking the chokeweed off it and throwing it in a heap on the grass.

"He hates yard work," Kim says, crying harder. "He doesn't care about those goddamn vines on the fence. He just wants to be out there because I think he shouldn't be." Her face is red and splotchy, her hair a mess. "Goddamn it, Oz," she screams out of the open window. "I *said*, get in here before you fall.

"I swear, I hope he does fall," she says to me. "This time I hope it knocks some sense into him. Look at him out there, Jackson," she says. "That asshole."

Dad sees me look out of the window this time. He grins, leans on one crutch, and waves. Both casts are muddy up to the shin.

"I've had it," he says when I go out to talk to him. "Over and out. I told her I'm not going back inside until she's out of here, and I mean it. Jesus, I told her I wanted her out just before I had the accident, when I was still in my right mind. I never should have let her talk me into letting her stay." He whacks at a bush with some clippers he's gotten from who knows where. I didn't even know he owned yard equipment. He says, "I want her out of here, Jackson. Now."

"Dad," I say, "what do you want *me* to do?"

"Tell her I'm not kidding. Help her carry her stuff out to the car."

Before I say a word to her, Kim says, "I know what you're going to tell me. I can't believe he hates me so much. God, after all I've *done*. I give him my whole life and what does he do? He throws it right back in my face."

I try to talk to her, to apologize for how my dad has hurt her.

"It's time you took a good look at your father, Jackson," she

201

says. "That friend of yours that ran away, for instance, that Brady—what would you think if I told you I came in and found his mom here that night you went out to eat with your mom and Ted? The two of them in the hospital bed, all tangled up, laughing like they were your age. This is their idea of something funny. She's such a slut. All you have to do is look at her and you can see it—"

"Layla?" I say.

"*Lay*-la," Kim says. "Is that her name? Oh, my God, that's perfect. They're perfect for each other. You know, Jackson, I'm sorry for you, having a father like that. I really am. I hope you survive him."

With that, she walks into the bedroom and slams the door behind her. When she comes out about ten minutes later, she looks like herself again. She has on tight jeans and a bright red sweater. Her hair is combed and pulled back. Makeup has covered the splotches, camouflaged the puffiness under her eyes.

"I'm sorry if I hurt you, Jackson," she says in a formal voice, a careful voice. "But I'm not sorry I told you the truth. I'd appreciate it if you'd take Oz somewhere tomorrow afternoon, so I can come by and get my things."

She gets all the way to the front door and opens it. Then she rushes back and throws her arms around me. "I am sorry, Jackson," she says, sobbing. "For everything. I really, really am."

I pat her awkwardly. It's not long before she pulls away. She walks to the door again and through it this time, closing it without looking back.

"Free at last," Dad says, hobbling through the back door a few minutes later. "Thanks, pal, I owe you." He looks at the long smear of makeup on my white shirt, sort of grins, and starts to say something—then thinks better of it.

I just look at him, not even trying hide my disgust. I swear to God, if he'd said one more word I would've decked him crutches and all. Later that night, when he glances at his watch and says, "You know, Jax, you must be getting tired of being cooped up here all the time. You ought to go out this evening, do something wild," I look at him the same way again. Is he so stupid it never occurs to him that Kim would've told me about Layla? I don't say anything though. Screw him. Right now I just want to get as far away from him as I can.

There's a party at Tom Best's house; the word went around yesterday. When I get there, Pink Floyd's on the stereo, and there are coolers full of beer. I grab a can.

"Damn," Best says. He grins at me, raising his beer in a toast.

I pop the tab and take a long drink. The beer is cold and bitter going down. I don't like the taste of it, but that only makes me want to drink more. In an hour, I'm so shit-faced I have to go into Tom's bedroom and lie down to keep from vomiting. It's after midnight when I come to, naked and sticky in the dark room, Stephanie sleeping beside me. It all comes back to me, what we've done.

"Shit," I whisper. "*Shit.*" And she stirs. She turns and puts her arms around me, and it's like someone turned on her talk button.

"Oh, my God, I've missed you so much, Jax," she says. "But I just knew everything would turn out okay. I just knew. It's too weird. Like, I went to this psychic after you broke up with me, you know? I was so bummed. And guess what? She goes, 'You are meant to be together; it is in the stars. Your souls must fly apart for a while, but in time they will come back and find each other.' Is that bizarre, or what? She saw it in the tarot cards. And, like, here we are."

Yeah, here we are—there's no denying that. And, who knows, maybe the psychic was right. Maybe if I'd gone to see her, I could've saved myself a lot of pain. She'd have seen Amanda in the cards and known why I wasn't writing to her. She'd have told me, "Forget the beautiful blond girl. She loves you, yes. But you do not deserve her."

I take Steph home. I drive the dark streets home to Dad's, the world spinning around me. Creeping to my room, I think, Hey, for once, we're normal. A drunk, sneaky teenage kid. A snoring, clueless father.

 he's back!" Dad says, when Steph appears the next afternoon. He glances over at me. He looks like he's about to wink.

Don't, I glare at him.

He just grins.

Steph unzips her backpack and starts pulling stuff out of it. Two tie-dyed shirts, one each for me and Dad. Some flat, pretty scary-looking home-made cookies with M&M's on them. The latest *Enquirer*. There's a mix tape for Dad that she's titled "Get Up, Stand Up" after the Bob Marley song. And one for me that has "Destiny" printed on it. I stick it in my jeans pocket and hope to hell she won't go off on all that garbage about the psychic with Dad. Fortunately—or unfortunately—Layla arrives before she gets the chance. She throws her arms around me and says, "Honey, you're a sight for sore eyes! And Stephanie! You come over here and give me a hug, too."

"Party!" Dad says.

Layla laughs and pulls a six-pack of beer out of the huge

canvas bag she carries everywhere. She pops a tab on one and hands it to Dad. "Jax?" she says.

I look at Dad and realize he assumes I've been drinking all along.

I shrug. "Sure."

Later, Dad says, "So, Jax, what do you think about Layla?"

"What's to think?" I say. "I've known her since I was five."

"About me and Layla," he says. "What would you think about us, you know, getting together?"

"Kim told me she'd been around," I say. "I'm not surprised."

"Kim told you?"

I shrug.

"Goddamn it," he says. "She had no business telling you that."

"It was true, wasn't it? So what's the big deal?"

"No big deal. It just wasn't her place to tell you, that's all. But what do you think, Jax?"

"I've always liked Layla," I say.

What I think is, God, what a great TV sitcom this could be— perfect for the nineties: *Like Father, Like Son.* The real-life adventures of a dad, a son, and their flaky girlfriends. Over the next few weeks, lots of possibilities for episodes present themselves in real life. Dad and son double-date, smashing the generation gap myth. The dad introduces the son to the evil weed: nice bonding theme. The son bravely parties on for days, worrying about whether his girlfriend is pregnant because they were both drunk the night they got back together and forgot to use a condom: *would* he insist on an abortion? Of course, it's television, and everything turns out all right, so he doesn't actually have to make the decision. I imagine an episode in which the prodigal son, Brady, comes home and discovers that his mom and his best friend's dad are getting it on.

He'd be ecstatic! I can just see him, wiggling his eyebrows like Groucho Marx. Grinning his knowing grin. He'd say, "Jax, bro!" He'd cook up a fantasy about how Dad and Layla would have a baby together that would turn out to be a weird blend of the two of us. A perfect child with only our best traits.

Yeah, it would make a great episode in the sitcom my life's

205

become. But I'm glad he's not really here to get obsessed with them and suck us both into playing family. The truth is, the whole scene disgusts me. Dad and Layla are as ridiculous as adolescents, the way they act. Life is one big party.

We blast some music, drink a few beers. Dad and Layla do the sit-down dance together and fall back on the pillows of the hospital bed, gasping for air. That's the cue for Steph and me to exit left and give them some privacy. We go to her house, smoke a little weed, listen to more music. Sometimes we talk about Brady. Steph's been dreaming about him again. She's convinced he's trying to send her some kind of message, and she thinks we should sneak into Layla's house, where, with his things all around her, she's bound to be more receptive.

"If he wanted to tell you something, why wouldn't he just call you?" I say. "I mean, don't you think this telepathic shit is kind of pointless when all he really has to do is pick up the phone?"

She gives me this look, lights a joint, and offers it to me. I take a long drag, then another. We pass it back and forth a couple more times, then I lie back on her bed and look at her. She's sitting beside me, Indian style, her head moving in slow motion to the Jefferson Airplane. A thin ribbon of smoke curls up from the incense that's burning in a little clay pot on the table. Her hair looks like smoke, gauzy—like the hippie blouse she's wearing. The more I look at her, the more I like the idea of going to Layla's. I imagine Brady, who-knows-where, all of a sudden getting a mental fax of the two of us in his bedroom—in *his* bed, not in the one I slept in when I stayed over. To hell with him, I think. Who needs him?

By the time we walk the half mile or so to his house, drinking the beers we swiped from the bar refrigerator, I'm feeling crazy with the idea of doing it there. We slip in through the front door, making a single shadow as we pass through the lighted hallway. In Brady's dark room, I pull her to me.

"Jax," she says. "We have to find totem things. You know, to bring Brady—"

I press against her, hard.

"Jax, I mean it."

"No you don't," I say.

She laughs then and lets me move her hand down to the zipper of my jeans. She lets me lead her to Brady's bed.

When we're through, she whispers, "He was with us."

For me, there was just the black void, the not-hereness I always feel with her. But I say nothing, just watch from the bed as she gathers some of Brady's things—the glitter yo-yo he carried all through sixth grade, the statue of Elvis he bought at a flea market, the old, beat-up cowboy holster with a cap gun in it. She arranges them in her lap. She closes her eyes and whispers, "Brady, Brady, Brady."

I want out of here. Brady never threw anything away, Layla hasn't touched his room since he left, and being here without him depresses me. We built that plastic dinosaur skeleton together one rainy Sunday; we raced the Hot Wheels cars on the orange track we propped against the back of his desk chair; we bickered over whose turn it was to sit on the beanbag chair. To tell the truth, it scares me. All those things, and the things Stephanie's touching, trying to call Brady back with, make me think of Grandma going through all Grandpa's drawers and closets after he died.

Brady's not dead, I tell myself. He sent me those postcards. He's not dead. And even if he were, we wouldn't find out about it by gathering totem objects and trying to commune with his soul. I don't believe in that crap. I came here with Stephanie because I wanted to screw her in Brady's bed. It was a crappy thing to do all the way around, and I knew it while I was doing it. Nonetheless, I keep going back. But after that first night I go alone.

It's easy, now that Layla has started staying over with Dad. I climb out my bedroom window at two, maybe three in the morning, and head over. I walk. I like walking in the dead of night; the empty streets look like I feel. Sometimes a car cruises by and I get scared. What if it's an undercover cop? But it never is. I walk on and cut into Layla's backyard from the alley. Once inside, I go straight up to Brady's room and just sit there in the dark. Sometimes I turn his stereo on real low or open his closet and look at his shirts hanging there. Sometimes I sit on his beanbag chair and try to convince myself he's just gone to the kitchen for food. Any minute, he'll come back and I'll say, "I'm so sick of this shit, man. I get up at dawn to go work out, I do my schoolwork, take care of Dad—he's driving me crazy. And what am I going to do about Steph?"

He'll grin at me, toss me a Coke and a bag of Doritos. "Jax," he'll say, "Jax, Jax, Jax," in this mournful voice, and I'll start laughing because I already know he's going to spout his favorite line from this poem we read in lit class: " 'Life for me ain't been no crystal stair.' "

The nights I don't go to Brady's, I drive to a hidden place I know near the reservoir and drink a few beers. I skip stones across the water and watch it ripple. I stare at the houses across the lake.

I feel like I did that time Mom decided it would be a great idea for me to go to camp and I got so homesick she had to come and get me. But how can I be homesick now? I mean, I'm living with my dad. His house is home, too, isn't it? I guess I'm just a weenie kid like I was at camp, missing my mom. I do miss her. I might as well admit it. I miss her taking care of me; I miss the way she used to keep me in line before she fell in love with Ted—that sixth sense of hers that honed in on me like radar when I so much as considered doing something I wasn't supposed to do. I even miss the stupid little things about her that usually drive me insane: the way she sings while she's working around the house, the way she's always so damn cheerful in the morning. If I could just go home, I think. But home isn't home anymore, not really. The new house is Mom and Ted's house, not mine. Jeez, I think. Get out the violins.

But being melodramatic and overly emotional is normal at my age, I tell myself. Not to mention that things have been weird as hell for a long time. All in all, I'm not doing so bad. Then one afternoon, I'm driving home from school and I see a guy in jeans and a jeans jacket walking past the library. From the back, for a split second, I think it's Dad.

No, I realize. It's not him.

And suddenly I'm shaking because all I can think about is how awful it would have been to have seen this guy who looked like Dad—to have thought for a second he *was* Dad—if Dad had died. I have to pull into the Kroger parking lot and sit there. I don't know how long it is before I stop crying.

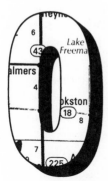utside, it's getting to be spring. The sky is blue, with big white clouds floating in it. The trees have a green haze on them. There are yellow and purple crocuses poking up through the grass. Inside the hospital, it's your basic antiseptic white, dotted with ugly-colored plastic furniture, like always. But it looks great to me because I'm here with Dad, who's getting the casts off his legs. He's his old self, joking with the nurses, making outrageous remarks. He's even happier when we get home and the men are there to take the rented hospital bed away.

"Good riddance," he says, as we watch them wrestle it down the driveway and into the truck. "That goddamn bed made me feel like a sick person. Things are looking up, pal. Another week, I'll be driving. I can think about getting back into the gym big-time, maybe even having a real life again."

He reaches over and messes up my hair. "Jackson, buddy, I couldn't have done this without you. But you've got to be getting tired of this crap. And I know your mom wants you back home. . . ."

"I don't mind staying a while longer," I say.

"Well," he says, "actually, I've been thinking maybe I'd take off for a while. Layla's got some time coming. She's got this wild idea to dress me up in a Hawaiian shirt like Ratso Rizzo and drag me down to Florida. Sit me in the sun. Christ, look at these legs." He yanks up his sweats and reveals them—dead white and flaking, from the casts. "I could use a suntan."

I shrug like I don't care. I don't tell him that I turned down a trip to Florida with Mom and Ted and the girls to stay at home with him. I must do something to give myself away, though, because he says, "Hey, you could go with us. Spring break's coming up, isn't it? I'll talk to Layla—"

"Can't do it," I say. "I'm going with a bunch of guys from school. I just hadn't gotten around to mentioning it. You know, waiting to make sure you were okay."

The truth is I turned them down, too. But it's easy enough to get back in, especially when I say I can drive. Dad thinks it's a great idea, spends a whole evening telling me stories about trips he took to Florida when he was in college. Mom's leery, though.

"You don't trust me?" I say.

"It's not that, Jackson," she says. "It's just, if something goes wrong—"

"Jesus, Mom. We're going to drive down to Florida, camp, drive back. Big deal. What's going to go wrong?"

"Nine times out of ten, nothing. It's that one time I worry about. You haven't had any experience traveling alone. . . ."

"I'm not traveling alone."

"Well, that's the other problem," she says. "I trust you, Jackson. I don't know about those other boys. Some of them are pretty flaky."

"Excuse me if I'm confused," I say. "Aren't you the one who's always saying, 'Jackson, why don't you go out and do something with your friends?' Now I want to, and you're acting like they're a bunch of criminals."

"Honey," she says. "What's wrong with you? You're not yourself lately."

210

"Jesus, Mom," I say, "you get married and drag us to a new house. Dad nearly offs himself. But I have to act like I always have or everybody freaks out. Give me a break, will you? Let me live *my* life for a change."

Bingo. Guilt does the trick. I'm gone.

We cut Friday afternoon classes so we can leave by four. Guys in my bus, girls in Tracy Perry's van. This is just one of the things our parents don't know about: that the guys and girls are all going together. Once we get out of town, we stop and regroup. Stephanie, Kate Levin, and Beth Barrett get in the bus with Tom Best and Eric Harmon and me. Kevin Todd and Matt Morris go with the other girls.

Liquor is the other thing our parents don't know about. We've been collecting it for a couple of weeks, pilfering what we could from basements and refrigerators and liquor cabinets. Then we pooled our money and gave it and a list of the rest of what we wanted to Tom's brother, who just turned twenty-one. The hard stuff we're saving. It's our plan to mix a bunch of it together, pour in some fruit juice, and have a Hairy Buffalo the first night on the beach. For the drive down, we have beer.

I'm careful. But I've drunk enough lately to know I can drink a couple of beers before I start feeling any serious effects. Tom pops one and hands it to me. I make it last. When I finish it, I'm just the slightest bit buzzed. Pleasantly buzzed. Mellow. I turn up the stereo.

Stephanie's having a sixties fantasy. She's decided we're only going to play music from the sixties the whole trip down. We listen to the Mamas and the Papas, Buffalo Springfield, Simon and Garfunkel. When we go through Atlanta in the dead of night, she puts in a Motown tape and starts telling us about her dad driving the very same highway we're driving now on the morning after Martin Luther King was shot.

"It was, like, barely dawn," she says. "And there were people everywhere. All along the highway fences and on the overpasses. Black people. My dad said it was really, really weird."

"You mean, *spooky*," Tom Best says from the middle seat, and cracks up.

211

"Jesus, just be a regular asshole, Best," I say. "Okay? There's no need to improve yourself by being a *racist* asshole."

"Really, you are disgusting," Stephanie says. The other girls agree.

"Oh, screw you guys," Tom says. "Don't be so goddamn politically correct. Where's your sense of humor?"

"Some things aren't funny," I say.

He shrugs and rolls his eyes.

"So anyhow," Stephanie continues, "my dad and his friends, they're, like, driving along, going, what the hell *is* this? And all of a sudden they hear on the radio that the plane carrying Martin Luther King's body has touched down at the Atlanta airport. Then, no lie, here comes the hearse toward them. This big black hearse. My dad could *see* Coretta Scott King in the front seat—"

"Oh, please," Tom says. "How could he see Coretta Scott King?"

"He saw her," Stephanie says. "She was all dressed in black. She had on this black veil. Her kids were in the hearse with her."

"That is such a bunch of bullshit," Tom says. "Your dad's driving probably seventy miles an hour, he's on the opposite side of the highway from this alleged hearse with Martin Luther King's body in it, there's a split second when the two cars are next to each other—and he *knows* it's Coretta Scott King wearing a black veil? Plus all her kids—

"Hey, how many kids, Steph? What were they wearing? And what about old Martin's girlfriends? Weren't they there? He had plenty of them, you know. Him and JFK."

"Why are you so cynical?" Steph says. "No matter what anybody says, you can always find a way to make fun of it. Is there anything you believe in?"

"Myself," Tom says. He pops the tab on another beer. "Bud, here. Yeah, I believe in Bud. That's it, though. I figure, if you believe in nothing, nothing can hurt you."

"I know," Steph says. "Life's a bitch, and then you die. I hate that."

"Prove it's not true then," says Tom.

"Oh, come on, you guys," Kate Levin says. "Quit. It's spring break, remember? We're supposed to be having fun. And pull over, Jackson. You've been driving since we left home. You've got to be getting tired."

We argue for a while about who's competent enough to take the wheel. Tom's been drinking steadily since Chattanooga. Kate can't drive a stick shift. Steph's a terrible driver, period. We wake up Eric Harmon, who's been sleeping and doing who knows what else in back with Beth. I pull over, and Steph and I wade through the empty potato chip bags and the chicken bones on the floor of the bus to trade places with them.

It's cold back there. We pull a blanket around us. Stephanie rests her head on my shoulder. "It did happen, Jackson," she says. "Why would my dad lie about a thing like that? He saw the hearse carrying Martin Luther King's body. He saw Coretta Scott King. It was like history coming alive, like being right in the middle of it for just one second, he told me. Like *he* was an important person himself."

"I believe you," I say.

"Don't you think it's weird," she says. "This? Now, I mean. Driving the same highway our parents did, taking the same trip they took when they were young. God, this is depressing, but what if we end up like them?" Then she falls asleep.

Tom and Kate and Beth fall asleep, too—one by one. At least they all stop talking. Eric pops in Pearl Jam, circa now, and sings along.

I sit in the back, my face against the window, my arm all tingly where Steph's leaning on it, thinking about what she said. What if we *do* end up like our parents? I get this black hole feeling, imagining myself years from now losing Amanda, losing the children we've had together—which is crazy, I know, since I don't have her in the first place; I've wrecked any chance I ever had of having her. It was all just a dream. But Mom and Dad dreamed, too, when they were young. Everyone dreams. And everyone grows up, grows into what life really is. It seems dense of me to have assumed that I'd be different, that I'd make all the right choices, that I'd never make myself or anyone else unhappy by something I believed I had to do. A dull ache settles inside me.

Eventually, it starts to get light. There was a dusting of snow on the ground at home, but in southern Georgia, the fields are green. The trees are bursting with color. Too strange, I think: we've driven right into spring. I remember watching a science movie in grade school—a flower opening—and wondering how they'd know exactly the moment it would happen, so that they could capture it.

"You moron," Brady said. "They sit a camera in front of it for about a week and then speed up the film."

Now the world itself speeds by. Florida is a long, straight road with billboards. Sea World. Busch Gardens. Weeki Wachee. Pathetic-looking trees hung with curtains of moss. Now and then, an orange grove. It's midmorning by the time we get to Clearwater. It's hot, in the eighties. We pull into the parking lot of the condominium complex where Beth's family has a condo, Steph's Beach Boys tape blaring. The beach is maybe a hundred yards away; the ocean beyond it is as blue as the cloudless sky. For just a second, I think of Amanda again and miss her as if she were actually a part of my real life.

"Yes!" Tom shouts, the first one out of the bus. He strikes a pose like Columbus sighting the New World for the first time. The rest of us tumble out, stretching and bending.

"Can you believe it?" Steph puts her arm around my waist, slips her hand in the back pocket of my jeans, then presses herself against me like a book closing. "A whole week with no parents. No bullshit. Jax, let's stay together. I'll camp with you. Who'd know?"

I knew this was going to happen. Just like I knew Tom would end up staying in the condo with Kate; Eric with Beth. I knew Matt and Kevin would be ticked off because they'd planned on a big stag party, the five of us meeting new girls on the beach. And Tracy, Pam, and Carrie—best friends since first grade—would be ticked off because they'd feel like Kate and Beth had used them. But for once in my life, I don't care.

Time goes by, one perfect, sunny day after another. Steph and I play Frisbee or zonk out on the beach, working on our suntans. We buy loose joints from guys cruising the beach and smoke them late into the night, talking about our lives. It's mellow. I feel so close to her in the darkness, with the sound of the waves crashing on the beach beyond us. I guess that's why I slip and mention Brady's postcards.

"What?" she says. "You got two postcards from Brady and didn't tell me?"

"I didn't tell anyone," I say. "Not even Layla. I still haven't told her."

"God, Jax. Why?"

"I don't know," I say. "I suppose I didn't tell because I didn't know what to think about them. I mean, I get these two postcards. So what? They didn't really say anything about how Brady was or even *where* he was. I mean, by the time they got to me, who knows how far away he was from where he'd mailed them? And they came right after Dad's accident. To tell you the truth, getting them made me mad. I thought, Brady's supposed to be my best friend, and he's sending me some stupid postcard when he ought to be here, helping me. I didn't really want to think about what that meant, you know? Like, is he really my friend? Was he ever really my friend, or have I been kidding myself all along? It was just one more thing to be freaked out about, when it seemed to me that being freaked out about Dad was enough to have to handle."

"Your dad's been fine for a long time, Jackson."

"Yeah. Well, I didn't tell anyone then because I'd have had to explain why I didn't mention it *before*. And I didn't hear from Brady again. So I figured, screw him."

"You still should've told. At least Layla."

"I just didn't, okay? So I'm not perfect."

"You don't need to get mad at me, Jax," she says.

"I'm not mad at you," I say, even though I am—a little. Annoyed, anyway. "It's just over, that's all. There's no point in arguing about it. I didn't tell before, and I'm not going to tell Layla now; it would only upset her. *We're* not going to tell—"

"Just don't be mad at me, Jax. Please. I won't tell Layla if you don't want me to. I only want to be with you. That's the most important thing to me."

"I said, I'm not mad, okay? Not at you, anyway. Maybe I'm going to be pissed off at Brady for the rest of my life. But that's my problem. I just don't see any point in us talking about him or anything that has to do with him anymore. He's gone. Period. Wherever he is, I guess I hope he's all right, but there's nothing I can do if he's not. I have to go on with my own life."

"Yeah," she says. "It's sad, though. It's so depressing. I mean, the way he's just—gone."

We're quiet for a while. We pass a joint back and forth between us. A few hits and I'm feeling calm again. I think of Brady, imagine him on a beach somewhere himself, with the Dead, and I do hope he's all right. I really do.

Beside me, Steph sighs. "Jax, do you think it means anything?" she asks. "All we go through? All we can't change?"

"I don't know," I say.

"I used to think so. Maybe I still do sometimes." She's quiet again, then she says, "I mean, I still believe in love. That love matters."

I lie still beside her, full of something; I don't know what. It isn't love. I don't love her. I can't make myself tell her that I do.

"I know," she says. "I shouldn't even say things like that. My mom's always saying, 'For God's sake, Stephanie, why do you have to say every single thing that pops into your head? No wonder people think you're strange.'

"It's true; I am strange. I know it. I mean, Kate and Beth and the others—they wouldn't invite me anywhere anymore, except for the fact that we were once real friends, in grade school. They feel sorry for me. I've been such a wreck since the divorce."

"You'll be okay," I say. "You'll get it all worked out eventually. Everyone does."

"I won't," Steph says. "Because no matter how I try I can't quit loving people. That's my real problem. Kate and Beth, all of them. You and Brady—

"My dad doesn't give a damn about me. He pays for me, that's all. He has his real family with Janeen. But I keep loving him. I even love my mom. I can't tell her, though. She'd say, 'If you really loved me, Stephanie, you'd get yourself together, you'd give Robert a chance, you'd want me to be happy.' "

She's quiet then, waiting for me to say what she needs to

hear, but I don't say it. I hold her, though, and we fall asleep together under the stars. In the morning, she seems better, as if the words she'd released into the darkness were, in fact, the sorrows she had spoken of. She's back to her old self, spouting a dozen theories about life, finding signs in sunsets, in the patterns the sand makes when the water recedes from the shore.

THIRTY-NINE

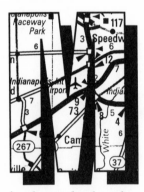

y head is killing me. Since Florida, I haven't been able to concentrate—maybe because now that I'm back at Mom's it takes all the energy I have to fake being the person I used to be. With Steph, I don't have to bother trying. We hang out, smoke a few joints, drink whatever we can get our hands on. We cut school a lot. On sunny days, we drive out to the reservoir and pretend we're back on the beach.

My grades the second six weeks are even worse than they were the first. Mrs. Blue stops me after class one day and says, "Jackson, are you all right?"

"Yeah, sure," I say, and exit as fast as I can.

But I'm not all right at all. I can't fall asleep until it's almost morning. Then when I do sleep, I dream I'm walking in water, and I wake up, my whole body aching, as if I've really walked all night against the terrible pull of the tide. It takes all I have to sit up, to drag myself to the shower. I sit and stare at my breakfast. It seems like a whole lot of trouble to pick up the spoon. I'm pissed off all the time. I hate myself, but I can't quit acting like an asshole to anyone who gets in my way.

Even Kristin and Amy. I'm sleeping, or trying to, when they arrive late one Friday afternoon. "Hey, Jackson!" they yell, clattering up the stairs to my bedroom.

"Haven't you guys ever heard of knocking?" I say.

Kristin steps back, disappearing down the stairs as quickly as she climbed them. Amy says, "Jackson, don't you like us anymore?" Then she's gone, too.

I stomp out the back door, filch a six-pack of beer from the refrigerator in the garage, and drive out to the reservoir, where I can be alone. I don't have my watch on, so I have no idea how much time goes by. All I know is that it's gotten dark. I vaguely remember that I told Steph I'd pick her up and take her somewhere. She won't be mad; she never gets mad. She'll just be sitting up in her room with her earphones on, listening to music, waiting for me. Still, I speed up, knowing how much she hates to be alone.

Oh, man, I'm blotto. I realize it when I see the red light flashing behind me. I stop the bus, sit there with my heart pounding, and seconds later, a tall black cop appears at my window. He shines his flashlight on my face, looks hard at me. "License, please," he says. "Registration."

I find the license in my wallet, fumble for the registration in the glove compartment. Shit, I think, glancing at the empty beer cans on the floor.

The cop reads the documents, then he opens the car door. "Step out. I want you to assume the position. That's hands against the side of the van, spread your feet. Spread 'em," he repeats, placing his hand just below my chest and pushing just enough to get me off balance. "Stand still," he says. He pats me down; his big hands make me flinch when they come near the private places.

He pulls me away from the bus by the back of the shirt, turns me so he's right in my face. "Son," he says, "your breath smells like beer. You been drinking?"

I don't answer; I'm too scared. I look down at the ground,

listening to the cars whiz by on the busy street. I can feel people looking at me. What if Mom drives by, or Ted? Oh, God, what if Grandma were to see me?

"Close your eyes now," the cop says. "Hold your hands out straight to the side, point your finger. Right one first, that's it— swing it around and touch your nose."

My finger falls somewhere around my collarbone.

He tells me to walk on back to the police car and follows, watching me as I do. He opens the back door, motions me in. It's just like in the movies: the wire-grille partition between the front and the back, the rifle in its holder on the dashboard, the radio with its fuzzy voices. I blow up the balloon device he gives me.

"Yep, point one all right," he says when it reads out. "I got to take you in."

He reads me my rights, handcuffs me, and locks me into the back of the car. Then he walks back to my bus, gets the keys, and puts some kind of tag on the front windshield. He doesn't say a word to me when he comes back. Just starts up the car and pulls into traffic.

The handcuffs hurt my wrists. I can't keep my balance in the seat because without the use of my hands, I slide from side to side every time he turns. I start feeling sick; there's no air, and there's a weird smell in the car. What is it? Some other kid's vomit, probably. Just the thought of that makes bile rise into my throat. I try to control it, but I can't, and I puke all over myself, all over the seat of the police car. Then, Jesus, I start crying. When I make a choking noise, the cop looks back, but he doesn't stop the car.

I must pass out, because the next thing I know, I'm lying on a steel bench in the holding tank. I sit up but lower myself again quickly when I feel light-headed, as if I might throw up again.

"You look like shit, man," a black kid says to me. He's tall, real dark-skinned, fierce looking. He's pacing the length of the room, from the cement block wall on one end to the thick glass wall on the other. The guard in the hallway watches him. So do a couple of guys who are sitting in the far corner, the only other people in the room. They're dressed in oxford shirts and jeans. Preppie types from North Central, maybe. Or Carmel. They look scared.

For the millionth time I think, Where's Brady when I need him? If he were here, he'd know what to do. In no time at all, he'd be holding court. Even the guard would be laughing. Then I think, Yeah, if it weren't for Brady, I wouldn't be *in* this mess! If we'd been together tonight, he'd have talked the cop out of arresting me. Jeez. It's amazing how, lately, I can get so mad at him for things he hasn't even done.

Finally, I hear my name called over an intercom. The guard opens the iron door. The officer who takes my statement is decent to me, makes no more judgment than to shake his head at what a mess I am: soaked with sweat from the nausea, vomit caked on my clothes.

"You can call your parents now," he says, nodding toward the phone on his desk when we're through.

Mom freaks. Driving drunk, I could've killed myself or somebody else. Plus, she's sure I've been terminally damaged by having to spend time in jail. Dad's pissed. "For Chrissake, Jackson," he says, "if you're going to drink, don't be so goddamn stupid about it." Layla says, "Wouldn't you think there'd be plenty of *real* criminals for them to hassle?" Stephanie feels guilty because I got arrested on the way to see her. Tom and Eric want to swap stories about what happened to them the night they got busted. Grandma's sure I'm headed straight for hell.

Ted says the only thing that makes sense. "Face it, Jackson, you're just not cut out to be an outlaw. You'll get caught every time. You might as well quit trying." He says it almost apologetically, as if he's condemning me to be a boring person for the rest of my life, the kind of person he thinks he is. But it's sort of a relief to consider the possibility that he might be right.

I think about Brady and how he loved being bad, how it energized him and made him larger than life. Brady Burton: the legend. He'd do anything. But being bad only makes me feel lost.

The problem is, if I can't hack being bad, what then? There's no way I can go back to being the way I once was. I've changed; I know more than I used to. But what I know doesn't make me smarter, only scared. Everything scares me. I go to drunk driving school—my punishment since I was a first offender. I sit there

with all the other losers, watching the gory movies—drunks ca-
reening across the highway into cars full of happy families or
teenagers on their way to a prom. I watch body after bloody body
being pulled from the twisted wreckage drunk drivers have caused.
Then the drunks themselves come on the screen, hunched over,
as if in prayer: "Sorry, sorry, sorry."

I drive home slowly, peering into car windows, thinking, Are
you going to die tonight? Am I? It scares me when someone passes
me too close, when a car pulls up right next to me at a stoplight.
I imagine gravity getting out of whack and all the cars in the world
going every which way, crashing into each other, spinning right
off the earth.

Steph scares me most of all. She loves me; she belongs
to me somehow. I feel responsible for her. When I quit drinking,
she quit. We're done with weed. We don't cut school anymore.
We stay on the treadmill of good behavior right up until late at
night, when we're finished studying and she says, "Jax, just hold
me," and I do and every time it's like that first night. It's the one
thing I can't make myself stop.

I dream of myself in mazes, in buildings with windows that
won't open. In one dream, I'm driving on a deserted interstate at
night, and the accelerator gets stuck. Then I dream Steph and I
are married. She's dressed like Mom was when she married Dad:
in a long white dress, a garland of flowers in her hair. I say, "Wait!
No!" But it's too late. Steph smiles and from the folds of the dress
produces a child, a little boy who looks exactly like me. I can't
leave her now; I can't leave this child. He looks at me with sad
eyes. He needs me.

The next thing I know, Mom's kneeling beside my bed, shaking me. "Jackson, Jackson," she says. "Honey, what in the world
is the matter? Why are you crying?"

"I can't take care of a baby," I sob, still tangled in the dream.
"I can't take care of Steph anymore. I can't."

"Oh, my God," Mom says. "Jackson, Stephanie's not—"

The urgent tone of her voice, the way she suddenly grips my
arm, brings me back. It was a dream, a dream.

"Jackson," Mom says again.

"No, no," I say. "I was dreaming. A nightmare. I'm okay."

But I know I'm in for it. I might as well tell her everything and get it over with. So I do.

"She really could get pregnant, then," Mom says when I've finished telling her about me and Steph. "Even if it was only a dream. I mean, the two of you have been—"

"Yeah," I say. "She could. We have. Mom, I don't love her. I never did, even at the beginning. But I don't know what to do about it."

"Oh, Jackson," she says. She gathers me up, and for a long time she just holds me the way she used to when I was little, one hand cupping the back of my head. I feel her heart beating, feel her breathing, feel her tears soaking my shoulder. "Well," she says finally. She takes a deep breath and lets it out. "What are we going to do? Oh, honey, I am so sorry I've let things go so far. I mean, I have to take some blame here, I know. I've been so wrapped up in Ted and the girls and the new house these past months. And you—"

"It's not your fault," I say.

"I didn't say it was my fault, Jackson," she says, and I almost smile. She's back, I think. The old Mom. No way she's going to let me get away with this shit anymore.

"Now," she continues. "First things first. Even aside from the fact that you're being reckless with your own future doing what you've been doing—if you don't love Stephanie, it's not right to stay with her. The longer you wait to tell her the truth, the longer it will be before she begins to put her own life in order."

"But she's a mess," I say. "She doesn't know how."

"That may be," Mom says. "But you're a mess yourself. And Stephanie is going to have to learn to take care of herself sometime, whether she's ready or not. It might as well be now. She's not your responsibility, Jackson. That's where you've gotten in over your head here. You can't save another person; you can only save yourself."

"But I can't just—"

"Yes, you can," she says. "You can and you will. I'm still your mother, remember? And I'm telling you that you're grounded until you get caught up with your schoolwork and until I see some evidence that you're getting your act together. I don't

223

care what you tell Stephanie. You can tell her I made you break up with her, or you can tell her the whole truth. But whatever you tell her, I want you here in this house every evening, every weekend, working your butt off and acting like a normal human being for a change. Is that clear?" She stops and gives me this funny look, as if to say, Are you really going to let me get away with this?

I mutter, "Yeah, yeah, okay," like I'm pissed out of my mind. But both of us know I'm not. I'm the one who has to take control of my life. For the first time in months, I feel like maybe, maybe I can.

figure I might as well tell Steph right off and get it over with. She gets in the car, coffee sloshing, as usual. She turns the mirror so she can see herself. She groans.

"I'm grounded," I say.

"What?" Her hand slips, and the mirror tilts even more so that I don't have to look at her to see her reaction. I can see her face in the mirror. She looks scared.

"From now till graduation," I say. "I'm going nowhere. My mom—"

"I can hang out at your house," she says. "We can do our homework there, watch the tube, you know. I don't care if we don't go anyplace. Your mom can't—"

"My mom figured out what we're doing, Steph. That's *why* I'm grounded."

"How?" she says. "How could she find that out, Jax?" She pauses. I can feel her looking at me, but I keep my eyes on the road. "Unless you told her. You did, didn't you? You told her. Boy, am I stupid, or what?" she says. "Duh. You're breaking up with me, aren't you?"

"I'm grounded," I said. "There's no point—"

"*Are* you breaking up with me or not? Because if you are, just do it, okay? I knew you were going to do it. You've been acting weird ever since you got busted. Things aren't the same." She starts to cry. "Well, are you?"

"I have to," I say. "Yeah, I am."

"Bullshit you have to. You know, Jax, you could at least tell me the truth."

And I know she's right. I should. So I drive past school, past the mall, out toward the reservoir. Neither one of us says a word until I pull into the secluded place where we used to go. It's a beautiful May morning. The water's like glass, shining, until a speedboat trailing a skier disturbs the surface.

"Okay," I say finally. "You're right; I'm full of shit. I am grounded, but only because I'm too messed up to ground myself. Steph, I can't keep on. It's wrong. I knew it was wrong from the beginning, what we did. I mean, me doing it when I knew I didn't love you."

Steph shrugs; she won't look at me.

"I do love you," I say. "I care about you. Just not—"

"So you don't love me *that way*," she says in a small voice. "So what? I knew that. I told you I knew. I told you I didn't care."

"You should care, Steph. You deserve somebody who loves you the right way. You're—"

"A wonderful person, oh yeah. Blah, blah, blah. Jesus, Jax, give me a break. I mean, big deal. I'm a wonderful person, just not the right wonderful person for you. I don't need that, you know? You want to break up? Fine, you did. It's over. So just quit being a dickhead and telling me how wonderful I am, okay? Just take me home."

"Steph—"

"I said, take me home, Jax. Will you just do that one thing for me?"

She sits quietly the whole way back, her eyes closed. I want to say something to her, so she'll know I'm sorry. So she'll know I care about her. But my mind is blank. I let her get out of my bus, walk up the sidewalk, and go into the house alone. I feel awful when, finally, she's out of sight. And at the same time, lighter. Relieved that it's over. Okay, incredibly relieved. If I'm really done lying, and I am, I might as well admit that that's true.

Next time I see her, a few days later, she's with one of the punks I've seen hanging around in the village. His bleached hair is cut in a Mohawk tipped with pink. He has on black jeans and black motorcycle boots with chains on them.

"Yo, Jax," she says in a dreamy, stoned voice. Then she goes on by as if I'm just some person she met one time, no one special.

I feel like I should go after her and say, "Steph, let's talk." Maybe if I explained again why I had to quit seeing her, I could help her figure out what she needs to do to get herself together. I could make her see that this weird guy can't be good for her. But I know if I tried I'd get sucked right back into her life.

Mom's right, anyway. I can't save Steph; I can only save myself—which I'm trying to do. In some ways it's fairly easy. I mean, I've totally lost the urge to do the really stupid things I was doing before. I really am done with all that. I just feel sad all the time.

I spend a lot of time in my room, staring at the photograph of me and Kristin and Amy. Mom thinks it's nice that I keep it on my desk. I'm sure she assumes that it's one of the pictures Ted took. How would she know that Amanda had sent it to me? How would anyone know that it's Amanda I see when I look at it? The ghost of her, the ghost of that day, the ghost of what might have been.

Amy and Kristin do matter to me, though. I'm still trying to make up for being mean to them. One Saturday night, I drive them downtown, buy them ice cream. It happens to be the night of my prom, and we sit on the steps of the Soldiers and Sailors Monument watching the girls in their formals, the guys in their tuxedos get out of the limousines and go into the Columbia Club. I remembered my mom telling me once that she and her dad used to do that when she was a little girl.

I point out people I know. "Tom Cruise—oops, I mean Tom Best," I say. "He just thinks he's Tom Cruise. And that's his girlfriend, Kate. She hated boys when she was your age, Amy.

Even when our teacher said we had to give valentines to every person in the class, Kate only gave them to the girls."

I tell them about Brady, who probably would've found something outrageous to wear if he'd been here: a Day-Glo tux, a squirting bow tie. I point out Mrs. Blue, whose husband drops her off and goes to park the car. She waits under the canopy, smiling, studying everyone who walks by, the way she always does. I shift sideways so she won't see me if she glances across the street. That's another thing I feel lousy about: disappointing Mrs. Blue, letting my grade in her class drop to a D, then avoiding her, even though she's told me point-blank at least five times that she knows who I really am and will never be convinced otherwise.

"How come you didn't go to the prom, Jackson?" Amy asks.

"Costs a fortune. More than a hundred bucks by the time you buy the tickets, rent a tux, go out to dinner. And flowers. That's probably another thirty bucks down the drain. That's a lot to spend just to take some girl to a dance. Unless she's your girlfriend."

Kristin looks up from her dish of ice cream. "You could've taken Amanda, you know. She could be your girlfriend. She still likes you, Jackson. She told me so in a letter. She thinks you don't like her."

It's almost too much to think about: Amanda here with me right now. The two of us all dressed up; Mrs. Blue smiling as we walk under the canopy into the dance. She would've come, too. If only I had called her. But she'd have thought she was coming to be with the person I was those few days we were together.

"How come you didn't invite her?" Amy asks. "Amanda would look really pretty in one of those long dresses." She looks stricken when Kristin says, "Maybe Jackson *doesn't* like her."

"I like her," I say. "I like her. You guys don't understand—"

"Oh, you are so dumb, Jackson," Kristin says. "Just because you got arrested—"

"How do you know that?" I ask.

"I know what's going on," she says. "I'm not a baby, you know."

I am flooded with shame. I hate Kristin knowing; I hate the way Amy's looking at me so confused. But I wouldn't even begin to know how to explain to them what happened. I still can't even explain it to myself. I just turn back to Kristin and say the one simple thing that I know is true. "Then you ought to have figured out that it wouldn't have been right for me to call up Amanda and ask her to the prom."

"You *are* dumb, Jackson," she says. "You got arrested. So what? I told this girl at school about it, and she said *her* brother was arrested five times. He was in jail, too. It's not that big of a deal."

"It is, too," I say. "You'd better think it's a big deal, Kristin, or you're likely to get in trouble yourself."

She flips her long hair back over her shoulder, her favorite gesture.

Brother, I think. Had she said "my brother" to the girl when she was talking about me? "Well, no sister of mine had better end up in jail," I say, testing her. "If you do, I'll spring you myself and lock you up somewhere else until you promise to be careful."

"Like Sleeping Beauty," Amy giggles.

Kristin rolls her eyes, but she doesn't say, "I'm not your sister." When she says, "Well, I still think you should've taken Amanda," she just sounds wistful, kind of sad—the way I feel myself, looking across the street at all the happy, laughing people dressed up for the prom.

229

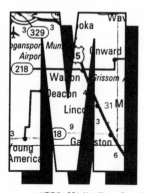emorial Day I go to the airport to meet Dad and Layla, who've spent the weekend in Las Vegas. They get off the plane holding hands, grinning. Dad's got on new cowboy boots and a bolo tie. He's still thin from the accident, limping a little, but he looks good, tanned. Layla's tanned, too. She's wearing jeans and a black leather jacket with fringe on it.

"Well?" Dad glances at her, and she blushes and kind of shrugs. He throws his arm around my shoulder, squeezes hard, and says, "Hey, pal, what would you say if you found out your old man got married?"

"Very funny," I say.

"We didn't plan it," Layla says. "We just did it. Jackson, it was too bizarre the way it happened. It's, like, after midnight and Oz and I are playing the quarter slots at Caesars Palace—oh, my God, you wouldn't believe that place! Everything gold or neon.

Slot machines everywhere, all of them making these weird noises. And blackjack tables, roulette wheels. And the people, well—

"It was a trip, but anyhow, like I said, we're playing this quarter slot machine with these stupid clown faces on it: I'm feeding the coins, your dad's pulling the arm, and we win the goddamn jackpot! Six thousand dollars, can you believe it? The coins start pouring out, bells go off—"

"So you decided to get married. Yeah. That makes perfect sense to me."

Layla giggles and gives me a hug. "Oh, Jax, I've always been like a second mother to you—now I really am. Honey, you know I've always been crazy about *both* you and Brady."

I look at Dad. "You're kidding, right? You guys are playing with my mind."

"No way," he says. "We really did it."

"You actually went to Las Vegas and got married." My voice comes out louder than I meant it to, and a couple of guys who are walking past us burst out laughing. They leer at Layla and give Dad the thumbs-up sign.

"He's upset, Oz. Oh, I was afraid this would happen just telling him, bam, like that. I mean, after all, getting married—"

"I'm not upset," I say. "But—"

"We honestly didn't plan to do it, Jackson," Layla says. "Honey, we never would've purposely left you out of the wedding if we'd known. It was a dumb wedding anyhow, in one of those tacky little places—at three o'clock in the morning—

"Honey, I know it's a shock. Believe me, I'm shocked myself. Your dad's shocked. Last night, after we did it, we looked at each other and said, 'Holy shit!' and drank two bottles of champagne. God, I'm still hung over."

"I'm pretty happy, pal," Dad says. By this time, we're halfway down the concourse. He's still got his arm draped around my shoulder. "I never thought I'd get married again, but it's the right thing, Jackson. Layla and I—"

"Who else could live with either one of us, right?" Layla says. "That's what made us finally decide."

For the next half hour or so, waiting for the bags, driving

home, they never quit talking at me—for the most part, simultaneously. For two people who haven't been married twenty-four hours yet, they have a hell of a lot of plans.

Dad will move to Layla's house. It's bigger than his house, nicer. "I'll tell you what," he says. "One thing I realized when I was down and out was I want a real home again, someplace that feels nice inside—"

"He just doesn't want to *stay* in it all the time," Layla says, leaning forward from the backseat.

Dad grins. "Yeah, a real house. Uh-oh. Sounds a whole lot like a real life, doesn't it? Pretty damn scary!"

He doesn't seem to notice that I'm not saying anything, that I'm stunned. In fact, he doesn't really seem to be talking to me at all. Neither one of them does. They talk and talk, but, in fact, they're talking to each other—and in a private, electric way that makes me uncomfortable, as if I'm witnessing something between them that I'm not really meant to see.

"And Oz is going out on the road again," Layla announces. "As soon as the doctor says he can. I made him call from Vegas—the road manager for the Moody Blues. You know, that guy who's always bugging him to go out. I mean, why not give it a try? He used to love it years ago. Jackson, don't you think it's a terrific idea? Go out a couple of months at a time. Then when he's home, we'll be together—

"You know me," she says. "I'm no good in the long stretch, anyhow. I never could keep a boyfriend more than a few months at a time. So Oz starts to think I'm a pain in the ass, and good-bye. When he comes back, it'll be exciting. Like starting all over every time. But without all the hassle of getting to know each other."

"Jesus, Layla." Dad laughs. "Don't explain things like that to anyone else but Jackson, okay? It sounds weird as hell."

"It is weird as hell," Layla says. "But it's exactly right for us, isn't it? It's what we want."

Dad reaches back and pats her knee. "Yep, it's what we want," he says.

"Oh boy." Layla sighs. "Can I really be happy?" She whacks herself on the side of her head with the palm of her hand a couple of times. "Yeah, I am. Now if I just knew it was really okay with you, Jackson—"

I'm not lying when I tell her that there's nobody I'd rather see my dad marry. I do like Layla; I probably even love her. And although I'd never have dreamed she and my dad would end up together, I can see the logic of it now that they have. I'm glad for them; I want them to be happy. But it scares me a little. I can handle one more change, yeah. I've got my life under control, and that's good. But it isn't the same as being happy. That's the thing that scares me: sometimes I think that I'll never be able to be happy again.

The truth is, I can't even remember the last time I was happy. Those few days with Amanda, of course. But I see now that that wasn't really happiness. It was joy. It couldn't have lasted. What I can't remember is when I last felt happy with myself and my life, day to day. I guess at some point after the divorce I just accepted the fact that I wasn't one of life's cheerleaders, like Kate Levin and some other people I know. I was sad a lot, but I got used to it. I got by. I knew who I was. I knew more or less what I wanted; I knew what I couldn't have. And we had fun, Brady and I. But now that he's gone, there's not even that.

God, I thought I'd gotten over his being gone. After I got arrested, I quit sneaking up to his room. I told myself, Screw him, you don't need him. He doesn't give a damn about anybody but himself. Now, I don't know. Maybe it's because graduation's so close—just days away—that I miss him again. I get up in the middle of the night and pace around my room like some cartoon guy whose wife is having a baby. Back and forth. Back and forth. Every time I get to the end of the room where the window is, I look out and see the same dead scene. Dark houses, black shadowy trees. Streetlights like a long line of targets.

I imagine myself shooting them out, one by one. I imagine how it would feel to have power over something.

Oh, who am I kidding? I wouldn't have the guts to shoot the lights out, even if I did have a gun. Ted was right about that. I have no talent for being bad. And why am I getting all bent out of shape because I'm not happy?

If Brady were here, he'd say, Jax, you've got to be simple-minded to be happy. Look at the world, man—kids kill each other for basketball shoes. It's *irresponsible* to be happy when stuff like that is going on.

I wish I knew if that were true. If I believed it was, maybe I could begin to figure out what it's reasonable to expect from life. What's possible.

Just stay sane, I tell myself. That's good enough for now. I concentrate on going through the motions, doing the right thing.

Mom says, "Jackson, let's have a graduation party."

"Great," I say, even though all I really want to do about graduation is get it over with. And I go through the last week at school as if I actually care: a yearbook signing party, awards night.

On senior cut day, it rains, but we all go out to Eagle Creek anyway and huddle in one of the shelters, laughing about things that happened when we were freshmen, or even in junior high.

Brady's name comes up. Someone says, "Remember when he let the boxful of crickets loose in the girls gym?"

This gets Tom and Eric talking about what our senior prank should be. Last year, some guys broke in and shot superglue into every single keyhole in the building. The beauty of it was, nobody even noticed till it was almost time for school to start. The teachers were drinking coffee, gossiping in the teachers lounge till the last possible minute. Then they headed for their classrooms and couldn't get in. Chaos. Security had to herd everyone to the auditorium to wait until a locksmith came. A tough act to follow.

"We could poison the food in the cafeteria," Tom says now, "but who'd be able to tell?"

Everyone laughs.

"Hey, they're still mad about last year," Kate says. "You guys had better be careful."

We settle on everybody buying a a dozen Ping-Pong balls, marking " '94" on each one, and dumping them from the stairwell into Grand Central, where all the hallways cross, two minutes before the last bell rings tomorrow morning.

It's a mess, of course. People crashing into each other, into the lockers. Girls screaming and acting crazy when the balls bounce down on their heads. Later, the principal gets on the intercom and tries to lay a guilt trip on us. "Someone could have been seriously injured," he says. But everyone knows that Grand Central is so congested in the morning that you couldn't fall down if you tried.

"Pretty pathetic prank," Brady would've said.

It's over with, though. Another thing to check off the list.

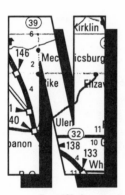

ext on my list is Layla. I pull up and she's out on the front porch, in the swing, reading. She waves wildly when she sees me, jumps up, and gives me a big hug. "Your dad's not here," she says. "He's working."

"I came to talk to you," I say.

"Really?" she beams at me. "Well. Come on in then. We'll sit." She heads for the kitchen, where we always used to talk.

I still haven't gotten used to seeing Dad's things there. His baseball caps on the hat rack, his favorite coffee mug in the sink. It's as weird as seeing the old snapshots of Brady and me on the refrigerator door.

Layla pops the tab on a Coke and hands it to me. "So, what's up, honey?" she asks.

I take the two postcards from Brady from the back pocket of my jeans and hand them to her. "I got these a long time ago."

"Jackson—," she says.

"I know I should have told you when I heard from him. I

don't know why I didn't tell you. I was screwed up, I guess. I know that's no excuse—"

Layla sits down at the kitchen table and stares for a long time at what Brady wrote.

I say, "I don't blame you if you're mad."

"Mad." Layla shakes her head and gives the cards back to me. "There's nothing in them, is there? I mean, not really. Nothing I had to know."

"That he was okay," I say. "I knew you were worried."

"Those postcards don't say he's okay," Layla says. "He's not okay, Jackson. That might be the only thing about this whole mess I understand. That and the fact that, aside from Jerry, who's such an asshole that *nobody* would care to be in touch with him, I'm the last person Brady would want to connect with. It's my own fault. I loved Brady; I really did. I do. But I failed him, Jackson. I very nearly loved him to death."

"Layla," I say. "It's not only the postcards I didn't tell you about."

For a second she looks scared, like I'm going to tell her something else about Brady, something terrible.

"It's me," I say. "Something I did."

"What?" she asks. "Jackson, you're not in some kind of trouble again?"

"No. It's something I did a while ago. Before you and Dad got married. I used that key you gave me a long time ago and came in here when you were gone. Once with Stephanie, a bunch of times by myself."

"Oh, honey, I know that," she says. "It's all right. Mr. Beaumont next door saw you. Old Mr. Nosy. I told him just to leave you alone—I figured you were still trying to work things out about Brady." She laughs. "You're just lucky he recognized you. Lord, he'd have been on the phone to the police in ten seconds if he hadn't. He's better than an alarm system. Jackson, listen—we've both had a lot to work out about Brady leaving. I'd have told you to come over myself if I'd've thought it would help. . . ."

"I know," I say.

"*Do* you have it all worked out now?"

I shrug.

"Well, I sure haven't," she says. "Boy, I can't believe I used to be so smug when you kids were little. So superior to those picky mothers who got all bent out of shape about homework and chores. Oh, Brady's so creative, I thought. I'm not going to spoil that by making him worry about stupid things like my mother did when I was a kid. I'd think of all the things I could've been if only she'd encouraged me. It's no wonder Brady hates me," she says. "I had my heart set on him being what I'd failed to be myself. I see now he must have felt like I was trying to eat him alive—

"I should've remembered that the more you want a kid to do something, the more likely he is to do the exact opposite just so you'll know for sure you don't own him."

"Like me," I say. "The way Dad's always telling me to relax, go with the flow, and I'm terminally uptight. Totally uncool. Brady used to say we should trade dads."

"Honey, don't even say that," Layla says. "There's no way your dad would trade you for anyone—especially not Brady. Those two are so much alike they'd drive each other crazy. And, my God, Brady was more out of it than either of us realized if he really thought you—or anyone—deserved *Jerry*."

I have to laugh at the way just mentioning Mr. Burton can still get her in a huff.

She leans over and gives me a hug. "You're more my other kid than ever, Jackson," she says. "I love you. God, you probably think *that's* the kiss of death, don't you? Well, how about this: I love you from my new, extremely realistic point of view?"

"Good enough," I say.

FORTY-THREE

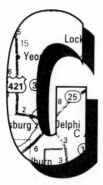

raduation day we meet in the gym for rehearsal at eight in the morning. There are two hundred and twenty-three of us, all in our own groups, all whacked out and edgy. Mrs. Blue tries to get us organized. But as fast as she gets one group dispersed and moving, the group she dispersed two seconds before re-forms and starts talking again.

She stands in the middle of the floor for a long moment, looking frazzled, then she steps up onto the stage, puts two fingers to her lips, and whistles a whistle any ten-year-old kid would be proud of. Some of us applaud.

She bows, grins. "Listen, guys," she says. "I want to get out of here as much as you do."

After that, things go relatively smoothly. We practice our entrance and exit without too much confusion. The principal appears and drones at us for what seems like an eternity about how graduation is a serious, solemn occasion and we and our friends and family should behave accordingly. He doesn't come right out

239

and talk about last year—the fact that Tyrone Meeks's girlfriend blasted the theme from *Rocky* on a boom box when his name was called and Tyrone strutted across the stage with his arms raised in a victory salute—but we know that's what he's referring to when he clears his throat and says, "Unfortunate episodes in the past cause me to make this reminder, which I hope you'll take to heart."

We're dismissed a little before noon. "Six sharp!" Mrs. Blue yells one last time as we rush for the door.

"Hey, where was Steph?" I hear Kate say.

"Not doing commencement," says Beth. "Do you believe that? I mean, wouldn't you want getting out of this place to be official?"

I feel a twinge of guilt. It seems to me I ought to go look for Steph, but what if I found her? It's none of my business, her cutting commencement. Maybe she's the smart one, after all—seeing all this phony crap for what it is. So I duck away before Kate and Beth notice me and ask me if I know what's going on with her.

At home, Kristin and Amy are waiting for me. Kristin hands me an envelope. "This came in the mail," she says. "It's from Amanda."

They both stand there expectantly.

" 'If one advances confidently in the direction of his dreams and endeavors to live the life which he has imagined, he will meet with a success unexpected in common hours,' " the card says on the front, a quote from Thoreau.

If only I *could* imagine a life, I think.

Inside it says: "Good luck, Jackson. Love, Amanda."

I can feel Kristin and Amy looking at me. "Nice," I say, sticking the card back into the envelope, pretending the sight of her handwriting hasn't affected me at all. "It was nice of her to send it. Weird it would've gotten here on exactly the right day."

"You're dumb, Jackson," Kristin says. "I told you before. She could be your girlfriend."

I yank on her long hair gently, tease her. "You know, I used to think I *wanted* a sister."

*   *   *

When I get to school at six, Mrs. Blue is standing at the back entrance of the gymnasium, smiling, making wisecracks, directing people to gather in the wide passageway between the locker rooms and the gym itself. She laughs when Tom and Eric turn and flip up their gowns as if to moon her, revealing madras shorts with "FREE AT LAST" on their rear ends. As the time for the ceremony nears, she wanders through the sea of black, straightening caps, adjusting tassels. She lines us up in two lines, one at each door.

We can hear the buzz of excited voices as the crowd settles on the bleachers. Laughter, babies crying. Then "Pomp and Circumstance" begins.

Mrs. Blue stands in the doorway of the line I'm in, pacing us, counting one-two-three after each person's exit so that we won't go out all in a clump.

When it's my turn, she leans close. "You're a wonderful person, Jackson Watt," she whispers fiercely, giving me a quick hug. "Don't you forget it. Go now—" I feel her hand on my back, pushing me forward, and I step out onto the basketball floor, my eyes burning with tears.

It doesn't take long to spot my family. They take up most of a row: Mom in a pretty new dress, Ted in a dark business suit, Kristin and Amy in party clothes, Grandma in one of her church outfits. There's Dad in jeans and a sport coat and Layla looking like a high-class gypsy. Her bracelets twinkle when she stands up and waves her arms at me as if flagging in a semi. Grandma casts her an embarrassed glance.

We sit through the predictable valedictory speech by the class nerd, about what a big responsibility faces us: the world. The senior choir sings a song about kissing today good-bye. Then a school board member takes the podium to address us.

It's hot in the gym. All over, people are fanning themselves with their programs. There's a collective sigh of relief when, finally, it's time for the presentation of the diplomas.

Things start cranking up around the Gs. A sprinkle of confetti in the bleachers, a burst of applause. Then Governor Grant's name is called and a bunch of girls start screaming. He's cool, though.

241

He walks across, takes his diploma, shakes the principal's hand.

But it's all over. The rest of the way through, people express themselves. Eric Harmon lifts his gown going down the steps, revealing his hairy legs. Jarmel Hart gives a deep bow when he takes his diploma. Betsy Nielson does a series of pirouettes across the stage.

The principal's voice grows deeper and more controlled with each act of defiance. "Benjamin Perez."

"Yo! Benny! You free!" someone shouts, and the whole audience laughs. Well, the whole audience, except Grandma.

Even I can't resist a thumbs-up sign as I start back to my seat.

When it's over, we stand, and in one fluid move, the last thing we'll all do together, we raise our hands and place our orange or gold tassels on the other side of our caps. We were instructed this morning not to throw our caps at the end of the ceremony, but like Tom Best said, "What are they going to do, make us go back to high school?"

We toss them as high as we can, and for an instant, it's as if the gym is full of wild silk bats.

It takes Grandma an hour to get over the rowdiness. Back at home, about every ten minutes, she sputters, "Honestly, I've never seen anything like it. No manners whatsoever. Jackson, what's wrong with those kids to make them act like that?"

Finally, when even Ted laughs at her, she gives it up and busies herself helping Mom put all the food out. There's ham and a half-dozen kinds of salad. Rolls and bread for sandwiches. Baked beans. Layla's famous broccoli and cheese.

Their timing is perfect. They put the napkins with silverware rolled up in them on the buffet, and the guests begin to arrive. We eat, and after I've opened my presents, Amy and I find a jar in the kitchen, punch holes in it, and the two of us go out to catch fireflies. Kristin has made friends with Tom and Mary Beth's kids, and they get a game of hide-and-seek going in the side yard.

"Want to play?" I ask Amy. "The two of us can be one person, then we can hide together."

"Yeah, okay!" she says.

We find a dark corner near the garage, sheltered by a lilac bush, and she tucks her thin body into mine, her heart pounding. I can see Kristin, the first fireflies of the summer blinking all around her, as she crisscrosses the lawn, searching for a place to hide. Her white dress shines in the moonlight. I can see her face plainly, the trouble she works so hard at keeping secret showing itself now in the little worries of the game, and I think, God, I'd die if I were that age again, all the broken pieces of my childhood still jagged and sore inside me. I'm about to go after her and bring her back to share the hiding place I've found, when she disappears into the shadows. So I wait, pulling Amy closer to me, holding her tight.

Through the leaves, I see Mom at the kitchen window. Dad appears, gets a can of beer from the refrigerator, and says something that makes her laugh. A car horn honks, a neighbor's screen door slams. Soon I hear one of Tom's kids shout, "One hundred!" Then the voices of the others as they're discovered, one by one.

"Ready, Amy?" I whisper.

She nods against me.

"Okay, here goes!" And I leap up, run for Home—the oak tree in the side yard—carrying her under my arm. Her legs flail, her arms clutch my waist. Pretty soon, she's upside down, screaming at the top of her lungs, "They're coming, they're coming!"

The others stream after us, but even carrying Amy, I'm bigger than they are, faster. They can't catch me. I touch Home, laughing like a maniac.

"Daddy, we won!" Inside, Amy throws herself at Ted, who picks her up and holds her in midair until she calms down. Kristin and the others burst in seconds later, their nice clothes all askew.

"Jackson," Grandma hisses at me. "You've gotten those kids all wound up now. Look at Kristin's pretty party dress, all muddy."

I turn and scoop her up like a bride.

"Jackson Watt," she demands. "What in the world do you think you're doing. I'm your *grandmother*, for goodness' sake. Put me down this instant. I said, put me down!"

She's as light as a feather. I could hold her like this forever, no problem. The kids start giggling. Dad's laughing his head off.

"Jackson," Mom says, but she has to put her hand to her mouth to hide her smile.

"Grandma," I say. "I'll be glad to put you down as soon as you say, 'As God is my witness, Jackson Watt is the best person I've ever met.'"

Even Grandma starts laughing then. She says it. When I put her down, she tries to act huffy again, straightening her skirt, patting her hair. "Jackson," she sniffs. "Honestly!" Then, in spite of herself, she reaches out and gives me a big hug, patting me on the back like she used to when I was little. "Honey, I just can't believe you're all grown up," she says.

FORTY-FOUR

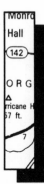

'm in a great mood when I get to the graduation party at Eric Harmon's house. I just laugh when I see the cluster of girls in the driveway, still boo-hooing about what great friends we've been and how it's all over now. And then Beth turns and says, "Oh my God, Jackson's here."

I stop cold. "What's up?" I say.

"You're not going to believe this, man," Tom says, coming down to meet me. "Steph. We just found out. Pills. She OD'd. Jesus, she's dead."

I want to believe he's making another one of his lousy jokes. I wait for him to grin his gotcha grin. But he doesn't. He walks over to Kate and puts his arm around her.

"What pills?" I say to Beth. "What happened?"

"All I know is her mom found her. Our phone was ringing when we got home, and when my mom picked it up, Stephanie's mom was screaming. They'd gone out to dinner, and when they came home, they found her." Beth starts to cry again. "In her bedroom, all by herself. We were all at commencement, and she—"

245

"Ah, shit," I say.

"She didn't even leave a note," Beth says, crying harder. "That's what really gets to me. She thought none of us would even care."

I turn away from them and walk back down the driveway.

"Jax," Beth calls.

"Let him be," I hear someone say. "He's upset."

What I am is pissed out of my mind. I don't need a note to know what Steph meant to say. Fine, don't love me; you'll be sorry.

Back in my bus, alone, I close my eyes, but I still see the empty seat where she sat every day this spring. I hear the music blaring from Eric's backyard. I hear Steph's voice, too—telling me some crazy story, bitching about her life. I remember lying by the fire with her that first night, the length of her body against mine, her slow breathing.

"Parts of me are all over the place," she said. I didn't listen.

I should go back where the others are, I think. But when Kate and Tom come over to the bus and ask if I'm all right, I tell them to go away. It's Brady I want to talk to. He'd know what to do.

"Where are you, anyway?" I say, pounding my fist on the steering wheel. "Where are you? Maybe I screwed up with Steph. Yeah, okay—I screwed up big-time. But you're the asshole, buddy. You screwed all of us. You left us all behind."

I'm still there, just sitting there like a zombie, when Mom and Ted pull up beside me.

Mom gets out and hurries to the bus while Ted goes to find a place to park. "Beth's mother called me," she says when she gets in. "Oh, Jackson. That poor girl. Honey, I'm so, so sorry." She leans over to hug me, but I put my hands up so she can't.

She gets this kind of frantic look on her face. "It's not your fault," she says. "You don't think that, do you, Jackson? *Jackson?*"

"I don't think anything at all," I say. "I don't think—" I shake my head. If I keep on, I'll start crying and I don't want to cry. It's stupid to cry now. It's way too late for crying. But I don't want to try to explain that. I don't even understand it myself. I don't understand anything. I close my eyes, try to breathe deeply. I could go to sleep right here, I think. What Steph did weighs so heavily on me, it's a kind of darkness pressing all around me.

Ted appears at the open window and says in a quiet voice, "Jackson, let's go home. Will you let me drive you home?" I move to the middle seat to make room for him, and he gets in the driver's seat. Mom's crying now, her face in her hands. Ted reaches across to pat her leg, then he turns and looks at me, his big face so kind, and he says, "Jackson, I'm just god-awful sorry this had to happen to you."

We drive in absolute silence. In the dark yards, fireflies are still blinking. Windows still frame families washed in yellow lamplight. But everything else has changed, everything. When we get home, I go straight upstairs to my room and lie down on my bed, still in my clothes.

"Jackson?" Mom calls up the stairs.

I'm grateful when I hear Ted say, "Leave him, sweetheart. It's all right. He'll come to you when he's ready." When Dad comes a little later, I pretend that I'm asleep.

I don't want to see anyone. I don't want to talk to anyone. I only want to talk to myself because if I do that I can stay angry. Stupid, stupid, stupid is all I say—aloud, in my head. Like a stuck record. But it gets me through the next few days until Steph's funeral.

We gather in the room full of flowers, all of us who might have helped her. Me, Tom, Kate, Beth, and all the others. That punk guy she was dating. Her father, clinging to his pretty young wife. Her mother, who stands beside the casket, wringing her hands, saying over and over, "Oh, dear God, why did she do this to me?"

If she could, Steph would say, "To *her*, Jax. I hope you heard that. The woman thinks of no one but herself."

She'd roll her eyes, go limp as a rag doll. "And if you still have any doubt about it," she'd drawl, "look what the bitch has got me dressed in. Would I be caught *dead* in a dress like this if I had any choice?"

It *is* a stupid dress—flowery and old-fashioned, with puffed sleeves. Steph would hate it. She'd hate the way they've fixed her hair, too. And the fact that they've put makeup on her. She hated makeup. If I had the guts, I'd sneak in later, wash her face, and paint a rainbow there.

She's dead, I tell myself. What she looks like doesn't matter. Nothing can hurt her now.

But I hate the thought of her wearing that dress forever, being buried in it. Oh, God—being buried at all. She was so scared of the dark. She had nightmares. Even on the beach, under a skyful of stars, she woke up crying at least once a night, and I had to light the kerosene lantern so that she could get her bearings. In her bedroom at home, she slept with the same Snoopy night-light she'd had since she was little. Her mother knew this. Why would she put her in a box now?

If I stay, I'll say something terrible. I have to walk away— walk outside and take a deep breath. The anger finally dissolves, but when it does, I go watery inside. I'm shaking. If I don't keep my grip on this stair rail, I swear I'll fly up, become nothing and everything the way Stephanie should be allowed to do now. She's dead. Dead. Time rushes through me. Someday I'll be dead, too. We all will.

That's the worst moment I have. Nothing afterward seems real. It doesn't hurt much to hear the minister's sermon because the happy, popular fantasy girl he describes is not Steph. It's as if some other girl has died. Once the casket is closed, I can't even imagine the real Steph in it. It seems easy now to think of her as she would want me to. A person lost to me in this life, like Brady is—but existing somewhere in the universe, existing inside me.

"We're supposed to learn something from all this shit we go through," Steph told me more than once, when she still believed there was something to be learned that might help her. In the days after her funeral, I believe this might still be true for me.

Then a voice on the radio announces that the Grateful Dead will be in concert at Deer Creek the second week of August, and I think, *Brady will be with them.* I'm absolutely sure of it. And that's when the real grief hits me, the howling, terrifying grief I should have felt all along. Steph wouldn't have killed herself if she had known Brady was coming back. I'm as sure of this as I am that Brady will come with the Dead. The news of the concert coming too late seems like a terrible, stupid misconfiguration of the stars.

If only, if only, I think. I lie awake at night, too overwhelmed to cry. I drive out to the reservoir alone and sit in the place where I broke up with Steph. Again and again, I replay that morning the way I meant it to be. I tell her the truth about how I feel and say, "Steph, I'm your friend. We've both got to get our shit together. We'll help each other the right way." And we do.

I tell no one how I feel. I lift weights. I run. I swim laps. I go on long bike rides. It's a game with me: how long can I go without thinking? I especially don't think about Amanda: I figure she's the price I paid for screwing up what my life might have been.

Dad's no problem; he's gone. Out with the Moody Blues as promised. Mom worries, though. "Maybe some counseling would be a good idea," she says. "It's been such a strange year. . . ."

"I'm fine," I say, "really." And to convince her, I keep on going about my business as if I've miraculously survived all that's happened in the last year, as if I'm looking forward to going off to college. I help her in the garden. I let her take me shopping for school clothes and dorm supplies. We take a family trip to Myrtle Beach, and I act the perfect brother. Every day I take Kristin and Amy to the boardwalk. We ride the rides. We poke through the souvenir shops. We get ice cream.

I'm just biding my time, waiting for Brady. It never occurs to me that I might not find him when the Dead come. I know I will. I lie on my bed, the Dead blasting on my stereo, imagining how it will be. Maybe I'll walk right past him, cool, like I don't care. Or act surprised. "Brady, whoa! What brings you here?" In one scenario, I hug him, say, "You've been gone long enough. Come home," and I save him, as I should have saved Steph. In another, I take a long look at him, step back, and deck him.

he afternoon of the Dead concert, I put on jeans and the tie-dyed T-shirt Steph made me, grab my backpack, and head out to Deer Creek. My VW bus fits right in, though its plain orange paint job looks a little dull next to some of the custom jobs on the ones the Deadheads drive. There are buses that look like they've been tie-dyed. Buses decorated with solar systems. Wild, distorted flowers. There are cars and people as far as I can see. There are makeshift tents and real tents. Sleeping bags and Indian blankets spread out on the grass, like a surreal summer camp. There's strange-smelling food cooking over open fires. There's the smell of marijuana and incense. Girls in hippie garb. Guys with shoulder-length hair lounging on rumpled blankets, smoking. Some pluck mellow chords on guitars, some finger flutes to make a lovely, random kind of music.

Methodically, I go up and down the rows. "You know a guy named Brady Burton?" I ask. Some shrug, some try to help, some act like they don't hear me, some are so stoned they actually don't.

"Brady, Brady Burton," I keep saying. "Blond hair. Yeah, same age as me. About my height. A little heavy."

I ask a woman dressed in a long woven skirt and a T-shirt like the ones she's selling: bright purple, with stars and planets on it. She leans toward me when I say Brady's name. Her long silver earrings jangle. She points toward a stand of trees, and I see him playing Frisbee with a bunch of grubby little boys.

I have to look twice to make sure it's really him. He's much thinner than he was a year ago. Really thin. He's wearing filthy jeans, a ratty T-shirt. His hair is long, pulled back in a ponytail. I watch him pedal backward, the Frisbee hovering just above him. In one fluid move, he catches it and sends it spinning. I remember him, fat and sweaty in his Little League uniform years ago, the biggest klutz on the field, always glancing anxiously toward the bleachers where his father sat. He's so graceful now. I almost wish Mr. Burton could see him.

"Hey, Brady," I call.

He turns, his face lights up, and he starts running toward me. "Jax!" he says. "Oh, man!" He throws his arms around me.

We go to the Hardee's where we used to go all the time, and get a back booth. I'm drinking iced tea; Brady's wolfing down the three cheeseburgers and three orders of fries I bought him.

"No way," he says, when I tell him what's been going on with our various parents. "Layla married Oz? Your mom married the IU freak?"

"I'm telling you, it's been a weird time."

"Weirder than that?" he says.

"Well, my dad nearly died," I say. "Is that weird enough for you?"

Brady stops chewing. "What?" he says. "Oz? What happened?"

"He fell off a rigging."

"Jeez, is he *okay?*"

"Now," I say. "But he broke practically every bone in his body. He was in the hospital a couple of months. Then I had to live over at his house all spring to take care of him."

251

"God, that is a bummer," Brady says, then he gives me this sly look. "Well, I guess he can't be too bad off if he's screwing my mom, though. The wild woman."

"He *was* very bad off," I say, sounding priggish, even to myself. "And that's not all that happened while you were gone. Dad getting hurt, I mean."

"Yeah, what else?"

His voice sounds so nonchalant, like there's nothing in the world I could say that would matter to him, that I have to wait a second before I speak, until I stop wanting to tell him about Stephanie in the most hurtful, shocking way. Finally, I say it simply, the only way I know. "Steph. She killed herself, Brady. She's gone."

He just puts his burger down and stares at me.

"Graduation night," I say. "God, I really felt awful when I found out. I mean, I'd been, well, seeing her, and—I guess if anyone's to blame for what happened to her, I am. I knew she was messed up. I shouldn't have dumped her the way I did. But—"

"You were doing Steph?" Brady says.

"You left," I say. "That's how it got started in the first place. The *only* reason it got started. Listen, I don't mean to lay a guilt trip on you, but you really freaked her out taking off the way you did. That's when she first started acting strange. Well, stranger than usual. It took me a while to figure it out—that you guys had been, you know—"

"I freaked *her* out?" he says. "Hey, what about me? I mean, I screw the chick one time last summer. One time. And she starts acting like she's my wife. Like I owe her all my time. She was a leech, man. She was goddamn suffocating me. She was driving me crazy."

"She's dead, Brady," I say. "Jeez."

But he just shrugs. "Well, it's a clear case of bad karma," he says. "Terminal karma. She knew it herself, you know? Steph was always telling me she had really bad karma." He shakes his head and sighs and starts eating again. Silence falls between us for a while, and then he says, "It's so cool with the Dead, you know?

Steph would've liked it. It's, like, *real*. No hassle. If you need something, it appears. And what do you need? I mean, really?"

He grins, picks up the last burger, and unwraps it. "Food appears, man. Witness. Clothes—screw clothes. Music. Yeah, you need music. But with the Dead there's music everywhere. No, Jax, need is not the problem. It's want that wrecks people. If you don't *want* anything . . ."

He goes on about how great the Deadheads are. The way he talks, you'd think everyone in his life before he took up with them was a complete and total asshole.

"Aren't you even sad?" I interrupt. "About Steph?"

He looks wounded. "Sure, I'm sad, Jax," he says. "It's a bummer, man. My point is, the truly sad thing is that she offed herself when she could've split, you know? Gotten a real life." He segues back to himself: unlike Steph, *he's* the kind of person who's not afraid to take a chance on life. He starts giving me a blow-by-blow account of his adventures on the road. He pulls a notebook from the back pocket of his jeans. "My book's in here," he says. "*My* road, man."

He hands it to me, and I open it, but the writing is so small and smudged that I can only make out an occasional word. I reach into my pack for the divorce notebook, hesitate with my hand on the cover, thinking, why should I show it to him when he's acting like such a jerk? But I still believe the way he's behaving *is* an act. Maybe if he reads the notebook and sees that I'm not kidding about how bad the year was, he'll calm down and start acting like he's my friend. So I go ahead and take it out.

"I've been writing, too," I say, and offer it to him. "I kept it up while you were gone. I figured you'd want to see it."

"You're too much, Jax." He leafs through it. "I can't believe you did this. All these people trapped in their stupid little dramas. You really ought to forget them."

I remember all the nights I wrote in it, the house dark and silent around me, how I'd close my eyes sometimes and imagine the moment I'm living right now. Brady would catch up on the divorce data, then I'd say, "Flip it over." He'd read the part of the book that was about my life, alone. I'd imagined this moment in a lot of ways, in a lot of places. But I'd never once imagined that Brady would hand the notebook back to me before I had the chance to speak.

That's what he does, though. He hands it back to me and says, "You ought to cut loose, you know? Hit the road with me."

"Can't," I say, making my voice light. "Sorry. Next week I leave for college."

Brady rolls his eyes. "Oh, man, have you bought the program or what? Dude, next thing I know you'll be on Wall Street." He laughs, reaches across the booth, and yanks at the sleeve of my T-shirt, which fits tightly around my bicep. "Look at you, man. I see you've been working on the yuppie body for it—"

"Hey, screw you," I say, my hands tensing to fists.

He grins then and puts his hands up, open, as if to say, Truce.

"Screw you," I say again. "I mean it."

"Come on, Jax. Lighten up, I'm just kidding."

"Bullshit," I say. "You take off, you screw me over, you screw everybody over—"

"Screw you over?" he says. "I decide to live my own life and that makes me an asshole?" He looks hurt, the way he used to when we were little kids, bickering, and I got the upper hand.

"We were supposed to live together this year, in case you've forgotten," I say.

"Yeah, well, I was done dealing with the Jer. That asshole. Not to mention Steph. I told you, she was driving me crazy, man. So I was outta there. Nothing personal. It was the only way."

"What about Layla?" I said. "What did she ever do to you that was so terrible? Jesus, you take off and don't even write her a letter. I bet you're not even going to see her while you're here now, are you?"

"No way," he says. "Are you crazy? I wouldn't mind seeing Layla—plus, there's some stuff I'd like to get. But I'm doing her a favor not going over there. I mean, if I go she'll get all freaked out when I don't stay. Why upset her?

"The concert's over tonight, I'm gone. I've thought about this a lot the last couple of weeks. I mean, I thought, should I maybe skip coming here all together—hitch to Louisville, where the Dead go next? But Emmett, this guy I hang out with, he goes, 'Mellow out, man. What happens, happens.' I figured, okay, I wouldn't call you, but if you found me, fine—you know, like it was meant to be." He grins and wiggles his eyebrows. "Maybe I should've skipped it, though. I mean, if I'd known you'd gotten so goddamn touchy—"

"I'm not touchy," I say. "I've been through a lot, and I'm sick and tired of worrying about everybody, okay? I mean, are you going to do this forever? Roam around with the Dead? You look like shit, Brady. I bet those cheeseburgers were the first real food you've eaten for days."

He cracks up. "Mr. Mom! The Jax I know and love." He jumps up, does a little dance, nearly knocking down an old man who's carrying a handful of napkins to his wife. "Sorry, sir," he says. "Really."

The old man nods and goes on.

"See? I'm still the swell guy I always was." He grabs my shoulder, pulls me out of the booth. "Come on, kemosabe," he says. "Let's blow. Time to boogie."

Driving back to Deer Creek, neither of us speaks. But Brady turns the stereo on loud the way he used to, and if I block out reality, it's like the two of us are just out cruising on a summer night, the way we used to be.

he band appears; the crowd shouts its welcome. But I've been to Dead concerts with my Dad before, so I'm not surprised when that's the last bit of attention anyone pays them. "The Deadheads aren't really into the music," he always said. "They're into how music is all there is."

Now, with Brady, I understand for the first time what Dad meant. The minute the music starts, he's dancing, oblivious. Alone, two-by-two, in groups. Bodies sway. Hair and smoke seem like the same thing. Arms reach like tentacles toward the light. Near the end, a huge grinning skeleton appears onstage. Bone white, puppetlike, it dances, too— its rickety limbs flailing.

I'm totally wiped out when it's over. Drenched with sweat. I haven't stopped for one second. I didn't dare take the chance of losing Brady, who danced like a dervish the whole time, spinning and wheeling dangerously out of sight. He's on something. His eyes are dilated; his speech slurs as we make our way outside. Acid, probably. I never saw it, but there were plenty of times I saw his hands touch other hands, plenty of times he turned away from me and could have tucked a tab under his tongue. Now he stumbles, witless, beside me through the parking lot.

I could just let him go. I could say, "Great to see you, man. Keep in touch," and let him drift back to the Dead camp with the others. But I can't do it. I keep thinking, You let Stephanie go, and look what happened. I'm afraid for Brady. He's a mess; there's not much left of the person I knew. But maybe if I stay with him, I can save him. Maybe I can get him home, get him someplace where he can get help. He's been so much a part of my life, I have to try.

"I'm starving," I say, when we get to the bus. "Want to go for pizza?"

"Groovy," he says. "Excellent plan."

I open the door of my bus, and wasted as he is, Brady climbs in without a glitch. That makes me feel a little hopeful. He's been gone a long time, but not long enough for his body to forget a move it made countless times before he left. Maybe he'll remember other things, too, once I get him away. Maybe this life, his real life, will start to seem familiar to him.

He leans back, closes his eyes, blissful, like an old man taking a nap. "Far out," he murmurs from time to time.

I want to shake him and say, I know, *the cosmos*. It's cliché, man. God in swirling colors, all the answers to life's questions in the dripping sky.

I just drive north. When I exit from the interstate about an hour and a half later, Brady sits straight up, looks out the window at a cornfield. "Where are we, man?" he says.

"Huntington."

"*Huntington?* What? I can't go to Huntington, Jax."

I have to laugh. The way he says it, you'd think I'd told him we'd just arrived in the darkest pit of hell. "You're already here," I say. "Congratulations. You, Brady Burton, have won a night in beautiful Huntington, Indiana. Second prize is a night in Huntington *and* a visit to the Dan Quayle Museum—"

"Very funny," he says. "Take me back. My ride won't wait all night for me. What time is it, anyway?"

"One," I say.

For a second, I think he's going to reach over and hit me. Instead, he slams his fist against the dashboard. "Goddamn you, Jax. Don't think I don't know what you're up to." He starts to open the car door, even though we're moving. I swerve and stop at the side of the road.

"Look," I say. "There's a Denny's over there. Aren't you hungry?"

Brady shrugs. "I'm going back."

"Yeah, okay," I lie. "I'll drive you to Louisville myself if your ride is gone when we get back. But I've got to get some coffee first; I'm fried."

"Well, I've got to take a leak," he says. "I guess we might as well stop."

He hits the john the minute we get to the restaurant. When he comes out and sees me on the phone, he says, "You're not talking to Layla, are you? You're not deluded enough to think you can set up some kind of scene from *This Is Your Life?*"

"Give me a break," I say. "I'm talking to Ted, my stepdad. Just get us a table, okay? I'll be right there."

"Jackson?" Ted says.

I continue with the convoluted story of how I ended up where I am.

"*Huntington?*" Ted says, just like Brady did.

"I know it sounds stupid. But Brady was really wasted after the concert, so I just put him in the bus and drove in the opposite direction of where the Dead were going."

"He's still wasted?"

"He's okay. Right now, he's pissed. So I told him I'd drive him to Louisville—that's where the Dead play next. But I don't know; I still might be able to talk him into coming home with me—"

"Well, you be careful, Jackson," Ted says. "Listen, you know there's a good chance you won't be able to get Brady to do what you want him to do, don't you? Some people, well—if you can't get him to go home, it's not your fault."

"I know," I say. "Hey, I've got to go—"

"Gotcha," he says. "Just take care, will you?"

I slide into the booth across from Brady, who's got the menu propped up in front of him. He lowers it and grins at me. "You'll drive me to Louisville?" he says. "No lie?"

I nod.

"Okay, let's stay up all night then. After we chow down, let's go to Steph's grave."

We order a whole tableful of food. Eggs, ham, pancakes, biscuits. We're the only people in the restaurant, and Brady entertains the waitresses, telling them about traveling with the Dead. When he wipes the last plate clean with his toast and says, "The Dead don't get much to eat, you know," they laugh and bring him an extra stack of pancakes on the house.

It's past two when we leave. I drive the speed limit back to Indy, in spite of the fact that he harasses me about being a good citizen.

"Good citizen, shit," I say finally. "If I get arrested again, my ass is grass."

"Grass!" Brady raises his index finger. "Excellent concept, dude." He produces a joint from his back pocket.

"Don't do it, man," I say. "If we get stopped—"

But he just laughs at me, tokes up, and zones out. He's not as out of it as I think, though, because the second I turn onto Sixty-second Street, toward home, he says, "This isn't the way to Crown Hill."

"It's locked at night," I say. "So let's just go to my house and crash. We'll go first thing in the morning. Then I'll drive you—"

"No way," he says. "Tonight."

"I told you, it's locked, man."

"Then we go through the fence, wimp. She'd like that anyhow. Us breaking in to see her. I know a place—"

"How?" I ask. "What place?"

"Dude, I just know one, okay? I'll show you."

We cruise the side streets until Brady finds a section of fence where the iron poles are bent, but once inside, I can't get my bearings. I have no idea how to find Steph's grave. I was only there once, the day of the funeral. It's somewhere behind the chapel; I remember that. But when Brady and I find the chapel, I don't know which of the different roads leading away from it to take. The place is huge; I read once that there are thirty-some miles of roads winding through it. Now they swirl out like black ribbons from where we stand. The graves glisten white. The usual rectangular markers, crosses, angels. Marble tree trunks—their carved ivy mingling with the real ivy climbing round them. Those funny graves that look like little houses.

I should have come before now. I should have brought flowers for her grave; she would've liked that. But I was afraid to come, afraid of remembering how Steph looked in the casket, afraid the headstone with her name on it would bring some shock of realization: it's Steph beneath me, in the dark, alone. So I stayed away.

I follow Brady, who's roaming among the graves, reading the names aloud. We come to one huge, pillared monument that has a bronze statue of a woman, prostrate on the steps. Brady throws himself on it as if to hump her, and I'm glad I can't remember where Steph's grave is. Even if I could remember now, I wouldn't take Brady to it. I don't want to know what he'd do there.

"Maybe we should go," I say. "There's no way we're going to find the grave tonight."

"She's here someplace," Brady says. "What's the difference where? She's dead now. She knows everything. She knows we're here, man. We don't have to actually find her."

I shiver to think this might be true. I feel the presence of all the finished lives around me, watching me with something more powerful than eyes, something that lets them see inside me, and it scares and shames me.

"Brady, let's go," I say. "Come on. We shouldn't be here."

But he takes off up the hill, and it seems to me that, having committed myself to getting him through this night, I have to follow. I know where he's going. Silently, staying in the shadows, we climb to the top to the marble pillars that mark the grave of James Whitcomb Riley. Once there, I feel the tight band around my heart ease a little. It's the highest place in the city, and I can look out and see cars and roads and houses. In the distance, I see the downtown skyscrapers, utterly real.

"Awesome view," Brady says. "What a city!" Then he leaps onto the steps of the monument and starts reciting "The Raggedy Man."

"Remember?" he says. "Mrs. Everly made us all stand right here and say it together that time? Man, she was practically bawling before it was all over. All us sweet little fourth-graders spouting Riley's poem. She thought he was a god."

"Mrs. Blue says he's terrible," I say. "An embarrassment to real poets."

Brady shrugs. "Mrs. Blue takes it all too seriously, if you ask me. What's the big deal? Poems. Hey, James must've done something right to get this megagrave. It's what I want someday. A monument. With one of those, you know—" He waves his hands around, as if he could catch the word he wants. "What do they call it when they carve in what a great guy you were before you croaked?"

"Epitaph."

"Yeah," Brady says. "One of those. Did they put one on Steph's grave?"

"I don't think so," I say. "I think just her name and her birthday and when she died."

"Bummer," Brady says. "That's not right. There ought to be something more than that. Just because she didn't win the Nobel Prize or anything. They could've just put something nice there, something she'd have liked. Maybe from the Beatles or something. Or Simon and Garfunkel. She liked them."

In my head I hear a strain of that song about the lovers riding on the bus: "Kathy, I'm lost, I said, though I knew she was sleeping—"

And it all floods back to me, the two of us this spring as lost as the people in that song. But Brady's already gone off on another track—about how hopeless Stephanie was. How, really, she's better off dead. She couldn't even screw up right.

"I used to tell her, 'Steph, you get too bent out of shape about this shit. You want an instant reaction. If you really want to make them crazy, you have to *sustain* screwing up. You have to screw up over the long run.' You know what I mean, Jax?"

It's dark. I guess he can't see me well enough to see I have no clue what he's talking about.

"I have a theory about this," he says, pompous as a teacher. "Take Jim Morrison, man. The ultimate screwup, you think. I know this guy who went to his grave in Paris. It's a mecca for screwups, he said. Every screwup in the world wants to go to Jim's grave.

"But I say Morrison was an amateur. He got to twenty-seven. Big deal. My theory is you haven't really screwed up until there's no way you can possibly redeem yourself. You catch my drift?"

My face must be blank because Brady goes on as if he's speaking to a retarded person. "Morrison was twenty-seven, Jax. A baby. Joplin, Hendrix. Babies. Mama Cass, stoned, choking on a goddamn ham sandwich. Belushi, even. Babies, all of them."

"But let's talk about Elvis! Elvis made it to forty-two, a fat, pill-popping slob. A spoiled brat. 'Bring me girls! Bring me cheeseburgers!' This guy made screwing up an art form. And the beauty of it is, he didn't even know he was screwing up. He didn't even try. It came natural to him!

"He was the king, all right! Of screwing up. Yeah, King Screwup." Brady laughs. "You know what we ought to do, Jax? We ought to go there."

"Where?" I say.

"Graceland. Graceland. The Dead go to Memphis next, after Louisville. And today's the fifteenth, right?"

"Yeah," I say. "Barely. So?"

Brady gets this look on his face like he's just seen God. "Oh, man," he says, sounding like Elvis himself. "Karma! Synchronicity! This is so cool. August sixteenth is the day he *died*. Every year the fans go back, and the whole night of the fifteenth, *tonight*, there's a vigil. Let's go, Jax. You always wanted to go to Graceland. You always said your old man would take you. But who needs him? Let's do it ourselves."

"Brady . . . ," I say.

"Come on, come on—one last road trip. The ultimate road trip. What do you say? You're going to college; I'm going back to the Dead. But first let's do Graceland together, Jax. One last, unforgettable act."

FORTY-SEVEN

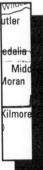

t was stupid to let Brady talk me into going. By the time we get to Louisville, I'm half inclined to say I've changed my mind—drop him off wherever the Dead are playing tonight and head home, cut my losses. But I know Brady. I'd drive all the way to the place and he'd sit there, his arms folded across his chest, refusing to budge. Once he's made up his mind about something, there's no changing it. We're going to Graceland. That's that.

When we stop for gas, I call Ted's office to tell him where I am and where we're headed.

"Yeah, Graceland," I repeat. "To Memphis. Brady wants to. There's some kind of big deal there because it's the anniversary of Elvis's death, and we're going to check it out."

"Elvis? Jackson—"

"I know it's weird. But just tell Mom I'm fine, will you? Tell her *not* to tell Layla I'm with Brady. It'll only upset her."

"Okay," he says. "Listen, you'll need money, won't you? Take that MasterCard I gave you to use in an emergency and get some cash. Almost any bank will take it. Get what you need." He laughs.

"And get me a souvenir. Be careful, though, Jackson. Really. Keep us posted."

As we pull away from the gas station, Brady lifts up his shirt and takes two packages of peanut-butter crackers from the waistband of his jeans. "Food for the poor."

"Did you steal those?" I ask.

His hand holding a cracker freezes halfway to his mouth. "Oh, man!" He smacks his forehead with his other hand. "I forgot. Right, it's a capitalistic society. We work for food. I guess we should take them back."

"Loosen up, Jax," he says when I don't laugh.

"Loosen up, shit," I say. "You want to end up in jail, fine. But leave me out of it." I make him wait in the bus while I go into the bank. I put fifty bucks in my wallet, fifty in the front pocket of my jeans. We drive through McDonald's and get some Egg McMuffins, then head back to the interstate.

Brady seems completely unaffected by the fact we haven't slept, but by noon, my eyeballs are scratchy, my head hurts. The lane markers on the highway start to blur. I'll have an accident if I keep on, so I let him take over, and I crawl into the backseat, expecting the worst. But, at least until I drift off to sleep, Brady drives like a sensible human being. The last thing I remember is the click of a tape going into the tape deck. Brady singing along with R.E.M.

When I wake up, we're not dead or in jail.

"Hey, we're bouncing into Graceland," Brady says, stopping at a red light. "I'm a weird-magnet, man. I drive into Memphis with no idea where I'm going, and here I am."

Sure enough, I sit up and there's Graceland, framed by my window. The house is big, but it's no Hollywood mansion. Just a nice two-story stone house with white pillars. There's a huge front yard, lots of trees, a long winding driveway. The stone wall has a set of iron gates made to look like an open music book.

We pull into the parking lot behind the Graceland Welcome Center with its strip mall full of souvenir shops. Brady and I pick one and go in. He's convinced we have to outfit ourselves so people will think we're real fans. Before we're finished, we've charged more than fifty dollars worth of stuff on the credit card. Black T-shirts with "Elvis" written on them in silver, aviator sunglasses with thick silver rims—the kind Elvis used to wear—buttons with a bolt of lightning and the letters "TCB" on them.

"Elvis's motto," Brady says. "Taking care of business with a flash."

"How do you know?" I say.

"I keep up on things, Jax. So just let me do the talking."

We change into our new shirts, buy our tour tickets—thirty more bucks. We eat in Heartbreak Café, people-watching out the window, and for a little while we're like we used to be together.

We crack up at the middle-aged ladies with ratted hair and lots of makeup, decked out in their Elvis fan club T-shirts, their Elvis jewelry, carrying Elvis tote bags. Kids our own age—one girl wearing a jeans jacket completely covered in Elvis buttons. An ancient lady in lime green polyester pants and a matching lime green Elvis shirt, hobbles past with a walker. But then I see the piece of notebook paper safety-pinned to the back of her blouse, "Shirleen Krebs/Hampstead, VT/ELVIS ALWAYS" written on it in green Magic Marker, and I don't know, it makes me sad.

Finally, they call our tour number, and we board a shuttle bus that takes us across the busy street, through the music gates, and up the winding drive to the house. Our guide is a college girl, winner of an Elvis scholarship, she tells us. She gives us a brief history of the house, tells us Elvis was only twenty-two in 1957 when he bought it for his mother, Gladys.

"Elvis had this thing about his mother," Brady whispers. "He was really wacky about her."

We file into the foyer; the dining room with a big console television and a long table set with Elvis and Priscilla's china is on one side, and the living room with Elvis's gold piano is on the other side. The staircase is in front of us, but the guide says we're not allowed upstairs.

"Aunt Nash Presley—Elvis's favorite aunt—still lives up there," she says. "There wasn't anything in the world more important to Elvis than his family. He put it in his will that no matter what happened, he wanted Aunt Nash to think of Graceland as her home."

She leads us through the blue-and-yellow television room with

265

its whole wall of TVs, six of them, so Elvis could watch all the football games that were on at once. There's a pull-down movie screen and a jukebox, wired for twenty-three rooms. The famous soda fountain where, in the early days, Elvis played soda jerk for his pals.

"Drug shakes," Brady cackles, falling a few steps behind the others. "Speed sundaes."

He can hardly contain his amusement at the jungle room, which Elvis himself furnished. It's all green and brown, the floor, walls, and ceiling carpeted for acoustics. There's a waterfall on one end.

"Oh, man," he keeps saying.

In the museum, we look at the display of Elvis's clothes, and when the guide says something about the fringe period versus the jeweled period, Brady asks her to explain.

"Well," she says, "you know how *active* Elvis was onstage. He'd get that fringe all caught up in his microphone! One night, it got to be such a mess, they had to stop the show and cut it free. Elvis like to died! The very next day, he called in the costume people, and they set to planning a new look for him. That was when they came up with the jeweled capes."

She points to the cape Elvis used in the Hawaiian concert. "It's beautiful, all right. But it weighs so much, Elvis couldn't wear it, except for getting his picture taken."

"Like a crown," Brady says, with a perfectly straight face. "I mean, like, Queen Elizabeth doesn't go around wearing her crown all the time for the same reason."

"Exactly," the girl says, beaming, and goes on to inform us that more people watched Elvis's Hawaiian concert on TV than watched man's first step on the moon.

"It's so nice to see you young folks here," a woman says to Brady as we turn away.

"I was raised on Elvis," he says. "I've been wanting to come to Graceland all my life."

Oh no, I think.

His mom was the ultimate fan, he tells the woman. She went to Elvis's last concert, in Indianapolis. She even caught one of the scarves Elvis threw out into the audience that night.

"She was buried with it," he says. "Last spring. Cancer."

"Brady—"

He holds his hand up to quiet me. I swear, he looks like he's about to start crying.

I can't get away fast enough. The graves of Elvis and his family are in the meditation garden, a little grottolike place near the swimming pool. I stand there, staring at them. Elvis's grave is piled with flowers. There's a little plastic guitar all wound round with plastic roses. At least a dozen teddy bears. Brady joins me, bows his head.

"Hey, how'd I do?" he stage-whispers.

"You didn't have to tell them Layla was dead," I say. "That's not funny."

"Everything's funny," Brady says. "You're losing your sense of humor, Jax. It's a sad, sad thing."

FORTY-EIGHT

CB in heaven."

"Elvis lives!"

"Elvis, I wish I had known you. Even so, I miss you. Brenda."

The stone wall along the front of Graceland is covered with this kind of stuff. Paint, Magic Marker, pencil, chalk, nail polish. We move along, reading, not talking.

"Boss—thanks. Rest in peace. Rock on. Dan R."

"It's midnight, and I miss you."

"He died at midnight," a voice says.

I turn around and there's a girl standing there, short and skinny with Dolly Parton hair. Fifteen, maybe. "He died at midnight," she says again in her deep southern accent. "I guess y'all probably know that." She blushes. "I'm Fay Beth Woodman, from Jonesboro. Where y'all from?"

"IndiaNOplace," Brady says.

She gives him a blank look.

"Indianapolis." I tell her our names.

"Wow," says Fay Beth. "Y'all came all that way?"

"You bet," Brady says, clicking back into his fan mode.

"You been to Graceland before?"

"No," Brady says, and of course he gives her the spiel about his mother. In this version, we're here because she never got here herself.

"That is just the saddest thing I ever, ever heard," Fay Beth says. "But it's so sweet y'all came for her. A tribute, kind of.

"We been coming every year since he died," she tells us. "My mama's president of her fan club at home; they all come down on a bus. My daddy drives down with my little brother. He says Elvis or no Elvis, they ain't about to drive two hundred miles with a busload of women—"

"Your whole family's here?" Brady asks.

"Yeah, we stay out at the Days Inn. It's real nice. There's a pool and all. Y'all want to come over there with me?"

Before I can say a word, Brady jabs me. "That'd be great," he says.

She talks nonstop all the way to the motel. Her brother, John Elvis, was born in Memphis, premature, on the fifth anniversary of Elvis's death. Actually, the exact same *time* Elvis died, it turned out: just after midnight. "Mama meant to call him John Ray Woodman," she says. "After her own daddy. But then when he got himself born the way he did, it seemed like a sign. So she changed and called him John Elvis. She would've changed it to just Elvis, plain, but she'd already told Grandpa Spivey that this baby would be his namesake.

"He looks like Elvis," she says. "You'll see. And he's got, you know, Elvis's way about him. He's real spiritual."

John Elvis is sitting on the balcony of the Days Inn on a lawn chair, plucking at a guitar that's about as big as he is. He's skinny like Fay Beth. He's got on jeans and a jeans jacket with no shirt under it. I'm almost sure his hair is dyed black. It's long and greased back like Elvis's was in the fifties.

"Hey," he says, when Fay Beth introduces us.

The picture window of their motel room is decorated with photographs of Elvis underneath red construction paper letters: "S.W.A.K."

269

"Sealed with a Kiss," Fay Beth says. "That's the name of Mama's fan club."

Inside, there's an old lady with bleached bouffant hair lounging on one of the double beds, reading a magazine.

"Where's Mama?" Fay Beth asks her.

"That laser light show over at the Pink Palace," the old lady says. "Her and Linda and Ray Ann went."

"Oh," says Fay Beth. "Grandma, this is Jackson and Brady. Brady's mama died in the spring, and he's come to Graceland on account of she never got to."

"My lord," Grandma says. She peers at Brady over her half-glasses. "Honey, I am so sorry about your mama. Fay Beth, bring those boys on in, why don't you? Give them a Pepsi or something. And there's chips there, over on the dresser."

She makes Brady tell her all about his tragedy. He's really cranked up now. He's got Layla wasting away in a hospital bed, bald from the chemotherapy. The last thing she hears in this world is the special Elvis tape Brady made for her.

All this talk about Layla dying gives me a creepy feeling; it seems like tempting fate. Plus, it's one thing for Brady to play a joke on those ladies at Graceland in passing, but it's mean to make a fool of this very real lady while we sit in her motel room drinking her Pepsis and eating her potato chips. And Fay Beth, too.

Fay Beth's grandma starts in telling us about how all the fan clubs are working together to get the government to let them have a big birthday celebration in Washington, D.C., next year. "Lord," she says, "I can't imagine why they're being so difficult. There was no better friend of the American government than Elvis Presley was. Didn't he serve his country when he could've been making millions of dollars making records and movies instead? And he was a personal friend of President Nixon's, you know—

"Are you boys eighteen?" she asks.

"Yes, ma'am," Brady says.

She whips out a petition and says, "Good, then you can sign this. It says you believe the government ought to say yes." Brady signs his name and puts Layla's address beside it. I sign, too.

Pretty soon three blond women about my mom's age come

in. "Mama!" Fay Beth says, and runs over to hug the one that looks exactly like her.

"Who's our company, honey?" her mother asks, smiling over Fay Beth's head at me and Brady.

"It's Brady and Jackson, Mama," Fay Beth says. "You know, I told you I was going down by the wall this afternoon? Well, that's where I found them, and—"

"It's really nice to meet you," I say, standing up. "Fay Beth's been so great, bringing us back here to show us all the stuff at the motel. And Mrs.—"

"Lureen," Fay Beth's grandma says. "Honey, just call me Lureen. Everybody does."

"Lureen," I say. "Listen, thanks a lot for the Pepsi and all. But, really, we should be going. You must have things planned for this afternoon."

"You're welcome to stay," Fay Beth's mom says, winking at Fay Beth. "I think Fay Beth would like for you to."

"Mama," Fay Beth says, blushing.

"Patsy," Lureen says. "Now don't you tease her."

I look at Brady, who's smiling this dangerous little smile. He seems rooted to the orange motel chair. I stare at him, hoping he'll see in my eyes that I mean business. "We've still got those tickets to see the *Lisa Marie*," I say. "And the tour bus."

"I *would* like to see those things," he says. "But, gosh, Jax, being here is so much like being with my mom again. I really hate to leave."

I keep staring at him, as if my eyes could say, look at these people, you idiot. They're serious fans. Look at them, with their pink fan club T-shirts—"S.W.A.K." printed in big red letters over a pair of sexy red lips. With their hair rolled up in curlers so it will look good at the candlelight ceremony tonight. There's no way you're going to get away with this crap with them.

But he just keeps smiling. At me, at Fay Beth, at the ladies. He's like an emaciated Buddha sitting there, so serene.

Patsy puts an Elvis cassette in the boom box on the dresser. "Love Me Tender" comes on; she sighs. Fay Beth's grandma—Lureen—pats the empty side of the bed, and Patsy plops down

271

on it. Linda and Ray Ann stretch out crossways on the other bed, facing them, their elbows bent, cupping their faces, looking like those pictures you see of teenagers from the fifties.

"Tell about your mama," Lureen says to Brady. "You girls listen, now, and see if this isn't just the sweetest thing."

Brady launches into his story again, this time ending with the fact that he'd brought a picture of Layla and left it with all the other offerings on the grave.

"Oh, it is sweet," Patsy says, wiping her eyes. "She'd be so proud to think you'd do that, I know. I just hope my John Elvis would be moved to do the same thing for me."

"God forbid he'll have to," Lureen says, and Patsy's friends agree.

Ray Ann asks Brady what fan club his mom was in.

Here it comes, I think—but he doesn't miss a beat. "She wasn't in one," he says. "Elvis was such a personal thing with her. Also, she raised me by herself, you know. My dad, well—he took off before I was born. So Mom had to work a lot. She said we didn't have enough time together as it was. She didn't like to leave to go off to meetings and stuff."

"I can understand that," Ray Ann says. "I don't know what I'd do without our meetings, though."

"It's a lot of fun," Patsy says. "Plus, it makes you feel so good about yourself. Last year we raised five thousand dollars for the children's ward in the hospital."

"That is so cool," Brady says.

Patsy beams. Then she glances at her watch and says, "My lord, ladies, we've got to get our rears in gear. You boys'll stay for supper, I hope."

"Sure," Brady says. "Gosh, that's really nice of you."

"Honey, it's no trouble," she says. "I'll just tell Travis to get extra from Kentucky Fried when he goes. Lord, it's beastly hot, isn't it? Maybe y'all ought to take a swim till it's ready."

Brady glances at me. "We didn't bring bathing suits," he says, "but there's a K Mart across the street. I bet we can buy some there."

FORTY-NINE

ay Beth sticks with us like glue at the K Mart, holding Brady's hand, babbling, so there's no way I can get a word in about why we should get the hell out of here before her dad shows up and nails us. They stay together in the pool, too. I stretch out on a chaise lounge, watching Brady swim up under Fay Beth and lift her, making her giggle wildly. She thinks he likes her; I can tell by the way she looks at him. When he kisses her, I look away. I think of the divorce club for the first time in a while and remember how close we all were, how Brady would fall all over himself trying to make us happy. I've never known him to hurt anybody on purpose—except his parents. Now I feel like I should warn Fay Beth against him, but I know it wouldn't do any good.

Why did I let him talk me into this? I should be at home right now, packing my stuff for college. I lie there in the sun, my thoughts dull, my eyes heavy. I could leave, but what would happen to Brady if I did? I've pretty much given up the idea of saving him, but it seems to me that I ought to stick around, at least until I can get him back to the Dead. He'll be safe there, or as safe as it's possible for him to be. I guess I fall asleep worrying, because the next thing I know, Brady and Fay Beth are standing above me, dripping cold water on me. "Daddy's back with dinner," Fay Beth says. "Come on."

They're all in Lureen's room now, helping themselves to chicken and all the trimmings that are set out on the side of the sink like a buffet. Her dad, Travis, is a big guy, a Vietnam vet with "Chu Lai" and a bleeding heart tattooed on his forearm. Fay Beth introduces us, and he gives us a suspicious look and a death-grip handshake. It's perfectly clear to me. When he finds out what we're up to, he'll simply kill us.

Thank God, just as Brady finishes his story—before Travis gets a chance to give him the third degree about it—John Elvis appears dressed in the black satin jumpsuit Patsy made him.

"Honey, look at you!" she says. "Lord, Elvis himself would be thrilled to see you."

"John Elvis is going to be an Elvis impersonator when he grows up," Fay Beth says. "When he was little, Daddy built him this bed that was a stage. It was bunk beds, actually, but with no bottom bunk. That was the stage part. It had curtains Mama made out of this gold material with little records on it.

"John Elvis was so cute," she says. "He'd get his little toy guitar and sing his heart out. Then he started getting tall, and he'd crack his head every time he got under there. Now he has to practice in the garage. He's good, too."

"He is," Lureen says. "John Elvis, honey, why don't you play just one thing for us before we leave?"

The kid doesn't have to be asked twice. He picks up his guitar, shakes his hair down into his face, and launches into a fairly decent rendition of "Love Me Tender."

I imagine Grandma saying, "Good grief!" to this whole scene, erupting into one of her what-is-this-world-coming-to tirades.

John Elvis winds down, and Patsy and Lureen make a big fuss, hugging and kissing him. Then the two of them leave to take the members-only fan club bus to Graceland.

"Daddy," Fay Beth says. "Can Brady and Jackson ride over for the candlelight vigil with us? Please?"

He gives us that look again, but he agrees that we can, so we all pile into his pickup truck. Travis and John Elvis sit in the cab; Brady, Fay Beth, and I in back. I feel weird, like I did one time when I was driving on an icy street and my bus slid and just barely missed hitting a parked car. My heart is racing; I can feel the blood pounding through my body. The cool breeze caused by the truck moving is a relief. I take some deep breaths to calm down, and I start trying to figure out how I'm going to trick Brady into losing ourselves in the crowd so we can get away from these people before all hell breaks loose—then somehow get ourselves back to the Days Inn to my bus. We'll find a place to park and get a decent night's sleep. In the morning I'll drive him back to the place where the Dead will play, give him some food money, and head for home.

It shouldn't be too hard, I think, when we get to Graceland. The whole street in front of the house has been blocked off. It's packed with people, at least five thousand, according to Fay Beth, who gives us a rundown of all the other candlelight ceremonies she's been to, describing how far in either direction the crowd has stretched from year to year.

Elvis is being blasted from big speakers set up near the gate. All day, everywhere we went, we heard his classic rock-and-roll cuts, but now it's gospel music and songs like "My Way" and "The Green, Green Grass of Home."

"Oh, man," Brady says in his Elvis voice, and Fay Beth giggles.

I hate him for making fun of everything, of making a fool of Fay Beth. It's depressing. I think of the Brady I used to know— the one who bought the coat for the old black man in the park, the one who used to get so mad and upset talking about the way the world treats people as if they just don't matter. What's hap- pened to him? Can't he see that Fay Beth and her family matter? Elvis is no joke to them. They believe in him; they think of him as one of their own. In fact, it's turning out that I'm not exactly immune to Graceland myself. I'd never admit it to Brady, but I envy Fay Beth's family for being so close, even if it is something as weird as Elvis that holds them together. There's something else, too. Those pictures of Elvis when he was so young, at the top of the world, and the later ones of him with Priscilla, holding Lisa

275

Marie—I don't know, they make me feel sad and happy at the same time, the same way I feel when I look at the pictures of my own family from when my parents were together.

"Haven't you had enough of this?" I ask Brady when John Elvis shows up and everybody gets distracted again about how cute he is. "Come on, you've had your fun. Now let's get out of here before Travis beats the shit out of us. He knows what we're up to. Didn't you see the way he looked at us at dinner? We'll find out where the Dead are playing tomorrow, and I'll take you there—"

"Screw the Dead," he says. "This is the source. Mecca. Where everything started. Graceland, man. Hey, without Elvis, the Dead never would've lived." He starts laughing hysterically, then repeats, "The Dead never would've lived," as if it's the funniest thing he's ever heard in his whole life.

Fay Beth turns. "What?" she asks, confused.

Instantly, Brady puts his fan mask back on and gets her talking about how the candlelight ceremony will be. He doesn't say another word to me, won't even look at me. I just stand there among the fans, hopeless, invisible, until finally it gets dark and it's time for Uncle Vester Presley to light the torch from the eternal flame that burns at Elvis's grave. A hush comes over the crowd as the old man walks down the driveway, the torch like a slow-moving comet, and one by one lights the candles of the Elvis Country Fan Club members. They're all lined up just inside the gates.

"It's not really fair the way they get to do it every year," Fay Beth whispers. "They ought to let some other fan clubs have the chance."

"Hush, Fay Beth," Lureen says. "This is no time for petty feelings." She reaches into her tote bag and hands all of us candles that she's stuck through aluminum foil pie plates so the wax won't drip on our hands.

It takes a long time to make our way to the gates, but everyone around us is patient and friendly; no one jostles. One lady who lives in Memphis tells Lureen about coming to Graceland the night Elvis died.

"It was a sight, I'll tell you. All these people carrying on. Crying like their hearts'd break. Some fainting dead away. Those they lined up on blankets there, just under the wall. It was awful," she says. "But I just knew I had to be here."

Then suddenly she's laughing, telling about how she and her girlfriends used to hang out by the gates at all hours when they were in high school, hoping for a glimpse of Elvis. They saw him one time. A limousine pulled up, and there he was in the back of it. "He had those sunglasses on," she says. "It was him all right, though. Lord, that smile . . ."

"Do you think he's really buried here?" another lady asks. "I've heard that some people think they just *say* they moved the casket over here from the cemetery. You know, to keep all the people from tromping through there like they had been."

"He's here," Lureen says, "God bless his soul. I feel it."

"Mama, look," Patsy says, smiling, nodding toward a family that's drifted near us. There are four of them, a mom and dad and two kids. They're fat as Pillsbury doughboys, all wearing Elvis T-shirts and plastic visors with "Elvis" spelled on them in blinking lights.

"Lord be," Lureen says. "It takes all kinds."

The line of candles snakes up the driveway; soon we're among them, adding our own light. The last part of the driveway, all the way to the meditation garden, is lined with floral displays: blue suede shoes made of carnations, blue music notes on a staff, blue teddy bears. There are gold records, American flags with Elvis's picture in the place where the stars should be. Envelopes with flowers spelling "Return to Sender." Guitars, lightning bolts, hearts—even motorcycles made of flowers.

When we reach the grave, Patsy, Lureen, and Fay Beth add the red roses they're carrying to the hundreds that are already there. They stand there a long time, all of them crying. John Elvis gets this unearthly expression on his face. Travis bows his head.

"The King," Brady says solemnly.

Fay Beth takes his hand.

I remember what he said about Elvis last night at the cemetery, and I have an almost uncontrollable urge to hit him as hard as I can, slam him all the way across the stone walk and into the swimming pool. But I think, What's the point? Hitting him would give me no more pleasure than hitting some obnoxious stranger.

277

It seems to me then that Brady is the one who died, that it's for him that I'm going through this weird ritual of grief.

If my face shows how bad I feel, anyone looking at me must think I'm one of the biggest Elvis fans that ever lived. I stand there with my candle, staring down at the grave, but what I see is Brady as he once was, the two of us together, but spinning so fast down through the years that no one picture holds, and in no time here I am again, smack-dab in the present, hurting worse than ever. I think of something I overheard my mom say a long time ago, talking to a friend: "Sometimes I think it would be easier if Oz had died, if I'd lost him that way." I felt so terrible when I heard it that I never could bring myself to ask her why she said such a thing, what she meant. Now it makes sense.

I can't stand to see Brady with his arm around Fay Beth, his head bent so he can whisper in her ear. I don't want to hear what he's saying. I hate the way he reaches up to brush away her tears. They walk back down the driveway, Patsy and Lureen trailing behind, murmuring how sweet they look, what a nice boy Brady is, what a pretty thing Fay Beth is growing into.

"Oh, Travis," Patsy teases, taking his hand. "Look at him scowling, Mama. He thinks Fay Beth is still his little girl."

I'm quiet going back to the motel—not that it makes any difference. Brady acts like I'm not there. He and Fay Beth snuggle in the corner of the truck bed, kissing. I don't want to see his hands moving on her; it's none of my business what he does. I close my eyes and let the hot air wash over me. Still, I'm glad when we get back and Travis says, "Fay Beth, you come on inside now."

"Daddy," she says. Whines, really.

"Fay Beth," Travis says dangerously. He gives me and Brady this look like, One word and you guys are going to get what you deserve. Apparently, even Brady can tell he's serious. "I'll walk you to the door," he says to Fay Beth. Travis lets him do that. The three of them and John Elvis walk toward the motel together.

"Goddamn," Brady says when he gets back to the bus. "Was that great, or what? Didn't I tell you Graceland would be a trip, Jax? Virtual reality, man: Elvis through the eyes of his true fans."

He laughs. "Too bad about Fay Beth, though. That would've been the perfect ending to a perfect day. Dude, I could've screwed her, you know? She was so ready. But, oh well, *c'est la vie*."

I'm sitting in the driver's seat of the bus, ready to go; he's just outside the window, grinning at me, and suddenly he breaks into a little dance. He hops around, playing air guitar, shaking and thrusting his pelvis forward like Elvis. I know exactly what he's up to. He's trying to make me laugh. He figures if he can make me laugh, I'll forget all the crap he's put me through since last night, all the pain he caused me by running away. That's how it's always been between us. But this time things have gone too far.

Calmly, I open the door and get out. I stand right in front of him, so we're eye to eye. He dances on. "You're pathetic," I say. "Do you care?"

He stops cold, splays his hands in that old helpless gesture, and, for just an instant, he looks sheepish. He looks like himself.

"Do you?" I ask.

His face darkens. "Pathetic?" he says. "Yeah? Well, screw you. You're the pathetic one, Jax. You're uptight and pathetic; you always have been. A goddamn drag. Everyone thought so. You don't know jack shit about anything."

I don't even realize I'm going to hit him until I do. Jesus, I hit him hard. He reels back, trips, and sits down on the asphalt. He puts a hand to his nose, which is gushing blood, and gives me this surprised look.

I don't say anything, just reach into the bus and get him one of the motel towels we used for swimming. The hand I hit him with is still in a fist. My knuckles sting, I guess from where Brady's teeth hit them. I stand there looking at him, breathing hard. There's a buzzing sound from the lights in the parking lot. Elvis singing through an open window.

"You didn't have to hit me, Jax," Brady finally says, his voice muffled by the towel.

I shrug.

"Okay, okay," he says. "I'm sorry I said what I said about you."

"It doesn't matter," I say.

"Pals," he says, and gives me the old Brady grin. He gets up and throws his bloody arm around me.

I let him do it. It doesn't matter—what I said was true. But it's not because I've forgiven Brady like I always used to, like he assumes I have now. It's true because the person he's become can't hurt me. Sorry or not sorry, it doesn't matter. Suddenly I'm so tired I can hardly keep my eyes open. All I want to do is sleep.

I might as well. There's no way thinking or talking will change anything between us now. I get back in the bus and lie down in the middle seat. Brady settles into the backseat, but he's too wired to sleep. He starts talking about old times, all the fun we used to have.

"Yeah, yeah," I say if he demands a response. But I keep drifting off, and what he's saying begins to seem like part of a dream to me, a dream life. The last thing I remember him saying is, "Tell Oz I met Garcia one time. *Garcia*, man. It was so cool."

In the morning, when I wake up, he's gone. I'm really not surprised. And I'm not mad, even when I check my wallet and all the money that was in it is gone. I don't feel guilty for hitting him, either. It seems strange to me that I hit him at all; in fact, I might even think it had been a dream except for the way that my knuckles are skinned up and sore. I don't feel any better for hitting him, or any worse. In fact, I could make a list of all the things I don't feel about Brady right now. God, for the first time in a whole year, I'm not worried about him. I figure he'll get by.

I get out of the bus, stretch, and go find a pay phone in the Days Inn to call Mom.

"Jackson! Oh, honey, I've been so worried about you," she says when she hears my voice.

"I'm fine," I say. "Really. I'll be home tonight."

"Brady?" she asks.

"Gone," I say. "I'll tell you all about it later."

Next I call information, get Amy and Kristin's mom's phone number, and dial it.

Kristin answers. I talk to her a little while, ask her what she's been up to. Then I ask her if she'll give me Amanda's address.

"Sure," she says. "Are you finally going to write to her?"

I tell her that's exactly what I'm going to do and she says, "Well, it's about time," in a prissy voice. I have to laugh.

Just a postcard to begin with. In the motel gift shop, I pick one with the music gates on it and write on back, "Dear Amanda, Would you believe it if I told you Graceland changed my life? I'll write you a real letter with the evidence when I get home." I hesitate a second, then figure, what the hell, and finish, "Love, Jackson."

"I can mail that for you right here." The clerk grins. "Even got an Elvis stamp for it, if you need one."

"Great, thanks." With the money I'd kept in my jeans pocket, I buy the Elvis stamp, an Elvis beer mug for Ted, the *Presley Family Cookbook* for Mom, and teddy bear earrings for Kristin and Amy.

It's still pretty early, just after nine. I look across the courtyard to Fay Beth's room, but the curtains are pulled. I wish I could apologize for what Brady and I did yesterday, but since she never figured it out, I'd probably just make her feel bad. I'd like to talk to Lureen and Patsy, though.

I'd ask them, "So, is caring the answer? I mean, having something that really matters to you—anything, as long as it's yours?"

But first I'd have to explain about Brady's running away and everything that's happened to both of us because of it—maybe everything that's happened in our whole lives. It's better just to let it be.

Climbing into my bus, I feel the last year settle inside me, become part of what I am. I know I'll never stop wishing that my parents were still together or that I'd listened—really listened—to what Stephanie was saying to me or that I could make Brady see that the person he's hurting most is himself. I'll never stop wishing that the world was a better place.

I turn on the engine, pull out onto the highway. At Graceland, it's business as usual. The barricades have been removed, and traffic zooms along where thousands stood last night. The buses are already ferrying a new crop of fans through the gates, up the driveway. It's hot and hazy. Poles of sunlight slant down through the trees.

The R.E.M. tape is in the tape deck, where Brady left it. I pop it in, and music blasts out: the song I heard yesterday, just before I fell asleep, "It's the End of the World As We Know It (I Feel Fine)" and I can't help smiling.

Fine? I think.

Well—okay, maybe.

Yeah. I feel okay.